LIVING ON
A PRAYER

Sheila started work at fifteen as a presser in Hepworths, a tailoring factory. She married at eighteen and had three daughters; Dawn, Janine and Diane and a younger son, Michael. Recently divorced, she now has eight grandchildren, and every Saturday and Sunday can be found at a football match for the Darlington Academy under thirteens and the Northern League.

Sheila has lived in Houghton-le-Spring near Sunderland for thirty years.

Praise for *Living on a Prayer*

'Sheila Quigley proves she isn't a one-hit wonder with this gritty follow-up to *Run For Home*' – *Bella*

'A good read' – *Literary Review*

'Sheila doesn't just write blistering crime novels, she creates a world of grim reality and a raw humanity that grips the emotions ⌐⌐⌐⌐⌐⌐⌐⌐⌐⌐⌐⌐⌐⌐he'

'A scary ⌐⌐⌐

'Tensi⌐⌐
– *Peterb⌐⌐⌐⌐⌐⌐ ⌐elegraph*

'This thriller flows at a tremendous speed, the gripping subject matter making for compulsive reading'
– *North East Lifestyle*

For Dale, Adam, Michael, Arron, Danny,
Carly, Shanine, and Leah

Acknowledgements

As ever, Susan, Kate, Alex, Justine, Darley and to all at Random House.

For the worst jokes in the world thanks must go to Julia Churchill, one of Darley's Angels, and to my son-in-law, Michael Simpson.

Thanks to my daughter Janine Forrest for listening.

Prologue

Sunday December 17

Debbie Stansfield's hands trembled furiously as she pressed Richard's pale-blue Nike T-shirt to her face. She breathed in deeply – to her this smell was as rare and precious as that of an exotic rose: the smell of her sixteen-year-old son. Her sixteen-year-old dead son.

Dropping her hands to her lap, Debbie stared at the photograph on the windowsill, a picture of her and Richard taken just a few short weeks ago at Debbie's birthday dinner. They were both smiling with the same deep dimple in their right cheek, inherited from Debbie's Irish grandmother. Everybody said that she and Richard were the spitting double of old Molly, with their black hair and green eyes.

Her eyes dropped from the photograph and she stared at her shaking hands. She was at once reminded of next-door's Alsatian bitch, Sandy. Sandy was dead too. Sandy had died in a fit, trembling just like Debbie was now. There had been nothing they could do to help the poor frightened dog except for gently stroking her head.

Richard had loved Sandy to bits, and Sandy, gentle as a lamb and frisky as a puppy to the end, had returned Richard's love a hundredfold. They were

3

the same age, Richard and Sandy, but Sandy had lived a good dog's life, whereas Richard had barely become a man.

Debbie sighed; she felt it well up from deep inside of her, right down where she imagined her soul to be. She lifted the T-shirt to her face again, and once more breathed Richard in deeply. Her throat tightened as she realised she was alone at last. *For the first time since . . . ?* She shook her head. *Since God only knew when.*

Time was gone. It had no meaning.

Time had taken Richard and left her behind.

She was sitting on the edge of his bed, having escaped at last all the well-meaning people who could think of nothing to say, yet all repeating the same nothings that had been spoken since forever.

A long, long line of nothings stretching back and back.

She was alone, but surrounded by Richard.

How many other parents had sat as she did?

Richard, her son, the only flesh and blood she had in the whole world. In the window his curtains, red and white Sunderland colours, fluttered briefly, then were still, as if Richard had paused for a moment on whatever journey he was on now, and breathed on them.

Debbie remembered the day she had hung them. Richard's tenth birthday. She smiled for a moment at the memory of Richard's excited face when Beefy Belmont had taken him to his first live football game, a derby between Sunderland and Newcastle. The curtains had been waiting for him when he returned, and Richard's face had lit up when he saw the surprise. Debbie had bought the curtains from the sale of her grandmother's silver watch to Sandra Gilbride, who had given it back to her the next day and said that she could pay her back weekly. Debbie never found out which kind neighbour had told Sandra that it was her grandmother's watch.

She sighed again. The curtains were faded now.

Ten years old he'd been then, and safe.

Next to his wardrobe, which was pasted thickly with pictures of Sunderland stars past and present, his comics were piled high in the corner, dozens and dozens of them. In the opposite corner, his punch bag hung limp and still, the brown leather scuffed in places, waiting for the kiss of Richard's fist.

On top of the chest of drawers a pair of goldfish swam round and round their bowl. Richard had won them three years ago at Houghton Feast and had named them Tim 1 and Tim 2, identical except for the black spot on Tim 1's tail. Richard had told Debbie that they only had a three-second memory span. 'So,' she asked, 'does that mean they think they're going in a straight line and swimming to the end of their little fish world?'

Richard had laughed, the deep dimple in his right cheek playing with her heart the way it always had. 'Don't know, mam,' he'd answered.

She could see, without having to open the cupboard door, the brown teddy with the missing arm. Debbie's grandmother had given it to Richard when he was born, and for years it had hardly left his side. Battered and worn, with the stuffing coming out where its arm had been, Richard had loved that bear. But Richard grew up, and had banished the teddy these last few years to the top shelf of the cupboard, away from the prying eyes of his friends. Debbie imagined the teddy waiting patiently for Richard to return, to smile at him one last time, to take him out and play with him, and love him like he used to. But Richard wasn't coming back.

Debbie raised the T-shirt to her face again, then dropped it to her lap. A tear quickly followed.

Suicide.

No way.

Not her boy.

Not her Richard.

Richard was a good lad, always had been, and any time now he'd walk through the door and wonder what all the fuss was about, reminding her that, hadn't he said he was spending the night at Kurt's?

''Course he will,' she muttered. That's right. It was all a mistake.

Then, like a bucket of ice-cold water in the face, she remembered calling Kurt hours ago – and he had told her that he hadn't seen Richard that day.

She'd brought Richard up to be a good lad, all on her own an' all. One of the good single mothers who never make the news. So what if some jumped-up little pen pusher had looked her up and down and taken great delight in writing 'Father Unknown' on Richard's birth certificate. So what if the local gossips had all but taken bets on who the father was.

Of course she knew who the father was. But he had buggered off as soon as she had told him she was pregnant, and good riddance too. She and Richard had managed very well on their own. But how was she going to manage now that she didn't have her Richard?

Debbie looked at the punch bag. It reminded her of her father, who used to bare-knuckle fight for a few bob. She sighed again.

This wasn't the first time death had danced with her. Her mother had died of cancer when Debbie was just fifteen, and her father had followed his beloved wife less than a year later.

Debbie's grandmother had come over from Ireland and had looked after her, and then, when Debbie was eighteen and found herself pregnant with Richard, she had asked no questions but had supported Debbie in the only way she knew how. She had fixed Debbie dry toast when that had been the only thing that she could keep down in the first few months of her pregnancy; she had unravelled old jumpers and knitted them up into baby clothes, as money was tight. And she had been so proud and happy when Richard was born. He was such a beautiful, perfect baby. And then, six months later she was gone too, leaving Debbie to cope by herself.

Debbie had managed with the help of a good neighbour whose own children had grown and moved away. Eventually the neighbour followed her eldest daughter south, but by that time Debbie knew she and Richard would be OK. Debbie had survived, made her mistakes and lived with them. She would manage again.

But would she?

The death of a child, she knew now, was far worse than the death of a parent, no matter how loved the parent was. It was the march of time, inevitable, expected even, eventually. But no one expects to have to bury her baby.

With a slightly bemused expression she stared at Richard's comics for a moment before shaking her head.

Alone again!

Richard was to have started his first Saturday job next week. In the tangle of disjointed thoughts this one hit Debbie hard. She sobbed and stuffed the T-shirt into her mouth. Terrified in case the sob turned into a scream, terrified in case the scream, once released, went on and on.

Adamantly she shook her head. No reason for it at all, no reason why her Richard should hang himself from one of the Seven Sisters trees at Copt Hill, and half frighten to death an old man walking his dog.

When the kind copper with a face full of freckles had come knocking at her door, she'd told him this: over and over she'd told him.

Somebody else's Richard.

Not hers.

Her hands wrung the T-shirt tighter as she kept on shaking her head. She knew she was right, even though the rest of the world said otherwise.

No way.

Not her Richard.

Monday 18 December

1

Detective Inspector Lorraine Hunt, of Houghton-le-Spring CID, eyed her mother suspiciously over the breakfast table, before saying. 'I know the pair of yer are planning something . . . I can smell it.'

She sniffed the air theatrically and nodded to herself as she buttered a slice of toast. 'Too much whispering going on around here, if yer ask me, like.'

Mavis, an older version of Lorraine, a tall leggy natural blonde with a deep abiding fondness for all things hippy, rested her chin on her hands and looked at her daughter with the same startling blue eyes that Lorraine possessed. 'Too much detecting going on around here, if yer ask me, like,' she replied drily.

'Huh.' Lorraine bit into her toast.

Peggy Monk, Mavis's lifelong friend who had arrived for a week's break a few months earlier, grinned at both of them as she came into the kitchen and moved to the table. She pulled out a stool with a loud scraping noise on the cream floor tiles. Lorraine and Mavis cringed.

Peggy was almost five foot, but had sworn for years that she was five foot one. Her hair, a deep auburn shade that could only come from a bottle, was piled on the top of her head in a style all of her own. She loosened the top of her pink satin dressing-gown. 'Phew, warm in here this morning, innit?'

When no one answered she looked quizzically from mother to daughter, then whispered in a conspiratorial tone, 'Something going down here I should know about?'

Lorraine closed her eyes and counted to ten. She had enough on her mind today without Peggy coming over all suspicious, like; it was hard getting Richard Stansfield's death out of her head. She slowly opened her eyes, looked at Mavis and said, 'She's been watching the gangster films again I see.'

Smiling, Mavis raised her eyebrows as she gave a slow exaggerated nod.

'I am here, yer know,' Peggy said, before quickly leaning over and taking a huge bite of Lorraine's toast.

'And don't I know it.' Lorraine glared at the remains of her toast.

Peggy turned to Mavis, cocking her head to one side. 'So, have we made our minds up yet, how many are coming for dinner on Greed And Gluttony Day?'

'What?' Lorraine frowned at Peggy for a moment. She had been thinking about Debbie Stansfield. PC Carter had broken the news to her, but she had not believed him, and she had not believed Lorraine an hour later either.

'What?' she said again, before realising that the older woman meant Christmas Day. Shaking her head, although secretly agreeing with her, Lorraine rose, pushed her stool under the table, without an

12

accompanying scrape, and said, 'OK, I'm off, see youse two later . . . Much later.'

'Nice suit, kiddo,' Peggy felt the dark-blue cloth of Lorraine's trouser suit as she passed.

'If there's butter on them sausages that yer call fingers I'll personally have yer deported.'

'Tut tut, such a thing to say to yer only godmother who worships the ground yer walk on.'

'Yeah, and thank God yer are the only one. Believe me, if there were two of yers I'd be deporting meself . . .' And with that she strode out the door leaving the other two women staring after her.

When she heard the front door close, Peggy said, 'She's working far too hard, yer know.'

'Yeah, not that that so-called Superintendent Clark appreciates her one little bit.'

'Huh, I remember him from school, right snotty-nosed little arsehole then, sucking up to the teachers every chance he got . . . Anyhow, I bet yer haven't asked her if she wants to have Luke round for Christmas yet?'

Sergeant Luke Daniels, Lorraine's most trusted colleague, was a tall, handsome black man, and the man that Mavis and Peggy thought, not-so-secretly, was perfect for Lorraine. *Will it ever happen though*? Mavis wondered to herself. *Not while she's still got those barriers up around her since her marriage ended.*

'The chance hasn't come up yet, Peg,' Mavis replied, shaking her head.

'Bloody hell Mave, there's only a week left now and if we're gonna have that beautiful bloke over

13

for the worst day of the year, you'd better get a move on.'

Mavis shrugged, 'Yer know what Lorraine's like though. Yer can't force her into doing anything she doesn't want to do. And remember, she's gonna have a hard time trusting anyone after John.'

Peggy tutted as she poured herself a cup of tea from the pot. She knew what she'd like to do to John if she ever got her hands on him. It wasn't only that he had lied to Lorraine before and during their marriage, he had lied to her about a fundamental part of his being. And he didn't even have the guts to own up to it. Lorraine had found out just what sort of man she had married when she went into a gay club undercover and discovered him with someone else – another man. At least John was doing the decent thing by not contesting the divorce. Mavis had confided to Peggy that it should come through any day now.

'Well,' Peggy finally said, reaching for another slice of toast, 'she's gotta get back on that horse sometime sooner or later. And yer can tell just by looking at her that she fancies Luke to bits. She better get in quick before someone else does.'

Mavis smiled. She couldn't imagine how anyone could pass over her lovely daughter for someone else. Especially someone like Luke who clearly only had eyes for Lorraine. But she humoured Peggy by saying, 'And just who would that someone else be?'

'That little bitch, Sara Jacobs.'

Sara Jacobs was a constable in Lorraine's station. It was rare for Lorraine not to come home and blow off steam about her. Jacobs, according to what Peggy and Mavis had picked up from Lorraine, was a perfectly adequate police officer, but had ambitions above and beyond her talents. And she was encouraged by her close relationship with Superintendent Clark.

Mavis shook her head. 'I don't think she's any threat to Lorraine.'

'You mark my words, she's just aching to get her horrible little paws on him.'

'Peggy, yer make it sound like Luke's got no choice in the matter. Anyhow, why have yer suddenly got a down on Christmas? Yer used to love it.'

With an exaggerated sigh Peggy screwed her face up. 'Aye, mebbe, but that was before that horrible twat Mark Cummings dropped me for that pole dancer, down Newcastle quayside, remember?'

'Oh, Peggy,' Mavis put her hand on Peggy's shoulder and squeezed gently. 'That was at least four Christmases ago, yer've bounced back from worse than that. Besides yer've had more than one bloke since then, three or four if I remember rightly.'

Peggy chewed her lip for a moment, then said, 'Aye, but it still rankles that she was ten years younger than me and that greasy bastard was ten years older.'

Mavis bit her lip to stop a laugh breaking out.

'Besides,' Peggy went on, 'Christmas is just plastic now, every flaming place yer look, plastic, plastic, and more bloody plastic.'

Making a mental note to leave the silver tree in the shed and buy a real tree this year, Mavis patted

15

Peggy's arm, 'Ha'way Peg, cheer up old mate, it's not like you to be so down, least of all over a man.'

After a moment Peggy smiled, 'Aye yer right, who the hell in their right mind would have one?'

Smiling, Mavis nodded. 'That's the spirit . . . And anyhow what if we're reading it wrong and our Lorry's not interested in Luke, have yer thought about that?'

Peggy shrugged, then grinning said, 'That's OK, if she doesn't want him, I'll have him.'

'Peggy!'

Peggy grinned. 'Just kidding . . . anyhow, of course she is, what's not to be interested in? Jesus Christ, the man's flaming well gorgeous.' She sighed heavily, 'If only I was a few months younger.'

'Months!'

'Well, yer know what I mean,' Peggy laughed.

Glad to see her friend back on form, Mavis laughed with her.

The death of Richard Stansfield was very much on Lorraine's mind. She had gone to sleep thinking about him, and had woken up with Debbie's voice in her mind – her son couldn't be dead because he wouldn't kill himself, it just wasn't possible. Lorraine had seen more than enough suicides in her time, had seen the grief and the hurt that it had caused families, and had once experienced that grief for herself. She knew what Debbie must be going through, but her insistence that Richard wouldn't have killed himself niggled away at other small inconsistencies in the case. So instead of going straight into her office as usual, she decided to risk the rush-hour traffic and call on Scottie, the pathologist for the Sunderland area.

Lorraine gave a light tap on his open door and walked in. Scottie was busy looking into one of his microscopes, but Edna, his surrogate mother, was facing the door and she smiled when she saw Lorraine.

Edna was small and dark and should have retired at least five years ago, but she stayed on because Scottie, who had become the child she'd never had, needed her. He was a brilliant pathologist, but like a lot of brilliant men, was absent-minded and disorganised. Edna looked after the administrative side of Scottie's life, freeing him up to concentrate on what he was really good at: taking care of the dead and discovering their secrets. Plus, Edna always said, she would only get into mischief if she wasn't working.

'Hello, love.' She smiled at Lorraine and Scottie looked up.

Scottie was dark and thick set. There was no vanity about him. His hair, aside from an ever-growing bald spot on his crown, was a thick black thatch with only a few silver threads running through it. His body hair was always trying to escape from his cuffs and the collars of his shirts, which, although clean, were always crumpled, as if he had put them on straight from the tumble dryer.

Over time, Scottie and Lorraine had developed a strong working relationship, and they liked and trusted each other. Although he was older than

Lorraine, Scottie had come to admire her for her policework and her strength of character. And she had time for him too. They would often bounce ideas off each other, which Scottie appreciated. Scottie felt that Lorraine truly respected the job he did. Other coppers looked on him as a necessary evil – somehow, in their eyes, he was tainted because of his proximity to the dead. He never felt that with Lorraine.

'Ahh,' he said in his deep voice, 'the day just got better . . . What can I do for you, kiddo?'

Lorraine smiled a hello to Edna but then her face became serious. 'It's the Stansfield boy. Scottie, my gut tells me it wasn't suicide. Why, I don't know . . . And I sincerely hope I'm wrong, but until yer tell me otherwise . . .' She spread her arms, palms up, wide.

'Not much I can tell yer, I'm afraid. It's inconclusive. There's bruising on the body, but at his age it could mean anything, football, messing around with his friends . . . His fingernails are broken, and by that I mean broken, not raggy and chewed, but broken, snapped off.' He paused for a moment. 'That could have happened if he'd changed his mind at the last minute and tried to get the rope off his neck.'

Lorraine shuddered at the thought.

'There are some other fibres under the bits of nails that are left,' Scottie went on. 'They aren't off his clothing, and they are definitely not rope fibres, though those are there too.'

'There was no note. Most suicides leave a note.' Lorraine looked at Scottie, a frown line appearing between her eyes. 'His mother said last night that he

18

had been a wee bit depressed a couple of months ago, but then he seemed to have come right all of a sudden. Mostly he seems to have been a pretty normal well-adjusted kid, and she's adamant that he didn't commit suicide.'

'That's not unusual. People look at their dead children and most just can't take it in . . .' Scottie perched on the side of his desk, almost sending a pile of paper over while holding his chin in his hand, contemplating what Lorraine had said. Finally he looked up. 'It's very unusual for suicides not to leave a note. As you know, most like to say goodbye, put their affairs in order . . . no chance that it was overlooked?'

'Nothing at all at the scene. Carter went over it with a fine-tooth comb and you know how thorough he is. Richard's mother, Debbie, couldn't find a note. Surely, if he left it in the house, it would have been somewhere obvious?' She stopped speaking and Scottie nodded in agreement. 'Scottie, I hate to ask you this, but is there any chance at all that you might not have noticed it? You went through his pockets and anywhere else he could have put it?'

Anyone else and Scottie would have been livid at the suggestion that he hadn't done his job. But he knew Lorraine couldn't help asking; she needed to cover all her bases. He shook his head. 'There's no chance we missed anything, I'm sorry, love. But maybe he didn't plan it? Maybe he got dumped by a girl he liked and went a bit too far?'

'Not according to his mother. Sounds like a well-rounded kid as far as I can tell. Apart from the temporary depression.' Lorraine shrugged, 'But I just don't know for sure. Teenagers: one minute they're up the next minute they're down.'

'Yup, we've all been there . . .'

'Found out anything about that night watchman yet?' Edna piped up, her legs hooked around the stool she was sitting on. 'What was his name?'

'Eric McIvor,' Lorraine answered.

'Now there was a mess if ever I saw one, poor soul . . . God,' Edna shivered.

'Yeah, metal spikes can certainly trash a body,' Scottie nodded. 'Five entry wounds, and thankfully the one through the eye would have pierced the brain almost at once. Otherwise death would have come slowly and agonisingly. So in that sense, you could say he was lucky. Found out what he was doing on the roof yet?'

Lorraine shook her head. 'Nope, it's a mystery. The warehouse was definitely broken into, but nothing was taken, so we can't really speculate as to why the intruders were there. We could be looking for a vicious murderer, or it could have been an accident.'

'Found any reason why anyone would want to kill him?'

Lorraine shook her head. 'Seems that he was a decent guy, nice family, no enemies that they knew of. He was just about to retire.'

Scottie shrugged. 'So what was he doing up on the roof?'

'Wish I knew for sure,' Lorraine replied.

'Looks like you're as busy as usual,' Edna said.

'Wouldn't yer think the villains would give it a rest at Christmas?'

'Huh, I wish.' Lorraine picked her bag up and slung it over her shoulder. 'Well, I better get moving. I'll come by later, see if you've turned up anything more.'

'OK,' Scottie said, then with a wide grin on his face he nodded with his head towards the door.

'What?' Lorraine said, puzzled.

He opened his eyes wide and nodded again.

'He's trying to tell yer he's got mistletoe hanging in the door, the big lump,' Edna said.

'It's not Christmas quite yet, Scottie,' Lorraine admonished, though she was smiling as she walked out the door. 'Bye.'

Half an hour later Lorraine walked into her office with the nagging feeling that something was missing from the usual morning ritual. She sat down at her desk, opened the top drawer and rummaged amongst the Post-it notes, rubber bands and other paraphernalia for her customary cigarette substitute. Finally she found a blue pencil stub hiding at the back of the drawer.

She studied the chewed stub for a moment, then sighed before muttering, 'Bloody hell.' She was about to put it between her lips when it hit her just what she was missing.

'Well, damn and blast.' Rising in one swift movement she quickly went to the door, opened it, stepped out into the passageway and yelled, 'Carter!'

As if she'd rubbed a magic lamp and an evil genie

had appeared, Sara Jacobs, the woman Lorraine couldn't help but hate, stood facing her across the desk. Jacobs was as dark as Lorraine was fair, and heightwise she barely reached Lorraine's shoulders. She kept her naturally curly hair cropped very short and lately, Lorraine had noticed, she had become very heavy with the powder and paint.

'Yes?' Lorraine asked, looking suspiciously at the other woman, who always seemed to have a fixed sarcastic smile on her face, as if she was better than anyone else. Lorraine would deeply love to wipe that smile off her face.

Jacobs preened herself before saying, in a voice only slightly higher than a child's, her voice being one of the things that grated on Lorraine's nerves, 'It's Carter, boss,' Jacobs paused for effect. 'He, er, he's in the hospital.'

'Hospital?'

'Aye . . . Apparently he was rushed in less than an hour ago, they reckon it's probably appendicitis.'

'Bloody hell.' Carter was one of Lorraine's inside team; she and her Sergeant, Luke Daniels, had taken the young constable under their wing six months ago. Although Lorraine found him aggravating at times, she also valued his hard-working qualities and his unstinting loyalty. Something the woman in front of her seriously lacked. Lorraine had a feeling that Sara Jacobs couldn't even spell the word loyalty, let alone know what it meant. But for a reason neither she nor Luke could figure, Superintendent Clark seemed to think the sun shone out of her backside.

But it was what Jacobs said next that had Lorraine gritting her teeth and fairly ruined her day before it had even started. 'Clark has assigned me in Carter's place.'

'Has he now.' Lorraine didn't even try to keep the dismay out of her voice.

'Yep,' said Jacobs sunnily. 'Last thing he did before leaving on holiday.'

Lorraine groaned inwardly. *That's right. Clark's off on an extended holiday to Australia. Jammy bastard.*

Then her thoughts turned to Carter. *Fucking hell, how long are yer off with appendicitis? If he'd come to me I would have plucked it out meself, anything's better than having to put up with her.* Silently she eyed Sara Jacobs up and down.

God help us.

Lorraine had always been ambitious, and she saw nothing wrong in other people's ambitions, helped them when she could, but some people would go way beyond the line to get what they wanted and these were the dangerous ones. She knew instinctively that the woman in front of her would cut her grandmother's throat to get what she wanted. In Lorraine's book, there were things yer did and things yer didn't. Simple as that.

That Sara Jacobs had her sights set on Lorraine's job had been made quite obvious months ago. And while Lorraine didn't see her as a threat, she didn't trust Sara to do the day-to-day grunt work that Carter was so good at. Things got overlooked if you didn't pay attention – important things – but it was

23

clear that Jacobs considered ordinary policework beneath her.

Lorraine frowned. 'So, where's Luke?'

Jacobs shrugged, 'Dunno, probably late again.'

Lorraine tutted at this blatant dig. She knew for a fact that Luke was rarely if ever late, but she was well aware that Jacobs would quite happily try to score points off him. She pictured Jacobs at home in front of her mirror, licking her thumb and rubbing it down her lapel every time she thought she'd got one up on somebody else.

Come back Carter, all is forgiven. I'll even make yer tea for yer.

'Phone the hospital and find out everything yer can about Carter.'

'But boss . . . I just told yer.'

'Just do it. Find out when he's gonna be out of the operating theatre. I might pay him a visit.'

Jacobs hesitated a moment, then said quietly, 'Yes boss . . . Er . . . here's what Carter was working on yesterday. I've looked through the files and as usual there's nothing urgent.' She shook her head to emphasise just how unimportant Carter's day had been. 'A few minor burglaries . . . A domestic . . .' She shrugged. 'He made one or two house calls.' She gave another indifferent shrug as she placed the files on top of the grey metal filing cabinet in the corner. 'I'll go and phone the hospital now, boss.'

'You do that . . . But just a few points before yer go. Those minor burglaries, well, they're damn important to the poor buggers who were burgled, especially if what's been taken was of great sentimental value,

OK? And as for the domestic, I'm certain that the poor sod involved, be it a woman or a man, will think it very important, especially if that person is now in the damn hospital along with Carter . . . Got that?'

Not meeting Lorraine's eyes Jacobs bit her lip in an attempt to keep her resentment under control, and nodded, before turning to go.

'Pass the files down, please,' Lorraine said. Jacobs stopped in mid-stride and reached for the files. Carter usually had everything arranged just so for her, so Lorraine wasn't surprised to find out she was missing him already. She sighed. Just as she was sorting through the disorganised files, Luke Daniels walked in, filling the room with his presence. Lorraine tried to ignore the effect that Luke had on her but it was difficult. Not only was he, objectively, a very handsome man, he was also kind, considerate, funny . . . and he understood Lorraine in a way that no one else did. He stepped smartly to one side as Jacobs left the room, but Lorraine didn't miss the way she deliberately brushed against him.

Slapper.

'Good morning, boss.' Luke gave her his slow smile.

Wish he wouldn't do that!

'Is it?'

'Uh oh, what's the matter?' Luke threw himself in the chair opposite Lorraine's desk and tilted it back so that it was balancing on its back legs.

'It's Carter, he's in the bloody hospital.'

'Never!' Surprised, Luke brought the front two legs of the chair back to earth with a thump.

25

As Lorraine began to tell Luke what little she knew about Carter, Sara Jacobs came back.

'Definitely appendicitis,' she interrupted, then smiled at Luke before turning her attention back to a livid Lorraine. 'He goes under the knife at precisely three this afternoon.'

Under the knife, under the knife . . . The callous bitch, I know who I'd like to see under the knife.

Lorraine's appendix had been taken out a few months shy of her seventeenth birthday; she remembered just how painful it could be.

'By the way, one of these unimportant cases that Carter was working on is a young boy's death.' She passed the file over. 'Take it, study it, learn something. Shut the door behind you on the way out.'

'Yes, boss.' Jacobs picked the file up and headed out the door.

Luke, who had observed the tension between Lorraine and Jacobs with a wry smile, waited until Jacobs was out of earshot before saying, 'So what's on for us, boss?'

'I'm calling a departmental meeting,' Lorraine said. 'I want to bring everyone up to speed on the night watchman case, not that we've got much on that. With Carter away, I'm going to assign Jacobs to Sanderson. He'll be able to keep an eye on her. And I want to warn people not to make assumptions about the Stansfield boy. I don't want anyone to get lazy and miss something just because they think it's a cut-and-dried case of suicide.'

'Something you not telling me, boss?'

Lorraine sighed. 'I saw Scottie first thing this morning. He's had a look at the boy and there are a couple of things that don't add up. I'll fill you in later, but I don't want to say too much right now – let's round up the troops.'

Lorraine and Luke stood up and went to the door together. As they reached for the doorknob, their hands touched and she felt a spark of electricity jump between them. Lorraine gasped and she quickly drew her hand back.

He must have felt it.

He had to have felt it . . . Jesus!

If he had, he chose to ignore it as, smiling, he opened the door for her.

2

Rachel Henderson quietly closed the door behind her. She held her breath, waiting for the soft snick that sometimes sounded more like a revolver being cocked than a latch clicking in place.

For a brief moment she leaned against the door, saying a quick thank-you to whichever saint, angel or god was listening. He hadn't heard her leave – wouldn't be coming after her demanding that she stay at home with him instead of going to school. Rachel had been careful – she was always careful – to shower and dress as quickly and quietly as possible but sometimes he'd catch her on her way out the door. Today she was lucky. Taking a deep breath, she launched herself into the new day and headed for the bus stop.

Rachel would be sixteen next month, and a few months after that she would be leaving school and job-hunting. That had been the plan, until lately anyway. Get a job and leave home. Leave Houghton if it was really necessary. But now? Now the plan had changed, now there seemed to be another way out that didn't involve stocking shelves or cleaning toilets or leaving town.

Rachel walked, head down so as not to catch

anyone's eye, and counted the paving slabs to the bus stop. She knew exactly how many there were, knew every crack, stain and discarded wad of chewing gum on each of the 431 slabs because she'd been walking with her head down counting them for the last three years. Ever since her stepfather had walked into her bedroom one dark winter morning a month after her mother had died, and said that she was now the woman of the house.

Trying to stop herself thinking about the horrible night she'd just endured, she began to silently count in French, her favourite subject. Until recently, thinking about running away to live in France had been her major escape route in the dead of night when all was quiet except the creaking of the floorboards, but now she had another.

Rachel shifted her bag over to her other shoulder and breathed in sharply. The action had made one of the cuts on her arm open, and she could feel a trickle of blood roll down her arm and stick to her shirt. She had been self-harming for over a year now, and the relief was tremendous for a while. The knife was silent, kept her secrets well and eased the pain. Until she escaped him, she used the knife to put the pain she felt inside outside herself, on her body, where it was easier to deal with.

Until reality moved right back in, as it always did. Slap bang in the middle of the night when her ten-year-old half-brother David and eight-year-old half-sister Mandy were fast asleep. Reality in the form of her stepfather.

The threats were endless, from telling everybody

that she was a spiteful shameless slut – that mouthful had come out the first night and had been repeated at least once a week since – to claiming that no one would believe her – they would think she was making it all up for attention, and why would they think anything else? He was a respectable, upstanding member of the community, while she was obviously just a sad little tart. And didn't the whole world know just how simply evil some teenage girls could be?

Lately he'd been threatening to use little Mandy the way he used her if Rachel told anyone. That made her feel sick: she couldn't let Mandy go through it and be ruined, the same way that she was.

And there were rewards for keeping shtum, fantastic ones some might think. *Yeah, fantastic if yer didn't care about a big fat bastard slobbering all over you, and doing stuff to yer that not only hurt, but made yer want to heave.*

The rewards ranged from the straighteners that she used on her hair every morning to the latest fashion gear. She guessed it was some kind of perverted guilt that made him treat her to whatever she wanted and pay for wherever she wanted to go. Treats that had already turned David and Mandy against her, because they had to do without whilst she was showered with stuff she didn't even want. She loved them both with all her heart but now she knew they almost hated her. Though she never asked for anything, at least once a week – sometimes more – under the envious gaze of her half-siblings, some gift or other would be waiting for her on the breakfast table.

Who wants gifts if it means yer life is pure hell?

Night after night she prayed for God to help her, but He never answered her prayers. *Too busy, look what else is going on in the world.*

Or maybe He didn't have time to answer prayers from girls like her.

But perhaps now He had heard her. Now there was hope, at least she had that. She might never end up with an ordinary bloke but there was someone special who cared about her. Who was gentle to her, in a way that her stepfather never could be. She didn't even need to run away to France because her life was going to change right here in Houghton. And if she was here, she wouldn't have to worry about Mandy alone, with him.

She reached *quatre cents trente et un* and knew she was at the bus stop. She looked up and her heart dropped, Claire Lumsdon and Katy Jacks were already there. Most mornings they were chasing the bus along the street.

She tried to avoid Claire and Katy as much as she could. It was a shame, because once they had all been close – extremely close, three best friends together. They spent all their time round at each other's houses, playing with their Barbies, plaiting each other's hair and giggling about the silliest things. But that was before her stepfather had made her grow up too quickly. Overnight, she lost her spark, had become sullen and withdrawn, unable to have fun the way she used to. Claire and Katy didn't understand why Rachel had changed, and called her stuck-up and a snob and had even stopped talking to her for a

31

while. It was better now that they were on speaking terms, but Rachel still felt the tension between them. Or, maybe, it was just her.

But today Claire and Katy weren't talking by themselves as usual. Instead there was a gaggle of younger children gathered about them, and Katy Jacks was holding forth about something or another, with the rest of the kids listening enthralled.

'Hi Rach.' Claire smiled at her. Rachel gave her a nod and self-consciously pulled the sleeves of her school blazer down to make sure they covered the cuts on the back of her wrists.

Claire's nearly white hair had been done up in hundreds of tiny plaits and Rachel grudgingly admitted to herself that she looked fantastic. Katy was nowhere near as cute as Claire, although if her nose wasn't so big she might come close. But both of them were attractive girls, and popular. Rachel sighed. What she would give to swap places with either of them.

What Rachel did not see was that she was just as cute as the other two girls. When she brushed her hair each morning she looked with loathing at the image in the mirror, her self-hatred preventing herself from seeing that she was, in fact, a very pretty girl. Her strawberry-blonde hair hung to her shoulders with the aid of the straighteners, her deep fringe rested on her eyebrows. She had hazel eyes and a petite figure that should have ensured a steady crop of boyfriends, would have, if Rachel gave any of them half a chance. Gave herself half a chance.

There had been times when she'd been really low

and had almost told Claire her dreadful secret. But at the last minute she always thought about what betraying the family would bring with it. If her stepfather was put away – that's supposing she was even believed – the other two would probably never forgive her. Especially if they were split up, like he said they would be, and put in separate homes.

Rachel stood away from the group waiting for the bus and tried to ignore Katy, who loved being the centre of attention. Rachel knew that Katy and Claire were popular with the younger kids, who liked to copy their style, but Rachel felt above all that now. She didn't need Claire or Katy as friends any more; she had others now, others who shared the secret.

She smiled inwardly thinking about that other secret. The one that wasn't shameful and hers alone – the one that was going to change everyone's lives. And now she had friends – proper friends, more like family to her than her stepfather ever could be – and their lives were going to change too. Kurt, Niall, Richard and Melissa. She smiled again to herself. They were real friends, true friends, they would do anything for each other. If someone had told her six months ago that she would be hanging out with Melissa Tremaine, much less counting her one of her best friends, she wouldn't have believed them. Katy and Claire could be as popular as they liked – they hadn't been specially chosen like she and her friends had.

Meanwhile, Katy, who was thrilled to see that she had an audience of at least half a dozen kids, who were listening to her with their mouths hanging open, said in a loud voice. 'Bet yers don't know the legend of the Seven Sisters? Yer know, the reason why the trees up at Copt Hill are called that? Well, in 1653, seven witches were found bollock-naked in a pond –'

'Ge'bye,' Simon Brown whispered in awe, his carrot-coloured head bobbing up and down. '*Real* witches?'

'Ner, pretend ones.' Jilly Bowmont, a petite auburn-haired girl a few years below them said, as she dug Simon in his ribs.

'Yeah, they bloody well were real ones,' Katy went on quickly. She was loving the limelight and was determined to hang on to it as long as possible. 'They managed to catch them, but one got away.'

'Katy Jacks, you're just making it all up to frighten us,' Jilly Bowmont put in, 'Cos I know for a fact there's only six trees at Copt Hill, so there.'

There were nods from some of the others.

But Katy wasn't having her glory stolen away from her that easily. No way. The attention was on her, and she was keeping it. Boring Saturday afternoons with her uncle Tony had finally paid off. Until that moment Katy had not realised just how much of the Houghton history he'd been spouting to her for years had actually sunk in.

'That's because, dummy, if yer'd waited until people were finished, yer'd hear the reason why,' she glared at Jilly Bowmont, wondering how the cockeyed little know-it-all had dared to contradict her in the first place, then turning back to the rest of the kids delivered her punchline with a flourish. 'They cut the seventh tree down as a warning to the witch what got away.'

34

'Bet yer don't know what sort of trees they are then,' Jilly replied, putting an edge on.

Katy glared at the little cow who seemed intent on stealing her thunder but then a saviour from the back of the crowd piped up, 'Beech, they're beech trees.'

'Aye, beech, that's just what I was gonna say an' all.' Katy quickly jumped in, praying that whoever it was that had opened her big mouth, had done her homework.

Deep in thought, Rachel was oblivious to Jilly and Katy's arguing. There were usually squabbles at the bus stop of a morning, about practically anything they could think of, and mostly just for the sake of it. But then her head whipped up when she heard Jilly Bowmont say loudly, 'So which one of the trees was it that Richy Stansfield hung himself from?'

Rachel looked up as Katy Jacks said, shrugging, 'Dunno. Does it matter?'

Rachel walked round to where Claire and Katy were standing and pulled them away from the group. 'Did I hear right?' she whispered urgently. 'Richard Stansfield hung himself?'

Claire replied, 'Aye, that's right. His body was found yesterday.'

'Yer sure?' Rachel asked, a lump forming in her throat. She felt like she was going to faint and be sick all at the same time. 'Yer sure it was Richy? It wasn't someone else?'

'Yeah, I'm sure,' said Katy Jacks aggressively. 'Me mam was round at his place last night, looking after his mam. What yer saying? That I would make something like that up?'

Rachel looked at Katy, hoping against hope that the other girl was just telling tall tales, but why would anybody make up something like that? Katy wasn't half as nasty as she pretended to be. She might love to be the first to have the goss, but deliberately making lies up just to upset Rachel? No, that was more than even Katy would do.

Rachel's heart was thumping wildly in her chest, and the lump in her throat was still hurting. *Richy dead? Killed himself? No, not Richy. Just can't be true.*

She looked back down at the pavement, still unable to fully take in the shocking news. She felt the tears well up behind her eyes and rubbed them furiously, not wanting the others to see how much she cared. She was closest to Kurt and Melissa but with Richy's ready laugh and cheeky ways it had been impossible not to like him. And now he was dead. It just didn't make any sense.

Aware that both Katy and Claire were watching her closely, Rachel pulled herself together and stared back at them.

'Where's the stupid bus?' she muttered. 'We're all gonna be in trouble at this rate.'

Rachel couldn't have cared less whether she got to school on time or not. But there were people she had to talk to and the sooner the bus came the sooner she'd get to the others and find out whether they were thinking the same thing as her.

Kurt Allendale rubbed at the bus window with his sleeve. 'Bloody manky dirt,' he said, looking out of the clean circle he'd made. He was looking for Rachel and it took every ounce of his will not to shout her name when he saw her standing at the bus stop. Rachel's attendance was not that hot, and lately he'd started to look forward to the short time they spent alone together on the bus to school

Kurt was sixteen years old, tall and athletic-looking. But, aside from wearing all the latest Nike gear, he wasn't sporty at all and would do anything to sit on the bench, even though he looked like he'd be a natural at anything he put his mind to. He even looked like a bit like a young Lee Sharpe with his dark hair and pale-blue eyes.

But even though he didn't play a contact sport of any kind, he usually sported a bruise or two from falling down the stairs or hitting his head on the doorframe or jamming his fingers in the kitchen drawer. The family doctor, who had treated both Kurt's parents since they had themselves been children, would shake his head at Kurt's latest injury, sympathise with Kurt's mother's latest explanation, and file his notes away in a folder that Kurt was sure had 'accident prone' stamped all over it. Kurt's parents, even though they weren't church-going, had been raised in the Catholic faith, and their romance was whirlwind. They were married within a matter of months after they first met and, as both families were well off, no expense was spared. The bride had three bridesmaids and was ferried to church in the family's vintage Rolls-Royce, and the honeymoon was spent in Barbados. But the couple had squabbled the whole time; what had been minor niggles became major incompatibilities, and they could barely stay in the same room as each other. Kurt had worked out that he must have been conceived in Barbados; he didn't have any brothers or sisters. And his parents didn't even seem to know that the word 'divorce' existed.

Kurt shifted on the bus seat and his hand went to his ribs. The bruise, the size and shape of an egg, was healing, its edges turning yellow though the centre was still a nasty, purplish black and hurt if he wasn't careful. He knew it was his own fault, always had been, he'd never been able to do anything right.

His mother was always telling him that even her best friend's twelve-year-old brat could play rugby better than he could. He was no good at art like his cousin Matthew; anything Kurt drew looked like a heap of crazed spaghetti. Neither was he much good at computers, though, according to his mother, his other cousin, prickly Paula, was a genius at computers, could practically make them talk, yeah, and sing and dance an' all.

The only thing he was good for really was upsetting his mother, top marks for that all right.

Yeah, and when the fists found their target he curled up into the tightest of balls.

Now that he was good at.

All it took was practice.

Practice and the ability to dream. Now that he certainly needed. To be able to dream of whichever country his father was in at the moment.

The box under the bed was brimming with postcards from all sorts of exotic locations. Every night he took them out, stared at them until his eyes hurt, then dreamed. He dreamed of boarding a plane and flying to Dubai or Sydney or wherever his father was doing business, and staying with him, perhaps even for good. There had been promises made but, what with school, nothing had ever come of it.

The family firm exported goods to just about every country in the world, which was a good excuse for his father to be somewhere abroad for at least ten months of the year. When he was at home, it was great. Kurt's mother would leave him alone and his body would start to heal. But then, when Kurt's dad left, his mother would find twice as many things to be angry about, would hit Kurt twice as hard, taking her rage at Kurt's dad out on him.

But things were gonna change soon, he thought as he moved along for Rachel to sit down. Pretty soon he'd be able to get out of there, now that he had somewhere to go; a place where they would never find him.

He sensed that something was wrong by her pale face and the stiff way she held herself when she sat down. He hoped her old man had not been nagging her again – from what she'd told him, the old sod sounded like a right moany git.

When she whispered just what it was, his face went as pale as hers and apart from making a quick call on his mobile, he sat in stunned silence until the bus reached the school gates.

With his left hand Niall Campbell checked that both of his T-shirts were tucked in properly underneath his pale blue hoodie, as he ran the tip of his cigarette up and down the wall, momentarily fascinated by the tiny shower of sparks. He watched until there was nothing left but the dead orange stub with a blackened end. Interest gone, he threw the stub on the ground and turned his attention to the schoolyard.

He gave a small nod of satisfaction when he saw Melissa Tremaine heading towards him.

Niall was seventeen years old, and tall. His fair hair was cropped as short as possible, otherwise it curled the moment it left his scalp. His eyes were a deep velvet brown. He could have been an incredibly handsome boy if he wasn't so painfully thin. He was so thin that he was difficult to look at; his skin was stretched tightly across his sharp cheekbones and his eyes had deep shadows underneath them, making them look unnaturally bright.

He glanced behind him, looking for the other two, but the bus hadn't arrived yet.

Normally Niall tried to stay in bed as long as he could but today, after he had heard Kurt's hushed, panicked voice, he had thrown on his clothes and run to school. It wasn't far, but he never ate breakfast, and last night he'd thrown up his dinner, and so the exertion had made him out of breath. He still felt a little dizzy.

Watching Melissa move closer he repetitively pulled at each finger of his left hand, cracking the knuckles. He knew how much this annoyed Melissa, but it was a nervous habit he couldn't seem to shake off. He shook his fingers out, then hugged himself (God, he was so cold) while he waited for the

40

frowning thundercloud that was Melissa Tremaine to reach him.

Melissa had to have the shortest fuse in the world. Niall often wondered why she even bothered to come to school because she was forever being sent out of the classroom to, as the teacher put it, cool off.

Melissa was beautiful. This she knew for a fact; she had good eyes and mirrors were everywhere. She knew her long dark hair was thick and shiny, her brown eyes were large and naturally heavy-lashed, her skin so creamy smooth that once she'd been sent out of class to wash off the non-existent make-up, which exasperated her so much that she had vandalised both rest rooms.

Yeah, Niall thought, *Melissa has a gorgeous face all right, but don't look down, don't, whatever yer do, stare at her outsize tits, or the rolls of fat that run down her body like waves every time she moves.*

Jesus, even her ankles have rolls on them.

Niall hadn't been to Melissa's house. If he had, then he might have been surprised. Her parents and her three older brothers were all slim. Melissa hated being the fat one in a house where appearance was the be-all and end-all. She hated the looks her brothers' skinny girlfriends, fake-tanned and bleached blonde every one of them, gave her when she walked in the room, hated the way that they whispered to each other behind their hands. Melissa hadn't always been fat, but when she was twelve she had been hit by a car and was bedridden for weeks. She developed a taste for food, and food became both her best friend and her enemy. It was a vicious cycle:

she would eat when she felt bad, she felt bad because she was fat. And when the teasing from her brothers got too much, or she couldn't forget the snide remarks from her schoolmates, she'd take refuge in food and binge, not even tasting what she shoved in her mouth, until there was no food left.

She couldn't even dress the same way as the other girls at school. Her school uniform, a pair of men's extra-sized black trousers and a man's white shirt, were clean, but even they were too tight for her.

Niall didn't much like looking at Melissa anyhow; she always reminded him of how fat he was.

Melissa was thinking pretty much the opposite of Niall. She looked at him worriedly; he was looking more and more like a drug addict every day.

Why was he so skinny? She had never once seen him take drugs, and he definitely only smoked fags. She knew that his parents, both busy lawyers who she had met and, amazingly, quite liked, had been dragging Niall around from doctor to doctor for the last year, but Niall just kept on getting thinner and thinner, just like she kept on getting fatter and fatter. The difference was she could see that she was fat, but no matter what yer said to Niall, he couldn't see that he was in danger of slipping through the cracks in the path.

'So, what yer after then?' Melissa demanded, her hands perched on the region that on anyone else would be called hips. 'It must be something extra special to drag you out of bed before dinner time,' she hissed impatiently. There were three packets of beefy crisps and a king-sized bar of wholenut chocolate in her bag, and the thought of them was starting to make her mouth water.

Niall took a deep breath, and ran his tongue over his teeth one last time before announcing, 'Richy Stansfield's dead.'

'Fuck off!' Melissa managed before her jaw fell open.

Niall nodded, 'Honest . . . he was found hanging from a tree at the Seven Sisters last night.'

The colour drained from Melissa's face. 'No . . . No . . . Do Kurt and Rachel know?'

'Yeah, that's why I'm here. Kurt phoned twenty minutes ago, good job I don't live far, innit . . . But where the fuck've they gotten to?'

'We're here,' Kurt called, as he and Rachel hurried to join them. 'A couple of idiots were clowning around on the bus and the driver refused to go any further until they got off.'

'Is it true?' Melissa asked, looking at Rachel.

Rachel bit her lip and nodded. 'Katy Jacks knows somehow. Why would she lie about that?'

'Shit . . . How?'

'It . . . they've been saying it's suicide.'

'Suicide,' Melissa gulped as her flawless complexion turned dull grey.

'That's what she said, you deaf or something?' Niall sprung forward from the wall he'd been leaning on as if it were made of rubber. 'But it doesn't seem like Richy, does it?'

Kurt spoke up. 'And remember, he was going to see Marcel . . .'

'What are you trying to say?' Rachel's eyes flashed

43

red with anger. 'We don't know what was going on in Richy's head. So he talked to Marcel, so what? We all know he was weak, we all knew that he wasn't serious . . .'

Melissa swallowed hard, and looked at each of them, 'I want out.'

'No, don't be daft,' Rachel said. 'Come on. Think about it. It probably was suicide. Marcel wouldn't do anything to hurt anybody, yer know he wouldn't.'

'But Rachel, it doesn't make sense,' Melissa replied. 'Richy tells us he's going to talk to Marcel and the next thing we know is that he's, well, dead. And have yer asked yerself why he would want to do something so, so horrible as . . . Why would he?'

Rachel shrugged, 'I don't know.' She looked at Kurt for help, but Kurt had none to give her.

Niall finally spoke. 'I don't know what happened. I can't believe Richy killed himself. I don't think Marcel had anything to do with it either. But he'll know better than any of us what we should do next.'

'We should talk to him after the meeting tonight,' Kurt said.

Rachel nodded her head in agreement.

'Yer all forgetting one thing.' Melissa stared at them, her eyes widening with fright. 'The night watchman.'

3

Aside from his kids, Danny Jordan only had one real love in his life. Elizabeth the third he called her, Lizzy for short. She was a white Nissan minibus and his pride and joy. He, Lizzy and a few mates had been wearing out the road from Sunderland to Calais for the last four years, and he proudly told anyone who would listen that, unlike a few women he could mention, Lizzy had never once let him down.

Danny called her Elizabeth because of his love for old films and the queen of his dreams was Elizabeth Taylor. He'd worn out at least four tapes of *Giant*, and his current girlfriend Julie was starting to kick up a fuss.

And who could blame her, his cousin Len had said when he'd admitted to once or twice, in the throes of passion, calling Julie Elizabeth. A common mistake, he shrugged. It only ever happened when he went up to bed straight after watching *Cat on a Hot Tin Roof*. Completely understandable. He still couldn't see how she could say he was obsessed with the film star. Fancy being jealous of a film star! His ex-wife Jade had been the same, and the evil bitch had even taken to kicking Lizzy's tyres every time he called round to pick the kids up. He just couldn't understand the problem. It wasn't as if Elizabeth Taylor was gonna walk through Houghton-le-Spring any time soon, for Christ's sake, nor was she ever gonna be perched on the top of Penshaw Monument where nearly the whole bloody world would be able to see her, worse luck.

He sighed. *Women. Bet they don't even understand themselves.*

Danny was tall, thick set and in dire need of a shave ten minutes after he'd had one. He had dark hair, green eyes and, usually, a friendly smile. He also had a mortgage that he struggled with monthly, and a maintenance bill that he swore supported half the kids on the Seahills.

He worked shifts at the Nissan car factory, which left him with ample time to make his frequent trips to the Continent for the duty-free fags and booze that helped keep his head just above water and his three bairns in shoe leather. He swore if it wasn't for the extra few bob he made on the booze trips, he'd be rising out of his grave every morning and clocking on well into the year 3006.

He was waiting outside his cousin's house in Tulip Crescent. When he was a kid, his friends had called it the House of Usher after an old Hammer horror, and now their kids still called it that, though they probably did not know the reason why.

Not that yer could blame them, Danny thought, as the red satin curtains twitched. It was an imposing building that had been in Len's family for years but was in desperate need of a paint and grass grew out of the drains. It wasn't so bad inside, or it wouldn't be if Len's daughters didn't insist on draping the furniture with black lace and spraying everything with patchouli. Danny was just about to give up waiting and knock on the door, when Len appeared, shutting the door behind him.

At forty-two, Len was as tall and dark as Danny, with green eyes that were a shade or two lighter than his cousin's, but the resemblance ended there. Len was extremely thin, with legs not much fatter than a pair of pipe cleaners. He had the look of a professional pall bearer off to perfection, especially since he had taken to dressing in top-to-toe black after his wife had died three years ago. It also didn't help that the remaining two ladies in the house, his daughters – nineteen-year-old Carol and seventeen-year-old Lucie – were both goths, who dyed their hair a deep shade of purple, hung heavy silver crucifixes around their necks, wore long, floaty dresses that laced up at the bodice and made up their pale faces with dark eyeliner and black lipstick. Danny often wondered where the hell they got black lipstick from, but seeing as both girls were firebrands, and very touchy on most subjects, Danny kept his questions close to his chest. He wouldn't be surprised if they got called Morticia or Vampira to their faces; it was what he called them behind their backs.

After locking the door, taking three steps up the path, then spinning round and going back to check that the door really was locked, a habit that drove the usually laid-back Danny up the wall, Len, blue plastic carrier bag swinging at his side, strode up the path and jumped into the minibus. Danny sniffed the air, praying that Len didn't have egg sandwiches again. Three days ago he'd very nearly caused a mutiny on the bus over the stink the eggs had made after being wrapped up and sweating in the heat of the van for nearly twenty hours.

God only knows what he's got in that carrier bag, but anything was better than day-old boiled-egg sandwiches, that's for sure.

Got to keep everybody happy, usually that's quite easy: just make sure that Adam doesn't take his trainers off.

'Morning,' Len grunted with his usual dour smile as he made himself comfortable. For the next day and a half, apart from their time spent on the ship, Lizzy would be home to five men. That's why Len always demanded family rights: he was the first to be picked up so that he could stake his claim on the best seat.

Len loved his comforts – always had. Danny had lost count of the times they had camped out as kids, and he'd woken up in the middle of the night stiff as a board, freezing cold and completely alone because Len's bed had called him home.

He watched Len through the mirror. Satisfied that he was sitting down and buckled up, he drove to the next pick-up, Brian Levy's. Brian was medium height, thick set and very strong as he worked out almost every day in the gym. He kept his long brown hair tied back in a ponytail that hung past his shoulder blades; his eyes were the same colour as his hair. No one knew too much about Brian. Len, whose opinions on every matter were frequently aired, reckoned that Brian was forty pretending to be thirty, a sign of vanity, according to Len. Danny didn't disagree with Len when it came to Brian – he noticed that he dressed young for his age in tracksuits and trainers, and occasionally wore a baseball cap; once or twice he'd turned up in a hoodie. And it all seemed to be the latest, trendy gear, the stuff you saw teenagers wear.

Brian had only lived on the Seahills for a couple of years, so no one really knew for a fact how old he was, and no one cared to ask. He'd come knocking on Danny's door one day six months ago to buy a packet of duty-frees and talked himself into a job. His accent was South Durham pit village, although which one was anybody's guess. As far as anyone knew he lived alone in the corner house in Daffodil Crescent. But he kept to himself and worked hard, and both were assets as far as Danny was concerned.

For some reason Brian had the same annoying habit of double-checking everything just as Len did. Only Brian wasn't content with just checking the damn door and maybe having a quick glance through the window. Oh no, Brian also went back into the bloody house to check everything out, and God only knows what else he did in there.

Resting his elbows on Lizzy's steering wheel and his chin in his hands, Danny sighed. Brian's ritual took four minutes each time they made the trip, and there was no way in God's known universe that he could be hurried along. And Danny certainly wasn't gonna try. He had a feeling that Brian could be hiding a real mean streak, and he wasn't gonna get on the bad side of him, not for a measly four minutes.

Brian finally jumped in the van and Danny felt like applauding. He said his good-mornings, sat down with legs stretched out in front of him and, using his rolled-up sleeping bag for a pillow, promptly went to sleep. This suited Danny, because in four hours Brian would take over the driving and Danny liked to think that Lizzy was in the safe hands of a fully rested driver.

Before they moved off to the next pick-up, Danny leaned over and opened the glove compartment to check the three grand he had stashed there. He would do this many times on the road to France, much to the annoyance of his passengers, who would look at each other then pull faces behind his back as they shook their heads at this silly little habit, none of them realising their own little habits annoyed Danny just as much.

Danny stopped outside of Adam Glazier's door, at the other end of the street to Brian's. Adam was already outside and waiting for them. He was twenty-six years old, tall and slim with fair hair that was already thinning on top, his hazel eyes had a slightly oriental slant and his right front tooth was snapped in half. Having broken away from home and tried life on his own in a council flat for three months a year ago, he'd decided that life was much easier with his widowed mam, even if he had to put up with shit from his teenage twin sisters. At least there was always food on the table, so he had moved back home. The three-bedroom semi-detached house was also home to four boxer dogs. Oscar, the eldest, was beaten, only marginally, in his lager consumption by Adam's mother, Brenda.

'Hi guys,' Adam said, his perpetual grin lighting up his face as he stepped over Brian's legs and flopped down next to Len. 'Wanna hear a good joke?'

Len looked him up and down, snorted loudly, then muttered something unintelligible under his breath before swinging his head back to the window.

'What?' Adam asked, his eyebrows raised in a picture of innocence.

Len turned back, gave Adam a calculated stare, and then said an emphatic, 'No.'

'Why not?' Adam held his hands out palms up and looked around the minibus as if he had a huge audience.

''Cos it'll be yer usual stupid crap, yer daft idiot, so what's the point . . . And if yer ask me yer just make them up as yer go along, 'cos believe you me, each one's worse than the one before, so there.'

'No, I don't make them up. Anyhow, yer've got no sense of humour at all. Yer as miserable as me cousin Jimmy. He wouldn't get a punch line if it stood up on two legs and bit his friggin nipple.'

'Aye, yer do make them up, yer tell the worst jokes I've ever heard . . . And half of them are blasphemous.' Len tutted. 'And, of all things, fancy mentioning yer cousin's nipples! See what I mean, depraved, that's what yer are . . . depraved.'

'Oh no,' Adam groaned, 'he's on his God trip again . . . And anyhow, yer git dopey twat, somebody's gotta make them up, else where the fuck do yer think

51

they come from, eh? . . . God's little joke shop in the sky?'

'See what I mean, do yer see what I mean . . . blasphemy.' Len practically spat the last word at Adam. 'Yer should be struck right between yer eyes.'

'Just tell the fucking joke, will yer? For Christ's sake.' Brian snapped, glaring at Adam with one eye.

'I thought you were asleep?'

'I was 'til you arrived, yer prick.'

'OK, OK, chill.'

Brian's other eye opened and Adam was just about to tell his joke when Danny said, 'We've got to pick Jacko Musgrove up, then we'll be on our way. The forecast's fine so we should make good time this trip.'

Adam's ears pricked up, but he wasn't interested in the weather forecast, he left that to Danny.

'Is Jacko joining the crew now, Danny?'

'Aye, just for the run up 'til Christmas like. Remember last year, there was nowt left come Boxing Day. And I had four days of hell with people knocking on the door. I'm certain half of them thought I was telling lies. Jesus, if I'd had the gear I would have been over the moon to sell it.'

'Good. I like Jacko.'

Len grunted his approval and Brian, who didn't know Jacko that well, shrugged his shoulders. As the last man to join the crew he had very little say.

Danny drove down the street. At the bottom he turned right then right again, which brought him outside Jacko Musgrove's house. He beeped the horn twice but it was from across the road, the house facing his, that Jacko came, the house Christina Jenkins shared with her father.

Hand in hand they walked down the path to the gate. Once there Jacko took Christina in his arms and kissed her. It was clear to all of them on the bus that she returned the kiss a thousand times over even though her face was as scarlet as the jumper she wore.

'Oooo,' Adam said. 'Since when have them two buggers been an item?'

'A few months now. They got together just after Christina was attacked and little Melanie went missing, remember, round about Houghton Feast time?' Len put in, pleased that he had the gen and it gave him one up on Adam.

'Oh aye, nasty business that, we were all out looking for Melanie, like. Me and me mam had the dogs out,' Adam replied, still ogling Christina.

'What I want to know,' Brian said, 'is what's a good-looking chick like her doing with an ugly bugger like him. He's got a patch on his eye for fuck's sake, and fucking scars on his cheek.'

Len snorted, 'Jacko's not ugly, at least not underneath where it counts. And he wasn't born like that, that happened in a bike accident. And he's not as ugly as some I could mention.' Len's eyes raked Adam up and down.

But Adam was still looking at Christina, wondering why he couldn't get somebody like that, and he didn't take the bait, thinking Len was now having a go at Brian.

Jacko kissed Christina again, then whispered

something in her ear which made her smile. A moment later he was climbing into the bus and saying hello to everybody.

They each returned the greeting then settled down for the long haul.

As they pulled onto the main road through the Burnside that led from Houghton, Adam winked at Jacko. 'When's the wedding then?'

Jacko laughed, 'Give us a chance, mate, we're not even engaged yet.'

'Slow, aren't yer?'

Jacko shrugged.

'How's her old man taking it?' Danny asked.

'Not good, but Christina's stronger now and the old git's not getting so much of his own way. Besides he's no match for Doris.'

Doris was Jacko's mother and a force to be reckoned with.

Len nodded, 'Aye, she'll show Jenkins the road home all right.'

'True,' Adam agreed. He'd been on the receiving end of Doris's wrath before. 'Anyhow, want to hear a good joke?'

Len groaned as Brian snapped, 'Just tell the fucking joke, will yer?'

'OK, OK, chill . . . Right, what's the difference between an in-law and an outlaw?'

Len couldn't help himself: even though he moaned about Adam's jokes he fell for it every time. 'What then . . . Come on, tell us.'

'An outlaw's wanted.' Adam slapped his own thigh as he laughed out loud.

As they pulled onto the A19 and the others groaned, Danny chuckled. He quite liked Adam's jokes.

4

The meeting had gone pretty much as Lorraine expected. Most of her staff hadn't yet heard the news about Carter and there had been an audible moan when she told them that she was going to have to spread his workload amongst them. They were always short-staffed, so one person off sick made a huge difference. Lorraine told them that there would be an inquest into Richard Stansfield's death and, until then, they should keep their minds open. She could tell Dinwall was sceptical. You didn't need to be long in the police force to see your share of young life wasted through suicide. 'But,' Lorraine stressed, looking Dinwall straight in the eye, 'a verdict of suicide can tear the lives of the ones left behind apart. They'll be constantly running through the "what ifs": what if they had been a bit nicer, what if they hadn't snapped that one time, what if they had been more sensitive to what was going on. We all know that if someone wants to kill themselves – really wants to – then nothing anyone said or did is gonna stop them. But I've some "what ifs" of my own: what if Richard Stansfield *didn't* want to kill himself? What if it was just a stupid game gone wrong? What if he wasn't the only one up on Seven Sisters that night? We owe it to his mother to find out.'

The police officers muttered to each other as they got up out of their seats. Lorraine ignored them and went on. 'Hang on for a minute, I need to divvy up Carter's workload, remember?'

Grumbling, they returned to their seats.

After the meeting, Luke had decided to nip out and get him and Lorraine a cup of coffee from the take-out place. He was carrying a couple of cups in a cardboard holder and he could smell the coffee, which he knew Lorraine would appreciate, when a loud shouting came from up the street just as he was approaching the zebra crossing outside of Peter's Bakery in Newbottle Street.

He frowned when he saw a white tracksuited youth with a blue cap perched on the back of his head, running away from Li'l Ole Daisy's, a recently opened dried-flower shop. In each hand he held a large flower display, one of them a huge basket full of red flowers and green ferns woven through with silver tinsel that was nearly bigger than he was. The other, which looked like a weird display of brown twigs gone haywire, was fast losing pieces of itself as the youth ran. Obviously, the thief had started his Christmas shopping.

Stopping the first person to pass by, an old grey-bearded man walking a small three-legged dog that looked as old and grizzled as the man, Luke handed him the coffee. 'Here mate, hold on to these for a minute.' The old man nodded eagerly, a grin neatly splitting the beard.

Luke didn't give chase because the youth was on a collision course with him. He waited patiently and when the flower thief was abreast of him and running at full speed, Luke stuck his foot out and a moment later flowers and thief were sprawled on the path.

Bending over, Luke took hold of his collar and hauled him to his feet. When his toes were barely scraping the path, Luke shook him.

'What the fuck yer doing, yer black bastard?' the amazed thief yelled.

'Placing you under arrest, got a problem with that? Eh?' Luke shook him again.

The youth struggled wildly. 'Yer can't do that, yer not a copper yer fucking idiot, get back in the fucking nut house and let me go, yer black . . .'

Luke shook him again. 'Save it, creep, unless yer can come up with something new, 'cos quite frankly, it's boring. What? Do yers all have a handbook on what to say to black coppers?'

'Piss off.'

Ignoring him, Luke used his free hand to take out his mobile and phone for a squad car.

'Me brothers will get yer for this, yer git fucking twat. I'm warning yer now, yer bastard, yer better let me go or else.' He struggled as hard as he could, but a man three times his size would not have been able to wriggle out of Luke's grasp.

'Just make sure yer tell yer brothers where they can find me, OK?'

Just then the shopkeeper, a pretty young girl, arrived. She picked the flower arrangements up and looked at the damage. Breathing a sigh of relief when she saw that there was nothing that couldn't be put right, she looked at Luke and said. 'Thank you so much.'

Luke nodded, then, overcome that the thief had not got away with her hard work, the flower girl impulsively flung her arms around Luke and hugged him. Luke smiled but, his hands already full, he declined to return the hug, although for one brief moment he was reminded of Lorraine.

'I'll send someone along to take a statement when we get this toerag duly processed and into a cell, OK?'

Nodding and smiling she turned and took her arrangements back to her flower shop.

At the mention of a cell, the toerag struggled even harder, and with a supreme effort managed to land a hard kick on Luke's shin.

Luke breathed heavily and glared at him. 'Nice one, we'll just add resisting arrest and assaulting a police officer to the charge . . . Like that, do yer?'

'Fuck off.'

A moment later the squad car arrived. Luke handed the thief over, by now not so cocky, and turned to retrieve his coffee. He was just in time to see the old man and his dog scarpering off round the corner, taking Luke's coffee with them.

'Well, isn't that just great,' Luke muttered, 'I hope yer enjoy them.'

'Well done, Luke,' two voices said in chorus. Luke spun round to see Mavis and Peggy beaming at him.

'We saw it all,' Peggy went on. 'Didn't we, Mave? We were just standing over there.' She pointed to

Barclays bank across the road on the opposite corner. 'We saw him kick yer, the cheeky little rat.'

Mavis nodded her agreement.

Then Peggy blatantly nudged Mavis as she said with a grin, 'By the way, Mavis has something to ask yer, bonny lad. Haven't yer, Mave?'

Luke looked from Peggy to Mavis and raised his eyebrows in a questioning look.

Mavis took a deep breath, mentally kicking Peggy for dropping her in it and said, 'Yes, well, we were wondering, Peggy and me . . .'

'And Lorry,' Peggy chimed in.

'And Lorry,' Mavis added, praying Luke couldn't see how tightly gritted her teeth were. 'If yer, er, if you weren't working, would yer like to spend Christmas dinner with us?'

For a moment Luke seemed taken aback, then he grinned, showing a glint of gold, and said, 'I'll have to check the roster but I would love nothing more, ladies. Believe me, it will be a pleasure.'

'Great.' Peggy smiled as widely as Luke had. 'We'll let yer know later when to come, yeah,' she said, nodding her head like the Churchill dog.

Before Luke had a chance to say anything else Mavis took hold of Peggy's arm, 'Well, we've got to be going now, catch yer later, Luke.'

As they hurried round the same corner that the old man and his three-legged dog had, Mavis hissed at Peggy, 'She's gonna kill us for this.'

'Ain't that a fact,' Peggy grinned.

Luke was wondering if he should pay the flower shop a visit, after all. He couldn't go on Christmas

Day without presents. He smiled to himself as he turned back to the café to replace the coffee that the old man had taken off with.

After the meeting Lorraine went into her office, where her phone was ringing. She picked it up on its fourth or fifth ring. She listened, a slow smile spreading across her face, and then dropped the receiver back into its cradle. Her lawyer, Dakis, had just informed her that she was now divorced, and a free woman at last.

'Thank God,' she muttered.

That's the last time I'm putting meself through that, no more men for me and that's a fact.

Lorraine had once, not so long ago, loved her now ex-husband, John. Standing at the altar she had believed with all her heart the words she was saying, *'til death us do part*. It was a cliché, but she had thought that she and John could make it through anything, as long as they had each other. But she was wrong. She had trusted him, but he had lied to her, and really, it was as simple as that. They just weren't cut out to last the distance. She wondered what John was feeling now. Sadness? Relief? But his feelings were of no concern any more. She had thrown herself into her work with extra vigour lately and hadn't allowed herself to consider how she would feel when this moment arrived. Certainly she'd not thought she would feel so elated. But she did; actually she felt quite giddy. Giddy enough to smile at Sara Jacobs when she came in a moment later.

'There's been a stabbing, boss,' Jacobs announced, half way between Lorraine's desk and the door.

Lorraine's smile dropped from her face. 'You're joking. It's morning. What inconsiderate idiot gets stabbed in the morning?'

'Looks like it happened last night.' Jacobs glanced at the paper she was carrying. 'Seems there was some sort of fracas at the Blue Lion. Nearby resident called it in last night. When the uniforms arrived, everyone had cleared off. But it turns out there was a victim, name of Jason Manners, made it home and was found by his aunt in her front room this morning.'

'Never heard of him . . . local?'

'No, he belongs to Durham, Esh Winning to be exact.'

'Bit off the beaten track for him round here, isn't it? Any idea what he's doing in Houghton, in the Blue Lion of all places? The biggest dive for miles. Is he still alive?'

'Don't know to the first, and yes to the last, but apparently only just. He lost a lot of blood.'

Standing up, Lorraine walked over to the coat stand. Shrugging into her jacket she said, 'He'll have been taken to Sunderland then?'

Jacobs nodded.

'OK, I'll take this one. It's time that Blue Lion was sorted out good and proper. Let's get them closed down.' She grabbed her bag from under her desk and slung it over her shoulder. 'Where's Luke?'

Jacobs shrugged. 'Deserted his post, most likely.'

For the second time that morning, Lorraine couldn't believe what she was hearing. If Jacobs had built up some sort of camaraderie amongst her fellow officers then that sort of comment could, perhaps, have been taken as gentle teasing. But Jacobs courted only those whom she felt could help her career. In fact, Jacobs had shot herself in the foot with that one snide comment. Lorraine had been impressed with the thoroughness and professionalism she had displayed when discussing the stabbing but now, for her, Jacobs was back to being a bitch.

'Well, track him down and ask him to follow me on to the hospital.'

'Oh, I er, I thought I might . . .'

Lorraine hated to mince her words, but as Jacobs was so tight with Clark, it wouldn't do to alienate her. She looked at her for a moment, then said, as diplomatically as she could, 'I realise you probably want to come along, and I don't blame you. But we need someone here. Sanderson and Dinwall are busy with the night watchman case and I don't want to distract them. The rest of the squad are equally as busy, and with Carter in the hospital, you're not just the most likely candidate to man things at the station, I'm afraid you are the only candidate. Got that?'

Jacobs nodded amiably enough, but Lorraine could practically feel the other woman bristling as she headed out the door.

She blew air out of her cheeks as she ran her fingers through her hair. These petty politics were the most annoying part of her job. 'God, I wish Carter was back,' she said to herself.

Car keys in hand, Lorraine was just leaving the

police station when Luke appeared holding two cups of take-out coffee.

He handed one to her. 'Thought you might need this, boss.'

She took it with a smile. 'Thanks. I do. Come on, we're off to the hospital. There's been a stabbing.'

'I'll just go and bring the car round, OK, boss?'

She nodded, as she stuffed her own car keys back into her bag. It was probably best that Luke drive as she was so distracted. There was that poor boy Stansfield and now there was a stabbing, possibly an attempted murder, to add to her list. And knowing the patrons of the Blue Lion, they would all have been there, but would amazingly have seen nothing. Didn't people care about each other any more? Her mind jumped from the stabbing in the Blue Lion, on to the impaling of the night watchman two nights ago.

Lorraine shuddered inwardly. She'd seen some grisly things in her time, but that was horrendous, five entry wounds and five exits. Scottie had said that part of his liver was missing, that it must have been on the last spike, slipped off and been picked up by rats.

She guessed he was right: they'd scoured the place and found nothing, nothing but the dark blood-stained earth into which most of the man's life's blood had drained .

She sighed as Luke pulled to a stop in front of her. She didn't imagine she was going to be able to get the thought of the night watchman out of her head – his mutilated body, the look of shock on his face, the

64

spike sticking out from where his eye used to be. Her mobile vibrated in her pocket. She flipped it open, listened for a moment, nodded and said, 'Thanks Jacobs. Let me know if you hear anything more.'

'OK, boss,' Luke tilted his head to one side as he gave her a questioning look. 'Hospital?'

'Change of plan. The stabbing has just gone into the operating theatre. Apparently there's some internal bleeding that they didn't catch when he was admitted. We'll try and see him later on if he's up for it.' She thought for a moment. 'Right now we need to pay a visit to the school.'

'School?'

'Yeah, when I talked to Scottie this morning he mentioned that Richard Stansfield's fingernails were snapped off. Perhaps he was trying to save himself at the last moment. Scottie's also found some unusual fibres on his person that don't belong to his clothes and don't belong to the rope. I can't put my finger on it but there's something not right . . . No suicide note for one thing, and it seems that a kid like that would have given his mum some explanation. I think we should go and talk to some of his friends.'

Lorraine had been back to her school many times since leaving, always in an official capacity, as a young uniform escorting truants back to school, and more recently as a Detective Inspector warning kids off drugs. Despite herself, she was usually overcome by nostalgia: the corridors painted in that same strange nothing colour, the smell – a potent mix of bleach and cabbage – and the kids, as innocent and as knowing, as wise and as stupid, as predictable and as mercurial as kids had been when she went to school.

The school receptionist paged the headmistress, Mrs Colley, whose footsteps were heard echoing down the corridors almost immediately. She was relatively new to the school, and Lorraine was struck by how well she resembled the traditional model of a headmistress: tall, solid and stern-looking. Mrs Colley shook Lorraine's hand. 'Detective Inspector, I'm sorry to meet in such circumstances.'

Lorraine introduced Luke. 'This is my Detective Sergeant, Luke Daniels.'

Mrs Colley shook Luke's hand. 'Come this way, it'll be easier to talk in my office. And you're welcome to conduct any interviews you might like to do there.'

Mrs Colley's office was very neat and ordered, its walls adorned with framed photos of students past and present. Lorraine and Luke sat on the chairs the headmistress pointed to while she took her seat on the other side of the desk. 'I was very sad to hear the news about Richard Stansfield,' Mrs Colley began, 'very sad. He was a great boy, well liked by everyone, it seems. Not the best student, but by no means the worst either. Just a decent boy who would have made a good man. I find the whole thing hard to believe . . .' She shook her head solemnly.

'Mrs Colley, have you talked to his teachers? Have they mentioned anything? Had Richard behaved strangely in the past few days or weeks?' Lorraine asked.

Again Mrs Colley shook her head. 'I talked to his teachers before our staff meeting this morning.

They're all in a state of shock too. He seemed the same – happy – I mean, you never can tell for sure, and I've only been here a short time so only knew him a little. I'm afraid I'm more knowledgeable about the more, shall we say, boisterous members of the school, but there had never been any concern about him falling into the wrong crowd or having problems at home – unlike his friends . . .'

'His friends?' Luke prompted.

'All good kids. But all troubled, I'm afraid. Melissa Tremaine has a temper on her, but she's got a heart of gold. I've seen her defending younger kids against bullies. She's been bullied herself though, on account of her weight. Niall Campbell who used to be a pupil here, is the other way – terribly skinny – very worrying. As for Kurt Allendale and Rachel Henderson, I'm sure they have problems at home – but of course, I can't act on suspicion alone, and they've never been persuaded to tell anyone just what their problems are. The five of them started hanging out together a few months ago, according to Richard's form teacher, and my impression was that Richard was the one who brought them together. I'm very, very sorry that this has happened. I feel so terribly for his poor mother, and I'm talking to the teachers about arranging a memorial service at the school for Richard.'

Lorraine had met teachers before who had been so twisted by bureaucracy and by hyperactive children strung out on E-numbers that they had lost whatever idealism about teaching they had when they began. She sensed Mrs Colley wasn't like that – she seemed the sort of teacher who made a point of trying to see the child behind the problem, and although she seemed a little stuffy and perhaps a little patronising, Lorraine had no doubt that she had the best interests of her students at heart.

'I would like to talk to his friends, if at all possible,' Lorraine said.

With assurances that she would bring Richard's friends to them as soon as possible, Mrs Colley left Lorraine and Luke in her office.

Kurt, Melissa and Rachel were huddled round the corner of the art building. Kurt had seen Lorraine and Luke get out of their car and head towards the school offices, and had told Melissa and Rachel that the police had arrived. Niall had sloped off back home to bed after he talked to his friends, claiming that he didn't feel so good. 'Yer don't look it either,' Melissa said.

'Do you think they're coming to see us?' Rachel asked Kurt.

'Don't know. But what are the chances? We have to get our story straight about Richy,' hissed Kurt. 'We can't have them sniffing around Marcel.'

'What if it's not, though,' Melissa whispered. 'What if they want to talk to us about,' she glanced hastily around, before going on, 'you know what?'

'Don't be daft, why would they?' Rachel stated bravely, even though she was practically shaking in her shoes with fear. 'If it was that, the coppers would have lifted us well before now.'

But Melissa wasn't easy to convince. 'How do yer know?'

'She's right, Melissa, they would have come to our houses,' Kurt said. 'So just chill, will yer.'

'Can't.'

'Yer have to.' Rachel patted Melissa's shoulder. 'Just let me and Kurt do the talking. Say yer have a sore throat or something. But whatever yer do don't let on if they mention the other thing, do yer hear?'

Melissa, looking far from happy, nodded.

'And all we need to say about Richard is that we don't know nothing. 'Cos we don't.' Kurt looked hard at Melissa but he was only just holding it together himself. He couldn't ever remember having spoken to a policeman before.

Under the watchful gaze of her two friends Melissa took a deep breath and nodded.

The headmistress had sent for Richard Stansfield's friends. She had also asked the school secretary for water and Lorraine and Luke sipped from plastic cups as they waited for Richard's friends to arrive.

'It seems like a very long time ago that I was wandering those corridors,' Luke said.

'Yeah, I remember seeing yer,' Lorraine replied. She had left her chair and was studying a class photo on the opposite wall.

Luke and Lorraine had had this conversation before, but try as he might, he couldn't remember ever seeing her at school. Lorraine smiled. 'Here I am,' she said.

Luke left his chair and stood next to Lorraine. He

69

was so close she could feel his breath on her cheek. She pointed at a blonde, skinny kid about fourteen or fifteen years old.

'Sorry, still nothing,' Luke said.

'Do you remember her?' Lorraine pointed to a shorter, dark-haired girl standing next to her.

'No, I'm afraid not.'

'Her name was Jackie Evans and she was my best friend.'

'Jackie Evans . . .' The name rang a bell in Luke's mind. 'Didn't she kill herself?'

Lorraine nodded, still looking at the photo. 'Must have been only six months after this photo was taken. She broke up with some guy – actually, Pete Fraser, you know him, works at the Kwik Fit down the road?'

Luke nodded.

'Anyway, he was her first boyfriend and she was distraught. Took paracetamol, wanting to end it all.'

'Damn.'

'That's right. She was sick as a dog for the first day or so and then she seemed to get better. She felt stupid, ripped up the note that she left for her folks, and told me not to tell anyone. So I didn't.'

'And then?'

'And then three days later she was in hospital with renal failure. It was awful; she was in fucking agony. Her parents by her bedside the whole time. She needed a liver transplant, but there was none available.'

Luke stayed silent.

'You know how I was talking about "what ifs"

before? Well, I have my own what if. What if I hadn't been so fucking stupid and had told her parents what she had done? By the time she was in hospital it was too late – and she knew she was dying and by then she didn't want to. She was so fucking scared.'

'Richard Stansfield . . .'

'I don't know whether or not he changed his mind but I can't help thinking, what if he had? What if he had spent his last few moments trying to get the rope off his neck? At least Jackie had her family with her when she died. Poor Richard was all alone at the end. All alone and terrified.

'I know yer not supposed to, but there are some cases that I can't help getting personally involved in. Just after Jackie died I made a promise to myself and, well, to her too, that I would try and think about her every day, even if just for a few moments. And then something like this happens, and I'm reminded about Jackie and I realise I haven't thought about her in years.'

Luke's hand hovered above Lorraine's shoulder. She was normally so powerful and strong, and these rare glimpses of vulnerability only underscored her strength of character. He liked the way she looked but he loved her for her spirit. But something stopped him from taking her into his arms. Something more than the fact that she was his boss and they were on the job. If anything were to happen between them, and Luke dearly hoped it would, then he was going to have to tread softly, show her the respect that he suspected she had never received from her ex-husband.

A soft knock interrupted Luke's thoughts.

'Come in,' Lorraine said, the spell of the picture broken. Lorraine took the headmistress's seat while Luke perched, more informally, on the side of the desk.

The door opened and Melissa walked in followed by Kurt and Rachel.

Lorraine smiled at the very large girl who planted her feet and stood there with a stubborn air about her. She noted that all three of them looked very anxious, and the petite girl with strawberry-blonde hair looked scared to death. 'My name is Detective Inspector Lorraine Hunt, and this is Detective Sergeant Luke Daniels. I'm very sorry to hear about your friend. You must all be very upset. But I hope you realise that I need to ask you some questions. We need to find out more about the events leading up to Richard's death, and I hope youse can help me.'

The three teenagers fidgeted, and Lorraine noticed that none quite met her eye.

'Do any of you know why Richard Stansfield might want to kill himself?'

There was a profound silence in which the very air seemed to stand still. Lorraine noticed Rachel shudder, then Kurt said in a clear voice, 'No, Miss.'

'You're Kurt Allendale, right?'

'Yes Miss.'

Lorraine looked at the girls who shook their heads.

'What's your name?' Lorraine said to the pretty, strawberry-haired girl, trying to catch her eye.

'Rachel Henderson . . . Miss.'

Lorraine swung her eyes to Melissa, 'So you must be Melissa Tremaine?'

Melissa nodded.

Lorraine looked back at Rachel, figuring her to be the easiest to crack. 'So where were you when Richard Stansfield died?'

Rachel swallowed hard, then rubbed her neck.

Lorraine and Luke looked at each other. They were getting nowhere. It would be better to talk to the teenagers one by one.

'OK, why don't you and Kurt wait outside, Melissa.' Together they turned to leave. Kurt was looking straight ahead. Melissa glanced once at Rachel, but Rachel was staring at Lorraine.

As the door closed behind them, it was Luke who spoke first, 'Hello, Rachel.'

She nodded at him.

'There's nothing to be worried about. Why don't yer take a seat and we can talk.'

As Luke continued along the same lines that Lorraine had instigated, Lorraine watched Rachel. Her bones told her that there was definitely something going on with the girl, with all three of them for that matter. Their obvious nervousness and reluctance to talk rang alarm bells in her mind. If she had only suspected before that there was more to Richard's death than the obvious, she was convinced now that her instincts were right.

But as far as concrete evidence went, they had no luck with Rachel and no more luck with Kurt. Just like Rachel, he'd refused to talk or had deflected their questions with the skill of a master secret keeper.

Lorraine thought that Mrs Colley was right – there was something about these two kids that made you feel they were used to lying to protect themselves: their closed manner, the way they didn't quite meet your eye when they spoke to you, and Lorraine was sure she had seen the tell-tale scars of self-abuse poking from the long sleeves of Rachel's jumper.

Melissa, however, seemed different. There was a stubborn air about her, but it felt forced, as if it was an act rather than a true part of her personality. Lorraine could understand that – she had built up enough walls herself in her time.

'What sort of boy was Richard?' Lorraine asked.

Melissa shrugged, 'Same as any.'

'Was he happy? Was there any particular reason why he should take his own life or do you think it was an accident – kids fooling around? Was there something he was into that might have pushed him over the edge?'

Melissa paled. 'We weren't into nowt, we didn't do –' She stopped short, as if she realised she was about to say something incriminating.

Lorraine picked up on it at once. 'Do what, Melissa?'

'Nowt, we never done anything.'

'Are yer sure? You won't get into trouble.'

Melissa shook her head adamantly and Lorraine could see the girl was terrified.

'Yer can tell us, Melissa, there's nothing to be worried about. Were you fooling about? Was it an accident?' Luke said gently.

'Shouldn't we have solicitors or something?'

'Why? You haven't been accused of anything. We are only asking you a few questions about your friend. Anything you can tell us will help,' Lorraine said with a smile, but there was an edge to her voice.

Melissa shook her head again. 'Don't know nothing. He was all right the last time we saw him.'

'Yes, that's what Kurt said. Exactly what he said, in fact. But yer know what, Melissa, I'm not sure I believe yers.'

Melissa didn't say anything, just stared at the floor.

'Listen, Melissa,' Lorraine tried more gently. 'We know yer all upset. Just take yer time, try to remember what yer can. Anything will be helpful.'

Again Melissa remained silent, her head bowed. But Lorraine didn't miss the tear that fell onto the floor.

'Hey,' she said gently. 'Hey, come on.' Lorraine quickly got out of her seat and went to Melissa. She put her arm around the large girl and led her to the chair that Luke had quickly vacated.

Melissa put her head in her hands and sobbed loudly. Lorraine, kneeling beside her, rubbed her arm in what she hoped was a consoling manner while Luke stood behind them, looking on, concern etched on his face.

'I'm sorry,' Melissa said in between sobs. 'I just can't believe that Richy's dead.'

'Don't be sorry, you're allowed to be upset. Here.' Lorraine reached over and pulled out a couple of tissues from a box on the headmistress's desk and handed them to Melissa.

'I'll get yer a glass of water,' Luke said, and left the office in search of one.

Melissa's sobs started to subside. Lorraine really felt for her. Out of the three friends that she had interviewed, Melissa seemed to be the only one who really cared that Richard had died. Lorraine suspected that wasn't quite the case, that Kurt and Rachel were hiding their emotions from her, but Melissa seemed the sort whose sensitive nature was hidden under a tough façade. Luke returned quickly with some water, handed it to Melissa and stepped back behind the chair. Melissa gulped the water down. Lorraine took the empty glass from her and set it on the table. 'You OK now?'

Melissa nodded, her eyes downcast.

'Yer know,' Lorraine said, stroking Melissa's hair back behind her ear, 'I know what yer going through. I had a friend who died when I was about yer age.'

Melissa raised her head and looked at Lorraine. Her face was red and puffy from her torrent of tears. She started to say something, then stopped, dropping her gaze to her hands.

'What were yer gonna say, Melissa?' Lorraine urged softly.

'I was gonna say,' Melissa stopped, as she let out another sob. Her chin trembled and she put her hand over it to try to stop it. 'I was gonna say that yer can't know. It's not the same thing.'

'I know,' Lorraine said simply. 'It's never the same thing. People are different, circumstances are different. Being in the force has taught me that. But there are similarities; I still can sympathise with what yer going through. I know what it's like to lose a friend.'

Melissa shook her head. 'Yer can't understand this. Yer just can't. Yer have no idea.'

Lorraine sighed. She didn't seem to be able to get through to her.

'Can I go now?' Melissa said sullenly, already rebuilding her barriers.

Lorraine looked at her, then she rose to her feet. She grabbed her bag from behind the desk, took a card out of it and handed it to Melissa. 'My number's on there. Any time yer want to talk, just give me a ring, any time, OK?'

Melissa nodded, then left as quickly as she could.

'There's something going on, Luke. Them three kids are terrified of something. Melissa is all hard on the outside, and I bet she can crack a few heads together, yet inside she's soft as putty and frightened . . . But of what?'

5

Louise Brown stared out the window and watched Melissa Tremaine, Rachel Henderson and Kurt Allendale walk from behind the art block and into school. She wondered what they had been up to. They looked sad and she didn't blame them – she didn't know how any of them could stay at school when one of their friends had died.

But mebbe it's 'cos it's better to be where your friends are. Mebbe home's not a great place to go back to.

'Louise Brown, are yer daydreaming again?' Her teacher's voice cracked into her thoughts and she turned her head to the blackboard, trying to ignore the giggles of the girls around her.

Small and unremarkable, Louise wore her mousey-brown hair long. She used her hair as a shield against the world, as a curtain between her and the bullies who tormented her about the scars that covered her right cheek and ran all the way down her body. 'Just ignore them,' her grandmother told her, 'remember, sticks and stones.' So Louise learnt to sit in dark corners, pretend she was invisible, hope that people forgot she was there. She had become very good at that. So good that she barely knew anyone.

Except that's going to change.

She concealed a smile when she thought about how she wasn't going to be lonely any more. That even when her father lost himself in drink and sobbed at the kitchen table, she would feel loved and wanted somewhere. Somewhere with another family, a different one, whose father wouldn't blame you for the loss of his wife and son. Who would love you for all of you, even your faults. Especially your faults.

Louise had only been four years old when the fire had swept through her house, greedy in its intensity. Her father had picked her out of her bed, clutched her to his chest and ran out of the house. He had been beaten back by the flames when he went back for the rest of the family. Louise couldn't help but wonder that if her father hadn't had saved her, if he had saved his wife, Kath, and baby son rather than her, perhaps he wouldn't need to drink so much. Perhaps he could find and keep a job. Perhaps he could bear to look people in the eye.

Louise thought back to the morning. She still couldn't believe the news about Richard Stansfield. Normally shy, it had been her who had shouted out what kind of trees the Seven Sisters were. She had arrived at the bus stop late, so when Jilly Bowmont had whispered to her just what had happened up at the Seven Sisters, Louise had been as shocked as the rest of them.

When the bus arrived, she had slithered quietly into the seat behind Rachel and Kurt, and listened to what little they had to say. When Kurt got out his mobile phone, she guessed that he was calling

Melissa or Niall. One or the other. The four of them had become very close. She had noticed that over the past few months.

Louise had a special interest in Kurt and Rachel. She remembered – and it wasn't that long ago – when Kurt, Richard, Rachel, Niall and Melissa hardly seemed to know each other. And then suddenly they were firm friends. Could it happen to her? Could she be friends with them?

Louise wanted nothing more than to belong, but she'd missed the first few important bonding years at school. Instead of being in the playground she'd been in the hospital enduring endless skin grafts, and her natural shyness had not been helped by the scars on her body. And because she had missed so much school, she had been kept back a year, and was in the class below Melissa Tremaine, even though they had been born only one hour apart in Sunderland General. Although she and Melissa weren't close, Melissa had come to her rescue when she had been tormented by bullies. Louise looked up to Melissa, seeing her for the genuinely kind person she was, despite the aggressive façade she had built around herself.

The class finished, and Louise decided to skip the next period. Gym. She hated gym. Hated getting changed and hiding her body so no one could see the scars. And she hated seeing the other girls' smooth skin. Even the chubby ones could slim down. But she could never get rid of the scars. And besides, it was almost time to meet Mary. Slipping out of the school gates, Louise hurried over to the park, then to Houghton town centre.

She'd first met Mary at the CD counter in Woolworths when they were both after the same single, and had seen her four times since then, once in a café and the other three times in the park where they had talked for hours. Well, Mary had talked for hours. Mary had promised to meet her this morning and she was going to introduce her to some other friends of hers. They all belonged to a club that Louise knew Melissa and her friends went to. She'd followed them one night but had been too nervous to knock on the door.

And now she was going to join the same club – she felt like hugging herself with delight.

Louise waited by the entrance of Woolworths, where they had agreed to meet. She looked at her watch; Mary was late. She got a little sinking feeling in her heart.

What if Mary didn't turn up? What if she had forgotten?

But then she gave a little gasp of surprise as someone tapped on her shoulder. Louise turned round to see Mary's face with that distinctive, tear-shaped mark on her cheek. She was smiling at her.

'Did I give you a fright?' she said, her voice betraying the fact that she came from the Somerset Downs.

'No, not really,' Louise replied. 'Just thought yer might not be coming, that's all.'

'You silly thing.' Mary said lightly. 'I'm just a bit late, that's all.'

And, smiling at each other, the two girls walked off.

Lorraine stared down at the unconscious figure of Jason Manners. A deep frown creased her forehead and she chewed her bottom lip. Manners was not a pretty sight. Even if his face wasn't so pale because of blood loss, it was still the sort of face only a mother could love.

He moved onto his right side and groaned. In moments a nurse was there, moving towards the bed with an energy and efficiency belying her short, plump stature and blonde, doll-like features. Luke moved along so that she could reach Manners. Gently she moved him back onto his left side. The doctor had told Lorraine that he had been stabbed on the right side. She watched as the nurse lifted the hospital nightgown up, took the dressing off and checked the wound.

'Shit.' Lorraine said under her breath.

'Yeah, nasty one, innit,' the nurse said.

The nurse, satisfied that the stitches were still in place, was about to put the dressing back on. Lorraine gently touched the nurse's arm. 'Look at this, Luke.'

Luke came round to the other side of the bed, took one look and muttered, 'Oh God.'

'Yeah, he hasn't just been stabbed; he's been carved. Look,' Lorraine followed the pattern of stitches with her finger. 'A large circle. How many stitches?' she asked the nurse.

'Forty-two.'

'And what would yer say this is?' Her fingers traced a shape inside of the circle.

Luke shook his head. 'It reminds me of something, but . . .' He shook his head again.

'Well,' the nurse said, 'the doctor did say when he was stitching that it reminded him of a fish.'

Lorraine nodded. 'That's what it looks like to me.'

Luke stared at the image. It was difficult to make out at first because of all the bruising, but then he squinted and the picture became clearer. 'I see it now. You're right. Definitely a fish inside a circle.'

'That's what the doc said.' The nurse replaced the dressing and made Manners as comfortable as possible.

'What's the prognosis?'

The nurse sighed. 'If he makes it through the night?'

'Odds being?'

'Thirty, seventy . . . Against.'

'Not good . . . And we need him alive.' Lorraine and Luke looked at each other. Luke said, 'He's a new face, boss, never seen him before nor heard of him either.'

'Me neither. Put a uniform on the door. I don't like this at all. Someone has really got something against this guy. Was that his aunt sitting outside?' This last question was directed at the nurse who was taking Manners's blood pressure.

Without looking up from her task the nurse replied, 'Yes, she's the one who found him.'

'We'll have a word,' Lorraine said.

Luke nodded. As if their bodies were in tune, they turned to leave together. Lorraine suddenly became aware of Luke's body, despite the circumstances. He was tall and broad, muscular, and she suddenly

83

reddened, conscious of the way he moved and of the fact that they would need to brush against each other to get through the doorway if they both kept the same pace up. She moved slightly quicker and Luke fell in behind her.

The woman who waited outside the door looked Lorraine up and down with a malevolent gaze. Lorraine had met her sort before: hard-faced, bitter women who always just stopped short of breaking the law. This particular woman was in her late fifties, had fluffy red hair that was grey at the roots and there were specks of black mascara below her eyes. Her purple top clashed horribly with her hair, and needed a wash four or five wears ago.

'Mrs Manners, is it?' Lorraine asked her.

'He's gonna be all right, isn't he?' the woman asked with a sixty-a-day wheeze.

Lorraine took her badge out. 'We aren't doctors, so really there's not a lot I can tell yer.'

'Oh, you lot,' the woman sneered.

Lorraine rolled her eyes at Luke, then said, 'Yeah, do yer mind if we ask a few questions?'

'Ask what yer like, it's up to you. It's a free country . . . Well, it used to be, like. Now yer can't say this or yer can't say that, in case yer step on somebody's friggin' toes.'

Lorraine chose to ignore her last sentence and said, 'Do yer know what yer nephew was doing in Houghton?'

'He never tells me nowt.'

Lorraine translated this into: *I'm telling youse lot nowt.*

84

She tried again, 'Does he live with you?'

'Now and then. Wherever he lays his head. Mostly in the first crack house he can find.'

'Heavily into drugs, is he?'

'I think I just answered that so if yer don't mind . . .'

Lorraine bristled at being dismissed in such a fashion. 'If yer don't want to answer my questions here, I'm sure a ride to the station can be arranged and we'll question you there.'

The woman curled her lip and huffed, but answered Lorraine's questions readily enough.

As they walked down the corridor to Carter's room, Lorraine said, 'Well, normally I would say that was sorted. He is a druggie, he owes money everywhere, according to his aunt, but that carving, it's weird . . . Why would any sleazebag who wants to get money carve a fish into his victim? Why waste his time like that? It doesn't make sense. If he was just stabbed, then we could just put it down to drugs, but I just can't believe this has anything to do with the usual lot of shitheads we deal with.'

Luke nodded his agreement. Then he smiled. 'Well, look who it is, boss.' They were outside Carter's room. Lorraine pushed the door open and strode in. Carter looked pale and drained, his carrot-orange hair and enormous amount of freckles contrasting starkly with the whiteness of his face. He tried a smile when he saw them.

'Sorry, boss,' he muttered, looking thoroughly miserable.

Lorraine smiled and walked over to his bedside. 'It's all right, Carter, yer can't help being ill.' As she saw how pathetic he looked, her chest filled up with a strange feeling. What was it? She remembered feeling something like it when her pet rabbit, Pookie, had escaped when she was a child and had been run over. She had cared for that rabbit, loved it, fed it her greens that she had smuggled off her plate . . . *Oh God, don't say I'm going all motherly over him.*

She stared down at him, shrugged mentally and thought, *And so what if I am? Carter's a good 'un, and I'm missing the aggravating bastard already.*

Reaching out she took hold of his hand. 'Yer'll be fine, Carter, up and about in no time, these days it's nowt, honestly.'

Carter, who had adored Lorraine since day one, took a deep breath and squared his shoulders. 'Yer right, boss, I'll be back to work in the morning.'

Lorraine laughed, as Luke said, 'Well, not quite that soon, Carter. We don't want yer stitches dropping out on the job, do we, mate?'

'Huh,' Lorraine added. 'Like to see what some stupid little pen pusher with his head up his arse would say to that one.'

'Probably quarantine us, boss,' Carter grinned.

They spent the next fifteen minutes talking to Carter, then, after saying goodbye and wishing him luck, Lorraine and Luke left, Lorraine making certain that she was way ahead of Luke when they reached the door.

Christmas decorations were being put up in the wards as they passed. In the main entrance a seven-foot animated Christmas tree wished everyone who walked by a Merry Christmas and a Happy New

Year. Lorraine grimaced, then rolled her eyes as Luke stared in fascination at the tree.

'Do they ever grow up?' she muttered to herself as she surged ahead of him.

'Going to Scottie's party this year?' Luke asked, catching up just as the doors opened for Lorraine.

Lorraine shrugged. Scottie had an amazing party every year. Most of it, of course, had to be down to Edna. Scottie was a brilliant pathologist, but he couldn't sort himself out of a paper bag, let alone organise one of the social events of the year. Scottie's party was always a laugh, and John had always been pleased to come along with Lorraine. They'd always had a good time, even if they had a little too much to drink. 'Why not?' John had always said. 'It's Christmas.' But she had to drag him to Clark's boring parties – truth be told, she had to drag *herself* to Clark's parties – and she thanked God that Clark was on holiday this year. His parties were staid, formal affairs where everybody felt obliged to turn up but by ten o'clock almost everyone had made their excuses and left. She'd laughed at some of the excuses she'd heard her colleagues come out with to escape. Come to think of it, John had come up with some pretty good ones himself over the last couple of years.

Whoa, she stopped herself. *Don't go down that road, kiddo. Not good to reminisce about the good times*.

'Not doing Christmas this year, OK . . . That's if it's all right with you.' She could have kicked herself. She hadn't meant to snap at Luke.

He stepped back and held his hands up in mock surrender. 'OK, boss . . .' he smiled. 'But, er, how can yer not do Christmas? It's all around yer.'

Lorraine stopped in mid-stride, spun round and said, 'Let's not get into that.'

Wondering what he'd said wrong, Luke shrugged. 'Yeah, whatever yer say,' he replied. Putting his hand in his pocket for the car keys, he moved around her and reached the car.

Kicking herself even more, Lorraine followed him. Why couldn't she keep her big mouth shut? She really liked Luke, but after John could she trust another man?

But that doesn't mean Luke's the same.

Shit. To hell with the lot of them. Even living with the Hippy and the Rock Chick's gotta be better than living with a man.

She felt in her pocket for a pencil stub and came up with nothing. She scowled as she fastened her seat belt. Luke looked over at Lorraine and said, 'You haven't had lunch yet, have you?'

Lorraine smiled, and shook her head. 'Too busy.'

'Well, we can't be having that. You need to eat, girl. I'm going to sit you down and make sure you have a proper meal.'

Lorraine couldn't quite believe her ears. 'Excuse me?'

'Sorry.' Luke flashed her a teasing grin with a hint of gold in it. 'I'm going to make sure you have a proper meal, *boss.*'

'OK, you win,' Lorraine said, a slow smile

spreading across her face. Luke grinned back at her, started the car and pulled out of the hospital car park.

The first couple of restaurants Lorraine and Luke went to were closed. They eventually found a pub that was still open for lunch. It was a homely sort of pub, comfortable, with mismatched second-hand furniture, a battered leather sofa set in front of a blazing fire and something soft and melodic playing on the stereo. Luke listened for a moment, and then, turning to Lorraine, smiled broadly and said. 'I love this "Desperado". That's my song.'

Lorraine felt herself going weak at the knees. *That's my sort of man*, she thought, *someone who looks all hard on the outside but isn't afraid to admit that he has a soft side, too.*

Lorraine took a seat at an empty table. She watched Luke through lowered lids, her heart beating just that little bit faster as he went to the bar to place their orders. He came back, clutching a drink in each hand. Setting one on the table in front of Lorraine he said, 'I got you a lemonade, since we're still on duty.' He pulled out a chair opposite Lorraine and sat down. 'So, what do you make of that Manners case?'

'Never seen anything like it. Being stabbed is bad enough, but I don't understand why someone would want to carve something like that into another person.' Lorraine shook her head. 'It doesn't make sense.'

Luke looked deep in thought for a moment.

'Someone's wanting to send a message. That's the only thing I can come up with.'

'But what? And to who?'

'That's the question, boss. We need to find out whether the symbol means something. Meanwhile I think it's probably best if we go round and talk to someone at the Blue Lion.'

Lorraine took a sip of her drink. 'Do yer now?'

Luke smiled wryly. 'Took the words straight out of yer mouth, did I?'

Lorraine smiled. 'Something like that.' She took a sip of her drink. 'Actually, I've sent Sanderson and Dinwall over to talk to the landlord.'

They leaned back as two plates of sausages and mash were placed in front of them. Lorraine didn't realise how hungry she was until she smelt the delicious aroma of onion gravy that wafted up from the plate. 'This looks great,' she said.

Luke grinned at her. They ate in silence for a while. Then he suddenly said, out of the blue, 'So how are things with you, Lorraine?'

Lorraine looked up at him. Luke hardly ever called her by her first name. He normally just called her boss. She found it vaguely unsettling.

'Um. OK, I guess. It's been a strange day.'

Luke raised one eyebrow in a question.

'Not just dealing with Richy Stansfield and Jason Manners. And not just remembering Jackie either.' Lorraine pushed her mashed potatoes round the place and said, as off-the-cuff as possible, 'My divorce came through today.'

'Wow. How does that make you feel?'

Lorraine looked up. Luke was looking at her intently. She smiled. 'It's funny. I don't feel sad. I feel happy. And free.'

Luke grinned. 'That's great.'

'I loved John. I really did. I don't think I've ever been as happy as the day we married. But there was an awful lot I didn't know about him. There was an awful lot that he kept from me. And then he changed.'

Luke nodded. 'It's the job, isn't it?'

'Not really, though it didn't help.' Lorraine sighed. 'You can't escape the fact that this job takes up all of your time. But it was more than that. We weren't the same people we were when we got married.'

Suddenly Luke put his hand over hers. 'That might be true,' he said seriously. 'But let me say what I think, Lorraine. Any man who threw away his chances with a woman like you, who didn't try to make it work, is more than stupid. He's crazy.'

Lorraine looked deep into Luke's eyes. They stayed, sitting that way, for a long time. Finally, Lorraine broke the silence. 'We better get out of here, Luke. Or I could do you for wasting police time.'

Luke smiled. 'Your wish is my command, boss.'

And as they walked out the pub to Luke's car, Lorraine felt her stomach turn over in knots. *Your wish is my command.* And she believed him.

6

The last few weeks, Melissa and Rachel had taken to walking home together. They lived two streets away from each other, but they had never been great friends, not until lately. Now, and today more than ever, they felt in need of each other's company. After all, they shared a secret that brought them closer than years of friendship ever could.

As they crossed the park a group of year seven kids started taunting Melissa. 'Hey, fatso,' two boys shouted together, then dug each other in the ribs and started giggling. Soon the rest of the ten-strong bunch joined in.

'Fat girl,' yelled another boy who obviously had no mirrors at home.

Another stuck two fingers up and shouted, 'Come on down, fat girl. In fact, roll bitch roll . . . Yer'll get here quicker.'

The others found this hysterically funny and laughed their heads off.

Rachel saw the sudden pain in Melissa's eyes, then the flash of anger that quickly replaced the hurt. She knew this happened all the time to Melissa, but this was the first time she had seen it first-hand.

Turning to face them Melissa planted her feet.

Gesturing with her hands she yelled, 'Come on then, yer little pricks, bring it here. Mouthy bastards . . . Come on, we'll sharp see who'll roll. I'll strangle the fucking lot of yers. Cheeky twats . . . Come on.' She took a menacing step towards them, and most of the bunch cowered backwards.

Rachel placed a calming hand on Melissa's elbow, which was angrily shrugged off as Melissa moved forward again.

'No,' Rachel said, shaking her head. 'Just ignore them Melissa, they're just a bunch of year sevens, who know nowt about nowt. Stupid kids, that's all. Besides, Marcel wouldn't like it if he finds out we've been fighting . . .'

It took a moment for Melissa to focus when she turned and looked at Rachel, but as she did the anger died and was replaced by a look of anxiety that had not been there when she'd faced up to the gang that had been tormenting her only seconds earlier.

Slowly she nodded, then they continued their journey through the cold and dreary park, the gang staring sullenly after them.

When they were approaching the Seahills, Melissa broke the silence between them. 'That's the first time anyone's ever said, "We".'

Rachel frowned for a moment, then understanding dawned and she matched Melissa's rare smile.

Niall stared at the plate of food in front of him: roast beef, Yorkshire puddings, mushy peas, turnip and the dreaded carrots.

Jesus.

93

For some damn reason known only to God, no matter how much yer chewed the flaming things, they always came up fucking whole. Bright orange and staring right back at yer as if yer had no right to chuck them back up.

He felt ready to burst right open just thinking about them. But he'd learnt a trick or two: eat the veg first, 'cos at the end of the day they are supposed to do yer good, then down a pint of water which makes it easier for the rest to come right back up again.

He knew his mother was staring at him, he felt his father was staring at him, and his ten-year-old brother was doing his damnedest to stare at everybody seated round the table at the same friggin' time.

Well, sod the lot of them.

It's OK for them.

Not an ounce of extra fat on any of them. Fucking bean poles all three, and the bloody grandparents, and the aunts, uncles and fucking cousins. The whole family, all sixteen of them, skin and bastard bone.

And pretty soon all of them would be watching him when they went to his grandma's for Christmas dinner.

He knew that at least half of them were convinced he was on drugs. He'd heard them whispering. Just because he was fat didn't mean he was deaf, for God's sake.

Why do I have to be the fat one?

It wasn't fair.

Think, think of ways out of Christmas.

Think of a way out of the frightening mess we're in.

He felt his insides turn to ice as he thought of what

they'd done. He wasn't sure that even Marcel could help them out of this one.

Under his lashes he stared moodily at his younger brother, whom he hated but would probably march into hell for. Everybody had said since as long as he could remember that they were like two peas in a pod.

Where the hell are they looking?

Jesus!

Andrew's skinnier than anybody has a right to be.

Sighing inwardly he dug his fork into the creamy mashed potatoes, stirred it round for a moment before harpooning a carrot. *Get them down first.* A moment later his dry lips closed over the carrot. He could smell melted butter on his fork from the potatoes. He quickly chewed then swallowed, an automatic reaction.

The first mouthful was always the worst.

Niall warily watched his parents, who moved their eyes back to their plates as soon as they noticed his eyes upon them. He sighed. He knew that his parents thought he was on drugs. He knew that they went through his room regularly, searching for them.

Huh, only fools take drugs.

In the heavy silence that had covered the table like thick hovering smoke for months, the sound of the family's cutlery hitting off their plates was preternaturally loud.

Niall sighed. *If they had to give evidence against me, they'd both have plenty to say. Probably wouldn't be able to shut them up.*

Then he paled. Pretty soon his parents just might.

Carter, still groggy from his operation, listened to the old man in the next bed complaining about the hospital meals.

'Pile of shite, we got better fed in the bloody trenches, son . . . They've got the right idea.' He nodded his head and looked across the room where a family of Sikhs were uncovering a variety of dishes they had brought in for their grandfather.

The thought of any sort of food made Carter feel sick. He sighed. His appendix was out now and the doctor had said everything went fine, and all Carter wanted to do now was to go home and get back to work. But out of politeness he agreed with the old man.

The last thing the old man needed was encouragement. 'Should we go on strike?' he said eagerly. 'Throw the bloody lot on the floor, maybe that way they'll get the message, especially if we jump on it . . . What do yer say to that, bonny lad?'

Carter groaned. 'No, no, I'm a policeman, I can't do things like that.'

For a moment the old man stared at him in stunned disbelief, then he said, 'Yer a *what*? A fucking *copper* . . . A fucking copper in the next bed to me!'

Carter nodded. 'Afraid so.'

The old man stared at him for an embarrassingly long time and Carter was starting to squirm when he said, 'Ah, what the hell, I suppose coppers end up in hospital an' all . . . But I'll never live it down, a copper in the next bed.' He shook his head.

Carter scratched his chin; the stubble was starting

to itch. He smiled warily at the old man, who still stared at him. He wished Luke was here; he'd promised to come in tonight. He glanced at the clock on the opposite wall, twenty past eight, visiting time was nearly over.

'So how long have yer been a copper for?' the old man said suddenly.

'Oh, a couple of years.'

'Like it, do yer?'

'It's what I always wanted.'

The old man shook his head, 'Never thought I'd see the day, lying in bed next to a copper.' Then he smiled, 'Ah suppose there's good and bad, son, and to tell yer the truth we'd be badly off without your sort, so, young copper, fancy a game of dominoes?'

Deeply relieved, Carter nodded. Dominoes he could handle, and he'd give the old sod a run for his money.

Kurt flung himself on top of his bed and lay down flat on his back, worrying at the slack tooth. He'd just been to yet another visit to the dentist, who unlike the family doctor had started asking questions.

Questions like: Why does a healthy boy like you have slack teeth?

Tripping up the stairs, or falling down them?

Why are you so clumsy?

Me mother slaps me around, he could say, but never did.

He'd been lucky tonight, his nan had phoned. Saved by the bell, he'd thought, then burst out laughing.

He shook his head in amazement, at his own stupidity, like he had a death wish or something. Why the fuck had he done that?

Must be going soft in the head.

Jesus!

He sighed. Yeah he'd been lucky tonight, the sound of the phone had been like an electric shock, stopping her at once, but she'd remember him laughing the next time she lost it – which could be tomorrow, next month, or in the next five minutes.

Oh boy, would she.

After the phone call she'd made him a ham salad – in the middle of winter a ham salad! He'd laughed at that an' all, but this time in the privacy of his bedroom, whose walls had absorbed much laughter over the years.

He held his arm out straight and, tilting his head to one side, he looked longingly at the picture of the blonde with the big tits. She slept in a magazine under his mattress, safe because his mother didn't come in here, not even to make his bed; she'd been handing out clean sheets with regularity since his eighth birthday. Once a week she poked her head round the door, her nose sniffing like a troubled bloodhound. Only rarely did she enter the room. He would come in from school to find the duster wrapped around the door handle and the Hoover standing to attention outside of the door. If she did not hear the Hoover in exactly five minutes all hell was let loose.

He worried the tooth again. Was it slacker than before?

No. He shook his head. With a bit of luck it might bed in like the others had.

He looked out the window: the night was full of stars, it would be frosty tonight. Perfect for using his telescope, but how could he look at stars with Richy Stansfield dead?

How could he look at stars knowing that he and his friends could face the same fate as Richy?

7

Jacko pulled into the truckers' café on the French side of the channel and cut Lizzy's engine. With a heavy wind behind them they had made good time this trip. Although it was bitterly cold even for December, it had, thank God, stayed dry. They had bumped into a van full of mates from Murton in the warehouse, and had a good natter. Jacko remembered Adam falling over one of the crates and knocking Jerome Bennett flying, and smiled. Trust the bloody daft idiot to knock the hardest man from Murton over. Lucky for Adam, Bennett had been in a good mood this once.

The moon shot from behind a fast cloud just as Jacko was getting out of the cab. He paused for a moment, looking at it, almost hypnotised. Then he shook his head in amazement, this same moon was shining over his three girls. He wondered whether Christina was staring at it at the same time. He thought about the way she looked at him, the way she moved, her shy smile and the sweet way she treated Melanie.

Man, he was lucky. He was the luckiest bastard in the world.

'Oi, Jacko,' Danny's voice took him out of his reverie. Danny was at the door of the café, his hands deep in his pocket, jumping up and down to try and warm himself up. 'Yer want something or not?'

Jacko locked the van, then shouted, 'Mine's a coffee, very very sweet.'

'OK,' Danny replied, waving his hand at Jacko and almost decapitating a small bald man who was coming out of the door.

'Sorry there, mate,' Danny said.

The man kept his head down and grunted something grumpily at him.

'Aye, whatever,' Danny replied.

'What'd he say?' Len asked, as they walked into the dimly lit café.

'Dunno, can't speak French, can I?'

'Bet yer a million it was fuck off,' Brian said, pulling out a chair and sitting at a table which looked like it had been carved in Neanderthal times, and the whole tribe had signed it.

'Fucking poison dwarf,' Adam said, sitting down next to Brian.

'Hey,' Brian glanced quickly around, and was surprised at the amount of faces peering at them in the dimness. 'There's more of them than there are of us, so just keep a lid on it, eh?'

Adam shrugged and reached for the can of Coke that Danny put in front of him.

A few moments later Jacko entered the café and walked over to the table. Brian was yawning and rubbing at the stubble on his chin. This set Len off, then suddenly all five of them were yawning.

'Infectious, innit?' Jacko laughed.

Danny put the tray laden with tea and coffee and

pop on the table. As each man reached for his own particular poison he sat down and said, 'If everything goes according to plan tonight, I reckon, that's if you lot are game, and the weather holds, we can maybe squeeze another trip in before Christmas.'

'Aye,' Adam said at once, as the other three nodded. Then Adam drained his can of Coke, reached over and grabbed another one. Brian snorted. Taking the can from his lips, Adam said, 'What?'

'Oh, for fuck's sake!' Brian exploded. 'Yer bloody gonna want to go and take a piss as soon as we get off again, aren't yer? It's all the fucking pop yer drink, can after bloody can, it's a friggin wonder yer guts are not dropping out the amount of pop yer drink . . . And yer did the same thing last trip.' He looked at Jacko, 'We missed the ship last time 'cos the tit needed to piss every five minutes. Added nearly five hours onto the time . . . Fucking idiot.'

'Yer starting to sound more and more like Dot every day.' Adam replied calmly. His response elicited a growl from Len.

'We're all right, we've made good time. We can spare a few minutes. Unless a wheel falls off we'll make the ship with time to spare,' Danny said.

'That's what yer said last time,' Brian grumbled.

'Well, we'd better get a move on then.' Danny stood up, rolling his eyes at Jacko. 'Come on, let's get Lizzy moving.'

But just as soon as they got in the van, Adam tapped Jacko on the shoulder. 'Umm, need to take a slash,' he said sheepishly.

Brian groaned loudly and said, 'Why can't yer tie a fucking knot in it! Jesus H Christ . . .'

'Yer taking the name of the Lord in vain . . .' Len began.

'Why don't yer put a fucking sock in it,' Brian said, his face reddening with irritation.

Jacko solved the feud by switching the engine off.

'Sloth,' Len muttered, grabbing the chance to get a dig in as Adam stepped over him.

'Oh, yer can't even go for a piss in peace now . . . And what the fuck's a sloth anyhow?'

'Never mind,' Danny the peacemaker said. 'Just go or we'll be here all night.'

'No, I want to know what the fuck a sloth is.'

'A sloth, yer daft bastard,' 'Brian answered, 'is a lazy, slow, tree-dwelling animal that only touches ground for a shite. So now yer know, OK?'

'Is that right?'

'Oh, for fuck's sake,' Danny said, his patience ending. 'Will yer just go and do what yer have to do?'

'OK, OK, I'm going.' With that Adam jumped out of the bus and ran back to the café.

A few minutes later, Jacko was looking in his rear-view mirror, when Adam came out of the toilet. Just behind him was the short bald man they had seen earlier.

It was pretty dark but Jacko thought he had seen them talking. Shrugging he started the engine. *Must have been seeing things,* he thought. *It takes Adam all his time to speak English, never mind bloody French.*

103

8

Sandra Gilbride shivered as she knocked on Debbie Stansfield's door. It was a freezing night and the cold wind seemed to blow straight through her, chilling her to the bones. She wore her hair in a plait, but damp tendrils blew across her face and she swept them back with her hand. Stamping her feet to bring the feeling back to them, she knocked on Debbie's door again. Still no answer. She jumped up and down on the spot to help warm up her feet. High heels weren't the most sensible choice for this sort of weather, but Sandra was a small dainty woman who wouldn't be seen dead without them. She was carrying flowers and a card signed by everyone in the Seahills Residents' Association. The Association had only been going for five months, but somehow Sandra had been designated the official bearer of flowers to the sick and departed.

But she would have visited Debbie anyway. Debbie was a good sort, God bless her. She would have come over earlier but she'd noticed that the house had been pretty full all day, so she'd decided to call tonight when things calmed down a little and Debbie was on her own and in need of a bit of company.

But part of her dreaded seeing Debbie. Sandra

knew that if it was one of her own four boys lying in the hospital morgue she wouldn't be able to bear it. *It would be worse than going through yer life with yer right arm missing.*

She heard barking and looked up the street. It was only Jess, Dolly Smith's black-and-white collie, barking to be let in. Then the sound of carol singers belting out 'Good King Wenceslas' caused her to swing to the left.

A bunch of kids were working their way from door to door up the street. She smiled: she loved seeing the kids carolling. And then, suddenly, her face dropped. *It can't be good for Debbie to open the door and see the smiling faces of kids, red-nosed from the cold.* She hesitated for a moment, then walked out the gate, her heels tapping loudly on the cold pavement, and talked to the eldest of the children for a moment. He nodded and she slipped him a coin from her pocket. Pulling her denim jacket tighter around her, she turned back, walked up to Debbie's door and knocked once more. She should have worn something warmer.

God, it was getting colder.

Come on, Debbie, pet, I know yer in. The bloody house is lit up like a Christmas tree . . . Jesus, I'm gonna turn into a flaming icicle if I stand here much longer.

When there was still no answer she tried the handle, and the door, a little stiff at first, slowly opened.

'Hi, Debbie, it's me, Sandra,' she said loudly.

She listened, then frowned. No sound at all, just

complete silence. She moved down the red-carpeted hallway, feeling more and more anxious with each step she took.

'Debbie?'

Where the hell was she?

Entering the sitting room, Sandra looked round the door.

No Debbie.

And it was nearly as cold in here as it was outside. Sandra was beginning to get seriously worried.

Sandra muttered, 'As cold as the bloody grave,' under her breath, but then mentally kicked herself, even though there was no one who could hear her.

Where was Debbie? She walked back into the hallway and took the door into the small kitchen. No one here either, though it looked as if someone had cleaned up for Debbie. The cups had been left to drain, as if the person who had washed them wasn't sure where they went. Sandra blew air out of her cheeks in frustration. She could see the warm air from her lungs hovering in the kitchen.

'Bloody hell.'

She went back into the sitting room, switched the gas fire on, then the radiators. From there she went to the bottom of the stairs.

'Debbie?' she shouted again.

When there was still no answer she hesitated, her foot on the first step, wondering whether she should go for help or search the bedrooms herself.

'Debbie, love, are yer up there?'

Nothing, just a stone-cold silence that seemed to reverberate through the house. Sandra, a feeling of dread lodged deep in her stomach, walked up the stairs.

With her heart in her throat, she pushed open the first door. She knew at once she was looking at Debbie's bedroom. It was decorated with a woman's touch, the walls and bedding were the same delicate shade of pink and the furniture had been given a new lease of life with a fresh coat of white paint. Debbie wasn't in here either. Quietly she closed the door and crossed the small landing. It was obvious that the door opposite, which had a large poster of Wayne Rooney on it, led to Richy's bedroom. She realised that she had been holding her breath for some time. She let it out slowly and put her hand on the door-knob. For some reason she was dreading opening the door in front of her.

What if?

No, *don't even think like that.*

Taking a deep breath she opened the door.

Please God, let her be all right.

Please.

Richard's room. Sandra saw immediately where the freezing draught was coming from. Richard's Sunderland curtains were being blown into the room from the wind that came in through the open window. At first glance Sandra thought the room was as empty as every other room in the house, and she quickly moved to the window, and slammed it shut.

Then her gaze travelled back to what she had first thought was a pile of clothes in the corner. If Richard was anything like her boys he'd have thought that corners were where yer keep clothes.

But then a movement caught her eye. It was Debbie, huddled in the corner, clutching a blue-and-white sweatshirt of Richard's to her face.

'Oh dear God,' Sandra gasped, her hands rushing up to cover her mouth. Debbie's face was pale and her lips were nearly as blue as the striped sweatshirt she held in her hands.

'For pity's sake. How long, love? How long have yer been sitting here?' Sandra whipped the blanket from Richard's bed and, crouching down, pulled it around Debbie's shoulders. She was only wearing a T-shirt, and the skin on her arms was mottled and purple. Sandra felt Debbie's cheek. It was ice cold.

Debbie stared forlornly at Sandra. Her face felt so stiff that she couldn't have answered even if she'd wanted to.

'Oh, yer poor bugger. Come on, let's get yer up and downstairs in front of the fire to thaw yer out.'

Debbie's huge brown eyes overflowed. 'No, no . . .' she cried. 'Richard's in here . . . I . . . I can't leave him all by himself . . . No, c-can't leave him, he's just a bairn, my, my baby. He's all I've got, just me and him. Debbie and Richard, that's all.'

Sandra knew the last thing she should do was leave Debbie in this room a moment longer. No matter how much she wanted it. In this weather, the cold was dangerous – lethal even. Sandra knew a family whose great-aunt had died alone in her house from hypothermia, her pension not enough to cover both food and electricity. That was an old person with an old person's constitution – she had never heard of someone young succumbing to the cold – and she hoped Debbie would be OK.

'No, Debbie.' Sandra was firm, even though her heart was breaking with pity for the woman in front of her. 'Yer have to come downstairs with me. I've already put on the fire, the room will be warm now. So come on,' she urged, 'we have to get yer thawed out, love.'

Debbie shook her head and made a noise like a drowning kitten. But Sandra was a force to be reckoned with, once she put her mind to something, and she pulled the barely responding Debbie to her feet.

'No,' Debbie sobbed, 'Please!' She shook her head, misery blazing from her eyes as she looked around her son's bedroom.

But Sandra was adamant. 'Come on, love, we have to get yer moving, and yer know me, I'm not going anywhere until we do.'

Gently but firmly she guided a sobbing Debbie from the room. Slowly she navigated the stairs, once or twice fearing that the taller, heavier Debbie was going to collapse and topple them both down the stairs head-first, but finally, after what seemed an age, she had Debbie seated in front of the fire.

She spent a good few minutes rubbing Debbie's hands and feet to get the circulation going, before going into the kitchen to make a cup of hot, sweet tea, then made sure Debbie drank every drop. Even then she was not content and tried to force another cup on Debbie, who begged off saying she would be sick. She had never tasted so much sugar in a cup of tea before.

Thank God, Sandra thought, sighing with relief as the colour slowly began creeping back into Debbie's face.

'Tell yer what, lovey,' she said, coming back in from the kitchen, 'I'll just pop over home, tell them where I am, grab me night things and I'll stay with yer, OK?'

She felt her heart ready to burst when Debbie grabbed hold of her hand and kissed it. For the first time in her life Sandra was lost for words. Indeed, if she could find any she knew she'd be too choked up to deliver them. Instead she gently kissed the top of Debbie's head then squeezed her arm.

Five minutes later, pyjamas and dressing-gown tucked under her arm she was on her way back over to Debbie's when Rachel Henderson and Melissa Tremaine passed by.

Now what are them two doing out on a freezing cold night like this? she wondered. She didn't even realise they were mates. Two more totally different kids would be hard to find.

Shrugging, she let herself into Debbie's and closed the door on the dark December night.

Tuesday 19 December

9

Lorraine had a strange feeling of déjà vu as she hung her black coat on the stand then looked around the strangely empty office. Usually, either Carter or Luke, mostly both of them, were already here and waiting for her. But this morning the office was empty, with a few stragglers from the night shift hanging around, finishing up their work and quickly being replaced by officers who looked just as exhausted.

Today she wore her hair down, brushed until it shone, a really good contrast to her black suit and black blouse, and felt she looked good: professional, yet, she hoped, a bit sexy too. She had hardly slept at all last night, she had just gone over and over in her mind the scene in the pub, thinking about Luke's hand on hers, his eyes locked on her eyes, his words: *Any man who threw away his chances with a woman like you, who didn't try to make it work, is more than stupid. He's crazy.*

Lorraine felt a flush heat her cheeks as she re-ran that moment in the pub. *There is something there, I just know there is.* She smiled to herself. Even though she was fuelled on only a few hours' sleep, she felt awake, energised, full of anticipation and nerves.

What was it going to be like with Luke today? She thought. *Will he ask me out?* she smiled again. *What the hell, perhaps I'll ask him out. After all, my wish is his command.*

She sat down at her desk and allowed herself to think of the future. They could make it work, she knew it, even if they did work together closely. *Perhaps we'd have to tone that down a little*, she thought, *but wouldn't it be fantastic to come home after a long day's work to Luke, have him wrap his strong arms around me and kiss all my troubles away* . . . She bit her lip and smiled, unconsciously twirling a stray lock of blonde hair around her finger. She was disturbed from her thoughts by a tap on the door. Sara Jacobs stood at the threshold of her office, holding a folder to her chest. 'Looks like Luke's late again, boss,' Sarah Jacobs said, her smile looking to Lorraine very false and sly.

But even Jacobs couldn't ruin her mood this morning. In fact, she wasn't going to let her get to her. Lorraine got the feeling that Jacobs knew that Luke was the better officer, could run rings around her in fact, and so the only way she had to make herself look better was to put him down. *She's barking up the wrong tree there*, Lorraine thought. *Those tactics won't work with me.*

Lorraine looked up from where she was sitting at Jacobs and said, very very sweetly, so sweetly in fact that Sara got the message, 'Is he, now?'

'Probably stuck in traffic,' Jacobs mumbled.

'Yeah, probably . . . So, if you could call everyone in, we have a busy day in front of us, thank you.'

Five minutes later Sanderson, Dinwall and Jacobs were standing in her office.

'Anything new overnight?' Lorraine was looking at Sanderson.

Sanderson, a small wiry man in his late forties, reminded Lorraine of a fox. Although he was older than Lorraine, he had been one of the first to congratulate her on her promotion to Detective Inspector. If he had ever felt any resentment over his younger colleague being promoted over him, he never showed it. In fact, he had been unstintingly loyal to her over the years, and Lorraine trusted and respected his judgement and his experience.

'Looks like we might have a lead on some of those robberies that have been plaguing Houghton for the last few months, boss.'

She raised her eyebrows expectantly.

Sanderson pulled a chair up to her desk, sitting casually with one leg resting on top of the other. He went on, 'Seems like it's a bunch of kids, teenagers, boss. A couple of witnesses say four, but the others say five, and they seem organised. The reason why they haven't been caught is because someone has been feeding them information about where and when to strike.'

'So, a bunch of kids.' She thought for a moment. 'Were they seen on the night the watchman died?'

'Still can't drag up any witnesses on that one, boss,' Dinwall put in. 'It was dark and the warehouse is out of town. It's not a part of Houghton where you'd like to take a date, if you know what I mean.'

Sanderson interrupted him. 'But it looks really

similar to the break-in at Johnson's garage last week. Quick strike, in and out, used bolt cutters on the chains, which is how these perps got into the warehouse. We know that money was kept on the premises in a fairly insecure way . . .'

'Which anyone could find out just by visiting the place,' Dinwall added. 'I went to Johnson's after the break-in. He's not exactly security aware.'

'And a group of kids were seen leaving Johnson's garage. Not that our witness got a good look at them,' Sanderson added.

'Well, I wouldn't want to approach a gang of teenagers by myself on a dark night,' Jacobs said, her only addition to the conversation.

The three other police officers stopped talking. Sanderson actually turned round in his seat to look at her.

'Well, I wouldn't,' said Jacobs, realising too late that she had said something stupid. 'Some of these kids are bloody scary,' she added, defensively.

Sanderson coughed and turned back to face Lorraine. She could see that he was raising an eyebrow at her, but she didn't want to betray her feelings so she avoided his gaze and shuffled some papers on her desk.

'OK, back to the case in hand,' said Lorraine. 'I can see where you're going with this, Sanderson. But it's still really sketchy and we need to fill in some blanks. Yeah, it looks like kids, but we can't be sure of that at this stage. Take Dinwall and talk to the owner of the warehouse again,' she looked down at her papers, 'a Mr Austin, and see whether he can shed any light.'

Sanderson and Dinwall looked at each other, then back at Lorraine and nodded.

'And yer've been to see the landlord at the Blue Lion?'

'Red herring,' said Sanderson. 'Yes, there was a fight but the landlord swears black and blue that that's all there was.'

'Do yer believe him?'

Sanderson nodded. 'Can't see why he'd lie about that, boss.'

'So we're back where we started.' Lorraine sighed. 'Great. And also, as if we didn't have enough to do, I received this off the fax late last night.' She held a letter up. 'It's gone out to all stations in the North. There's going to be a crackdown on cigarette and booze smuggling. This cannot leave these four walls. No one knows which day the sting will be on. We will be told one hour beforehand, so we have to be prepared for this. Of course, that will give us four or five hours to prepare ourselves for the ones that escape Dover. It does concern the whole country and it's gonna be in the next few days, just before Christmas.'

Lorraine watched Dinwall's face drop. *There goes his duty-frees for Christmas then*, she thought to herself.

The ship had been delayed because of the harsh weather and when they finally reached port three hours later than estimated, Jacko and Adam, along with most of the people on board, were desperately ill, even though they had lain flat on their backs for most of the trip.

When the ship docked, however, Jacko started feeling better, though he was still a little bit shaky on his legs. He looked at Adam who still had a slight greenish tinge, shook his head slowly and after taking a deep breath, said with a low growl, 'I ask yer, for God's sake, is it fucking well worth it?'

Adam laughed, not one of his heartiest, then, stretching his long limbs, replied, 'When yer desperate for dosh, mate, yer know as well as I do, just about anything's worth it, even this fucking torture.'

Together they followed the crowd down the packed stairs towards the deck where all the vehicles were stored. At the top of the second flight Jacko was jostled by a small bald man.

'Hey mate, watch what yer doing.'

The man looked Jacko up and down, sneered, then hurried away.

'Could have killed yer there, mate. If yer'd gone over the side yer would have bounced down all them decks,' Brian said quietly from behind him.

'Yeah, thanks for that. Just what I needed to know.' Jacko glanced at Brian and did not like the way he curled his lip up into a sneer good enough to match that of the bald man, before barging in front of him.

What's eating him? Jacko thought. And then, *Isn't that the bald man from the caff?*

'Come on,' Adam shouted from the bottom of the steps.

Danny, who had never suffered from seasickness in his life, was already at Lizzy's wheel when they got there and raring to go. Len was looking out the window searching the crowd for them and Brian was sitting in the back with his eyes closed.

'Ha'way man . . . Yer wouldn't believe it's Christmas in a few days. We've got to get a move on if we want to get home and back across one more time before then.'

Jacko groaned inwardly. Already the prospect of another trip, before they'd even finished this one, was sounding decidedly unwelcome. 'Huh, don't I know it's Christmas in a few days, how the hell could I not know? Some daft bastard has been singing carols in me ear for what seems like the past year.'

Danny nodded, 'Yeah! heard him, flat as a fart the old bugger was an' all.'

'Where were you?' Adam said to Brian. 'I looked up once or twice and yer were nowhere to be seen.'

Brian shrugged, 'If yer only looked up once or twice how do yer know I wasn't there?'

'I know yer weren't there,' Len declared, 'I'm like you, I don't need to lie down, seasickness doesn't bother me, so where were yer?'

'Well, for all it's got to do with anybody, especially you, Dot, I was talking to some old mates that I used to knock about with from Durham. Is that all right with yer?' Brian said irritably.

'What do yer's keep calling Len Dot for?' Jacko muttered at Adam.

Adam grinned, and leaning towards Jacko used a stage whisper calculated to be loud enough for Len to hear. 'Well, yer know Dot Cotton from *EastEnders*?'

'Aye,' Jacko did because his mam Doris and their

neighbour Dolly were addicted to it. If they weren't watching it together and dissecting Martin and Sonia's marriage or tutting at Jim Branning's latest shenanigans, they were discussing the previous night's programme over a cup of tea the next morning. Jacko always had a private laugh when he caught them at it; they talked about the characters in *EastEnders* as if Walford was just down the road.

'Ha'way man, think about it,' Adam urged.

'I'm thinking.'

Adam could see that Jacko's thinking was getting him nowhere. Tutting, he said, 'It's obvious yer not a real *EastEnders* fan, are yer, Jacko?'

'Ner, I'm more into *Emmerdale*.' Jacko laughed. 'Though I have caught a couple of episodes.'

'Huh, well yer know how Len keeps on spouting all that stuff from the Bible?'

'Aye.'

'Well, so does Dot Cotton of *EastEnders* . . . Get it?'

'Oh aye.' Jacko laughed out loud and glanced over at Len's scowling face. He'd known Len for years: no way would he ever see the funny side of this. He laughed again, not out of spite or cruelty, because Jacko had a good heart, but because he was wondering how nobody had ever come up with that nickname before.

'Shh,' Danny said, when it was their turn to come off the ship. 'Gotta concentrate, and when we go through customs don't nobody make eye contact. If yer look at the buggers they'll surely pull us in just for the bloody fun of it. I know what the greedy bastards are like at this time of year.'

'Get behind that clapped-out blue van, the one with the black bags up at the windows,' Adam said. 'That's bound to be pulled in, practically asking for it.'

'Somebody should have told the poor buggers that they'll be pulled in if they try to hide something . . . Must be first timers . . . Bet they lose the lot,' Danny said, watching the old blue van cough and splutter its way down the ramp.

He pushed his speed up as far as he dared as they came down the ramps and edged in behind the blue van, narrowly missing a silver Mitsubishi jeep which beeped at them.

'Fuck off,' Brian growled, curling his lip and glaring out the window at the jeep, whose occupants hastily looked in the other direction.

Things were going slow up ahead and Jacko was starting to worry that everybody was getting pulled in. Impossible, of course, given how many cars came off the ferry compared to the number of customs officials that were available. Everybody knew that they had to pull a certain percentage in, but most got home quite safe – it was the luck of the draw, really – but Jacko knew that Danny's run of luck must come to an end soon.

'Where do yer find a duck with no legs?' Adam grinned at everybody.

'Here we bloody go again,' Brian twisted his body round to get in a more comfortable position. 'Non-stop chat all the way home.'

'Who else will help yer while away the hours until we reach Houghton?'

Brian didn't answer, just shifted down further in his seat, closed his eyes and pretended to sleep.

'Now we're got that cleared up,' Adam clapped his hands together, 'where do yer find a duck with no legs?' he repeated.

'Where?' Len snapped.

'Where yer left it.'

'Very funny,' Len growled sarcastically.

'Yeah, I thought so too. What about you, Jacko?' Adam turned to Jacko but was suddenly struck silent as both they and the blue van in front of them were pulled into the bays. Brian suddenly sat up, as he realised, from the movement of the van, that something wasn't right.

'Oh God. Oh dear God,' Danny said.

They all watched silently, each heart in the van beating faster and faster as customs men and their sniffer dogs descended on the blue van, knowing that it would be their turn next.

'What we gonna do, Danny?' Adam practically screeched, as three men got out of the blue van and stood at the side of the bay as the dogs went over the van. 'What we gonna do?'

'Nowt we can do, just stick to the story, OK? Yer know we've got the proper quota. The exact amount of fags, the exact amount of booze; we only have to prove it's for our own use and not for resale,' Danny said as calmly as he could, but there was an edge to his voice.

'Aye, but when they find out most of us are on the

dole they're gonna want to know where we got the money from, aren't they? Oh God, I'm gonna go to jail, I'm gonna lose everything,' Jacko said. He put his face in his hands. Images of Doris, of Melanie, of Christina, the three people he loved most in the world and who depended on him, came into his head. What were they gonna do if he couldn't care for them?

'A loan, Jacko, chill, yer got a loan, and the fags and booze is for yer own use. Stick to the story, OK? And try not to look so goddamned guilty.'

'What about me?' Len demanded.

'The same, Len, for Christ's sake,' Danny shot at his cousin.

Len glowered at him but for once kept his mouth shut as the five men sat in stunned silence.

A minute later Danny gasped as one of the customs men who had been inside the blue van got out and waved them forward.

When they reached him, another man came over and walked around the van looking in the windows. Danny wound his window down. 'Hello sir, we've only . . .' he started to say, but was interrupted.

'Count this as your lucky day. These mugs in front of you are for the high jump.'

Danny's heart started to beat with excitement. He saw the man at the back of the van give a nod to the man in front, 'OK, you can go.'

'What?' Danny knew if he'd been standing up his legs would have given way.

Jacko felt like shouting with glee, and Adam

couldn't contain himself. 'Want to know a good joke?'

The customs man looked at Adam as if he wasn't quite right in the head.

'Shut the fuck up, yer git daft twat,' Brian growled at Adam. 'If they hear yer jokes they'll lock us all up and throw the bloody key away.'

Danny didn't need to be told twice. With a huge sense of relief, he pulled Lizzy out of the bay and soon they were on the road back to Houghton.

'Why do yer think they let us go?' Adam asked as Dover was disappearing from view.

'They were probably just doing routine checks, and found more than they bargained for on that blue van,' Danny answered.

'Aye,' Len agreed. 'They looked like a right shifty lot to me. Bet the van was full of drugs.'

'Whatever,' Adam smiled at everyone. 'It was good for us.'

Jacko shrugged, while Brian silently agreed.

They were thirty miles from Scotch Corner and an hour from home when the front tyre on the van blew. 'Not again,' Brian, who had taken over the driving from Danny, moaned as he safely steered them to the side of the road.

'It's OK, guys, got a couple of brand-new spares.' Danny jumped down from the front passenger seat, as the rest of them piled out of the van.

'I thought yer said these tyres were brand new?' Adam complained, as he rolled a tyre to the front of the van.

'Aye, brand-new second-hand.'

Len snorted.

Danny glared at him, 'Have yer any idea how much brand-spanking-new tyres cost for this van? . . . Have yer? An arm and a leg, that's what . . . These beauties are fine – they do the job all right.'

'They're not that bad,' Jacko agreed. He was at the front of the van where he and Brian already had the wheel off.

'Did yer hear about the scarecrow who won the Nobel prize?' Adam said, then waiting until he got all of their attention, he went on, 'He was outstanding in his field.'

Jacko groaned as he tightened the bolts on the tyre, and slowly straightened up. The men got into the car and Brian started up the engine.

Every one was a lot happier now that they were nearly home. Brian turned the radio on. Goffy was playing his tunes on Metro radio and Lizzy was purring along.

What more could yer ask for? Danny was thinking contentedly. *And if we manage to get that last trip in in a day or two, and the customs men behave themselves instead of being silly buggers like they were today, then it would be a good time all round. Especially for the kids, new trainers for the girls and new footy boots for my pride and joy.*

Adam opened a can. 'Do yer want one, Jacko?'

'No thanks, not much of a drinker actually.'

'What, yer don't drink?'

'Aye, sometimes.' Jacko shrugged, 'But mostly I can take it or leave it.'

'Not everybody sinks to gluttony and has to have a can in his hand nearly every minute of the day as if it were an extension of his body,' Len said.

'Oh for God's sake . . . Judge not lest ye be judged,' Brian spat at Len.

'Where did yer dig that up from?' Len sounded quite amazed.

'There's not only you that can read the bloody Bible, yer know. It hasn't got a tag on it, saying "hands off, sole property of Len Usher", yer sanctimonious git.'

'Well, excuse me.' Len sounded as if his nose was properly put out of joint.

'OK, Dot.'

Adam burst out laughing, as Jacko, hiding a grin, looked out the window.

'Ha'way lads, not long before we're home now. I know yer all tired, but try and chill, eh?' Danny looked pointedly at Len.

Len scowled at his cousin then transferred his gaze to the fields and hills whizzing past. Danny could tell by the way he held himself that Len was far from chilled. He was gonna have to have a quiet word with all of them. He wanted to do another run, but the level of antagonism in the van was high this time, and he was sick to death of all the sniping and bickering. It was just gonna have to stop.

Jacko looked around the living room, a huge smile on his face. Melanie was going to love this. In one corner stood a Christmas tree with paper ribbons all around it and peppermint sticks hanging from its branches.

Christina had made a silver star out of tin foil that she placed right on the top of the tree. And all around the room, light glinted off tinsel and fairy lights sparkled and twinkled. The room had been transformed, and Jacko couldn't wait to see the look on his daughter's face.

'I see Christina's done a hell of a job.' He'd promised Melanie the decorations would be up today, so when he found out that he had a chance to go to France, which meant he couldn't fulfil his promise, Christina had stepped in and put everything up.

'Aye, she's gonna love this all right,' Doris smiled. 'Cup of tea, Jacko?'

'None for me, mam. I'm gonna hit the sack for a few hours.'

'OK, son. Good trip?'

Jacko sighed, 'Not really. We got pulled in by the customs, but they let us go 'cos they had their hands full with the van they pulled in just before us. It was all a bit nerve racking. I don't think I'll be going again, can't stand the bloody tension. Yer sitting there when yer come off that ship and yer bloody terrified.'

'Then don't bother no more, son, it's not worth it. Anyhow,' Doris's smile faded from her face, 'yer'll not have heard about poor Richard Stansfield.'

Jacko had always liked Richard: he and Beefy took him fishing now and then. 'What's the matter with him?'

Doris looked at Jacko sadly.

'Well?' Jacko demanded, knowing with a chilling feeling that something terrible was wrong.

10

'Melissa, would you *please* stop doodling on your textbook and pay attention?' Miss Adams's exasperated tone rang out round the class.

Melissa raised her head and sullenly looked at her teacher. 'I am paying attention.'

'Then what did I just say?'

Melissa shrugged and cast her eyes back down, tracing a circle round and round the front cover of her book.

Miss Adams's high heels clacked towards her and then suddenly the teacher was standing in front of her desk. 'I'll take that,' she said, plucking the ballpoint out of Melissa's hand. 'And these,' she continued, sweeping the rest of Melissa's pens off her desk. 'You will get them back after class. Now concentrate on the board *please*, Melissa.'

As Miss Adams walked briskly back to the front of the class, Melissa mouthed swear words silently at her back. *Prissy cow.*

Melissa's face was a silent study in built-up anger and resentment. She slumped on her desk, folded her arms across her chest and stared at the board. It wasn't even ten o'clock yet and already she and Miss Adams had been at each other's throats.

Why couldn't the bitch just leave her alone?

Christ, it's not as if I don't do the bloody work.

All she ever does is pick, pick, pick.

She put her head in her hands, and her long dark hair fell forward, hiding her face. She wanted to smash things, pick the bloody desk up and throw it at the wall. *I hate them all, every bloody one of them. Who the fuck's worried about flaming geography, for fuck's sake. What does stupid geography matter when Richy's dead? How the hell is knowing the annual rainfall of Western Australia gonna get me out of this mess?*

'Bloody hell,' she muttered out loud, then ground her teeth in frustration.

Miss Adams heard her and looked up from the sentence she was writing on the blackboard. 'Right, Melissa, that's it. See me after class.'

Then the tight rubber band that was Melissa snapped. 'Fuck this!' she yelled, and she heaved her bulk out of the chair, nearly knocking the desk over in the process. Without saying another word she stomped out of the classroom.

'Melissa,' Miss Adams shouted after her as she followed her out into the corridor. 'Come back here at once.'

But Melissa only speeded up. She went through the double doors so fast that they swung loudly behind her. Not caring who saw her leave, she strode out of the school gates.

Pausing, she leaned against the wall and breathed deeply. She felt calmer already, just being out of the stifling classroom. It had seemed as if it was shrinking by the minute, until all she could see was a huge Miss Adams, with Marcel standing behind her. She shuddered at the picture in her mind of the pair of them.

Bloody woman.

A moment later she felt a touch on her elbow. Startled, she looked round. Rachel Henderson was standing beside her.

'What?' Melissa demanded.

'Miss Adams sent me out to see if you were all right.'

'She's doing me friggin' head in. I don't know how yer do it. How the fuck can yer concentrate? Everything's going round and round in me bloody head, and her banging on about nowt. Jesus, all I can see is her face and Marcel's in me bloody mind, I wish to God I'd never got involved . . . What are we gonna do, Rachel?'

Melissa looked desperate, almost on the verge of tears, and seeing her like that frustrated Rachel. Hadn't Marcel shown them the way? Hadn't he picked them out as special? Weren't they all chosen? She sighed. She supposed she could almost understand it if Melissa was scared. She herself sometimes forgot what Marcel had promised them. Day-to-day life was difficult – it was difficult to remember those promises when your stepfather came banging on your door at two in the morning like he had last night. He'd just got in from his shift where he'd had another row with his foreman so he'd taken it out on Rachel in more ways than one.

She was sore and bruised. She'd tried sitting in a

warm bath, but before it had time to do any good, her stepbrother had been yelling at her to hurry up. It seemed the older he got the more angry he became, and Rachel was beginning to think he knew what his father was doing.

She leaned against the same wall as Melissa, and sighed again.

'I'm sorry,' Melissa said.

Rachel nodded. Yesterday evening she'd confided in Melissa on their way to the club. It had felt good to tell someone at last.

They had been walking across from Richy Stansfield's place, and had seen Sandra Gilbride enter his house. 'She must be going in to check on Richy's mam,' said Rachel.

Melissa looked stricken with guilt. 'We should go to see her, tell her how sorry we are.'

Rachel sighed. 'According to Katy Jacks, she's in a bit of a state. Perhaps we should leave it for a couple of days.'

Melissa nodded. 'Do yer remember when Richy and Kurt first came to Marcel's?'

Rachel smiled. 'Yes. It was my third time. I was surprised to see them, actually, but it was good to see them there.'

'How did yer know about the meetings?' Melissa asked.

'It was Mary. I met her in the caff on Newbottle Street. She told me she liked me hair.'

'That's what she told me too,' Melissa interrupted, 'and then she told me about the club, about how I'd make friends there and,' she said quietly, looking at

Rachel with a slightly nervous expression on her face, 'I did.'

Rachel smiled at Melissa. 'Mary told me about the club and I went because I thought it would be good to go, if only if it meant that I'd get away from my stepfather, just for a few hours.' And then she was quiet for a moment before saying, 'Actually, I found something much better than that.'

'Marcel,' said Melissa. She knew what Rachel meant. When she first met Marcel, she had felt the same way. He had taken her hands in his and had told her that he could see past her weight, past her stubbornness, past all the barriers that she put up between her sensitive soul and the rest of the world. Melissa had felt, for the first time, that someone understood her. But then he had turned to Niall, and had said very much the same thing to him, and she had felt unaccountably disappointed. And if Melissa was honest, a little bit jealous too. She looked at Rachel, who had her head down and was chewing her bottom lip, deep in thought. After a couple of seconds, Rachel looked up and met Melissa's gaze. 'He knew me,' Rachel said. 'He understood me. He knew about me stepfather.'

Melissa looked puzzled. 'What about yer stepfather?' she said, but then she looked at Rachel's expression and thought that she could guess.

Rachel swallowed. 'Me stepfather. He's been coming into me room at night. He's been . . .' She looked at the ground and said, 'Well, he's not gentle.'

Melissa still couldn't quite believe what she was hearing. 'Yer mean he's . . .' she looked at Rachel who was looking straight back at her. Melissa shook her head. 'That's disgusting,' she said finally. 'How long has it been going on?'

'About three years,' Rachel said, her voice small and broken. 'Since mam died.'

'Rachel, yer should have gone to the police. They would have helped yer, they would have put him away!' Melissa said passionately. 'He's a sicko, yer know that? Yer were twelve when he first . . .'

'I can't go to the police,' Rachel said strongly. 'What do yer think they'll do? They'll break us up, Mandy and David would be put in care and that's if they believe me. But who would? It's my word against his.'

'But can't they, yer know, examine yer or something?' Melissa asked, but regretted the words as soon as she said them. Rachel looked stricken.

They walked in silence for a while. Then Rachel said, 'Yer see, Marcel never asked me anything like that. He understood what I needed. The first night I went to the club, he asked me back to his chambers. He asked me what was wrong. I told him, but somehow he already knew. He wanted me to trust him enough with my secret. And then he told me the story of Mary Magdalene, how she was a prostitute, but who was saved by her faith in Christ. And then,' Rachel dropped her gaze and said in a voice so quiet it was almost a whisper, 'he let me wash his feet.'

Melissa frowned. 'Rachel, don't yer think that's really strange?'

Rachel shook her head adamantly. 'No. It was beautiful.'

They reached the gates of the house and Rachel had turned to Melissa and said, 'Yer've gotta promise me that yer won't tell Kurt or Niall. They wouldn't understand.'

Melissa shook her head. 'I won't,' she had said in a quiet voice.

But now it was daytime, and the confidences of last night were replaced by something else. There was a wariness to Melissa's tone that Rachel didn't like. She wasn't trusting in Marcel as much as she should, and that worried Rachel.

'What are we gonna do?' Melissa said. Rachel could hear the strain in her voice.

Rachel shrugged, then switched her weight to her other leg. 'What can we do?'

'We could run away, go to London. They'll never find us there.' Melissa took her pale blue hairband out, shook her hair then ran her fingers through it before replacing the band.

'But there's no need, Melissa. Marcel will take care of us, he knows what's best.'

'No,' Melissa cried. 'Richy was right. We should have gone to the police. It was an accident what happened to the night watchman. We weren't to know he'd follow youse up on to the roof . . . What the fuck did yers go on the roof for anyhow? If yer hadn't we wouldn't be in this friggin' mess.'

'But Melissa, we're not in a mess! I've told yer, Marcel will sort it . . . A blessing will be delivered.'

Melissa shivered, 'Listen to yer, yer starting to sound just like bloody Marcel.'

Rachel smiled. 'Richard was so soft, such a baby wanting to go to the police. You know the Blessing Guides are good, you know we'll be safe with them . . . That Richard was weak. He didn't like it that Marcel paid less attention to him than he did to us. Richard didn't give him the chance. He didn't believe. And that's why he killed himself, because he knew that he would never receive what Marcel tried to offer him. He wasn't worthy. Anyhow, aren't you looking forward to the ceremony on Christmas Eve?'

'No,' Melissa said softly. She wasn't looking at Rachel, just staring at the ground in front of her feet.

Rachel sighed. 'Melissa, we belong to the Blessing Guides now. They helped us when we needed them, when nobody else was there. You know they're right. Look at us, remember we had nobody until we found the Blessing Guides, nobody wanted to be my friend.'

'That's only 'cos yer wouldn't let them.'

Rachel shrugged. That was true, but she'd felt so ugly and tainted that she'd felt everything was her fault. Then Marcel saw her true self, he saw underneath her skin, he knew her in a way no one else had. She knew he could make her pure again.

Melissa shook her head and started to walk away. She didn't like what Rachel said about Richy. She was starting to sound too much like Marcel. Out of the five of them, Richy was the one who seemed to have his head screwed on the straightest. Now that he was gone, would they still be friends? Or would they drift away from each other? Melissa hated that thought. These were the best friends she'd ever had. But she couldn't be around Rachel at the moment.

She couldn't bear to hear any more about Marcel. It was strange how reassured he made you feel in his presence, but as soon as you left him, the doubts and the fears came flooding back.

'Where are yer going, Melissa?' Rachel asked, catching up to her and walking by her side.

'Don't know,' Melissa snapped.

'Come on, we'll go and see Mary. She'll help, yer know she will.'

'Do we have to? She's almost as bad as Marcel.'

Rachel laughed, 'No she's not, yer just feeling bad over the night watchman. You mustn't. It was an accident. And remember what Marcel said. At the end of the day he got in the way of the Lord's work. He shouldn't have tried to stop us.'

'You sound like you're glad he died!'

'No, of course not. I wouldn't have wished that to happen to anyone. But it wasn't our fault. You know it wasn't.'

Melissa kept walking. She had her hands thrust deep inside her pockets and her fingers touched the two items there: one was the card she'd got from the policewoman who her instincts told her to trust, who she wanted to trust; the other was a silver coin, embossed on one side with the symbol of the Blessing Guides, a circle enclosing a fish.

Niall lay on his bed with his hands behind his head and studied the ceiling. He had felt weak and tired when he tried to get up that morning, so he didn't bother getting out of bed. It was almost lunch time and he really should eat something, but he was way

136

too tired to even contemplate getting out of bed, never mind facing last night's leftovers in the fridge.

It must have been well after four when he got in last night. Slowly he shook his head.

What the fuck had he got into?

His knees hurt like hell from all that friggin' kneeling. He was certain the left one was skinned and bleeding, though he couldn't really be bothered to look.

Blood was the last thing he wanted to see. Christ, that watchman had bled plenty.

Whose fucking idea had it been to go on the roof?

Whoever it was hadn't expected the old man to follow them, pretty nimble an' all. Surprisingly.

Until he fell.

Niall's fists crumpled the sheet as he clenched and unclenched them unconsciously. The thing was he'd seen the man around Houghton before, more than once, pushing a woman in a wheelchair.

Who's gonna push her now?

Point is, he sighed, watching a small spider wriggle out of the light fitting, *me and Richy only went for a laugh.*

Aye, and because I was lonely.

And bored.

And sick of people telling me what to do.

And look at Richy now.

And they think it was suicide . . . but that doesn't make sense.

Fuck it.

Turning over, he punched the pillow until it was plump then sank his head into its softness.

'I'll get up later,' he murmured as he drifted off.

Kurt, shoulders slumped and head down, slowly shuffled into school behind everyone else. This morning Miss Adams had become increasingly worried as neither Melissa nor Rachel came back to class. After half an hour she had told them to read from their geography books, then disappeared.

Now it was after lunch and they were still both missing. Miss Adams, though, had found her way back and given them a surprise test on what they'd read.

He'd tried Rachel's mobile, over and over, but it was switched off, and he knew that Melissa's was broken again. *So where the hell are they?*

But he knew where they would be, the only place they felt safe these days – with Marcel.

What really happened to Richy?

Kurt made his way to his desk, pulled out his chair and sat down. Niall had texted him this morning to tell him there was no reason to get out of bed. And Melissa and Rachel's desks were also empty. He saw that Mr Fallowes, the maths teacher, had noticed the empty desks and made a couple of marks on the roll. Kurt sighed. A large part of him wished that he was wherever Melissa and Rachel were now. He stared out the window in the direction of the Seven Sisters.

Not that he could see them. They were hidden from view by houses and other trees. As if brick and wood had joined forces and placed themselves between the Seven Sisters and the inhabitants of Houghton, trying to protect them.

I should write that down, he thought, smiling to himself.

But then he pictured Richy hanging from one of the tree branches and shuddered.

Was his body hanging limp, when the man had found it? Or was it swaying in the wind?

He tried to remember if it had been windy that morning, but he couldn't for the life of him. Then he did his best to put the picture of Richy out of his mind.

Richy had been the happiest one of them all. People loved him, he had oodles of confidence and a fantastic mother. Kurt sighed and bit his bottom lip. *He only become involved because of me. He wanted to get out ages ago but I asked him not to 'cos I didn't want him to break up the group.*

And now he's dead.

Kurt squeezed his eyes shut. His head was starting to hurt with the worry of it all. Nearly as much as his heart was hurting. He really should go and visit Richy's mother, but he didn't dare. She might guess and start asking questions. And he knew that when he saw her face, all crumpled and red from crying, he wouldn't be able to lie.

He sensed somebody standing beside him and opened his eyes.

'Were you falling asleep, Mr Allendale?' Mr Fallowes asked.

'No, sir,' Kurt quickly replied.

'Of course you weren't. Nobody falls asleep in my lesson. Do they, boy?'

Kurt sighed. Did he really have to take this shit?

He was sixteen for fuck's sake.

Swallowing his pride, he looked Mr Fallowes in the eye and said, 'No sir,' but really he wanted to be where his friends were. Wherever they were.

11

Lorraine was on her way to visit Debbie Stansfield and angrier than she could ever remember being. The good mood of the morning had evaporated as the minute hand on the clock had ticked by and Luke still hadn't shown up. She was worried about him, because it wasn't like him at all, but then Jacobs had come in to tell her that Luke had phoned in to say that he wasn't coming into work that day.

Lorraine had leaned back in her chair. 'No reason why?'

'No, boss,' said Jacobs. 'Just that he would call in tomorrow if he wasn't going to be able to make it. Otherwise to expect him as usual.'

Lorraine's reaction was, at first, worry that someone in his family had died. *But that can't be right*, she thought, *because he'd need more time off.* And the more Lorraine thought about it, the angrier she became.

Didn't even bother to ask to speak to me!

Well, that's men all over.

Give them an inch and they'll take a bloody yard. Bastards.

What was yesterday about, if he doesn't have the guts to face me now?

All in all, it had been a frustrating morning. Sanderson and Dinwall came back after talking to David Austin, the warehouse owner, with little to report. Austin had told them that, after he had heard of the break-ins in Houghton, he had taken any money off the premises at night, which was probably why the intruders didn't find anything to take. He showed them around the deserted building. 'If Eric had heard something, he would have come up these stairs,' he said as they climbed them up from the main floor to where the offices were.

Sanderson explained to Lorraine that this would have blocked the intruders' escape route. 'There was only one other way out,' he told her. 'Up a ladder fixed on the floor that led to the roof. We went up there. You'd need to be pretty nimble. But there was no escape once they were on the roof either, so they must have been panicking.'

'And then Eric McIvor went up behind them . . .'

'And either they pushed him or he fell. But I tell you something, boss, it's pretty slippery up there. And you're an elderly man, out of shape, up on the roof in the dead of night – well, I wouldn't rate his chances.'

Lorraine sighed as she drove her car further along the road. They still were no closer to finding out what happened with the night watchman. *And no closer with Richy Stansfield either,* she thought.

She had called Scottie to see whether he had found anything more.

'I'm sorry to say it's still inconclusive, love.' His accent was even more pronounced over the phone.

'Aside from those fibres, there's nothing to tell me that it's anything other than a suicide. I know that's not what you want to hear.'

'I just wish I could believe it, Scottie,' she had replied. 'But there's just something not right.'

'I'm sorry, love,' Scottie had replied. 'I can only tell you what I discover.'

Lorraine sighed as she thought ahead to her destination. It wasn't a call she was looking forward to making. But now, at four o'clock with the evening drawing in dark and cold, she could make no more excuses.

She stopped her car outside Debbie Stansfield's house and sat for a few minutes while she calmed herself down.

The poor woman's just lost a son. Last thing she needs is an edgy cop pestering her.

She breathed deeply using some karate techniques she'd been taught. After checking her phone for missed calls – *None. Damn . . .* – Lorraine got out of the car, locked up and walked up Debbie's path, knowing she was being watched from all sides. *I must have been watched from the house an' all*, she thought as the front door opened and Sandra Gilbride smiled at her.

'Hello,' Sandra said, opening the door wider.

Lorraine returned the greeting and was about to step inside when Sandra whispered, 'She's not too well, mind yer.'

Lorraine nodded. Of course, she had not expected Debbie to be on top form. And she took Sandra's news for what it was – the concern of a worried good neighbour and friend. In fact, there were a lot of good neighbours on the Seahills, and Debbie was going to need all the good neighbours and friends she could get over the next few weeks and months.

Sandra showed Lorraine into the living room, where Debbie sat by the fire, a rug over her knees. 'I'll just go and make us a cup of tea,' Sandra said quietly. 'Debbie,' she touched her friend gently on her shoulder, 'can I make you something to eat? Some toast?'

Debbie remained sitting still, staring at a picture that she held in her hands. 'No, thank you,' she said quietly, in a dry, cracked voice.

'You've got to eat, Debbie love.'

Debbie just shook her head.

Sandra smiled thinly at Lorraine and then went into the kitchen. Lorraine stood on the threshold of the room for a moment, and then moved into the room. 'Is that a picture of Richard you've got there?' she asked.

Debbie lifted her head and regarded Lorraine for a moment. She then turned her gaze back to the picture and ran her hand over its surface. 'Yes. It's my favourite one of him,' she said, holding it up so that Lorraine could see. 'Look.'

'He was a handsome boy.' Taking her handbag from her shoulder, she sat on the settee opposite Debbie. The poor woman looked so distressed. She was only in her mid-thirties – about the same age as Lorraine – but the last two days had aged her dreadfully. Her face was lined with grief and pain. The women sat silently for a while. Lorraine wished she could think of something to say that would help Debbie, but she knew that words would not be enough. With Richard gone, nothing ever would be enough.

In fact, it was Debbie who broke the silence. 'He didn't murder himself, yer know,' she said straight-forwardly, as she kissed the picture. 'He wouldn't do that. No reason, yer see, officer, no reason at all. He was happy, my Richard. Very very happy.'

Lorraine stood up. There were pictures on the mantelpiece, pictures of Richard as a toddler, playing in a sandpit; Richard on his first day at school, knobbly knees hanging out of shorts just that little bit too big for him; Richard muddy and laughing, a football under his arm, grabbing Kurt Allendale round his neck. It was an old photo, but Lorraine definitely recognised Kurt. She picked up the photo and turned to Debbie.

'This is a good photo.'

Debbie looked up and smiled. 'Yes. That was taken after Richard scored two goals off Herrington Burn when he played striker for Glendale. That's Kurt Allendale. He likes to watch but he's not really one for sport. I took them to McDonald's for a treat afterwards.'

'Were Kurt and Richy good friends, Debbie?' Lorraine asked casually as she looked at the other photos.

'Kurt used to come round here and do his home-work,' Debbie answered. 'Nice kid.'

'I hear Richy was also particularly good friends

with Niall Campbell, Rachel Henderson and Melissa Tremaine.'

'Well, yes . . .' Debbie answered, with a questioning tone in her voice.

'I just ask because, according to the teachers at his school, they seemed like an unusual group of kids to start hanging out together. Yer know, nothing much in common.'

Lorraine couldn't help but notice the defensive tone in Debbie's voice when she answered, 'Well, yes, but Richy was friends with everyone. What's all this about?'

Lorraine hated intruding on Debbie's grief like this, but she needed to ask her questions. Questions she hoped would give her the answers she knew Debbie needed. 'It's really nothing,' she said gently, 'but I have to check all avenues and make sure that I've got the right picture. There was nothing about his friends that worried you?'

Lorraine could see that Debbie was thinking hard. Eventually she said, 'Well, they hardly ever came round here, and when they did I left them to themselves. They all seemed like nice kids.' Then her expression darkened as she thought through the implications of Lorraine's questions. 'What are you saying?' Debbie's voice became higher, 'Are you saying that I shouldn't have?'

Lorraine kicked herself. God, she needed Luke. He'd be able to say exactly the same thing but in a way that wouldn't offend. 'No, Debbie, that's not what I meant,' she said soothingly. 'As I said, just trying to build up a picture.'

Debbie nodded and turned her head back to the photo of Richard. Lorraine took a deep breath and sat down again. 'I'm sorry to have to ask you this again, Debbie, but is there anything more that yer can remember about that day? Anything at all, no matter how insignificant? It's all helpful.'

Debbie held the picture to her chest and began shaking her head, rocking back and forth. 'No, I've told yers over and over, no.'

'It's OK, Debbie love.' Sandra came in from the kitchen where she'd made tea. She put the tray on the coffee table, then sat on the arm of Debbie's chair and put her arm around her. 'Help yerself.' She looked at Lorraine and gestured with her hand towards the pot of tea.

'Thank you.' Lorraine filled all three cups.

Lorraine took a sip of tea while she thought how she was going to phrase her next question. She had to tread carefully – Debbie was clearly hanging on by a thread. She wished that Luke was here – he was so good in these sorts of situations. He knew not only what questions to ask but also how to ask them in a way that put people at ease. 'This is a difficult question to ask,' Lorraine began tentatively, 'but I'm afraid I have to ask it. Do you know whether Richy and his friends were into anything unusual? Did yer ever get the feeling there was something he wasn't telling you?'

'What are you saying? My boy was decent and my boy did not murder himself.' Debbie was staring intensely at Lorraine, then she hung her head, and tears splashed onto Richard's picture. She then

147

clutched the picture to her chest and let out a heartrending howl.

Sandra looked sternly at Lorraine. She was rubbing Debbie's arm while her friend sobbed into her shoulder. For a few minutes, Lorraine listened uncomfortably to Debbie crying, but then, after Debbie had gulped down a few tears, she said to Lorraine, 'Yer can't know unless yer've children how scared you are, how scared yer are everyday that they're not gonna get hit by a car or run over by a bus or something dreadful like that. But yer also know that yer've got to let them go, be free to live their lives. Richy was just a lad, aye, but he was turning into a man. And I trusted him. Yer know how rare that is? For a mother to actually trust her son? Especially with all these drugs and gangs and everything today. But Richy just isn't into that. I know my son, and he's not like that.'

Lorraine flinched at the present tense. And she heard Debbie take a deep intake of breath as she too realised what she had said.

'Listen, Debbie,' Lorraine said, leaning forward and putting a hand on her knee. 'I'm not implying your son or any of his friends were into anything illegal. And I am so, so sorry that I have to ask you these questions, particularly at this difficult time.' She leant back and took a card from her handbag. 'Here is my card. It's got my office number on it. Call me if anything suddenly comes to mind.' She passed it to Debbie, who took it from her and stared at it.

'I best be going now.' Lorraine put her cup back on

148

the tray and stood. 'Thank you for seeing me, Debbie. I'll see meself out, Sandra.'

Sandra nodded, as she stroked the back of Debbie's neck.

'What a fucking day,' Lorraine muttered as she started the car. The visit had only upset Debbie even more.

She was nearly back at the station and swallowing past a lump in her own throat when her mobile rang. Quickly she pulled over to the side of the road, telling herself for the millionth time that she had to get a hands-free set, hoping and praying that it was Luke.

Unknown number. *Shit, who's this?*

'Hello?'

A minute later she ended the call. 'Fuck.' Jason Manners was dead. He had never woken up from the anaesthetic. For the time being he was residing with Scottie, who would very much like to see her.

She turned the car at the next roundabout and headed towards Sunderland.

Lorraine stared down at Jason Manners's dead body. 'So how did he die?'

'Internal bleeding. He was cut up pretty badly and his veins were weak from all the drugs he'd been taking. The doctors did try and replace the blood but as quickly as they were pumping it into him it was pumping back out.' He lifted the sheet. 'You've already seen this, I take it? This wasn't the cause of death, but to partially flay the skin off someone when they're still alive . . .' Scottie shook his head. 'It's agony.'

Lorraine was looking at the symbol carved on Manners's body. Even though she had seen it before, its impact hadn't lessened and she felt sick. Carved had been the correct term: whoever had done this had taken his time, and seeing as Manners was still alive and probably conscious he would have felt everything and been in pure agony.

Lorraine shook her head. She'd seen some horrific things but this was hard to swallow. 'Ever come across anything like this before, Scottie?'

Scottie was staring at Manners's mutilated body. 'No, and neither has anyone I know.'

Lorraine took a step back and leaned against the bench. 'What sort of person could do this?'

Scottie gently drew the sheet over Manners as if the man were still alive and Scottie was afraid to hurt him. 'Like Edna said, Lorraine, a pretty sick one.'

Lorraine took her notebook out and from memory sketched the marks on Manners's body. 'This obviously means something to the person who cut him. I'm hoping that if we found out what it means, it might lead us to the person who carved him up.'

'Where was he found, again?'

'Somehow he made it to his aunt's place. I don't know how the hell he did, though, with his injuries. She's the one who called the ambulance.'

'Wasn't he at the Blue Lion?'

Lorraine shook her head. 'Sanderson and Dinwall went to see the landlord. Yes, there was a disturbance that night, and knives were flashed around, but apparently, it was all bluff. Couple of punches thrown but that was it.'

'Typical Sunday night at the Blue Lion then,' Scottie said.

Lorraine smiled wryly. 'And we just assumed that was where Manners got stabbed.'

'Not like you, Lorraine,' Edna said.

Lorraine shrugged. 'Now it's a murder enquiry, we can't afford to make any more mistakes. I don't feel good about this one. You have to be pretty cold-blooded to cut someone up like that.'

'I think you're right about the symbol though, Lorraine. Find out what it means, and I'm sure it'll lead somewhere.'

'Thanks, Scottie.' Lorraine slung her bag over her shoulder. 'OK, then, I'll catch you guys later.'

'Good night,' they both said in unison.

Outside, Lorraine slid into her car, and checked her mobile. Still no missed calls.

Should she phone him?

I hope he's OK. I hope whatever it is that's keeping him from work isn't serious.

But why didn't he want to talk to me this morning?

Lorraine sighed. *Here you go again, girl, reading too much into things. Yesterday was really nice, but what was I thinking?* She looked out the window into the night and smiled at herself. *Get me thinking of a future with him based on what? A nice chat over a lemonade and bangers and mash? God, I'm sad.*

He was just being kind, after I told him about the divorce.

And obviously he just thinks that we're colleagues, nothing more, otherwise he would have called me, surely?

The problem was, Lorraine admitted to herself, that after months of suppressing her feelings for him, she had finally given in to the fantasy of sharing her life with Luke. *I'm not sure that I can see him just as someone I work with now.*

She sighed as she started the car and drove off into the lonely night.

12

Louise was so excited she could barely keep still. Mary was calling for her. Actually calling at her house. Any time soon she'd be knocking on the door.

Nobody had ever called for her before. She smiled at her father who was reading the paper so he never noticed the smile. She loved her dad to bits when he wasn't drinking. He seemed to be laying off the booze a lot more lately. Louise hugged herself. Life had suddenly started being good. And it had all started with meeting Mary. She must be good luck. She'd had to warn Mary though, told her about her dad's scars, which covered most of his face, arms and chest and were even more noticeable than Louise's. But Mary had understood. 'Scars also have their place in the universe,' she'd said. 'They're a mark of where you've been, of what's happened to you, They're a mark of who you are. And they mark you out as someone special. And I should know.' As she smiled wistfully, the tear-shaped mark on her cheek moved.

No one had ever talked about her scars like that before. Instead of feeling ashamed about them, as she had ever since she could remember, she now allowed herself to feel proud of them. It felt good, if strange, to look in the mirror and be happy with what you saw there.

And Mary knew what she was talking about, of course. She also had a mark, a tear-shaped port-wine stain on her cheek. Louise thought that this mark must have been part of the reason why Mary had approached her the first time. They were so similar in lots of ways – Mary had said so.

Even though she was expecting it, the knock on the door still startled her. Grinning, she practically ran to open it.

'Blessed be,' Mary said, when she was faced with Louise's happy smiling face.

'Blessed be, Mary.' Louise answered as she stood aside for Mary to enter. 'Come and meet me dad.'

Louise was so happy she practically skipped down the hallway ahead of Mary. When they entered the sitting room Louise's father had his back to them.

'She's here, Dad.' He put his newspaper down and turned.

Mary had been prepared for a few burn marks but nothing as bad as this. It looked as if Louise's dad's nose had been burnt off, and his skin was slickly covered with moisturising lotion. He looked scary.

'It's all right, Mary,' he said as he recognised the shock on her face. 'I'm used to it by now . . . Sit down, won't yer.'

'I'm sorry,' Mary murmured.

'No reason to be, love. I'm just pleased our Louise has found a friend at last. She gets pretty lonely sitting here with only me for company. I've told her to get out more.'

Mary nodded, and this time she managed a full smile. 'She'll enjoy herself.'

'Sort of a youth club, is it?'

'Sort of.'

Louise returned with her blue coat and stripy blue and cream scarf, and Mary stood up. 'Good night.'

He nodded to them both, adding to Louise, 'You be careful now, Louise, it's dark out there.'

'Sure I will, Dad, the bus drops me practically at the door.' Louise raised her eyebrows at Mary and mouthed, *dads*. God, this felt great, her dad acting normally, sharing a private joke with someone that she could call a friend.

'OK, you enjoy yerself now.' He smiled at them both as they walked out the door but his smile faded once he heard the door shut. He couldn't help but notice that Mary looked an awful lot like Louise; both were petite and dark, but where Louise had burn marks from the fire that had claimed his wife and son, Mary had a dark, port-wine stain on her cheek in the shape of a teardrop. And Mary looked young, very young, but not nearly as young as Louise did. Should he be worried about that? He shrugged his shoulders. He wasn't about to start lecturing Louise on her friends, not after he had let her down so many times. He sat down down at the table, picked up his newspaper, and tried not to think about the off-licence down the road.

The bus dropped Mary and Louise close to a large house at the end of a leafy street. It was private and partially hidden from view by the large trees that grew well above the five-foot wall.

'Is this where it is?'

Mary nodded as she opened the gate.

'Never really noticed this place before, it's so well hidden away.'

In the hallway Mary took Louise's coat and scarf and hung them in a cupboard, before removing her own brown coat. Louise noticed that there were loads of coats in the cupboard. Her stomach twisted with anticipation and nerves at the thought of meeting all these new people. 'Come on,' Mary said. Louise followed her. They passed two doors on the right, then Mary stopped at the third door on their left, turned the handle and walked in.

Louise gaped. This was definitely not what she'd been expecting. She was in a huge room, almost as big as a hall. A wall had obviously been knocked through to make more space. The heavy red curtains were closed, and there was barely any furniture, only a few cushions piled in a corner. A large table with two pitchers of orange juice and a dozen or so glasses on it was set up at one end of the room. The wooden floors were carpetless, except for a rug that was placed in front of a huge fireplace that took up most of one wall. Instead of crackling logs it had a gas fire at its centre. Around the table stood twelve or so people, chatting quietly together.

Louise picked Melissa out immediately. She and that boy Niall, who she'd overheard people saying at school was on drugs, were standing apart from the group, looking a little uncomfortable. Kurt Allendale and Rachel Henderson were there too, talking to some people she didn't know, though Kurt kept throwing what looked like worried glances at Melissa and Niall. *Perhaps they're just nervous, just like me,* Louise thought. It made her feel better. Rachel, on the other hand, looked happy and animated as she talked to a tall, older man dressed in a black suit. As Louise looked over to Rachel, the man turned his head and met her glance. There was something in the unsmiling way that he looked at her that Louise didn't like, and all of a sudden she felt intensely uncomfortable. But then, a door on the other side of the room opened and Louise forgot all about the man talking to Rachel as in walked the most gorgeous person she'd ever seen. This must be Marcel. He wasn't very tall or big, just a medium-sized man dressed simply in jeans and a white tunic top, but he had a presence about him. He was the type of person who, when he stepped into a room, people took notice of. Louise saw that he had olive skin and a lot of dark, curly hair, but she was entranced by his eyes which were so dark and intense that she couldn't take her own off them. Marcel smiled as he walked over to them, the most beautiful, benevolent smile. Louise was awed by the graceful way he moved. He kissed Mary's cheek, then held out his hand to Louise.

'Mary, you told me she was special but you never told me how pretty our newest member is . . . Hello, darling, I'm Marcel.' He took her hand and kissed it.

That was it for Louise. No one had ever told her she was special, let alone told her that she was pretty.

And it wasn't just anyone telling her these things, it was someone so beautiful and so kind that, it struck Louise, he didn't seem quite of this world. When he smiled at her and looked into her eyes, Louise felt as if she was the only person in the room. Never in her life had she met anyone even half as charismatic, and her cheeks reddened, while her stomach seemed to flip right over. This time it wasn't nerves: Louise was in love.

Still holding her hand, he led her to the centre of the room and gently eased her down into a sitting position, never once lifting his eyes from hers. Taking this as a signal, the others peeled themselves from where they had been standing and formed a circle around Marcel and Louise.

Marcel held his hands in a praying position, only instead of the fingers resting on each other they were intertwined. When Louise noticed the others doing this she took it as a signal, and did the same with her own hands. Marcel smiled kindly at her, then he began to hum. Slowly his voice rose and fell. One by one the others joined in.

It was electric.

Mrs Reardon, stooped with arthritis and ready for bed, old tartan dressing-gown on top of her green pyjamas, cigarette in one hand and cat cuddled to her chest with the other, peered out of her bedroom window. She lived in one of the highest houses in Hall Lane, and from upstairs she could see most of the Seven Sisters, and beyond.

For weeks now she had seen lights bobbing about

in the middle of the night up there, but them bloody fools down at the police station didn't believe her.

'Not once,' she muttered to Timmy, her fat grey-and-black tomcat, which she carried around all day. 'Not once have they ever got back to me. Idiots, the whole lot of them. Aye, that's what they are, Timmy, bloody idiots. All been took over by bloody aliens if yer ask me.'

Timmy purred contentedly, and Mrs Reardon took a puff of her cigarette.

'Might even be Russian spies up there, yer never know, do yer, Timmy?'

She blew smoke out of her nose, momentarily clouding her vision. When the smoke had cleared, she saw that the lights had formed a circle. One by one as she watched, the lights went out, leaving one lone light shining.

'Huh, if I phone the coppers they'll not come, could be them there bloody terrorists for all they care, might be planning on blowing Houghton to kingdom come.'

She stroked Timmy. 'Aye, Timmy, I hope they get the bloody cop shop first. And if they come raping and pillaging, they'll find me already in me bed and waiting.'

'Shut up, shut up,' she yelled a moment later staring at a tiny red flower on the wallpaper, as she took her slipper off and slapped the adjoining wall to next door.

'Noisy noisy people.'

The noisy people next door, a quiet old couple in their seventies who hardly ever made a sound, shook their heads. They were used to Mrs Reardon and her ways: she had good days and she had bad days, and she'd been like that since her husband Desmond had died eighteen years ago.

Wednesday 20 December

13

The alarm went off at eight o'clock, filling the room with the sounds of the Black Eyed Peas. But Melissa was already awake, lying on her back and looking up at her bedroom ceiling.

How am I going to get out of this? What the hell am I gonna do?

Last night, after the service, Melissa, Rachel, Niall and Luke had all been called into Marcel's office. He was sitting behind his desk, looking gravely at them. The door slammed, and Melissa jumped with fright and turned round. Adrian, Marcel's brother, had shut the door and was standing before it, his hands clasped in front of him. There was no way out.

Marcel gestured that they should all sit down, and Melissa took a seat on the white leather sofa that faced his desk. Niall sat next to her, and she could tell, even though he wasn't looking at her, that he was as nervous as she was. Kurt and Rachel sat on chairs that were placed closer to Marcel's desk. The atmosphere was still and deadly quiet. Marcel regarded them all with concern in his eyes.

'You know why you're here, don't you?' he said quietly.

Melissa fidgeted in her chair.

'You're here as initiates, not yet Blessing Guides. You're here because you know that the life of a pure Blessing Guide is one of peace, love and harmony. You're here because you know that the life I offer you is better, far far better than the one you have now. But you're in this office because I fear you all don't quite believe this yet. You know all this, you know what I bring to your lives, and yet, you don't have faith.'

'Marcel, I do have faith, I do –' Rachel said passionately.

Marcel smiled at her. 'I know you do, Rachel. And you're an example to your friends. But you could set a better example, couldn't you? Otherwise none of you would be here. Now,' he said, turning back to the group, 'the Blessing Guides is a community. But all communities have needs. Although we don't believe in the material world, we do understand that we need to live in it. Until we find our base, until we find somewhere where we can live off the land, we need to find the means to live. You understand this, don't you? You understand that every single one of the Blessing Guides out there was an initiate. Every single one confirmed their place in this community by bringing something into it. But what have you brought? Nothing.'

'We tried though,' said Niall. 'But the night watchman . . .'

'The night watchman was a complication, that's all. Haven't I told you that everyone on this earth has a destiny? Everyone is chosen for something? We don't know the chain of events that led that man to follow you up on to the roof, but his destiny led him down that path. This is what I mean when I say you don't have faith. Trust in destiny and you'll find that your path through this life is much easier.'

Melissa couldn't bear it any longer. The stubborn streak in her urged her to speak out. 'But what about Richard? Was that his destiny?'

'Richard didn't have faith.' But it wasn't Marcel who had said those words. Melissa turned round. It was Adrian, and he was staring at Melissa as if he could see the torment in her heart.

The wintry morning sun fell over Lorraine's desk. It was freezing this morning, but at least it was bright. Taking a sip from the coffee she had picked up before coming to work, Lorraine flicked through the few notes she had on the night watchman. God, it was a hopeless case. She wasn't any closer to the truth than she was a couple of days ago, and there was nothing new in the file. Sighing she pushed the file away from her and thought through the options. Either he was pushed or he fell, no two ways about it. Lorraine sighed again and took another sip of her coffee. Sanderson had told her that he had talked to the usual suspects but they all seemed to have watertight alibis. They were clutching at straws there anyway. There was nothing they could find to link the break-in to anyone.

She sighed once more, and looked at her mobile. No missed calls.

He's off again. Jacobs had taken great delight informing her of Luke's absence.

But why isn't he answering my calls?

Why can't he tell me what's wrong? I thought we had really connected at the pub the other day.

She bit her knuckles with frustration, feeling her face go red as she remembered, yet again, lunch in the pub.

I shouldn't have told him all that personal stuff. It was unprofessional. I stepped over a line that he's not prepared to cross.

'Shit.' She rose and picked her coat up.

Time to visit Carter. He says he's bored. I'll give him something to do. Plus, Luke was supposed to visit him a couple of nights ago. I'll test the water, see what he had to say.

She drove down to Fence Houses, turned right at the cross-roads and was just passing the Beehive when she saw Melissa. Quickly she stopped the car, opened the door and leaned out.

'Like a lift, love? I'm sure I passed the bus, so it looks like yer gonna be late.'

She noticed Melissa swallow hard. She took a look behind her and then hurried over to Lorraine's car. As she drew closer Lorraine was again struck by how pretty Melissa was, the white hairband she wore contrasting beautifully with her dark hair. Lorraine wondered whether she should mention that a piece of the headband was frayed, but decided against it. Poor kid had enough on her plate without someone drawing attention to a trivial detail. Dreadful shame about her weight though. Surely her parents could do something, even if it was just for her health's sake.

'Hop in, love.'

Melissa got in, and Lorraine could swear the car actually groaned. She pulled away. Making sure the road was clear up ahead she glanced quickly at Melissa.

She looks chewed to bits about something. Not surprising, I guess. Her friend's dead.

'Not long before the holidays now. Are yer looking forward to Christmas?'

Melissa nodded, staring straight ahead.

Christ, it's like pulling teeth.

'So, going to any good parties?'

Melissa shrugged then muttered, 'Don't get invited to any.'

'Why ever not?'

Melissa snorted. 'Probably frightened in case I eat everything in sight.'

'And would yer . . . eat everything in sight?'

Melissa shrugged again, and Lorraine took that as a yes.

Poor kid. She looks really cut up. She's having a rough time.

'So, what do yer like best at school? Anything yer particularly good at?'

Melissa heaved a totally exaggerated sigh, which screamed 'leave me alone', then answered. 'Not really.'

Lorraine had just about given up when Melissa suddenly said, 'I used to like history and stuff like that.'

'Oh, I was good at history . . . What about Kurt and Niall? Do any of your friends like history?'

167

Melissa shrugged. 'Dunno.'

They were nearly at the school gates and Lorraine stopped the car. As Melissa got out, she looked at Lorraine and said, 'Got some new friends, but I don't much like them . . . Bye.'

What a strange thing to say.

Frowning, Lorraine looked in her mirror. A black car that she was certain had been behind her as she'd left Fence Houses, quickly pulled in front of her and drove off. Lorraine was so intent on watching the car that she never noticed Melissa bypass the school and go into the park.

The black car pulled around the corner and parked outside Collins's shop. The driver watched in his rearview mirror until Lorraine's car passed the end of the street.

Taking out his mobile, he dialled, spoke two sharp sentences, switched off, and drove away.

When Lorraine walked into Carter's ward he was sitting on the edge of his bed, talking to his domino buddy. She'd grabbed some oranges and a bunch of flowers from the shop downstairs.

'Here,' she thrust the gifts at him. 'Don't say I never get yer nowt.'

Carter went pink with pleasure. 'Thanks, boss.'

The old man's eyes widened, 'She your boss?' he asked Carter in amazement.

'Oh aye, that's the boss all right.'

'Bloody hell . . . How come I never had a boss like that down the bloody pit?'

Carter laughed and the old man turned back to his newspaper, but not before he gave Lorraine a lecherous wink.

Lorraine smiled, then said to Carter, 'Is there anywhere we can talk in this place?'

'Aye, there's a small quiet room down the corridor.'

'Can yer walk or will I have to push yer there?'

'No, I'm supposed to be moving about.'

'Good, come on then.'

Carter shrugged into his brown velvet dressing-gown, then followed Lorraine.

'Good luck, mate,' the old man shouted as Carter left the ward.

Carter blushed again, this time with embarrassment as the other four men in the ward, knowing which sort of luck the old man wished on Carter, started to laugh.

'So, how yer feeling?' Lorraine asked, sitting down at a small round table that had three seats.

Carter took one of the other seats and said, 'Fine, I can go home in a few days, but it's gonna be the New Year before I can come back to work.'

'Oh, well I'd be lying if I said I wasn't missing yer, Carter . . . Jacobs can't fill yer shoes and that's for sure.'

Carter had never heard such praise from Lorraine before. He wanted to get dressed and rush right back to work. 'So are things building up, like?'

'Building up! Jesus. That's an understatement . . . Listen, I'll tell yer what we've got, yer can think about it then give me your input, OK?'

'Sure thing, boss.'

'We have a dead night watchman who seems to have fallen off a roof. We have a dead man with a carving on his body . . . which was done while he was alive.'

Carter whistled.

'And we have a teenager who may or may not have hanged himself. I've spoken to his mother a couple of times and she is adamant that he did not commit suicide. And I haven't the slightest idea where to start with all this.' She held up her hands. 'There's just too many things happening and nothing seems connected.'

'Business as usual then.'

Smiling, Lorraine nodded. 'We have a feeling that it's a group of teenagers that have been targeting small businesses, but there's no witnesses as to the warehouse robbery. And we can't exactly bring in every teenager in Houghton, can we?'

'No, but I think I remember someone saying that Andrew Duffy's back out.'

'Shit. That's right. I'd forgotten about that little toerag. I was hoping he'd be banged up for at least two years.'

'Yeah well, boss, yer know what happens. We catch them but the prisons can't keep them.'

'That's all we need, that little shit back on the streets.' Shaking her head she took a sheet of paper out of her bag. 'That's the symbol that was carved on Jason Manners's body. See if yer can come up with something. Let me know if there's any books you need, unless yer like me to bring in yer laptop?'

'Can't go online in here, boss. Mucks up the machines.'

'That's right. Call Jacobs if yer want her to bring in anything you need. Anyhow yer've given me an idea. I just think I'll give Andrew Duffy a visit.' She stood to go. 'Did, er, did yer have a good visit with Luke the other night, Carter?' she asked as casually as she could.

'He didn't come in, boss.'

'Oh. Well, he's taken some personal time off work lately. But have yer heard from him?'

'We're not allowed mobiles. The nurse said he's phoned the ward a few times to see how I am and all that, but he didn't come in last night.'

'OK, I'll try to get in some time tomorrow, see if yer've found anything out about that.' She nodded at the piece of paper on the table. 'See yer later, Carter.'

'OK, boss.'

'Oh, by the way, didn't I see you playing dominoes with that old codger as I came in?'

'Yes, boss.'

'Who won?'

Carter's face split into a huge grin. 'Me.'

Lorraine smiled. 'Carter, is there no end to yer talents?' Carter went bright pink for the second time in twenty minutes, and remained so, even after Lorraine had said her goodbyes and walked from the ward.

14

Mavis and Peggy decided that, as they were to have a special guest this Christmas, they should have all-new decorations. Mavis had bought a home decoration magazine that had a special Christmas edition, and she and Peggy had pored over it, deciding, in the end, to eschew the normal red and green colour scheme for one that was silver and white. 'Very elegant,' Mavis said to Peggy. 'Lorry will like that.'

So, having made their decision regarding the colour scheme, a shopping expedition was called for. After a late breakfast, Mavis and Peggy wandered round Gateshead Metro centre, practically dazzled by all the bright lights and fantastic Christmas decorations.

Shop after shop competed for the best window display and already they had changed the colour of the decorations they wanted three times, and still, after two and a half hours, had only picked up half what they came for.

'I'm flaming well fed up,' Peggy complained. 'Me feet are killing me, and what did I tell yer eh, nowt but plastic. And,' she spun round and stared at two passing teenagers, 'look at the state of her, the one in blue. She's pretty much blue herself. Christ, they wander round half bloody naked in the middle of winter.'

She stared at the young girl's back, her skirt nothing but a strip of material with at least six inches of skin between the top of her skirt and the bottom of her top. 'I mean, dear me. There's no mystery these days, is there? Ten years' time, you mark my words, we'll all be living in bloody nudist camps.'

'Why, Peggy, you'd love to live in a nudist camp, right up your street.'

Peggy pulled her stomach in. 'Huh, not with the likes of her to compete with.'

But Mavis wasn't listening to Peggy. She had just seen Luke, with a young girl on his arm, entering Debenhams. There was something about the girl though – she didn't look all there.

'My God,' she muttered.

'So what's the matter, then?' Peggy demanded.

'I've just seen Luke go in there with a woman. And I think she was drunk or something.'

'Fuck off, yer never have.'

Mavis nodded.

'Are yer sure it was Luke?'

'Well, it certainly looked like him.'

'They reckon everybody's got a double, yer know. Should we go and spy on him?' Peggy asked eagerly.

'Peggy, we can't do that!'

'Why not? I'll tell yer one thing, the bugger's not sitting down to Christmas dinner with us if he's got a tart in tow, and that's for bloody sure. Especially not a tart who can't hold her liquor.'

Mavis shrugged. 'It is very strange. It must have been a lookalike . . . Has to have been.'

'But yer really do think it was him, don't yer.'

Mavis sighed, 'Not really sure now . . . Anyhow, it couldn't have been, he'll be at work.'

'Them coppers don't work regular hours like normal people do. For Christ's sake, look at our Lorry.'

'Hmm,' said Mavis. 'But it really looked like him, though. I could have sworn it was.'

'What was the girl like?' said Peggy, her curiosity well and truly roused.

'Hard to tell. Very pretty . . .'

'Not as pretty as our Lorry though,' Peggy blustered. 'I'll tell yer something for nothing, if that Luke is stringing our Lorry along, he won't know what's hit him.'

Mavis was amused, despite herself. 'I thought you said that it couldn't be Luke? That it was probably his double?'

'Aye, I did. But men. Yer just can't trust them. Not even the good ones.'

Mavis smiled at her friend. Men's inability to be trusted was a running theme in Peggy's conversation, one that Mavis often tuned out. But Luke, was he one of these men? *He can't be*, thought Mavis. *He adores our Lorry. Yer can see it in his face.* But, with a sinking feeling in her stomach, Mavis thought, *Well I've been wrong about men before. And so has Lorry.*

'Come on, Peggy,' Mavis said to her friend. 'Let's get home. I want to get these decorations up, so Lorry can see how pretty they are.'

But as they walked past the glittering window displays, Mavis prayed that she was seeing things. That it wasn't Luke, shopping for Christmas presents, with a beautiful young girl in tow.

Jacko, Danny and Len were propping up the bar in Newbottle Workingmen's Club.

'Sorry, Danny,' Jacko said, 'but Doris won't let us sell the fags from the house, mate. She's scared the coppers will find out, but she's more scared that them teenage gangs what's robbing people will find out and come in and take them. Remember, she did take a beating a few months back.'

'That's all right, Jacko, I just thought yer might be able to shift a few packets, yer know, so we can get down again. But Brian took some to the gym and they're crying out for them. Want a freshener?'

'No, yer all right, a couple does me.' Jacko took a long drink from his pint of lager.

'I thought these keep-fit guys didn't smoke?' Len said.

'What keep-fit guys?' Danny asked his cousin.

'Yer know, at the gym.'

Danny looked at Jacko, who grinned and shook his head.

'Well?'

'Well what?' Danny said.

'If yer keeping fit yer don't smoke.'

'Len, it doesn't matter. Mebbe they bought them off Brian for their girlfriends or something.'

'Aye why, hypocrites if yer ask me.'

Danny groaned.

Jacko finished his pint. 'I'll have to be going, lads, OK.'

'All right for the next trip?'

Jacko hesitated. He'd been wondering how to broach the subject. 'Well, if yer really want to know, Danny, I'm not all that keen on going back . . . If something happens . . . I've got three of them to look after now, yer know.'

'What's gonna happen?' Danny said.

'Yer heard about that van from Murton. Lost the lot and they're all looking at time.'

'That's 'cos they were carrying drugs an' all.'

'Aye but it's nearly Christmas yer know. What if we get stranded over there?'

'We won't . . . Think about it, yeah.'

'OK,' Jacko nodded. 'See yers later.'

Jacko left the club and crossed the road to the bus stop just in time to catch the bus down to Houghton. He was meeting Christina at the library for a quick bit of Christmas shopping. Christina wanted to know what to get for Doris.

When he got off the bus he could see Christina waiting for him, and his heart thrilled. Every time he saw her he couldn't imagine what he'd done to deserve such happiness: all he knew was that he had the best three girls in Sunderland city, if not the entire universe.

'Hi love,' he said when they were in touching distance.

Christina smiled shyly, and blushed a pretty pink when Jacko gently kissed her cheek. Then, holding hands, they walked through Houghton until they were outside of Makay's.

'I thought a nice hat and scarf for yer mam, but I'm not sure which colour. What's her favourite?'

'Purple, she loves purple.'

They went inside and Christina rummaged through a full rack of scarves. Jacko spotted a full-length black coat that would fit Doris a treat, then he looked at the price tag. 'No way,' he muttered.

If I do just one more trip, he thought, watching Christina go up to the counter and pay for the purple wool scarf, matching hat and gloves she had in her hand.

No, it's not worth it . . . Too risky at this time of year.

Doris needs a new coat badly. If she gets wet taking the bairn to school then she's stuck in for the rest of the day.

Christina looked over at him and he smiled at her.

No, I'm not taking the risk.

Lorraine stopped the car outside Andrew Duffy's house. Two of his younger brothers were leaning against the wall smoking. The Duffys were a handsome family. All six boys possessed their father's baby-blue eyes and high cheekbones and their mother's fair hair.

Drew was number four and, so far, the worst of the bunch. Lorraine knew the parents had tried, but they were both far too weak and had let the boys get away with murder from day one. 'They're just bairns,' was one of the adult Duffy's favourite sayings, no matter what they did. Well, they were known to the police and now they were starting to spend quite a lot of

177

time in court, with their 'just bairns'. With everything from petty crime to harassing the neighbours.

'Me dad's not in,' Scott Duffy said, blowing smoke at Lorraine as she walked past him, while the other brother sniggered loudly.

She gritted her teeth as she smelled the smoke.

Yer dicing with death, kid. Do that again and I'll have yer in the cells for something, she thought, glaring at him.

Whatever Scott saw in her eyes caused him to drop his own, and the younger boy to stop his sniggering.

Lorraine banged on the door, far louder than she'd intended to, but it helped to get out some of her frustration. It was opened a moment later by a small fair-haired woman with what looked like a permanent frown crease between her eyes.

'Aye?' she said, staring at Lorraine.

Lorraine took her badge out, 'I'm here to speak to Andrew Duffy.'

'He hasn't done nowt. He's hardly been outta the house since he come home.'

'He'll be in now, then.'

'Well, er . . .' she said, knowing that she'd dropped her son right in it, and Mrs Duffy stepped aside to let Lorraine enter.

'Andrew, the police are here to see yer,' Mrs Duffy announced as she walked up the hallway followed by Lorraine.

They entered a small sitting room, made smaller by the fact that it was painted red. *But other than that, the place is quite clean and tidy,* Lorraine thought, *especially bearing in mind that there's all those men in the house.*

Andrew Duffy was sitting with his jean-clad legs hooked over the arm of a chair facing the television; he had the remote in his hands and had been idly channel-hopping. He looked up at Lorraine and stated in a matter-of-fact voice, 'It wasn't me.'

'What wasn't you?' Lorraine helped herself to a seat on the settee.

'Whatever it is yer here about. OK?'

'I'm here about the death of a night watchman, Andrew.'

'Then it definitely wasn't me . . . Read me files, no murders in there, and that's a fact.'

'Yeah, but yer fond of breaking into warehouses, aren't yer?'

Lorraine heard a snigger and turned round to the doorway. Scott was there, insolently cracking gum, and she revised her earlier opinion. Perhaps this one was gonna be the worst of the bunch.

'Do yer mind . . . And shouldn't yer be in school?'

He shrugged and moved away from the doorway. A moment later Lorraine heard his mother pleading with him to go back to school. If it were her kid she'd be reading him the riot act and no mistake. But these parents just didn't understand that kids needed some discipline, some boundaries. She turned back to Andrew to see him grinning.

'I don't know what you're grinning at, Andrew. If there's anything to link yer to the warehouse robbery, yer could be looking at murder, even if it was an accident. Don't worry, I'll find something that'll stick.'

179

'It wasn't me,' he said adamantly as he threw the television remote onto the floor and sat up straight. 'Look, it really wasn't.' He paused for a moment, staring at the big red swirls on the carpet. Finally he admitted, 'I had a bit of a rough time inside,' blushing to the roots of his blond hair.

With those looks I just bet yer did, Lorraine thought, feeling a twinge of pity for the boy in front of her.

'I'm not a grass,' Andrew went on, 'and besides I don't really know anything about it.' He sat back down on the chair. 'When was the break-in?'

'Saturday night.

Andrew smiled. 'You should have asked me that when you came in. I was staying the whole night at Jane Dawson's house. She's me new girlfriend. Yer can ask her mother if yer don't believe me. She cooked me dinner an' all.'

Lorraine did believe him, but she'd get Jacobs to check it out. She rose. 'OK, Andrew, keep yer nose clean.'

'I intend to. I'm never going back in there again,' he said, not looking at her as he reached for the remote.

Lorraine let herself out. When she was in the car, she stretched her legs. She was bone tired, and it was bloody dark already. She hated the long nights.

And still no messages or missed calls on her answer phone.

Fuck it. She threw the phone onto the passenger seat in much the same fashion that Andrew Duffy had thrown the television remote.

180

15

Kurt stood on the opposite side of the road to the school gates. He nodded to a few classmates who caught his eye, but otherwise kept his head down. He didn't need Mrs Colley catching him and demanding why he hadn't been to school today. But what else could he do? He really wanted to make sure that Melissa and Rachel were all right but neither of them were answering their mobiles. He'd last seen Melissa at the gathering at Marcel's house, and she had hardly said a word then. Just looked as if she was going to cry. He sighed. The last of the stragglers had come through the gates and were heading off home. There was no sign of Melissa or Rachel. He had missed them or they hadn't come to school that day. Kurt turned and walked down the road. He had to pretend to his mother that he was still going to school, but he had spent most of the day hanging out in the shopping centre. His fingers were stiff and sore from the cold. With a sinking feeling in his heart, he wondered just how long he could keep up the pretence before his mother found out. And what would she do to him then?

*

Rachel had spent most of the day with Melissa and now she slipped into the house like a silent wraith. Everyone was sitting round the table eating. Rachel didn't have to look at their plates to discover what was for tea; the smell of fish and chips had her mouth watering. She suddenly realised she'd hardly eaten a thing since yesterday.

She shed her coat and knew he was watching her.

She met his eyes across the silent table and knew exactly what he was thinking.

She had to get out of here.

She had two choices, stay and let things go on as before, because she knew in her heart of hearts that it would never end. As long as she was under this roof she was fair game.

Or she could leave this house, and him, forever and go back to where she'd just come from, where the sex was dealt out with something that seemed like love. Subconsciously she'd known before she came back that she was only coming for what was hers, her clothes, her bank book.

And to say goodbye to the kids, who might or might not miss her.

Rachel sighed. He had threatened her with what he'd do to them if she ran away before. But Marcel helped her to see the truth. He'd only used them to chain her. And they had been complicit in his abuse; they had made her life hell. And although she didn't want anything to happen to them, she didn't want anything more to happen to her.

Silently she headed for the stairs expecting at any minute for him to come after her.

But he didn't. At the top of the stairs she breathed a sigh of relief. Then she went into her room and began to pack.

She looked fondly at her mother's picture for a moment and ran her fingertip over her sweet face and placed it on top of her holdall. Then she looked around the room for anything she may have missed. But there wasn't anything more she wanted to take. Marcel was right. All the gifts he had given her only tied her to her stepfather and to this house. Everything her stepfather gave her cost money but was worth nothing. And being with the Blessing Guides meant living without the trappings of the material world. She looked at the gifts he had given her to buy her silence and wished she had the guts to take them outside and burn them. That would show him how little she cared about what he had given her, how little she cared about him.

But that would set him off and she might never get out of here.

Silently she walked back down the stairs. No one had moved. It was as if they were all part of a painting and the painter had left an empty chair.

It could stay empty forever as far as she was concerned. She was going to a better place. A place where they accepted her for what she was and didn't care about her past. A place where she knew she'd find peace and happiness. As long as she was near Marcel, she'd be safe.

And anyway, there was nowhere else for her to go. At her age she would never get a house or even a flat. And the four hundred pounds she had in her bank book that he didn't know about wouldn't last long.

It was back to the people of the Seven Sisters. It was back to Marcel. Rachel smiled softly, remembering the morning. He had been so kind today, so gentle. So different from her stepfather.

She looked at each member of her family, giving each of them time to say something, but nobody spoke. Her stepfather started eating and the kids followed his lead.

Silently, into the freezing night she left, closing the door behind her.

The sitting room was quiet and dim, lit only by a street lamp outside. Kurt tried a light switch: nothing. He moved towards the lamp on the far side of the room, but then, out of nowhere, his mother rose up and planted her fist on Kurt's bottom lip.

This was not the first time she'd lain in waiting for her victim. And, if truth be told, Kurt had been half-expecting it.

His mother's ring had caught his lip and it burst open, filling his mouth with that hot metallic taste. He put his hand to his mouth, then took it away again. He had been cut badly. Blood was streaming down his face and dripping off his chin onto his white T-shirt. For a brief second he felt nothing, then the pain came, hitting him almost as hard as the fist had done.

He stood stunned for a moment, staring at the blood on his fingers. He looked up and met his mother's eyes. That enraged her. She clenched her fingers in a fist, and launched another punch at him. But this time something changed. Something inside of him finally woke up, sprang to life and screamed: *No more!*

For the first time in his life he raised his hand and grabbed his mother's arm.

She screamed, far louder than was necessary, for Kurt was merely trying to restrain her, and the noise she made sounded as if she was the one hurt and bleeding, not her son. But it was fear Kurt could hear in the depths of her voice, and not pain.

He yanked her arm downwards, far more gently than she ever had, and pushed her quickly away from him. She fell backwards onto the settee, narrowly missing hitting her head on the coffee-table lamp.

'No,' she gasped, as Kurt stared at her. 'Please don't hit me. Please.' There were tears in her eyes when she said this, as there had been tears in his, many times.

How many times have I said that? Kurt thought sadly as he stared down at her.

And how many times has she ignored me?

He moved towards her, her eyes grew wider the closer he came. When he was close enough to touch her, he stopped dead. Pulling his T-shirt over his head, he used it to try and stem the blood from his lip. After a few silent minutes in which mother and son stared at each other like two strangers, he dropped the T-shirt onto the floor and quietly asked, 'Why?'

Niall felt waves of anxiety coming from both of his parents as he walked into the sitting room. His father, sitting in his much-used leather armchair, didn't say anything. He never did.

Just looked once, then looked away.

Given up already.

His mother would try and force food onto him like she always did.

He wondered if other families were like this, never talking to each other.

Perfect strangers.

Why didn't they ask him if he took drugs?

He knew that's what they thought. Knew that idea was burning away in their heads. Deep down inside they thought their oldest son was a drug addict.

Come on, he mentally egged them on.

Get it out into the open.

He'd answer honestly.

He sat down on the settee, and sighed. Weren't they bothered at all?

'Have yer had something to eat, Niall?' his mother said, trying her best to smile.

He groaned out loud and she dropped her head.

Yeah go on, make me feel good.

For fuck's sake, he should yell at them, tell them that no, he didn't take drugs, and food, well, food was the last thing on earth he wanted.

Which reminded him that he'd pretty much kept those chips down.

Too late now to upchuck them.

He sighed, but it was a sigh of deep irritation, and his mother sidestepped past him.

Oh fuck.

He should tell them that he was in deep shit and

that it had nothing to do with food or drugs. That he was mixed up in something that he didn't mean to be and now one of his friends was dead and he was scared, very scared.

That might get a rise out of them.

He watched as his father picked up the television remote and began channel-hopping.

Niall sighed again and left the sitting room, dragging his tired legs upstairs. Once in his bedroom, he took his mobile out of his pocket and started to text.

Melissa sat on the settee, her face set in a stubborn expression, and she had folded her arms across her chest. Her parents sat opposite her on the other settee, her mother looking worried, her father's countenance looking blacker and blacker. Apparently the school had rung, asking why Melissa hadn't come to school today. Her parents had been questioning her relentlessly.

Nothing new there. She screwed her mouth into a tight line of resistance.

Where have yer been, where have yer been, girl? Don't you know we've been worried sick?

Where have I been? She snorted silently to herself. Sitting inside Marcel's house for hours, listening to the Blessing Guides rabbit on and on about how great Marcel is and how excited they were about the forthcoming ceremony. Adrian had creeped her out by staring at her the whole time. And then Rachel reappeared, her face flushed and happy, after her private consultation with Marcel. Melissa, despite herself, had felt a twinge of jealousy. Why had she never had a private consultation with Marcel? The Blessing Guides was the one place where she thought she was accepted, but even there she didn't measure up.

'Melissa, yer not listening to me, are you?' Melissa's mother's voice cut into her thoughts.

'You show some respect to yer mother, young lady,' her father said.

Melissa raised her eyes to meet her parents'.

Fucking cruelty this is, like.

Any minute now, it'll be, 'Our David never went on like this.'

'Really, Melissa, our David never went on like this,' her mother kindly obliged her.

Over to you, Dad.

'Neither did our Allen.'

Right on cue.

And now for the trainee lawyer.

Together Melissa's mother and father chorused, 'And neither did our Simon.'

For fuck's sake.

'I'm going to take a shower.' Melissa announced, standing up.

'Yer what?' her father blustered.

'Yer heard me.'

'Oh, I know what you need, madam.'

Yeah, yer just try it, buster.

'Please, Malcolm,' her mother said, placing her right hand on his arm.

Her father had never raised his hands to her and Melissa knew he never would. But sometimes, oh sometimes she was tempted. She would do it; she would lash out at him just to see the shocked look on their faces.

Not as shocked as they'd be if she told them what she had got herself into. But she couldn't tell them. They wouldn't understand anyway. Probably think everything that happened was her fault. But it hadn't been her up on the roof that night.

She moved towards the stairs and left her parents staring after her. A few minutes later she was standing under a red-hot shower and sobbing her heart out.

After she'd calmed down, she dressed and put her coat on. She put her hand inside her pocket and drew out Lorraine's business card. It had her mobile number on it but Melissa's mobile had ran out of credit ages ago. Damn. She needed to tell someone and Inspector Hunt seemed kind, if a little brisk. She quietly closed her bedroom door behind her and walked as quietly as she could downstairs and slipped outside. *Let them think I'm having an early night, or something.* She drew her coat around her tighter, against the biting wind that had sprung up.

She looked up the street then down. After a moment's hesitation she paced upwards in the direction of the police station. At the end of the street she changed her mind, turned right and headed towards Marcel's house, where she'd promised to meet Rachel. Half way there she had another change of heart, and turning, headed back towards the police station. The black car that drove in front of her was just one of many she saw on the road.

Lorraine put the phone down, then sat with her chin resting in her hand. Wisps of hair had escaped the tight bun at the back of her head and curled softly around her face. She had just had a very disturbing talk with Carter, who was due out of the hospital tomorrow. She played it through her mind again.

No, boss, Luke didn't get in to see me today.

What? He didn't make it?

No, boss, there was just me and the old man in the next bed, who I thought was gonna lynch me at one time, 'cos I beat him at dominoes again.

Yer sure about that?

Aye.

OK then, I'll call round tomorrow and see yer when yer get home, right, Carter?

Thanks, boss. Ta-ra.

Yeah, bye.

And that had been that. She couldn't have questioned Carter further; the poor sod was in the hospital for Christ's sake.

She gazed out the window, and for some reason her next thought made her feel sad.

Luke wasn't here today.

She'd tried his mobile twice: no answer. *Three times and the bugger will mebbe start thinking I'm in love with him or something.*

And I'm not.

No way.

Why would I be?

Because he's fantastically gorgeous, kind and very warm-hearted. In fact a joy of a man, fantastic sense of humour. A stray treacherous thought wriggled into her head.

But he's let me down this time. Why couldn't he phone me? Why isn't he answering his mobile? What the hell happened between that lunch and now?

But even though her fingers had been itching to dial his number, she couldn't bring herself to call him, yet again. Even though she was his boss and had every right, there was something about lunch that day that had switched their relationship from being colleagues to something more intimate. Or had she been reading the signals wrong, yet again? And now she was angry with herself for feeling this way.

Why the hell won't he even speak to me? she thought for the hundredth time that day.

If somebody had told her a week ago that she would miss having Carter and Luke around as much as she was, she would have laughed.

But the truth was she missed them both, and in two entirely different ways. They were both good coppers, both cared for the community they worked in, both were loyal and supportive. *Well, until now that is*, Lorraine thought. But Carter was Carter, just a lad really, someone she would do her best to help up the ladder. But Luke . . . Lorraine admitted to herself that she had been imagining something more with Luke. And while she missed him professionally, she had to acknowledge that there was more to it than that.

Lorraine sighed and leant back in her chair while she thought through her depleted staff. Sanderson was a good man and as loyal as the day was long.

And he was a good copper, too. He was experienced, he knew Houghton-le-Spring like the back of his hand, and he had seen her through some very tight patches. But he was a little set in his ways and did everything by the book. He didn't have Carter's enthusiasm and energy, nor Luke's instincts. Lorraine smiled wryly. He did have a good marriage though. He adored his wife, Joan. They were a damn good match for each other and one of the happiest couples around. They even looked like each other.

It just seemed so easy for some people. You met someone, you liked them, like turned into love and that seemed to be it. Lorraine winced. *What is it about me? Why can't things run smoothly for once in my life?*

She stood up and reached for her coat.

He better be in tomorrow. He better answer, at least answer, his bloody phone. He better give me some sort of explanation for his behaviour.

Lorraine walked down the corridor. It was quiet tonight. Her high heels echoed in the hallway. She seemed to be the only person in the building, though she knew there were other people in the station. The thought made her feel more isolated and lonely than before. She waved goodbye to the duty sergeant and walked through the front door. It was dark, freezing cold and drizzling when she reached her car; the miserable weather was reflecting her mood perfectly. Throwing her bag onto the back seat, she loosened the buttons on her black full-length wool coat and pulled her silver-coloured scarf from her neck. There was nothing worse than the feeling of being trussed

192

up in the car. Lorraine slid behind the wheel, started the car, put a CD in the stereo and pulled out of the car park.

Ten minutes later, Lorraine, having left Houghton's lights behind her, was singing along to 'Angels' by Robbie Williams when a sudden movement caught her eye and she felt the thud of a body hitting her bumper.

'Oh my God,' she said, standing on the brakes. The car came to a halt with a screech.

Her heart filled with dread. What she had seen was small, definitely not an adult, and she prayed that she hadn't hurt a kid. She jumped out of the car and ran to the front of it, her stomach twisting in knots.

She had hit a dog. Lorraine leaned on the bonnet and felt sick. In the dull light from the street lamp the blood looked almost black.

'We saw it, missus,' a voice said.

Startled, Lorraine gasped, and spinning round saw two boys come out of the trees. They were wearing hoodies, but neither seemed threatening at all. In fact, she recognised one of them as Kurt Allendale, which meant the other one must be Niall. He was just as skinny as Mrs Colley had said. He looked like a stiff breeze would blow him over.

'Do yer think he's dead?' Kurt got down on his knees and gently stroked the flank of the dark brown Alsatian Collie cross, while Niall looked on.

Lorraine sighed, 'I hope not.'

The dog whimpered as Kurt gently felt his limbs. After a moment he said, 'I think he's just been cut on his muzzle and he's hurt his leg. Look,' he pointed at the dog's mouth where drops of blood steadily hit the road, then at his front leg, which was twitching and losing quite a lot of blood from a deep gash.

'That must be where I hit him, the poor thing. Thank God I wasn't going too fast. Yer sure nothing's broken?'

'Aye, not for definite but ah think so.'

Trusting his judgement Lorraine quickly shrugged out of her coat and placed it down on the road. 'Right lads, if yer can ease him onto the coat we'll lift him into the back seat of the car and I'll take him home and call a vet.'

'He looks half starved an' all,' Kurt added as he gently started to ease the dog onto Lorraine's coat. 'No collar either,' he said as they raised the coat and the dog into the air.

'Aye,' Niall added. 'Not very old either . . . Do yer have to tell the coppers when yer run a dog over? 'Cos if yer do, we'll tell them he jumped out into the road and it wasn't your fault.' Lorraine noticed that Niall was staring at her with a goofy look on his face. *God, spare me from hormonal teenagers*, she thought wryly. 'It's all right . . . I am the police.'

'Are yer?' Niall said in amazement.

Lorraine chuckled to herself. 'Oh, yes.'

'Yeah, I saw her at school,' Kurt said, and Lorraine caught the look that passed between him and Niall.

'Let's get this dog sorted,' Lorraine said, and, with Kurt's help, moved the dog onto the back seat. Seeing that the dog was safely placed in the back of her car, Lorraine looked at the boys, and for the first time noticed that Kurt's lip had recently been cut. 'Looks nasty,' she said to Kurt.

'Oh,' he put his hand to his mouth. 'It's nothing really. Fooling around with Niall here, and he accidentally planted one on me.'

Lorraine caught the quizzical look Niall threw at his friend, and also saw Niall rearrange his features as if realising too late that he was supposed to cover for his friend. 'Ah yes,' he confirmed, then shrugged. 'Just messing about.'

Lorraine regarded them for a long moment, sure that there was more to Kurt's split lip than both boys were saying, because Niall didn't look strong enough to last a round in the ring with a butterfly, let alone actually hurt someone, but knowing that she wouldn't get anything more out of them.

'Well, thanks for your help, lads, it was good of yers.' Lorraine quietly closed the door so as not to frighten the poor dog even more.

'No problem,' Niall said, as they both backed off to the other side of the road. 'Bye.'

'Yeah, bye.' Kurt nodded.

Lorraine smiled and gave them a wave as she drove off.

The two boys watched the car's headlights grow smaller and then disappear as it turned the corner.

'So that's the copper,' Niall said. 'She seems all right. A bit of all right, if you ask me.'

Kurt glanced at Niall. 'Yeah, I guess. But I wouldn't trust her. She's a copper after all.'

Niall nodded in agreement and they set off together, passing the last house in Hall Lane just as the downstairs lights went off. No lights were on in any of the houses, and the entire street was lit only by the outside street lamps.

'Everyone's in bed now,' Kurt said, wistfully.

'Aye,' Niall replied. Then, taking a sideways glance at his friend, he said, 'So are you going to tell me what really happened to your lip?'

Kurt didn't say anything for a few minutes, and Niall thought he wasn't going to answer him, but then Kurt said abruptly, 'Me mam.'

Niall stopped in his tracks. Kurt walked on for a couple more steps, realised that Niall wasn't by his side and then turned back to look at his friend. The two of them stared at each other, before Niall finally said quietly, 'Yer mam? Jesus, Kurt . . .'

Kurt nodded solemnly. The boys started walking again, in silence. They crossed the road and entered the field in front of the Seven Sisters.

Kurt was slightly in front when Niall took hold of his elbow and stopped him. 'You're telling the truth, aren't you? Yer mam really did do that to yer.'

Kurt nodded.

'And all of the other stuff as well?'

Kurt stared into Niall's eyes and nodded again.

Niall couldn't stop shaking his head in disbelief. He managed a quiet 'Wow.'

'Yeah, wow,' Kurt replied, 'the mother from hell. Look, let's get a move on. Marcel's expecting us and yer know what he's like.'

Niall hadn't moved, couldn't move. 'Bugger Marcel . . . But . . . why, does yer mam . . . ?'

'I might tell yer later.' Kurt started to hurry,

leaving Niall staring after him. After a moment he
quickly followed.

Lorraine ran into the house. Mavis was sitting on the
settee, watching one of the soaps she was addicted to.
Lorraine looked round for Peggy, but found no sign
of her.

'Quick mam, yer have to help, I've . . . I've just ran
a flaming dog over.'

Mavis sat bolt upright, 'Yer've what?'

'Aye, yer heard right, so come on, I need yer help
to get him outta the car.'

Together they hurried outside. 'Where's Peggy?'
Lorraine asked as she was opening the boot.

'Upstairs reading.'

'Good. Give her a shout, she can make herself
useful. She used to work on a farm once, didn't she?'

'That was when she was going through her back-
to-nature stage, but the truth was she just fancied the
farmer.'

Lorraine peered into the car, praying the dog had
not bled to death.

'Working on a farm hardly qualifies Peggy as a
vet . . .'

The dog was staring up at Mavis with the saddest
brown eyes imaginable. 'Oh you poor thing,' she
said. 'Really Lorraine, you should have looked where
you were going.'

'What! He ran out in front of me.'

'Hmm.'

Lorraine had never in her life heard a more
accusing 'hmm'. She swore an axe murderer would

197

have had more sympathy. She sighed before saying, 'You get hold of that side and I'll get this.'

Together they managed to ferry the dog from the car to the kitchen table.

'Poor thing,' Mavis repeated, managing to make Lorraine feel even more like England's most wanted.

'Who's a poor thing?' Peggy asked as she came into the kitchen. Her view of the table was blocked by Mavis and Lorraine, who moved away so that Peggy could see. 'What the . . .?' Peggy stared at the dog then at Lorraine. 'Yer've knocked the poor sod over, haven't yer.'

Lorraine looked at the ceiling, then back at Peggy. 'Well, rub it in, why don't yer. As if I don't feel bad enough as it is.'

'Move over.' Peggy pushed Lorraine out of the way and took control. Mavis was up by the dog's head, and he licked her hand, then gave two thumps of his tail on the table.

'Oh, would yer look at that?' said Mavis. 'The poor dear is feeling better.

'Nowt broken there.' Peggy's fingers gently moved over the dog's body, while Mavis and Lorraine watched anxiously. 'He doesn't even need a vet really. None of the wounds are deep enough to need stitches, and look, they've stopped bleeding already. Wounds to the head always bleed heavy and mostly look worse than they are.' Smiling, she stroked the dog. 'If yer ask me he's enjoying the fuss.'

'Really?' Lorraine raised her eyebrows.

'Aye . . . Yer can call a vet if yer want, but I guarantee he'll just charge yer a small fortune and tell yer to give him a sweet drink for the shock.'

'Well, now.' Mavis gently patted the dog who, in pain or not, looked like he had died and gone to doggie heaven.

'Hmm. Well, I think I'd like to get him checked out by a vet anyway. And perhaps he can help me find out who he belongs to.'

'Yer can't send him back!' Mavis said in horror. 'Look at the state of him, why he's nothing but skin and bone . . . If he belonged to anyone, they haven't been treating him very well. And he hasn't got a collar – you have to put a collar on a dog if he's going anywhere outside the house. Whoever had him obviously wasn't looking after him.'

'We still have to find out who owns him, mam,' Lorraine said through gritted teeth as she watched Peggy move briskly to the fridge, remove a packet of sliced ham, break it into pieces on a saucer, put a spoonful of sugar on another saucer and fill it with water.

They're gonna want to keep it.

Her heart sank; the last thing she wanted was some flea-bitten mongrel roaming about the house. Dogs were as bad as people: they moved in, wrapped themselves as tight as they could, then either ran away or died on yer.

The dog eagerly swallowed the meat, drank the sugar and water then offered Mavis a paw.

Lorraine groaned.

'Ohh, isn't he gorgeous,' Peggy said.

Before Mavis could agree, Lorraine said, 'No.'

They both looked at her, disapprovingly.

'Well, look at him,' Lorraine pleaded her case. 'He's downright ugly. He's mangy, he's skinny as a rake . . . And I must point this out, he looks like he's a puppy and so he's gonna grow a lot bigger than he is now . . . And, how do yer know he's not rabid?'

'If that dog was a biter he would have bitten yer when yer bloody well knocked him over,' Peggy said.

'Of course he would.' Mavis patted the dog and he snaked a long pink tongue out and licked her other hand. 'Ahh, isn't he cute?'

Lorraine shook her head, 'I don't think so.'

As if she'd never said anything or was standing somewhere on the moon, Mavis went on, 'Duke, I think we'll call him Duke. He looks rather royal, don't yer think so, Peggy?'

'Oh my God, he's a dirty scruff, mother, the least royal-looking dog in England. Are the pair of yers blind or what? And yer can't keep somebody else's dog, it's against the law. I should know, shouldn't I? It's like kidnapping.'

'Don't be silly, darling,' Mavis replied.

Lorraine gritted her teeth. 'First thing tomorrow I'll have some flyers printed.' She looked at the dog who was watching her with his head tilted on one side.

'Hmm. My money's on him being a stray,' Peggy said. 'His coat's a mess but there's nothing a good bath and brush won't put right once his cuts heal, isn't that right, Duke.'

Duke wagged his tail in agreement as he nudged Mavis's hand with his nose.

Lorraine shook her head: she was beaten and she

knew it. *A dog for Christ's sake.* She looked Duke in the eye and said, 'One chewed slipper, just one, mutt,' she waved her finger at him, 'and yer outta here.'

Later when Peggy had gone to bed and the dog was curled up on a blanket in the kitchen, Lorraine and Mavis were enjoying a last cup of tea in the sitting room when Lorraine said suddenly, 'Luke phoned in sick today. Can't find what's wrong though. He's not answering his phone.'

If Lorraine had expected her mother to come up with the answer she was sadly disappointed, and Mavis was strangely quiet as she sipped her tea.

Sanderson and Dinwall were the last two in the office. Dinwall was sitting at his computer, typing away with two fingers, while Sanderson was sitting in his chair and swinging it from side to side.

'Go home, Sanderson,' said Dinwall, 'you're doing my head in. Don't you have some paperwork or something to finish off?'

'Finished it,' said Sanderson.

'Well, go home or stop swinging your chair around. It's bloody annoying.'

'Joan's mother is visiting from Doncaster.'

'Ah,' said Dinwall. 'Mother-in-law. Enough said.'

Sanderson didn't make a move, but he stopped swinging on his chair. The office was quiet, the only sound being Dinwall's irregular tapping on the keyboard and the low hum of electricity. Suddenly, the phone rang and both men jumped. Dinwall answered it. 'Uh huh,' he said, looking straight at

Sanderson. 'Yup. Right. I'll send someone up there straight away.' He smiled as he placed the receiver back in its cradle. 'I have just the job for you, Sanderson.'

'What?'

'Dear old Mrs Reardon,' he chuckled as Sanderson groaned. 'This time it sounds serious. She's been robbed. I volunteered you.'

Sanderson sighed. 'OK, I'll take it on me way home.' He grabbed the keys off his desk and his coat from its hook.

While Sanderson drove up to Mrs Reardon's place, he thought of all the false alarms she had called over the years. For example, the time she accused her next-door neighbours of spying on her, when they were just an elderly couple who put up good-humouredly with all her accusations, or the time she had chased the postman down the road, and lately she had been ringing up the police station complaining about lights up at the Seven Sisters. She was an eccentric, batty old thing, but Sanderson liked her for all that and hoped that she was OK. He pulled to a stop outside of Mrs Reardon's house to be greeted by half a dozen neighbours. Alec Harvey, who had something about the child catcher from *Chitty Chitty Bang Bang* about him, had taken it upon himself to be the mouthpiece for the group, and as soon as Sanderson got out of the car he started in on him.

'About time an' all . . . She's an old woman yer know, all on her own.'

Sanderson stood on the cigarette end he'd dropped

as he'd got out of the car and replied, 'I'm sure you lot will have looked after her, Mr Harvey.'

Harvey looked at his watch, 'Aye why, that's as might be, but it's nearly twenty minutes since yer were called. What if the slimy robbing bastard had a gun?'

'Rest assured, I'm certain armed response would have got here in half the time if there was any chance that the robber was armed.'

'Yeah, right,' Harvey said in a disgusted voice. He turned his back on Sanderson and walked away.

Sanderson sighed, nodded at the other neighbours, then went into Mrs Reardon's house. She was sitting on a chair by the fire with a rug around her knees. One of the neighbours who Sanderson didn't recognise, was passing her a cup of tea. Sanderson smiled. She looked OK to him, in fact, she looked as if she was enjoying all the attention. 'All right, Mrs Reardon?' Sanderson asked as he sat down on a chair opposite her.

'Hello, officer,' she smiled coyly at him. 'He was a biggun, he was. Ran right past me and nearly knocked me flying, the rat.'

'Do yer think yer can recognise him?'

'Oh, don't think so, he had a hood on and a cap, both were pulled down . . . And it happened so fast . . . Took me ring, he did.'

Sanderson had just been going to ask her if anything was missing. 'Can you describe the ring?'

'Aye, I've had it fifty years.' She took a drink of tea, and her neighbour patted her shoulder.

'Yer doing great, Mrs Reardon.' Sanderson,

thanking his lucky stars that she was in the here-and-now, went on. 'Do yer think yer can describe it for me?'

'Describe what?'

'I'll let you get on with it,' the neighbour said. 'Just let me know if you need anything else, Mrs Reardon.' The neighbour let herself out, leaving Sanderson alone with the old woman, who looked crestfallen.

'The ring,' he prompted again. 'What did it look like?'

'Blue, big blue with shiny white diamonds all around. Beautiful it was. My husband brought it back for me from South Africa.'

Sanderson made a note and then checked through the house. The robber had got in by breaking a window by the kitchen door, putting his arm through and turning the key that was in the lock. 'You really shouldn't leave the key in the lock, Mrs Reardon,' he called out. 'I'm just going to secure this window and then I'll be on my way.' Finding an ancient hammer, nails and a piece of wood in the garden shed outside, he quickly banged the wood into place, returned the tools to where he found them and locked the kitchen door behind him. He then took the key from the lock and went into the living room.

Mrs Reardon was out of her chair, and was standing with her back to him, staring out the window, her blanket around her shoulders.

'Mrs Reardon, I've locked the door and have put a piece of wood up to block the broken window. Here's the key. You might want to put it somewhere safer.'

Mrs Reardon didn't say anything, just continued to stare out the window.

'Mrs Reardon?' Sanderson said, touching her gently on her shoulder.

Mrs Reardon turned to look at him. 'The lights,' she said quietly. 'They've gone.'

'What lights, Mrs Reardon?'

'The lights at the Seven Sisters, the ones I've been calling you lot about.' She turned back to look out the window again. 'They were there, but now they've gone,' she said, in a small tremulous voice.

Sanderson groaned inwardly. 'It'll just be kids with candles or something, Mrs Reardon. Now, do you have someone who can stay with you tonight?'

Sanderson managed to track down the neighbour who he had met in the kitchen. She was happy to stay with Mrs Reardon for the night, and after he had talked to her, he said his goodbyes to Mrs Reardon. She clutched his arm. 'I don't think it's kids, officer. It's like a procession or something.' She shoved his arm away angrily. 'Why won't anyone believe me?'

Later, wrapped around his sleeping wife, Sanderson, even though he was bone tired, couldn't get to sleep. He kept thinking about Mrs Reardon and her lights and how adamant she had been about them.

If she's right, he thought, *what the hell is going on up there?*

Thursday 21 December

16

Louise's father, Jeffrey, watched as his daughter quickly swallowed her cornflakes. It looked to him as if nothing at all was touching the sides, and he was greatly surprised when she finished without choking. He had fallen off the wagon yet again last night, but this time, instead of Louise asking him how he felt and could she make him a cup of tea, she had come to the table with barely disguised contempt, and she was now bolting down her breakfast as if she couldn't even bear to be in the same room as him. His mother had warned him that his drinking and self-pity would some day alienate his daughter from him, and today seemed to be that day.

'Yer seem to be in a hurry, pumpkin?' he said gently. Pumpkin was his pet name for Louise; he had called her that since she was a baby. Well, he called her that when he wasn't sobbing into his beer.

Louise sighed the sigh of those who suddenly think they know it all. 'Yer know I've made some new friends now, Dad,' she said with an annoyed tone in her voice.

'Yes, pet, and that's good, yer can never have enough friends in this world. This I've told yer before . . . So when am I gonna meet the rest of them?'

'Yer don't have to meet everybody I know. Do yer?' she snapped. For a moment he was stunned, and felt as if his ears were deceiving him. Louise had never once in her life, despite all the pain she'd been through, and the fact that she'd grown up without a mother, ever been stroppy. *God knows, I've given her enough reason.* Jeffrey silently promised himself that he would stop drinking, for Louise, for his little pumpkin. He wanted her to be proud of him. He replied quietly, 'Sorry, love, didn't mean to pry.'

Louise's mood was certainly changeable. She looked contrite, and smiled at Jeffrey, which only made him feel worse. She kissed the top of her father's head. 'I might be late in, Dad, like really late, play rehearsals.'

'You're in the school play?' He was amazed, Louise had never taken part in any extra school activities before.

She smiled, and nodded.

'Which part?' He suddenly felt a wave of pride rush over him. He couldn't wait to tell his friends down at the Buffs Club that his daughter was gonna be an actress. That would blow them away all right.

Louise hesitated, then she said, 'Mary.'

He frowned, 'The nativity?'

'No, some musical, I've forgotten the title,' she said unconvincingly. 'I really have to go now, Dad.'

'OK, see yer tonight.'

'Yeah, bye.' She hurried out and ran along to the bus stop.

The usual crowd was there, and Louise hovered at the back of the queue doing her invisible trick. When they piled on the bus, Louise slipped away, and when the bus pulled away from the kerb, she was nowhere to be seen.

'Don't look at me like that, dog, yer just a guest in this house until I find yer real owners.' Lorraine was standing by the kitchen bench, eating a piece of toast. 'And anyway, they're the ones who want you here, they can feed and water yer an' all.'

Duke stood at the kitchen door, wagging his tail.

'Oh shit.'

It was obvious the dog wanted to go out. *Where the hell are they?* Lorraine went to the bottom of the stairs – not a sound – then she glanced at her wrist-watch. It was seven-thirty. She sighed. She didn't expect Mavis to get up for another half hour at least and Peggy loved her lie-ins.

Duke gave a whine that set Lorraine's teeth on edge. 'Jesus.' She rummaged in the cupboard for a length of rope that she knew was there, found it, then made a loop and slipped it over the dog's head.

'Right, come on.'

Duke limped down the path. 'OK, there's no need to overact, yer've got yer own way and yer better be quick.'

Duke trotted quite happily by her side and, after a couple of turns round the block, Lorraine decided that was enough for her this morning. She let herself back into the house, took the rope off Duke, grabbed her car keys and hurried out the door. Fifteen minutes after that she was at her desk and writing out a rota for walking Duke for Mavis and Peggy.

The building started to liven up shortly after she came in and Sanderson was the first one in to see her. 'I think I made a mistake yesterday, boss,' he said as he walked into the room and sat down in front of her.

Lorraine frowned. 'Not like you, Sanderson. Why do yer think yer've made a mistake?'

'It's Mrs Reardon, and that business with the lights.'

Lorraine looked confused.

'Mrs Reardon has been ringing up the office, saying that she's seen lights up at Seven Sisters. No one's taken her seriously, yer know what she's like . . .'

'Yeah, sees ghouls and gremlins as clearly as real people sometimes.'

Sanderson nodded, and carried on. 'Anyway, last night she had a break-in –' Sanderson raised his hands to stop Lorraine from interrupting him. 'She's OK. A ring of sentimental value was stolen, and that seems to be it. If yer ask me she's enjoying the attention more than anything. She seemed coherent and, well, sane last night, but then she started talking about the lights again . . .'

'What, yer really think there's aliens and hobgoblins up there amongst the fairies now?' Lorraine asked.

But she couldn't fool Sanderson. 'No, and yer know I don't, boss.'

'Well, thank God for that then. So . . .'

'Well, I don't think it would do any harm to go up and have a look. Put her mind at rest, for one thing. It's probably just kids fooling around, maybe even

212

keeping a vigil for poor Richy Stansfield, but I'd just like to check it out and make sure.'

'OK, I'll go with that. Take Jacobs up later on this morning and investigate to yer hearts' content.'

Sanderson nodded but before he could say anything else, Sara Jacobs knocked and entered Lorraine's office. 'We've got a Mr and Mrs Tremaine outside. Apparently their fifteen-year-old daughter didn't come home last night.'

Lorraine was still thinking about Mrs Reardon and the mysterious lights, so couldn't quite figure out why the name sounded so familiar. 'Tremaine,' she muttered. 'The name rings a bell . . . Show them in, please.'

A few moments later Mr and Mrs Tremaine entered. One look at Mr Tremaine was enough for Lorraine to know which fifteen-year-old girl was missing. He may not have carried Melissa's weight, but she certainly took after him in looks. Mr Tremaine was an extremely good-looking man, with the same dark hair and eyes as his daughter. His wife was a pretty woman, but she could never hope to compete with her husband.

'You're here about Melissa,' Lorraine said.

The Tremaines looked startled for a moment, then Mr Tremaine said, hesitatingly as if he didn't really want to know, 'You've found her?'

'No, no . . . Sorry, please sit down.'

Sanderson rose and offered Mrs Tremaine his seat while Mr Tremaine took the other one.

'You know our daughter?' Mrs Tremaine asked, a puzzled frown on her face.

'I met her the other day at school. I talked with her and a few others about Richard Stansfield.'

'Oh,' Mr Tremaine said, and clutched his wife's hand. She had taken a great breath, and looked pale all of a sudden. Lorraine knew the woman seated in front of her was seeing Richard Stansfield's dead body in her mind's eye, and trying really hard to keep her grip on things. 'And I dropped her off at school yesterday morning.'

'We had a call from the school yesterday. She didn't make it to any of her classes,' Mr Tremaine said, his fingers nervously playing with something in his pocket. 'And then last night we had it out with her. She went upstairs to her room and that was the last we saw of her.'

Lorraine was remembering the strange behaviour of the black car. She wondered whether that had anything to do with it. She leaned back in her chair and regarded the two people sitting in front of her. Could they be blaming her in some way? She hadn't noticed Melissa go into the school gates but then she was watching the movements of that car that had followed her down the road. Finally she said, 'I picked her up because she would have been late and I dropped her off at the school gates . . . Naturally I assumed she had gone in but at the time my attention was on something else . . . Is this the kind of thing she does often?'

Mr Tremaine sighed. 'I don't quite know how to put this, officer, but if you've spoken to my daughter then you will possibly have already realised how awkward she can be . . . We have three sons who have never . . .'

He was interrupted by a sob from Mrs Tremaine. He clutched her hand harder.

'Something's happened to her.' Melissa's mother lifted her reddened eyes to Lorraine's. 'I know it has . . . I can feel it.'

'Nonsense, dear.'

Lorraine felt like Melissa's parents were decent people, although the father seemed a bit stuffy. But Lorraine couldn't think of why Melissa would have gone missing. She didn't seem the type to run away, but then, she did seem to be terrified of something, something that Lorraine felt she was on the verge of telling her in the car yesterday morning. And then Lorraine felt a lurch in her stomach. She hoped that Melissa hadn't followed Richy's lead and done something stupid.

'Has she been acting differently than usual?' Lorraine asked. 'I got the feeling when I talked to her yesterday that there was something on her mind. Do you have any idea what it could have been?'

Melissa's parents looked at each other, stricken. They looked back at Lorraine and shook their heads. But then Mrs Tremaine seemed to remember something and she said, 'Well, Melissa has always been a bit of a loner. But then she started hanging out with Rachel Henderson and,' her voice fell, 'Richy Stansfield and staying out at night later and later. We tried to talk to her about it, tried to ground her so that she'd stay home. But she always managed to find a way out of the house.' She put her hand to her mouth, and her husband stroked her arm.

'OK, I'm gonna leave yer with Sergeant Sanderson,

here. He'll take all the details and I assure you we will do everything we can to find Melissa.' Lorraine stood. 'You can use my office. I have something I need to do.' She picked up her bag and brown suede jacket and tried to smile at Mrs Tremaine in a reassuring manner.

When she reached the door Mrs Tremaine said, 'She's just a little girl inside.' Lorraine turned and for a moment both women looked at each other. Then Lorraine gave her a nod of understanding and softly closed the door behind her.

The corridor was empty and she leaned against the wall.

Why the hell do I do this job?

With a sigh she pushed herself off the wall. She had just reached the outside office when Debbie Stansfield walked through the door and spotted her immediately.

'He didn't do it . . . My son did not kill himself. He was murdered.'

Oh God!

'Ms Stansfield, please, we are doing our best.'

Debbie started to cry and Lorraine moved forward and put her arm around her shoulder. She guided her to a seat. 'You have got to let us do our job, Debbie.'

'But . . . But I can't even bury him.'

Lorraine felt her slump in her seat and for a moment she thought the woman was going to faint, but she pulled herself together and sat upright.

'He did not commit suicide.' Debbie was adamant. 'My Richard was a happy boy . . . Always has been . . . You never met him, you didn't know him . . . Ask

216

anybody. He was murdered and you lot are just dragging your heels.'

Debbie's eyes looked raw from days of crying, and she was wearing a blue Nike T-shirt under a black cardigan. Lorraine assumed the T-shirt belonged to Richy, and her heart went out to Debbie. Her grief was so much on the surface, and Lorraine could see why she would need to hang on to her belief that Richard hadn't killed himself. But Lorraine had to be firm with her. She couldn't have Debbie come into the police station and cause a scene, no matter how sorry she felt for her. 'I promise you we're doing all we can, Debbie . . . Look, let me drive yer home.'

'Don't want no lift off you . . . I just want yer to find out who murdered my boy, and I want it official that he was murdered. He did not commit suicide . . . Why would he?'

'I can't tell yer why, Debbie . . . there can be all sorts of reasons. Sometimes things just get on top of some of us, that's all, things just become a bit too much to take. And the ones left behind, they're looking for an explanation why, and it's so hard for them, so hard for them not to blame themselves. But really, it's no one's fault. Come on, love, let me take yer home.'

Debbie sighed, and Lorraine felt like crying for her. 'Come on.'

Debbie nodded, as she choked on a sob. Gently, Lorraine led her outside to her car.

Jacko knocked loudly on Danny's door. A moment later it was answered by Len. 'Hi Jacko, what yer after, mate?'

'Is Danny in?'

'Oh, aye . . . Forgot where I was for a minute there, here's me thinking I'm at home and yer knocking on my door.' Len laughed, then said, 'Ha'way in.'

Jacko smiled as he followed Len down the passageway. He'd been in Danny's house a few times. Danny was fond of the cards and now and then a few of them got a game going. He smiled to himself. Not a single picture of his current girlfriend or his ex-wife on the walls; rather, the passageway was covered with portraits of Elizabeth Taylor, and posters of films she had starred in.

Danny was in the kitchen making dinner. His youngest, three-year-old Samantha, was sitting at the kitchen table, knife and fork in hand, waiting patiently for her beefburger and beans.

Jacko patted her curly blonde head and she grinned up at him. 'Lo Jackso'.'

'Hello cutie, been a good girl?'

She nodded solemnly.

'Hi, Jacko, anything special or just a visit?'

'I just thought I'd call round and tell yer I won't be going on the beer run any more.'

Danny looked amazed. 'What for?'

'It's too risky, it's been in all the papers again, they're cracking down on it, man.'

'Oh Jacko, man, come on, yer know everybody likes having yer along.'

'Aye,' Len said. 'Ha'way man. Change yer mind.'

Jacko shook his head. 'Sorry, mate, they reckon yer can lose yer dole money now, and . . . Well, me and Christina are talking about getting married in the spring. She wants a big white wedding and I know I desperately need the money and all that, but I can't risk losing what I've got. I'm really sorry if I've let yer down.'

Danny sighed. He really didn't want to lose Jacko, he kept the others calm. 'Look, just think about it, will yer? I'll give yer a buzz just before we go. If yer change yer mind we'll be glad to have yer along. Oh,' he added sheepishly, 'and congratulations.'

Jacko shrugged, 'Thanks mate, but I don't think I'm gonna change me mind about the trip.'

'Well, the offer's gonna be there if yer do. Will I see yer this afternoon at the nativity play?'

'Why aye, our Melanie's singing.'

'Our Jimmy's one of the wise men, would yer believe it?' Danny shook his head in amazement.

'He's wise all right that one.' Len put in. He held out his hand to Jacko. 'Sorry to hear yer won't be coming mate, but all the best with the wedding and that.'

Samantha chose that moment to start banging her cutlery on the table. 'Me hungry *now*!'

'Yeah, OK,' Danny said, turning to his daughter.

Jacko smiled and said, 'I'll be off then.'

Half an hour later Jacko was sitting outside the Peppercorn café, nursing a glass of Diet Coke as he waited for Christina. He couldn't help but glance wistfully at the passersby, their bags full of shopping. He sighed. It was going to be hard to stay firm, especially when he could imagine all the brilliant things he could get for his girls.

Aye why, better luck next year, he thought to himself.

17

Always the gentleman, Sanderson opened the car door for Sara Jacobs. She got in without a smile or a thank-you, and made herself comfortable as Sanderson pulled away.

'Reckon this is all a bloody waste of time, if yer ask me,' she whinged.

Sanderson shrugged. It was on his lips to say, who asked you? but instead he countered with, 'Well, we won't know until we get there, but there's no harm in checking it out. Could be nothing, could just be kids . . . but the boss agrees with me that it's worthwhile taking a look.'

'So here we are, going out in the freezing cold on some wild goose chase.'

Sanderson shrugged, trying to hide his annoyance from the younger officer.

'Come on, Sanderson, we're only going here because of some silly old biddy, who sees fairies for God's sake, has now said she's seeing lights.'

Sanderson frowned. 'Mrs Reardon was once a respected school teacher, she also served her country in the war, and she happens to own a medal to prove it. And anyway, she's probably a bit shaken since the burglary. If we just put her mind at rest about one thing, it's worth going up there for me.'

None of this impressed Sara Jacobs and Sanderson could see he was wasting his breath. He fell silent and a few minutes later they came to a stop next to the field where the Seven Sisters stood. Although the Sisters could be seen from a distance, up close it was impossible to see them because of the large hedge that ran the length of the field.

'I think we'd better park in the Copt Hill pub, much safer, this is a pretty fast road.'

'But we'll have to walk that much further,' Jacobs complained.

'Nonsense. It's just across the road and up a bit.'

Five minutes later they stepped into the field and were immediately cut off from the outside world. They walked down a narrow stretch that just about passed for a path and was hidden from the road, then turned sharp left. Suddenly they were in the field, and facing the Seven Sisters.

'What the –?' Sanderson exclaimed.

'Must be a bunch of travellers.'

Four caravans were parked in a circle just below the tree line. As they watched, two young girls left one of the caravans and entered another.

Sanderson and Jacobs moved across the grass. When they reached the circle five people came out of the last caravan. A medium-sized man, slightly on the thin side with black curly hair and large luminous brown eyes, was obviously in charge. He walked towards them, his face a study in benevolent calm.

Sanderson noticed that the four other people who stood behind their leader, all girls, had the same beatific smile on their faces. The girls were all young – he'd be surprised if any were older than twenty – and poorly clothed. Something did not feel right here, and he distrusted their leader immediately.

'Welcome. Have you come to join us?' the leader asked, his face wreathed in smiles.

'No, certainly not,' Jacobs spat, distaste written all over her face.

Sanderson silenced Jacobs with a look before taking his badge out. 'Just checking one or two things out.'

'Like?'

'Like, what yer doing here?'

'Is there a problem, officer?' The smile didn't leave the leader's face. But there was steel to his tone. Sanderson's dislike for the man in front of him increased even further.

'Not sure about that yet,' Sanderson conceded. 'But could you clarify what you're doing here?'

'We are just resting. Come the New Year we will be on our way. If that's all right with you, officer?'

'Well, I'm just gonna have to check on that one, OK . . . What's yer name, by the way.'

'My name is Marcel, and these,' he spread his arms wide, to encompass the four girls, and the others that were now standing on the caravan steps watching, 'are the Blessing Guides.'

'Oh aye, got another name have yer? Yer know, other than Marcel, like?'

For a moment the smile left his face, then he replied. 'Marcel Gottsdiener.'

*

222

'So you reckon they're nowt but a bunch of religious nutters?' Lorraine looked at Jacobs with one eyebrow raised.

'Without doubt. I mean, come on, the Blessing Guides, have yer ever? And they all seemed pretty harmless to me. Most of them were kids.'

Lorraine looked questioningly at Sanderson, who pulled a wry face, 'Hmm, not so sure . . . I didn't like the fact that most of them were kids. And he's obviously set himself up as some sort of charismatic leader. He must be at least in his late thirties, if not older. So why's he hanging around with kids twenty years younger than him? I just didn't get a good feeling about them at all.'

Lorraine nodded. 'So, did he give a name?'

'Aye, Marcel Gottsdiener.'

'So he's German.'

'Yup, that's what I thought.' Sanderson scratched his cheek. 'But he definitely didn't have a German accent. He sounded more, more . . .'

'French,' Jacobs put in. 'But even that was watered down with,' she shrugged, 'I dunno, his accent was American more than British.'

'That would account for the Marcel . . .' Lorraine searched her mind. Gottsdiener sounded somehow familiar from the German classes she had taken at school years ago. Suddenly it came to her. 'By the way, Gottsdiener means God's servant . . .' She looked at Jacobs, 'Though I doubt very much that's the name he was born with.'

Jacobs blinked. For once she looked in awe of Lorraine.

'I'd like to find out more about this Marcel Gottsdiener, what he's doing here and why we haven't come across him before.' Lorraine looked at Sanderson. 'And I think you're right to worry about the fact he surrounds himself with kids twenty years younger than him. Sure, he could be harmless, but until we're sure of that, I want him, and the Blessing Guides, thoroughly researched. Later this afternoon, Sanderson, you and I might have to pay this God's servant and his Blessing Guides another little visit. In the meantime,' she turned back to Jacobs, 'get online and see what yer can find out about these Blessing Guides. OK?'

As Sanderson and Jacobs left her office, Lorraine slumped into her chair. Luke still hadn't come in. She picked up her phone and dialled his number. Straight to answerphone. She put the receiver down without leaving a message, allowed herself a few moments to look out the window, and then turned to the paperwork she had on her desk.

18

As usual, chaos reigned in the Lumsdon household. Most of the primary school children had been sent home at lunchtime to get ready for the nativity play, and the house seemed to be overrun with screaming kids.

'Not going back,' Emma declared suddenly. 'Don't wanna be no Mary.'

'Nonsense, Emma, it's just nerves,' her mother, Vanessa, said. *Dear God, if I ever feel like hitting the bottle it's at times like these.*

But I won't. She straightened her shoulders, knowing, with four girls, there were worse battles to come. They had been through a lot this last year and she wasn't about to crumble over a nativity play.

'Not going,' Emma shouted again. 'Forgotten everything.'

Kerry, Emma's older sister, walked past and clipped Emma on the back of her head. 'Oww,' Emma yelled even louder, then she stuck her tongue out.

'It didn't even hurt,' Kerry said. 'Enough of yer overacting, save that for the stage, so move it. Yer not having everybody saying that the Lumsdons let the side down, OK?'

Emma glowered at her sister, checked her bag that she had everything she needed, then, as changeable as the wind, she said sweetly to her mother, 'Come on then.'

'OK, see yer up there, Kerry, and don't forget to tell our Robbie the right time.'

Kerry yelled something, but it was muffled by the door closing behind them. Vanessa and Emma crossed the road and Vanessa waited at the Musgroves' gate while Emma ran to see if they were ready.

'Hi, Emma,' Jacko said as he came down the path with Melanie and Doris, before nodding at Vanessa. They set off for the school and were joined a few moments later by Sandra. Emma and Melanie skipped in front while the adults walked behind.

'You'll never guess what I read in the paper yesterday: only that some schools have cancelled their nativity plays,' Sandra said.

'Never, what for?' Doris asked.

'Oh yes, I read that an' all.' Vanessa agreed. 'Bloody disgraceful if yer ask me, something to do with this political correctness shit.'

'Ge'bye.' Doris's mouth hung open. 'Yer taking the piss aren't yer . . . I don't believe it . . . That's bloody shocking that is . . . What the fuck for?'

'Yeah, I think it's disgraceful an' all,' Sandra went on. 'It's because . . . Well, to tell yer the truth I can't really understand it meself . . . Apparently, it's because some other religions might get upset, so some schools lost their bottles and cancelled the nativities.'

'Why, that's just pathetic,' Jacko said in

amazement. 'What sort of people are running the bloody country?'

'Aye, yer bloody right, son. Oh, I bet Dolly's never heard of this.'

Dolly, wrapped up in her false fox fur coat, was waiting at her gate for them, and she was as shocked as Doris had been when told of the nativity ban.

'Jesus, I don't know. Bunch of bloody idiots who come up with all this politically correct shit, but the worst ones are the weak-willed fools who follow through. Instead of laughing in their faces and telling them to fuck off with their daft ideas, what nobody wants to hear.'

They continued their discussion until they reached the school gates, by which time more than a dozen of them, of all religious groups and nationalities, all thought it a stupid pathetic idea. 'No more nativity plays,' Mr Chang shook his head sadly. 'My Yann is one of the Three Kings this year and his brother is hoping to be one next year.'

'Relax, Mr Chang,' Jacko consoled him. 'Somebody somewhere has got to see sense in this.'

Nodding their heads in agreement, they all filed in to see their children perform.

Kurt watched in amazement as Niall scoffed the egg, chips and beans his mother had cooked for them. He didn't seem to need to stop to breathe. Kurt watched his friend with mounting incomprehension as Niall chased the very last bean round his plate, and used the bread to scrape up what was left of the egg yoke and the bean juice.

Kurt was only half way through his, and thoroughly enjoying the simple meal purely because someone else had cooked it for him. When a bowl of peaches and ice cream was put beside him, he smiled up in thanks at Niall's mother who ruffled his hair in return.

Niall wolfed the sweet back as quickly as he'd swallowed the dinner, and asked for more.

Kurt wondered how such a thin body could pack so much away, but out of manners he couldn't bring himself to say anything. Then Niall suddenly pushed himself away from the table and ran upstairs. Kurt felt embarrassed that Niall had left so quickly, so he made a point of thanking Niall's mother, who went pink with delight. He then followed Niall upstairs to the bedroom they were sharing now that Kurt had decided to leave his mother alone for a while.

Kurt was passing the bathroom door on the way to Niall's bedroom when just above the sound of running water he heard Niall vomiting.

Concerned, he knocked on the bathroom door. 'Are yer all right, Niall?'

He was answered by the sound of running water, much louder this time as if Niall had turned another tap on. Shrugging, he went into Niall's bedroom and sat down on his bed. He wondered how Niall could stand living in this room where everything was green: green carpet, green bedding, green walls. Thankfully, there was some contrast in Sunderland's red and white football stars on the walls, otherwise Kurt thought he might feel seasick.

Looking for something to occupy himself while

228

Niall was in the bathroom, Kurt found a stack of cookery books beside Niall's bed. He picked the top one up and was leafing through it when Niall came in.

'What yer doing?' he demanded.

'Nothing I . . .' Kurt shrugged, 'Didn't know yer like cooking.'

'Don't.' Niall took the book off Kurt and reverently put it back in place.

'So what's with all the books?'

'I like looking at them.'

Kurt was at a loss to explain Niall's behaviour. He looked down at his shoes, and then out the window. With a painful groan that sounded as if his bones belonged to a much older man, Niall opened his drawers. Kurt looked up from the scene outside and saw his friend take out two white T-shirts and two Nike sweatshirts, one grey, one blue. To these he added two pairs of black jeans and three pairs of underpants. Ignoring Kurt's wide-eyed stare, he went back to the bathroom.

But Kurt noticed something he'd never noticed before. Niall was wearing two pairs of jeans. The hems were barely noticeable, but it was definitely another pair of jeans under the top pair. Mystified, Kurt thought to himself:

He's wearing two sets of clothes now. No wonder he wasn't as cold as I was last night.

Why would he wear two sets of clothes?

To keep him warm?

But why would he be so sneaky about it?

Then, suddenly, the answer came to him in a flash of understanding.

He's chucking up his food.

Kurt felt goose-bumps all over again. He knew his friend had big problems. Most people thought Niall took drugs, and that that was the reason why he was so thin. But Kurt had never once seen Niall off his head, nor had he seen him take or smoke anything more than the odd cigarette.

He thought then of Niall's mood swings, how he frequently got out of breath, his leg and joint pains. How he would often trail behind them if they bought food, almost as if he didn't want them to see him eating. How he was hardly ever at school.

But he gulped his dinner down today.

Then it dawned on Kurt what was wrong with his friend.

He's starving himself, then he's binge eating, and then he's throwing up.

He's got that bulimia or anorexia or something.

Just then he heard water splashing from the bathroom. Kurt decided right then and there that he would challenge Niall when he came back out of the bathroom. He figured it was the least he could do, because Niall was his friend. He'd taken him in and fed him when he had nowhere else to go, but he was gonna kill himself if he was left to it and nothing was done.

Sighing, he sat on the edge of the bed, and went over it all again. Niall had all the classic symptoms of bulimia, and he should have noticed it before. Kurt was never more certain of anything. One of his cousins had been in and out of hospital for years before she finally succumbed to the illness. She had been the only relation that Kurt had liked. It had been terrible watching her sicken and die over many, many months.

The door opened noisily and Niall, dressed in his clean clothes, came in. The two boys looked warily at each other. Kurt felt that Niall already knew what he was going to say. So he took a deep breath and launched right in.

'Yer chucking yer food up, aren't yer.' It was not a question but a statement and Niall knew it.

'No,' he denied.

'Yes yer are . . . And yer double dressing an' all so you look fatter.'

Niall shook his head. 'Yer fucking daft yer are.'

'No, I'm not. I've seen it before.'

Niall's face coloured. 'I said yer fucking daft.'

'Yer can't deny yer've got two sets of clothes on.'

'It's fucking cold out there.'

'It's not in here.'

'Oh fuck off.'

'No.'

Niall growled. His fists were clenched into tight balls at his side. He stared at Kurt, then said through gritted teeth, 'Yer better back off.'

'So yer can just die quietly.'

'Who the fuck are you to say I'm gonna die. There's nowt wrong with me, yer fucking thick, man.' Niall was pacing up and down the room, his face red.

Kurt wasn't about to take Niall's denial at face value. 'Should I tell yer mam? She might be able to get yer the right help, before it's too late.'

'Too late for what?' Niall was spitting. 'Don't be fucking stupid, there's nowt to tell her, yer round the fucking bend, off yer trolley, as mad as them bastards up at the fucking Seven Sisters. Go on, fuck off and join them, see if I care. Yer nothing but a fucking nuisance. No wonder yer mother bashes yer up all the fucking time.'

Kurt flinched at that.

Seeing the hurt in his eyes, Niall felt terrible for what he'd just said, even though it was in temper. He sat down hard on his bed.

'I'm sorry,' he murmured.

Kurt sighed, 'It's all right. I used to think that, but I don't any more.'

That sentence just served to make Niall feel even worse. 'Look, I really am sorry, it's not your fault and,' he took a deep breath, 'I guess yer right.'

Niall was facing the mirror on his dressing table. After a moment he said, 'What do you see when yer look in there?' pointing at the mirror.

Kurt frowned. 'What do yer mean – when I look at me or when I look at you?'

'When yer look at me.'

'I see you of course, what the hell do yer think I see?'

'Want to know what I see?'

'Ha'way then.'

Niall took a deep breath, then he said what he had never told a living soul before. In one respect he welcomed Kurt's intrusion: no one had ever really sussed out what had been going on for the last two years. 'I see a huge fat body with a tiny pea head, and no matter how hard I look, that's all I see.'

'Wow.'

'Yeah, wow.'

'But that's not right, how can yer see that? Yer need help, Niall, 'cos if yer don't get it yer gonna die, trust me on this, I knew somebody like you . . . My cousin Jen. She died.'

Niall had been looking at Kurt through the mirror. Now he turned and faced him. 'I know I have a problem. But what I know and what I feel are two different things. All I see when I look in that mirror is a great big bloated fat body.'

'Not true, Niall . . . Honest, yer as thin as a rake . . . Have yer not looked at the size of the labels on yer clothes.'

'Makes no difference, it's the size of me in the mirror what counts.'

They sat in silence for a few moments, then Niall said, 'Rachel cuts herself.'

'What!'

'Yes, she told Melissa.'

'Jesus.' Kurt shook his head in disbelief.

'She says it makes her feel better . . . In a way I can understand that.'

''Fraid I can't.'

Niall shrugged.

'You like Melissa, don't yer?' Kurt asked.

Niall smiled slightly. 'Yeah, I suppose . . . She over-eats, because she feels like she's not as good as her brothers . . . I throw up, God knows why . . . Rachel cuts herself, God knows why that is . . . And you get beaten up. Prize specimens, eh?'

Kurt nodded ruefully. 'We're also thieves and murderers.'

'I'm not proud of that, but who would have known that the warehouse guy was gonna follow us onto the roof? Christ, it took me all me time to get up there, I swear he had hold of me foot at one time . . . But it was an accident, nobody pushed him, he fell.'

'I don't know, Niall,' Kurt added. 'Whichever way yer look at it, we're in deep shit . . . I can't see no way out except to go with the Blessing Guides when they leave.'

Niall shook his head. 'That Marcel will only have us robbing more people . . . That old wife up Hall Lane nearly caught me an' all. Did yer see him go all gaga about the ring though? Christ, I got plenty of blessings for that all right.' Niall smiled. 'It was the sort of thing I'd like to give to Melissa. Haven't heard from her all day. I wonder where she is?'

'She might just be keeping her head down.'

'We didn't see Rachel for long last night either . . . Tell yer the truth, I'm beginning to get a bit edgy for the girls, and I think Rachel's becoming obsessed with that Marcel. See the looks she was throwing at the new girl Louise, 'cos he was making a big fuss of her?'

Kurt sighed. 'What the fuck have we got ourselves into?'

Niall stood up. 'We've got to get the girls outta there before that stupid Mary ceremony takes place.'

'What do yer think's gonna happen?'

'Don't know, but the more I think about it the creepier it gets . . .'

19

You couldn't find two prouder parents than Vanessa Lumsdon and Jacko Musgrave. Emma was word perfect and played the part of Mary as if she'd played it all her life. She never once stumbled over her lines and she even managed a very small, very quick smile for the audience when she took a curtain call.

Melanie brought the house down when she sang a medley of Christmas carols, with the whole audience standing up to join in at the end. Jacko had a lump in his throat as he was thinking:

Just one more trip.

One more trip and she can have the best Christmas ever. I'll be able to get the bairn everything she's asked for.

He made his mind up, he would catch Danny outside. He had to do just one more run.

He smiled down at Doris as she looked up at him. *God, I owe her so much. She deserves a fantastic Christmas too.*

They filed out of the row, nodding to friends as they caught their eye, and walked outside into the cold air. As they waited for Danny, Doris was dabbing her eyes as she said to her friends. 'Where that bairn got that gift from I'll never know.' She nudged Jacko in his ribs, '''Cos you can't sing to save yer life.' She turned to the others and went on, 'Yer should hear him in the bath.'

'Have yer heard yerself?' Jacko laughed.

'Oh me, well I know I sound like a frog farting up a drainpipe.'

They all laughed, then Dolly said, 'And little Emma, eh? Quite the star of the show.' Everybody agreed, and Vanessa felt like she had clouds underneath her feet.

Especially when Mr Shillings had asked in passing, 'Could that have been a smile I saw from Emma?'

Emma was notorious for not smiling. So Mr Shillings's comment made them all laugh again, and just then Danny arrived. He looked uncomfortable. His wife was on one side, and his girlfriend was on the other. Both of them were throwing daggers at each other. Jacko grinned. They should know by now that the only person they really needed to worry about was Elizabeth Taylor.

Before Jacko could say anything, Vanessa piped up, 'Got any ciggies on yer, Danny boy?'

'Aye, there's some in the van.' He handed the keys to his girlfriend. She tossed her head but went to the van and came back with two packets of Regal king size.

'Here Vanessa, love.' She thrust the packets at her.

'But I er, I only . . .'

'It's all right. I've got no change so I'll get it tomorrow.'

Thank God, Vanessa thought. She only had

enough on her for one packet. Buying them from Danny saved her two pounds a packet.

'Got a minute, Danny?' Jacko asked.

'Aye, plenty for you, Jacko.'

They started to walk towards the van leaving the ex-wife and the girlfriend to natter with the others. 'God,' Danny breathed. 'Yer don't know what it's like, mate. Every time there's something like this on, I have the pair of them. I'm not just walking on eggshells, I'm eating the damn things.'

Jacko laughed. 'It's about the next trip. I'd like to go, that's if you'll have me?'

'Have yer . . . To tell yer the truth, mate, I was thinking about kidnapping yer. I'll let yer know the time, OK?'

'Yeah, great.'

They parted, and Jacko told Doris he was going to the library to pick Christina up. But he couldn't help feeling apprehensive as he walked towards Christina's work.

20

Louise and Mary left the house on the Seahills and began their walk up to the Seven Sisters. It was freezing, and Louise shivered inside her coat. She dug her hands deeper into her pockets. She was nervous – good nervous – but nervous all the same.

'Yer sure I'll be able to do everything right, Mary?' Louise asked anxiously.

Mary looked straight ahead. 'That's why we're going up there now, so you can rehearse.'

Louise fell silent. She looked from side to side in case she saw anybody who knew her. But the cold street was deserted. Then something tugged at her mind. She glanced sideways at Mary. Was it her or had Mary sounded a bit bad-tempered, cross even, when she'd asked her if things would go all right at the ceremony on Christmas Eve?

No, I'm just imagining it because I feel so happy and don't want anything to wreck it. Mary's so nice, really.

At last, to feel wanted by other people.

To be the most important one. She looked almost with awe at the girl by her side. *How marvellous to be Mary.*

They reached the Seven Sisters, where they were

greeted with respect by everyone. Louise saw Rachel Henderson standing alone, hugging herself to keep warm. Louise waved at her. Rachel returned the wave with a little smile, and Louise was about to go over and talk to her when Marcel stopped her. He had been waiting for them.

'Louise, Mary,' he said, taking their hands in his, 'you've come just in time. We're about to have a thanksgiving service, because life is good, and we're so happy.'

With a signal from Marcel, the Blessing Guides stood in a circle, holding hands, while Marcel began the chant.

'Blessed be to the weak, for they are made strong. Blessed be to the forgotten, for they are remembered. Blessed be to the lost, for they are found,' he said in his strong, mellifluous voice.

'Blessed be to us,' the Guides chanted back.

'Blessed be to those in pain, I will heal your wounds. Blessed be to those in chains, I will set you free. Blessed be to those in despair, I will give you hope.'

'Blessed be to us.'

Marcel lifted his head. He looked over to a tall, blonde, willowy girl who stood on the opposite side of the circle. 'Blessed be to Inge, for bringing to us the fruits of her labour.'

As the Blessing Guides murmured, 'Blessed be to Inge,' Marcel and Inge broke the circle and walked towards each other. The Blessing Guides now had their arms by their sides, and each was swaying slightly. Inge gave Marcel an envelope and dropped to her knees. Marcel placed his hand on the top of her head, murmured a few words over her and raised Inge to her feet. Louise noticed that Inge had tears in her eyes as she went to rejoin the circle.

As Marcel called more people to be blessed, Louise felt her heart swell with so much love for him she thought it might burst.

Marcel finished the last blessing and, still standing in the circle, said, 'Blessed be to us all. I have some news, some exciting news. On Christmas Eve our old friend, Mary,' Louise looked at Mary, who was standing beside her, staring at Marcel with an odd look on her face, 'will depart to spread the word and I will call a new Mary, to travel with us all.'

He took Louise by the hand and led her into the circle. 'Louise will be our new Mary. She will take her name and she will live with me and be my Blessed One.'

'Blessed be to Louise,' someone behind her said, but she couldn't work out who.

Marcel inclined his head in response. 'Every three years a new Mary is called. Every three years the old Mary leaves us to carry on our work elsewhere.' The Blessing Guides murmured, 'Blessed be,' before going over to a caravan where they each took a lantern.

Louise looked again at Mary, who dropped her eyes as soon as she saw that Louise's eyes were upon her. But Louise suddenly felt uneasy. Mary was unhappy with her. But why?

Lorraine opened the flask of home-made broth which Mavis had made up for her. It smelled delicious.

One thing about living with two good cooks, I ain't ever gonna starve. She filled a bowl, then tightened the lid. She knew Mavis had put extra in because Luke loved her broth.

But Luke isn't here.

'Damn him,' she muttered, as she dipped the spoon into the thick ham broth.

Sanderson entered a few minutes later. 'Something smells good,' he said, stretching his neck and peering into the bowl.

'Want some?' Lorraine passed the flask over. 'There's a clean bowl and spoon in the filing cabinet. Filed under B for bowl.'

'Carter's idea?'

Lorraine laughed, 'Yeah.'

Sanderson filled the bowl up, and devoured the broth in moments.

'God, yer must have been starving,' Lorraine said, grinning, as she took a sip from her spoon.

'Missed lunch. Been on that damn computer all afternoon with Jacobs. Haven't managed to find anything concrete on the Blessing Guides yet.'

'Yeah, Carter phoned, he's been poring over books to try and find what the hell that symbol carved on Manners's body means. He's found the circle and the fish. Apparently one represents Christianity and the other is a protection symbol. Early Christians used the signs together when they were being persecuted. To show where to meet and as a sign of defiance, according to Carter's research.'

Sanderson didn't say anything. Lorraine looked up at him. 'Yes, that's what I thought. Doesn't bring us anywhere closer. But doesn't it sound odd that there's a group of religious nutters up at Seven Sisters at the same time a religious symbol is carved into someone's body? And,' Lorraine added, 'their leader's name, Gottsdiener, means God's servant. Plus, this is the second time we've needed to be up at Seven Sisters this week.'

Sanderson saw what she meant. 'Richy Stansfield.'

'Richy Stansfield,' Lorraine confirmed. 'And now one of his friends, Melissa Tremaine, has gone missing. There might not be anything in it, but there's just too many coincidences for my liking. And you know what they say about coincidences in our line of work, Sanderson.'

Sanderson smiled. 'No such thing.'

'That's right. I want to go to the Seven Sisters and pay this Marcel Gottsdiener a visit.'

Sanderson nodded. 'Sounds good to me, boss. I'll bring the car round.'

When Sanderson left the office, Lorraine looked at her mobile phone. No calls. *What the hell is Luke playing at?* Lorraine picked up her mobile and scrolled down the numbers in her address book until she found Luke's. She sighed, locked her phone and put it in her bag. She shrugged her jacket on, wrapped her pink scarf twice round her neck, then went to the front entrance to wait for Sanderson.

They were passing Mrs Reardon's house and Lorraine noticed the curtains move. 'She's on guard.'

Sanderson smiled. 'If she's watching, there just might be something going on.'

He parked the car in the same spot he had used

earlier that morning, and he and Lorraine made their way over to the Seven Sisters.

'Oh my,' Lorraine said as they stepped over the rise in the field.

'Lanterns,' Sanderson said. 'She's been right all along.'

'Yeah, in this instance. Don't forget the others,' Lorraine countered, with a smile.

They saw about a dozen lights bobbing and weaving about, which then formed a circle, and a chanting noise carried to them in the still dark evening. Lorraine and Sanderson carefully moved forward up the grassy field. Lorraine had her boots on with flat heels, but it would be quite easy to break an ankle in the dark.

Just before they reached the circle of lights a man stepped in front of them. 'What do you think you're doing?' he asked, in a thick, threatening voice.

'What's it gotta do with you, like?' Lorraine demanded, giving no quarter.

Everything about the man was threatening, from the way he stood to the way he glared at them. His short, cropped hair appeared to be dark but with the absence of light it was hard to tell. He was tall and muscular with a large bulbous nose. 'You were here this morning,' he said, looking at Sanderson.

'Yeah, and . . . ?'

The circle had turned to a cluster as each bearer of light paused and looked at them. From the centre a light broke free and moved towards them.

'Step aside,' Lorraine said to the man.

'What?' he asked, amazement that this woman showed no fear of him creeping into his voice.

'You heard, Mr . . . ?'

'Strieber,' said the carrier of the lone light, as it bobbed up and down and now reached them. 'His name is Adrian Strieber.'

Lorraine took a look at the person who had spoken. He was tall and slight, with large, luminous eyes.

'And you must be Marcel Gottsdiener?'

His eyes narrowed in the glow from the lantern. 'You are well informed.'

'Detective Inspector Hunt.' Lorraine took out her identification from her jacket and showed it to him. 'What exactly are you doing here?'

'We are doing no harm, just a group of friends gathering for a spiritual meeting.'

'And is Melissa Tremaine one of your friends?'

He waved his hand in the direction of the group. 'See for yourself.'

Was that a note of sarcasm? Lorraine wondered. She'd known before she'd asked that Melissa was not present tonight. She would have stood out, but he'd used her size to evade the question.

'Is she one of your friends?'

A look of irritation covered his face as he said, 'Yes, we know Melissa, but we haven't seen her for some time.'

'Right. Exactly how long, would you say?'

'A day or two.'

'OK, where do yer live?' She waved at the caravans. 'In one of them?'

244

'No, I live in Houghton, on the Seahills.'

Say no more, Lorraine thought. *I bet yer haven't lived there very long.* 'OK, what's the address? I'd like to ask you a few questions.'

He reluctantly gave her the street and number. 'OK,' Lorraine said after Sanderson wrote it down. 'We'll be in touch tomorrow.'

They watched as Marcel turned and went back to the group of people.

'Come on, Sanderson, not much we can do here seeing as they're hardly breaking the law.'

'Fancy a drink, boss?' Sanderson asked as they walked down the hill.

Lorraine looked at the Copt Hill pub. It had always been a friendly place and she'd been in once or twice, with a few friends.

Why not, she sighed, *a glass of wine won't hurt. I might be able to sleep, get Melissa and Luke off me mind. Melissa especially. Where the hell are yer, girl?*

'OK, Sanderson. I must say though, yer will go to any lengths to keep out of the road of yer mother-in-law. Even to taking the boss out for a drink.'

'Mother-in-law or not, Lorraine, it's always a pleasure to escort you anywhere.'

'Thanks, Sanderson.' Lorraine had a theory that people like Sanderson were good for the soul, and tonight she badly needed some soul comfort.

'Let me out . . . You fucking prick!' the girl demanded, kicking the door so hard the sound reverberated around the room and through the walls to the rest of the house.

'Let me out now now *now!*' she screamed, over and over until it echoed and came back word upon word. Each scream was followed by a punch to the door. Her fist was tattooed in red ink with the letters H.A.T.E.

Her raven-black hair had been hacked short by a street hairdresser whose only qualification was he could hold a pair of shears steady enough to do the job, his payment a puff of smoke. Anger, hate and sheer frustration at her plight blazed steadily from her dark brown eyes that were ringed with red. The clothes she wore were shabby, second-hand, and so badly in need of a wash a scarecrow would have hung his head in shame. Her jeans were ripped in places the fashion designers had never intended them to be.

She was five foot four, dusky skinned, far too thin and stunningly beautiful. The right chances and she would have smiled from the covers of the best magazines around.

Selina, though, never had a chance, not one in her sixteen years, never mind the right one.

For three days she had been the captive of her estranged father. A father she had never once met, who she knew of only by name, but a father she had cursed frequently in her short life.

Her mother had died in childbirth, much the same age as she was now. Selina was born seven months after her grandmother had moved her mother down south, away from the boy who had got her daughter pregnant. Now the grandmother who had named Selina after her mother, was in the last stages of terminal cancer. She had made contact with Selina's father, who had not even known of her existence until less than a week ago.

He had come in the middle of the night, this unknown father, this figure of hate, seemingly as shocked by her existence as she was by his presence. He'd promised the grandmother that he would take Selina and do what he could to put her back on the right path.

The first item on his agenda, even though he knew it would breed even more hate in her tainted soul, was to wean her off her cocaine and dope habit.

'I'll fucking kill you . . . Bastard . . . Let me out.'

'No,' came a quiet, calm answer from behind the door, which only succeeded in enraging her more. Eyes bulging, she glared at a spot in the door where she imagined her captor's face was.

'You have no right to keep me here,' she screamed. Some of the screaming was from sheer temper. No one had ever kept her from doing what she wanted, no one had ever tried to curtail her freedom. But most of the screaming was born of a terrible craving.

Her body was shaking uncontrollably, and her insides were on fire. She needed, and her need was overwhelming.

She knew from some of her friends the effects of cold turkey and the pain that went with it, knew also that it was the only answer: methadone was a joke, they only mixed it with something else. She was frightened. Some idiots were of the idea that it took three days to come off drugs: fools, five weeks minimum. Then the fight went on, every single day, never able to fulfil the craving.

She chewed on her fists, drawing blood. Then stared at the blood for a moment before once more banging the fist on the door.

'Let me out, bastard.'

'No.'

'I hate you,' she cried.

Turning, she leaned against the door and slowly slid to the floor.

In the same position on the other side of the door, Luke sat with his head in his hands.

Friday 22 December

21

Lorraine was walking down a dark corridor towards a door that seemed to retreat further away the faster she tried to get there. She knew without a doubt that if she could only get to the door, then everything would be OK. She'd open the door and light would spill out, illuminating all the solutions to every problem she'd ever had. But she wasn't alone. Out of the corner of one eye, she could see a large figure with his face in shadow gliding a pace or so behind her, and he seemed to be ringing a large bell. Lorraine had the feeling that the large figure was Luke, but she couldn't turn her head to find out whether or not she was right. Moisture dripped from the ceiling and onto her face, and the door started to slowly open and suddenly Lorraine was terrified about what lay behind it, and all the while, the large figure behind her rang his bell. With mounting horror, Lorraine turned round only to find . . .

She woke up with a start. Duke was nudging her face with his damp nose, and the telephone beside her bed was ringing. Lorraine groaned, pushed the dog off her bed and fumbled for the phone. 'Hello,' she said into the white plastic mouthpiece as she glanced at the bedside clock. The digital display read 5:15. 'This had better be good.'

'Sergeant Delany here, Inspector. A body has been found half an hour ago at Fatfield river.'

'Shit.'

He ignored that and went on, 'It's the body of a young girl.'

'OK, I'll be right there.'

With a terrible sinking weight in her stomach, Lorraine swung her legs over the side of the bed. Quickly she dressed in jeans and blue jumper. Downstairs she shoved her feet into her boots, grabbed her jacket and scarf but just as she put her hand on the doorknob, she remembered that Sanderson had driven her home last night, and her car was still at the station. 'Damn, damn, shit and damn,' she said under her breath. She called the minicab company and promised them an extra tip if they got someone round there pronto. The driver showed up less than five minutes later, still too long for Lorraine's liking, and he took her to the station where she picked up the car and drove to Fatfield. It took Lorraine exactly eight minutes to drive to the crime scene and every one of them she spent in dread. She had a bad feeling about this.

She pulled up outside of a tent that had been erected beside the river. Quickly she jumped out of the car and ran to the tent. She lifted the flap and went in. Scottie was kneeling beside the body.

Lorraine sucked air in through her teeth. The sight was just as she had feared.

'You know her?' Scottie looked up with a puzzled frown.

She was quiet for a long moment then said, 'Yes. It's Melissa Tremaine.'

'You're positive about that?' Scottie said.

Lorraine nodded her head. 'I'm afraid so.'

'Well, that means we've got a positive ID. That makes life a little bit easier.'

Lorraine knew that Scottie really cared about his work. And if he seemed flippant, it was only a coping mechanism. God only knew how someone managed to cope with seeing damaged and brutalised bodies day in and day out, without respite. But today Scottie's tone grated a little on Lorraine. This girl, Melissa, she had tried to help. She couldn't help feeling that this was another teenager she had, in some unknown way, let down.

She went outside. She was staring at the river a few minutes later when Scottie came and stood by her side.

'Knew her well, did yer?' he asked gently.

Lorraine breathed deeply before replying. 'Not really, just this last few days. She was one of Richy Stansfield's friends. I talked to her up at the school about him, and there was something about her that I liked. Sure, she was bullish and stubborn, but I felt . . .' She shook her head. 'Then I saw her walking to school the next morning. She was going to be late, so I gave her a lift there. Her parents reported her missing yesterday . . .' She hesitated, deep in thought. 'What do you think, Scottie?' she asked, her voice low. 'Could it have been murder?'

'I don't want to say at this stage. But there's ligature marks on her wrists. I'd say this is very suspicious, but I'll have to get her back to the morgue to be 100 per cent certain. At the moment she's covered in mud so there's not a lot I can say . . . Once I've cleaned her up I'll be able to tell yer more . . . If yer come by later this morning.'

Still staring at the river she nodded, then turning, went back to the car.

It wasn't yet six o'clock, but Lorraine decided to go straight into work. She found some printouts that Jacobs had left on her desk about the Blessing Guides. She looked up from her reading as Sanderson walked in. 'Yer in early,' she said with a smile. 'Mother-in-law again?'

Sanderson smiled in response, then said, 'Same could be said about you, boss. How's yer head?' he said, referring to Lorraine's state after he had taken her home from the pub last night.

Lorraine gave him a wry glance. Then her face became serious. 'Melissa Tremaine was found this morning. She was found floating in Fatfield river.'

'Oh damn, the poor kid. Was it an accident?' Then he saw Lorraine's face. 'It wasn't suicide? Murder?'

'Scottie won't know until later, but it looks suspicious.' She studied Sanderson's face for a moment, then said, 'I can't help but feel we . . . I . . . could have prevented it . . . That day in the car,' she shook her head, 'I, er, I think she was trying to tell me something. She said . . .' Lorraine thought for a moment, making sure she had it right. 'She said she had some new friends but she didn't like them. At the time I thought it a very strange thing to say.'

Sanderson frowned and nodded. 'Can't fathom that one, but yer know what kids are like, always talking in circles. Sometimes I think they can barely understand themselves.'

Lorraine, in an attempt to change the subject, said, 'Have yer read this?'

He shook his head. 'What is it?'

'Sara Jacobs pulled some information off the web. Seems like the Blessing Guides are mentioned in a discussion board that some parents have set up about their children being sucked into a cult-like group. Marcel Gottsdiener is all over these reports. He's their charismatic leader or brainwashing pervert, depending on what you read.'

'Hmm.' Sanderson picked the pages up and Lorraine went on. 'According to these printouts, the group targets kids that are unhappy or in some way damaged. They become like an extended family to these poor teenagers, offer them love and acceptance, and by the time the group is coming to the notice of the authorities, they're off again, taking their children with them. And not just England, they've been in Germany . . . France, where Gottsdiener himself was questioned regarding the deaths of two teenage boys. They couldn't make anything stick though. '

'No.'

'This is what we know.' Lorraine started ticking off points on her fingers. 'Melissa Tremaine was, according to Marcel Gottsdiener, a "friend" of the group. She is now dead. Richy Stansfield, who we know was a friend of Melissa's, was found dead at the Seven Sisters, where the group seems to be holding their meetings. Look at Richy and Melissa's friends: Kurt Allendale and Rachel Henderson's headmistress suspects them of being abused at home. Niall Campbell is either a drug addict or has an eating disorder – I met him the other night, he's terribly skinny. And Melissa overate to overcome whatever was troubling her. All, except for Richy, could be seen to be at risk.'

Lorraine and Sanderson looked at each other.

'I say that we need to call on the Blessing Guides again, boss.'

Lorraine nodded. 'I agree with you. But I'd like to go armed with a bit more information first. I want you and Jacobs to research them more, perhaps email some of the parents on the discussion boards, see if you find out anything relevant from them. But be careful. We don't want to scare them off.'

'Right boss.' Sanderson stood up. 'I'll make a copy of these.' He held the pile of papers in the air.

'Good. I've got some phone calls to make, then I'm going back to the morgue. See if Scottie's found anything.'

'Oh, by the way.' Sanderson stopped at the doorway. 'How's the dog?'

'How's the dog?' Lorraine repeated scornfully, 'I'll tell yer how he is . . . He's a better bloody actor than Lassie, that's how he is . . . He's got them two wrapped round his paws.'

Sanderson laughed and left her office.

Lorraine sat at her desk for a moment, postponing for just a second the moment when she'd have to go and tell Melissa's parents that their daughter was dead. It never got any easier.

As she stood up to leave, the phone on her desk rang, and she picked up the receiver on the second ring. 'Detective Inspector Hunt.'

'Boss, it's me, Luke.'

Lorraine sat back in her chair. After days of not hearing from him, his voice unexpectedly gave her a shock. 'Where have yer been?' she demanded, far more harshly than she'd intended.

'Sorry. I know I've let you down. Look, I need another day. I'll come in tomorrow and I promise I'll tell yer everything.'

'Not good enough, Luke.'

'It's personal, boss, yer know I wouldn't take the time off if it wasn't important. And I just don't want to tell yer over the phone.'

Lorraine drummed her fingers on her desk. Luke never took time off, so she knew it had to be important. She just wished she knew what it was. This uncertainty made her act like a bitch. What she would give for a cigarette, right now. She sighed then said, if a little stiffly, 'Yer OK . . . Take all the time yer need.'

There was silence on the line for nearly a minute, then Luke said, 'See yer tomorrow, boss,' and hung up.

'Damn.' She felt like throwing the mobile across the room.

Not for the first time she wished she'd thought before she'd acted.

Damn.

Anyhow, what was so wrong that he can't tell me over the phone?

She sat still for a moment, and then stood up slowly. It was time to speak to the Tremaines.

Lorraine knocked on the Tremaines' door. She was dreading it opening.

They'll know by my face. They always do.

Do you have some sort of sixth sense when it comes to yer children?

Or is it just simply the lack of a smile?

Lorraine was just about to knock again, when she heard footsteps on the stairs. The door opened, and she was facing Mrs Tremaine, her delicate face red with tears. This never got any easier.

Taking a deep, silent breath, Lorraine said, 'May I come in, Mrs Tremaine?'

The woman stepped back, never once taking her eyes off Lorraine. She swallowed hard and Lorraine saw her throat muscles move. Her eyes, once a pretty hazel colour, were almost black with pain.

'You've found her, haven't you?' It was said in a quiet, polite whisper.

Lorraine gave a silent nod as she closed the door behind her.

Lorraine spent about an hour with the Tremaines, holding Mrs Tremaine's hand while she sobbed and telling both the parents that, even though she had hardly known their daughter, she had liked her very much. It was the hardest part of her job, and by the time she arrived at the morgue, she was already drained of energy.

Edna was at her usual post and Scottie had Melissa's body laid out on the table. There was no trace of the mud that had covered her like a second skin, and her hair looked like it had been freshly shampooed. Lorraine was struck again by how beautiful Melissa had been. How much more beautiful she could have been if it hadn't been for her enormous bulk. But this was just a body. The spark that had given Melissa that special something had disappeared.

'Just been round to the Tremaines',' Lorraine said.

Scottie looked up at her with concern in his face.

'They're devastated, of course. But they want to see the body. Edna, I told them to call yer, to arrange a time.'

Edna nodded her head.

'So, Scottie,' Lorraine said, looking at the body in front of her. 'Anything?'

'Quite a lot,' Scottie answered. 'First, I'm certain beyond any doubt that she was murdered, but whoever did it tried to make it look like suicide. But they did a really bad job. Can't have helped them that it looks like she fought like a she-devil, the poor kid. Look,' he pointed to the ligature marks around her wrists and ankles, then at dark bruising on her shoulders and arms. 'The bruising has developed over a period of about twelve to twenty-four hours. Looks like she was hit from above with something long and heavy – I would say a baseball bat, but it could be anything similar. And I would say that she was tied up with plastic ties with her hands behind her back for about that long too. The cuts are really deep, and look as if they've been reopened – as if she struggled to get them off her, then didn't, then tried again.' Scottie turned Melissa's body over.

'She's been hit on the back of the head.' He pointed to a large bump that could easily be seen. 'Which must have knocked her out, because it's so heavy it actually put a dent in her skull. Again, I think it was something with a similar heft to a baseball bat. It would have knocked her out immediately, and after that she wouldn't have had a chance.'

Through all of this Lorraine was staring at Melissa's face. She looked peaceful, untroubled; you would never think she'd been in the water for God knows how long. She shivered as she turned back to Scottie.

'So, she was tied up somewhere for a period of time, and hit with something like a baseball bat, not hard enough to break bones.' Lorraine met Scottie's eyes. He looked more serious than he had for ages. 'Then she was transported to the river somehow, I'm thinking back of a van or perhaps in the boot of a car, hit on the back of the head again and thrown in the river. It's so damn cold she won't have survived long. She hasn't been in the river for long, has she, Scottie? Perhaps two to three hours. The scavengers haven't had a chance to get to her yet.'

'Why would someone want to keep that poor girl tied up for all that time?' Edna said.

'I hate to think,' Lorraine said, but really her mind was turning over fast. Melissa was abducted, then taken somewhere, tortured so that she'd tell whichever bastard did this to her what she knew, then dumped off a bridge.

'And look at this.' Scottie pulled a test tube from the rack. It had four or five slender black threads in it. 'These are the same fibres under her nails that were under Richard Stansfield's. I've taken a look under the microscope and it's a definite match.'

Lorraine took the test tube from his hands and looked at it. She thought for a moment. 'So what do you think now about Richy Stansfield. Still suicide?'

Scottie shook his head. 'I think there's more to his death than his body is revealing. You were right, Lorraine.'

'Does this make sense to you, Scottie? Richard was somehow transported to the Seven Sisters in, say, the boot of a car. Once there, he was strung up – quite literally – and that's when he tried to get the rope off his neck.'

'That could work.' Scottie agreed. 'Do yer have any idea who could have done it?'

Lorraine nodded her head. 'A fair one.'

'There's one other thing.'

Lorraine allowed herself a small smile. Scottie loved to dramatise, especially if he thought he had found something.

He moved to the bench and opened a small drawer. He came back and held out his hand. Inside a small plastic bag was something that looked like a coin. 'Go on, yer can open it, the river's washed it clean. It

261

was in the pocket of her jeans, which were a tight fit. That's why it didn't get lost in the river.'

Lorraine opened the bag, took the coin out and gasped. She turned it over in her fingers. Embossed on both sides was a circle with a fish. Scottie liked to leave the best for last.

22

'Yer don't have to go, son. We're not that bloody hard up for Christ's sake. I've got me stamps I've been saving all year, at least we'll have a nice fat chicken. Yer know I don't care that much for turkey, and the bairn's got plenty presents to open.'

Jacko shook his head. 'Yer know she hasn't, mam. Half a dozen paltry little knickknacks don't make a good Christmas.'

'Two of them paltry little knick-knacks cost twenty quid each, son, and one cost fifty, which yer will be paying for until next bloody Christmas. And bloody hell, it's not as if the bairn demands anything. Yer know the little angel's always happy with what she gets.'

'Aye, but half the kids in her class have mobile phones, portable tellies, videos . . . you name it.'

'Aye, and some of them have a hell of a lot less than our Melanie does because their fathers are either out pissing it up the wall or shoving it in their arms . . . Anyhow, none of them have you, Jacko. Only our Melanie's got you. Some bairns are blessed in different ways, and some poor bairns have a rough road of it all right. From the day they're born till the day they die.' Doris sighed deeply. 'Anyhow, yer never know, I might win at the bingo yet, then we'll have a hell of a Christmas.'

Jacko laughed hollowly. 'Yeah, and pigs might fly. But if I do one more trip, just one more, it'll make a big difference.'

'It's up to you, son, but I don't want yer wasting money on me and Christina's not a greedy girl. And what if yer got caught? What would happen to us then, Jacko? We need you here.'

Jacko was staring out the window. What Doris had said had not put him off. In fact, it had just made him more determined to go. He didn't want to, he hated being away from home even for a short time, and he was nervous as hell in case he lost his dole money. But all of that paled beside the thought of what he could buy for them with the money he made from the trip.

Plus he'd already told Danny he was going.

Oh to hell with it, nothing risked, nothing gained.

He walked into the hallway and put his coat on. He already had an extra jumper on, ''Cos by God it's bloody freezing out there,' he muttered to no one in particular, and judging by the state of the grass the frost hadn't lifted at all yet.

Just then Danny pulled up and beeped his horn.

'Right, I'll see yer when I get back. And make sure yer behave yerself, Doris.'

'I'll Doris yer,' he heard her grumbling behind him as he closed the door. When he got in the van he spotted her at the window. He gave her a wave, and smiling she waved back, then stuck her middle finger up at Danny.

264

'No change there I see,' he laughed as he pulled away.

A few minutes later they were parked outside Len's house. Danny and Jacko watched as he did his usual double-check, then came to the gate and looked up and down the street twice.

'For God's sake,' Danny muttered, feeling like he wanted to bang his head on the steering wheel. 'Don't fucking well say he's adding that to his routine.'

'Looks like it, mate.' Jacko grinned as he moved along so Len could get his usual seat.

'That wind's raw out there,' Len said, giving an exaggerated shiver as he climbed into the van.

'Well, there's no wind in here,' Danny assured him.

'Only when you open the window so yer can have a fag,' Len retorted.

'Yeah, OK.'

They stopped outside Adam's house. He said something to one of his sisters, who merely looked him up and down before walking away, then he jumped into the van and practically yelled, 'Yo guys.'

'Been watching them old Rocky films again?' Len said scornfully.

'Here's a good one for yer . . . What goes "oooooo"?'

Len groaned and turned his face to the window. He had more on his mind than this moron's stupid jokes.

Jacko and Danny waited. They knew it wouldn't be long before Len demanded the punchline.

And, true to form, a moment later Len snapped, 'Well come on then, get on with it, yer git stupid idiot, what goes "oooooo"?'

'A cow with no lips.'

Jacko laughed, and Len glowered at him. 'It wasn't that funny.'

'Why, aye it was, man,' Jacko answered.

Danny drove the few metres to Brian's place, who was, unusually for him, waiting outside his house.

'Move yer fucking legs,' Brian snarled at Adam as he got in.

Danny frowned. Watching through his rear-view mirror, he caught Jacko looking at him and raised his eyebrows in a question. Jacko shrugged, then looked out the window and thought, *Perhaps Brian doesn't want to be here either.*

At the first service stop, Danny pulled up Len as he walked back from the toilets. 'What the fuck's the matter? Yer've had a face like a slapped arse all the way down.'

Len looked at his cousin, then after a long moment, said, 'There's no need for that sort of language.'

'Fuck that, yer not getting out of it that bloody easy. Now what the fuck's the matter with yer, eh? Come on, yer can tell me.'

Len sucked his teeth for a second before saying, 'It's our Carol, man. She didn't come home again last night.'

Danny sighed. 'Well, yer know Len, she is nearly bloody twenty years old.'

'Yer don't understand, she's been doing it a lot lately. She won't tell me anything . . . It's not right. A daughter should respect her father. Honour thy father and thy mother, that's what it says in the Bible.'

Danny rubbed his chin. 'Don't think I can help yer with this one mate, yer know how stubborn she is, chip off the old block there all right . . . If she doesn't want to tell yer anything.' He shrugged.

'But it's not right.'

'I don't think the kids of today's ideas of what's not right quite match up to ours . . . Too many rights these days, that's yer bloody do-gooders for yer, they all think they can do what they bloody well want . . . Do you, er, she might be . . . Well, yer know?'

'Yer know what?'

'Like er . . .'

A moment later Len exploded, 'Yer mean pregnant?' He was outraged, as if his little girl would ever. 'Why would she be out all night if she was pregnant?'

'Well, drugs then.'

'*Drugs*.' That was, if possible, even more shocking.

Danny patted Len's back and guided him towards the café. 'Whatever it is, Len, I'm certain it'll sort itself out. Yer probably worrying for nowt . . . She's not a little girl, yer know.'

'I know that but it's worrying, especially since that lad was found at the Seven Sisters . . . And there's rumours going around that he was murdered.'

'Come on, man, if anybody tried to do anything to our Carol, she'll sharp sort them out. Give her some space, will yer? And I thought you never took any notice of rumours.'

Len tutted, before asking, 'Will you have a word with her?'

Danny knew he was gonna regret this, but

anything to get him moving and lighten his mood; the whole lot of them seemed pretty edgy today for some reason. Why Brian should suddenly decide to sit at the back was a puzzle an' all. Only Adam seemed to be his normal, cheeky self.

'Aye, I'll have a word. Does that make yer feel better.'

Len nodded.

'Good.'

What the fuck I'm gonna say to a lass nearly twenty years old, I don't fucking well know, he thought as they reached the others who had ordered McDonald's and were sitting with their food at the restaurant table. They sat down just as the door opened and four men who, unknown to them, had been following them in a black car walked in.

23

Lorraine had a lot to think about after seeing Scottie at the morgue. She picked up Sanderson from the station and now they were at the Seahills, pulling up outside the address Marcel had given her this morning. Lorraine had to practically push past the hedge to get down the path.

'Must never have heard of shears,' Sanderson muttered, as Lorraine knocked on the dark green door, and he picked a couple of stray leaves off the back of Lorraine's brown jacket.

A moment later it was opened by Marcel. 'Detective Inspector,' he said. 'And Sergeant.'

He smiled at them, but Lorraine wasn't convinced. There was something disconcerting about him, something in the way that he held her gaze without blinking, something in his smug, supercilious smile that made her feel more than uneasy. Perhaps, having read about him on the discussion boards, she had become biased by the sad stories parents of lost children had to tell, or maybe her instincts were right. She didn't like this man. Not at all. Without waiting to be invited she stepped over the threshold, with Sanderson close behind.

In what Lorraine took to be the sitting room, a

young girl with a port-wine teardrop mark on her left cheek smiled up at them from the black leather settee. She was small and dainty, with a pretty smile that dimpled her cheeks. She looked very young. Lorraine took in the rest of the furnishings. A black full-length dining table was surrounded by matching black leather seats. In the centre of a table was a huge black vase filled with blood-red roses. Nothing in the room looked cheap. The floor was dark wood, and the bare walls were painted white. The Virgin Mary smiled down from a huge picture above the mantelpiece.

'This is Mary, my wife.' Marcel introduced the girl.

'Hello.' Mary smiled again. Lorraine couldn't help thinking that she looked rather vague and very young. Mary asked, 'Could I get you something. Tea, coffee?'

'No thank you,' Lorraine said as Sanderson smiled down at her and shook his head.

'So, what can I do for you?' asked Marcel, an edge still in his voice.

'You can start by telling me more about the Blessing Guides cult.'

Go boss, Sanderson thought, *straight for the jugular*, as he watched Marcel's face.

'You have been misinformed. We are not a cult . . . We are only a group of people who like the same things and worship in our own way, and not the predictable way of the established church.'

How fucking sanctimonious does he sound? she thought, but said, 'Tell me what happened, then, in France and Germany.'

'What do you mean?'

'Well, according to my research, a group of very irate parents sent you packing in Germany, and the heat followed yer all the way to France, where there were . . . how many suicides, Sanderson?' Lorraine, of course, knew exactly how many deaths there had been in France.

'Two, boss. Two young men, both associated with the cult.' Marcel swung his head to Sanderson, eyes blazing.

'We were absolved of any blame,' he said turning back to Lorraine. 'Two teenagers racing each other on motorbikes? How could it have been our fault?'

'Might have something to do with the fact that the same two teenagers were members of your cult.'

'We are not . . .'

'Yeah I know,' Lorraine cut him short. 'Let's just say they, er, knocked around with yer, eh, 'cos it certainly looks like yer like knocking around with kids.'

Marcel was decidedly irritated now. 'Yes,' he snapped. 'They had visited with us once or twice, but I'm afraid we were rather tame for them, and, if you don't mind, I went through all of this in great detail with the French police.'

They all turned their heads as a door somewhere in the house banged and a moment later a young girl entered the room. Lorraine noticed the burn scars on the side of her face even though her hair was hanging forward over it. She was very small and dainty and Lorraine couldn't help but notice her resemblance to Mary.

She turned back to Marcel, studied him silently for

271

a moment, then said without preamble, 'Melissa Tremaine was murdered.'

She watched his face, but he remained impassive.

'Poor Melissa,' Marcel said. 'She was such a lovely girl. I do hope you find whoever did this.' He seemed to have regained his composure.

My God, he's good. But them two aren't, she thought. She looked at the girls now, and both of them were very, very pale. She was sure that the younger-looking one of the two seemed as if she was about to cry.

She swung her head back to Marcel. 'She went missing night before last. Do you have any idea where she could have gone?'

'Sorry,' he said. 'Like I said to you last night, we last saw her a couple of days ago.'

'What do you know of a Jason Manners?'

'Now you have me, officer, never heard of him.' He spread his hands wide. 'We have a lot come for a night or two, when they find out we're just plain homely people . . .' He shrugged.

'Well, he was murdered,' Lorraine interrupted. 'While he was alive some sadistic brute carved this on his side.' She took out the coin.

'And?'

'And, it's funny, isn't it, that the very first time we see this symbol, which we know has to do with the ancient Christian church, it's carved into the flesh of some poor bugger. And the second time we see it, it's in the pocket of a poor, murdered girl.' Lorraine watched Marcel closely. He was sitting still, the muscles in his jaw working. 'I don't believe in coincidences. And I think that you – or someone in your cult – knows more about this than they're saying.' She stood up to leave. 'I wouldn't leave the Seahills, if I were you.'

A few minutes later Lorraine and Sanderson discussed their feelings, hunches and guesses in the car, then Sanderson pointed out something Lorraine had missed.

'Did yer see the ring on Mary's finger?'

Lorraine frowned and shook her head.

'I'd swear to God it's the one that was stolen from Mrs Reardon's.'

'But yer don't know that for sure, do yer, Sanderson?' Lorraine replied. 'If yer don't know that for sure, we can't go in with all guns blazing over a ring. He's a slimy fish this one, if yer'll pardon the pun.' Lorraine was rolling the coin around her fingers. 'That's why we have to be careful, and gather plenty of evidence before we pounce. Obviously the French police, as good as they are, couldn't pin anything on him, that's why he's still walking free. I need to talk to whoever it was in France and Germany meself, get the true gist of things . . . Also,' she looked at Sanderson and nodded her head, 'he's arrogant, very, very arrogant. Thinks he can't fall from grace, but he'll trip, bet yer life on it, and when he does I'll be there to pick the bastard up by the scruff of his neck.'

Aware that Lorraine was using him as a sounding board, Sanderson sat quietly while she seemed to be thinking.

Lorraine could see Melissa's face in her mind's eye, hear her last sentence as she got out of the car. *The kid was crying for help and I missed it.* She felt a lump in her throat as she pictured Melissa's face on the morgue table. *She was so young, she had everything to live for. God, why couldn't I have seen it before it was too late?*

She turned to Sanderson, who was nearly breaking his neck in an attempt to keep his cigarette out of the window. 'I want this bastard, Sanderson. So we go softly, very softly, we make sure that the barb is so tightly entwined in this fish's mouth that he'll never be able to wriggle off the hook.'

Sanderson nodded again, took a puff from his cigarette and said, 'Why don't they see it, these people who get involved in such things? Ninety-nine per cent of the time there's no religion in it, no true Christianity. It's just power, control and manipulation. People like Marcel would gladly tear people's lives apart.'

'Vulnerability, Sanderson, that's what it's all about. Kids with exaggerated ideas, overblown imaginations. Kids that have never fitted in, people that were never wanted anywhere else . . . These clever bastards suck them in. And sometimes, I suppose, yer ordinary regular kid, who for no reason other than a bit of excitement or for a dare, gets reeled in, wakes up one morning and finds out it's too late.'

Sanderson thought for a minute. 'Were those caravans there when Richard Stansfield was found?'

'No, I already checked.' She was watching the

smoke blow quickly away from Sanderson's cigarette in the wind. She sighed. Sometimes life was like a puff of smoke.

24

'Get upstairs, you, and send Rachel down. I want her now.' Mary hung her head as Marcel glared at her. She felt embarrassed that he should talk to her like this in front of Louise, who was looking anxiously from one to the other.

'Now,' he said again, this time more threateningly. Mary jumped.

Quickly she ran upstairs to the room that Rachel slept in. Her hand was shaking as she knocked quietly on the door and opened it. Rachel was lying fully clothed on the bed staring at the ceiling.

'Rachel . . . Rachel,' Mary said urgently. Rachel turned her head and looked at Mary.

'Marcel wants you, now. You have to go now. Please, hurry.'

'OK,' Rachel smiled at her and Mary felt a twinge of jealousy. Rachel was pretty and Mary was certain Marcel was sleeping alone with her. *After all, he used to with me*.

Mary walked over to the window and looked out of it. She heard the door close softly behind Rachel and now that she was alone she let the tears fall.

She'd been terrified when that policewoman was questioning Marcel. She knew it would put him in a bad mood, that he would take it out on her, that he would be downstairs now, controlling himself with Louise and Rachel, but once they were alone, she knew what was going to happen to her.

Why was I so stupid to become involved in the first place? Please God, help me find a way out, please.

She looked down into the empty street, and almost laughed.

God! God would have nothing to do with the likes of her, a fallen Catholic worshipping a false prophet.

And prophet he thought he was. Joseph, reincarnated in time for the Second Coming. He taught that Mary, that is, the first Virgin Mary, was impregnated with God's divine seed, but instead of it coming down in a shower of light, God sought out one holy man, the only man who deserved to be blessed in this way, Joseph, and gave him the divine seed. Marcel said that he had a vision, where God told him that he was Joseph incarnate, and he had to form a new church, and find a Mary, so that she could give birth to the Second Coming of Jesus, and the three of them would form a holy trinity on earth. *Unless I prove pregnant before tomorrow night, there will be another Mary.*

But what will become of me?

That first Mary charmed me into the Blessing Guides in much the same way that I was ordered to charm Louise.

What happened to her when she failed to become pregnant? Will the same happen to me?

Did she just leave?

Mary hoped so. Mary hoped that she was living

happily, somewhere else, somewhere warm. Perhaps she had a boyfriend? That would be nice, Mary smiled to herself, to find someone who loved you and only you. Who you didn't have to share.

But Mary doubted that the first Mary would have had that sort of luck. Marcel wasn't the type to let anyone go, and his brother was there to make sure they didn't escape, run away, or talk to the police. Anyway, everyone was implicated in the Blessing Guides; they were all guilty of something. Though most of them followed Marcel willingly and would walk through glass if he told them. And if you decided enough was enough . . . Mary shivered as she thought of Jason Manners.

No one had really liked Jason. He was rude, didn't wash, and there were rumours that he was into drugs. No one was sure why he was in the Blessing Guides, but for a time, Jason and Marcel had been close. But then came more rumours. Mary knew these to be true. Jason had been creaming off Marcel and using the money to buy crack. When Jason didn't appear for days, Mary assumed that he had run away. But Mary had assumed wrong.

Late one night, they had all been summoned to a ceremony. Most were blurry-eyed from sleep, but all were scared, not so much of Marcel as of his brother, Adrian. Jason Manners had been tied to a chair in the centre of the room, stripped to the waist. It was very late at night. Mary could remember the stink of alcohol that came off the terrified man. Marcel stood behind him. He put his hand on his shoulder and spoke to the group, not in his usual honeyed tones, but in a stern, commanding voice. 'All of you, you know what it is to be blessed.' He looked around the group; everyone was silent. 'You all know what it is to be loved, to have love in your hearts. You know that this is a community, and all communities have needs. All communities have rules.' He placed his other hand on Jason's shoulder, so that it looked like he was holding the man down. 'But this man, this viper who we have brought into the nest, is not like us. He does not have love in his heart. And he is not loved. But he is going to be blessed.' Adrian walked through the circle, a large knife at his side. 'We will mark him with our mark so that he can understand what it is to be a Blessing Guide, he can understand what it is to betray us. And he will walk alone, in shame, for the rest of his days.' And then Adrian started to cut into Jason Manners's flesh. His screams were horrible, and by the end, he had passed out with the pain.

After his brother had finished Marcel turned to the group. 'Make no mistake,' he said gravely, 'the same punishment will be visited on any of you who decide to betray us, betray me. Let this be a warning to you all.'

Mary didn't know what had happened to Jason. Not until today. She didn't know he had died. That was terrible. She bit her knuckles. But not as terrible as Richy Stansfield. He hadn't done anything wrong. All he had done was to try and stand up to Marcel. She had been there when Richard had come in to talk to Marcel, obviously scared, but also defiant. She had watched while Adrian had stalked up to him and wrestled him to the floor. She had stood at the doorway while Adrian pushed the still-struggling Richard into the boot of the car. And then the next thing she knew was that he had been found hanging from a tree up at the Seven Sisters. He had defied Marcel; he had paid the price. And now Melissa had too.

Mary felt so sick that every fibre of her body ached. She sighed, and wiped away tears. She was an accomplice to murder, had been more than once. There was no way out, and Marcel knew it.

Home, home was a place far away, in time as well as miles, the edges of Dartmoor, a cottage she'd shared with her mother and grandparents. And because she couldn't have her own way over a stupid bloody party, she'd slapped her grandmother for interfering.

Too frightened to go home, too ashamed to go home, she'd walked right into the arms of Marcel.

At first it had been good, much the same as it was for Rachel and Louise . . . *And that other Mary, the first Mary, must have been as miserable as I am now.*

Had she guessed what was going to happen to her?

She shuddered again, remembering Marcel's hand on her head. Over and over he would say, 'Suffer the little children to come unto me, suffer the little children to come unto me.'

'Help me, somebody,' she cried softly to the gathering dusk, as tears coursed down her cheeks. 'Please.'

*

In the communal room, the one that had been sound-proofed, the one Lorraine and Sanderson had not seen, Marcel, Rachel and Louise sat cross-legged on the floor. Marcel held each of their hands, and the girls gazed at him with utter adoration. He was their God, their Joseph, their Blessing Guide. Like Mary before them, and the Mary before her, they would each do anything he asked, and more.

He was explaining what their roles would be on Christmas Eve and they both listened with rapt attention.

He brought Louise's hand to his lips and slowly, looking deeply into her eyes, kissed it. Then he did the same with Rachel's.

'Rachel, you are to be the handmaiden. You will care for my wife at all times and you have a very important role in the purification ceremony. It is the handmaiden's job, among other things, to anoint the nine entries to the body with special oils, thus sealing them from dark entry.'

He turned back to Louise. 'Louise, soon you will take the name of Mary, soon you will be my bride.'

Louise felt her heart swell with pride. If only she could tell her dad. But Marcel had forbidden it. Marcel had told her that her father couldn't – wouldn't understand. She had told him about her father's drinking, and Marcel had nodded wisely, as if he had already guessed. He had then told her that her father wasn't worthy, he didn't deserved his daughter, he didn't even deserve to know his daughter was happy.

Never mind. She gazed lovingly into Marcel's eyes.

He was so different from other adults, so under-standing, so kind to allow the kids off the street into his home, to listen to their problems, to help them however he could and even offer a home to a special few, his chosen ones, the ones whose light shone the brightest.

Home. Tonight would be her last night at home. She gasped at the enormity of it all. Dad had been better lately, he might even miss her a little. But he would understand, everybody has to grow up and leave home at some time . . . She would leave a note in the morning.

But what if that upsets Marcel?

Luke was sitting outside the hospital waiting to pick Carter up. He was bone tired and practically falling asleep when Carter tapped on the window.

'Thanks, mate,' Carter said, grinning as he climbed into the car.

'No bother. Are yer all right now?'

'Aye, right as rain and as hungry as a starved dog.'

'Fish and chips at Roker?'

'Great.'

Twenty minutes later, having caught an almost empty fish shop on the way over, and with the Eagles' 'Desperado' playing softly on the CD, they were sitting on the seafront watching the most spectacular waves crash against the pier.

'So it sounds like big trouble yer've got, man,' Carter said.

'You bet.'

'So who's with her now?'

'I left her alone. She's asleep at last, I think. And I locked the door, secured the windows and she can't get out.'

Luke finished eating, rolled his paper into a ball, wound the window down and threw it into the bin, ten yards away.

'Good shot, mate.' Carter tried the same shot and missed, 'Bloody hell.' He got out of the car, picked the rubbish up and deposited it in the bin.

'So,' he went on, pulling his coat tighter around him when he got back in. 'Bloody freezing innit . . .'

'Aye.' Luke sighed.

'So,' Carter started again. 'How did they find yer, after all this time, like?'

'Social Services. A phone call right out of the blue, man, let me tell you, it was like a punch in the gut. Apparently her grandmother knowing she was dying had told a neighbour about me, seems she's still got contacts up here. The neighbour told the police, the police informed Social Services, so on and so on.'

'And yer never knew.' Carter's jaw hung open in amazement. 'All this time yer had yerself a daughter and yer never knew anything about her.'

Luke shook his head, and sighed deeper this time. 'We used to come down here, when we were fifteen, sixteen . . .' He broke off for a moment, thinking back, before saying, 'When I went to collect her I got the shock of me life, she's the spitting image of her mother, the absolute spitting double, only darker. Her grandmother had just died, and she was sitting in this room all by herself. She looked so lost, so lonely.'

283

Luke looked at Carter, 'And then she opened her mouth.'

'Oh.'

'Yeah, she's wild, man. And I mean really wild . . . Been living on the streets with God only knows what, until she was picked up for shoplifting . . . They showed me her file. Drugs, prostitution, you name it.'

Carter could hear the pain in Luke's voice. 'Well, maybe she had no choice, yer know, she did what she had to do . . . Nothing's cut and dried these days, mate.'

Luke nodded. 'Yer right, but she's gonna get the chance now all right, as soon as I get her cleaned up. It's been hell these last few nights . . . She doesn't want to be here, wants to go back where she comes from, so she's assured me more than once.'

'What's the boss say?'

Luke dry-washed his face with tired hands, then went on, 'I haven't told her.'

'Shit.'

'Yeah, I know I should have told her from the beginning. Now when I do tell her she'll probably go ape shit . . . Because it's worse than that.'

Carter looked dumbfounded, then flinched as a particularly large seagull screeched and flapped close to the window. He turned back to Luke. 'How on earth can it be worse than that?'

'Because finally, after all this flaming time, we had, well, a sort of date. It didn't start off that way, but we really talked. I don't think I've ever felt so close to her before.'

'Well, that's great. About time too.'

284

'And then, an hour before I was to leave for work the next day, all ready to ask her out properly, I got the phone call and went haring off to Doncaster.'

'She'll probably boil yer head in oil, or tar and feather yer. Remember, she's a black belt in karate.'

'Thanks, Carter.'

'I need yer to look in the missing persons register, Jacobs. Yer looking for a small petite female with a port-wine tear mark on the bottom of her left cheek. She uses the name Mary, but that could be an alias. Don't put it in the search unless yer have to, it could lead us up a blind alley.'

'OK boss . . . How far back?'

'Hmm . . .' Lorraine thought for a moment. 'Go back five years; this creep likes them small and young.'

'OK.' Jacobs left and Lorraine looked in her drawer, then half-heartedly moved stuff about, knowing full well that there were no more pencils left: she must have gone through hundreds in the last few months.

Well, no one said it was gonna be easy.

She puffed out her cheeks, warm air wafted up and disturbed her fringe.

Then sitting back she made a steeple with her fingers. She was nearly convinced that the Blessing Guide cult was at the bottom of everything. The problem was connecting it all together, gathering concrete evidence and making it stick. And with two of her best men down, that was gonna be hard to do.

285

Thank God Sanderson was around. He had proved himself invaluable over the past few days.

She bit her fingernails as she stared at the mound of paperwork slowly mounting up. 'Friggin' hell,' she muttered.

Standing, she quickly shovelled most of it into a briefcase. She would take it home, get through as much as she possibly could, have a good long soak and an early night. God knows, she fairly needed it.

Reaching for her jacket, she hesitated and ran her hand down the sleeve.

Luke's coat usually hangs next to this.

Oh for God's sake. She snatched the jacket off the hook. *I'm behaving like a love-struck teenager now.*

Must find some time to get a new coat. Could drop a hint to the Hippy or the Rock Chick, seeing as their pet, the great Duke, ruined mine.

She switched off the light and headed down the corridor. She could hear people talking in two of the rooms as she passed. A third door opened and a young Asian WPC, came into the corridor. She smiled, said hello, and Lorraine returned the greeting.

Reaching her car she flung the briefcase onto the back seat, then headed for home.

'Oh my God, will yer look at that.' Lorraine parked on the drive and sat for a moment staring at her mother's house. Peggy, hanging brightly coloured lights around the third window spotted her and waved, then turned her head and looked inwards.

Obviously telling her best friend I'm home.

286

25

Jacko was in the driving seat as they pulled into the old seaport of Dover. It was twenty minutes to eleven and traffic was heavy, as it usually was, all heading for the Continent.

But at least everything's moving, Jacko thought, nodding to himself, just as a motorbike came roaring up beside him and nearly mounted the pavement, rattling Jacko's already frayed nerves.

'Fucking hell, yer fat twat,' Jacko growled, his heart throbbing somewhere in the region of the roof.

'Think they own the road, them bastards, one law for them and a different one for the rest of us.' Danny nodded, as he calculated in his head roughly how long it would take them to reach the actual port.

'Forty minutes, tops,' he muttered to no one in particular.

Terrible trip down though, he thought, stealing one more glance into the glove compartment. *Traffic jams all the way, and that crash outside of Coventry, oh man, two lorries, a bus and four cars, all rushing around in the pouring rain as if there was no tomorrow. Well some folk wouldn't be home for Christmas, not out of all that tangled mess, and that's a fact.*

Adam woke up from a doze, yawned, stretched then cracked his knuckles. Len scowled at him.

Adam grinned. 'Think yerself lucky, mate. I usually fart when I wake up.'

Len groaned then looked towards heaven, as if praying for a thunderbolt to wipe Adam off the face of the earth.

'Anyhow, what do yer think of this one? A man walks into his mate's fancy-dress party wearing normal clothes and his girlfriend on his back. "What have yer come as?"' asked the puzzled host. "I'm a tortoise," says the bloke. "This," he points to his girlfriend, "is Michelle."'

Danny laughed while the others apart from Len groaned.

'Ahh,' Adam said, looking at Len who for once had a ghost of a smile playing around his thin lips. 'Don't try too fucking hard, man, it's gonna hurt.'

Catching Danny's eye, Len shrugged, then turned back to the window; the rare smile had melted as quickly as it had come.

As they approached the port, the black car was four cars away. It was very dark as the van crossed over the border between France and Belgium, but Brian had excellent night vision which was one of the reasons he mostly drove in the dark.

'Fucking hell,' he said. 'Did yer see him?'

'Who?' Danny and Jacko echoed, while both Len and Adam strained to see out of the back window.

'That fucking guard. He was at least eight foot tall and his gun was as big as him.'

'He wasn't,' Adam said, disbelief in his voice.

'That's a slight exaggeration,' Len said.

'Did you see him?' Brian demanded.

They all kept quiet. No one had seen the guard except Brian. Then Danny said, 'Are yer absolutely certain he had a gun?'

'I'm fucking well telling yer . . . It was huge, nearly as big as he was.'

'Oh, never seen any of them with a gun before.' Len sounded nervous. 'We've come over this border a few times and I've never seen a guard there yet.'

'It'll be nowt, man,' Danny said, squinting into the make-up mirror on the sun flap. 'It's probably because it's dark. He might be there to stop refugees or something.'

'Bet yer anything yer like he knows what we're here for,' Jacko said as two white vans overtook them. 'I knew we shouldn't have come for baccy. Yer never bother any other time. We're all gonna end up in the nick for Christmas through your fucking greed.'

'Why no, Jacko, just chill man, it'll be nowt.' The last thing Danny wanted was an irate Jacko. Good as gold Jacko was, salt of the earth, but Danny knew if Jacko lost it he could easily wipe out any of them on the bus, including Brian and his body-building ways.

Danny went on, 'I've never heard of anyone being stopped in Belgium before . . . They have no quarrel with us taking stuff out of the country. We are paying for it . . . It's them greedy twats back in England, charging all the fucking tax and VAT on the bloody tabs.'

'Aye, but we wouldn't have a job, would we?' Adam said as three white vans passed them on their way back to France. 'And, I heard on the ship that there's a serial killer on the loose: that's why the guard's there.'

'Never.' Len looked at Adam.

'Aye, and the way they described him, I'd be careful if I was you, Len.'

'Why's that.'

''Cos he's the spitting double of you.'

Len glowered at him, 'Ohh there yer go again, lies lies lies, that's all that drops out of yer mouth. Yer the Devil's spawn, that's what you are.'

'Ooo. Heavy.' Adam laughed.

Ten minutes later they were outside the warehouse. Danny, Jacko, Len and Adam went inside while Brian reversed the van up to the warehouse doors, then waited for the others to come out.

The car park was full of vehicles: mostly English, and mostly white vans with the odd smattering of jeeps, cars and minibuses. Brian recognised a few vans from Hetton-le-hole, which lies roughly two miles from Houghton.

The van was already loaded from the French warehouse with slabs of lager, bottles of wine and cigarettes, the exact amount that they were allowed apart from two or three extra cartons of cigarettes – seeing as it was Christmas, Danny had said as he hid them under the seat. And now all four of them trooped out of the warehouse carrying a cardboard box on their shoulders.

As they put them in the van, two large boxes with

two smaller ones on top of them, Brian said. 'I thought yer were only getting two boxes of baccy?'

'Ornaments,' Danny replied, tapping the top of one of the smaller boxes with his index finger.

'Fucking ornaments, it's three o'clock in the morning, how the fuck can yer shop for ornaments?'

'Special offer,' Danny replied. 'Christmas sorted, one for the ex-wife and one for the girlfriend.'

Brian held his right hand up, 'Don't, please . . . Tell me that they aren't the same bloody ornament.'

Standing behind Danny, Jacko nodded at Brian, who whistled and said, 'I never knew yer were so cheeky, lad.'

'Sinner,' Len spat at his cousin as he sat down.

'Don't you start,' Danny replied, taking over from Brian in the driver's seat.

'Can yer mind yer foot, son,' Len said to Adam, who turned to him, his face wearing a look of pure horror.

'No.'

'What?' Len demanded.

'Don't, after all these years, no, it can't be,' Adam said dramatically.

'What do yer mean, yer little shit?' Len was practically shouting. By this time they had the attention of everybody in the van.

'Don't tell me after all these years that you, you of all people, are me dad. What me mam must have been thinking about . . .'

'No, no,' Len blustered, his face registering real horror. 'No, I'm not yer dad . . . Oh no.' he shook his head adamantly, unaware that the others were fighting to keep from laughing out loud.

'But yer called me son.'

'That was just a, a . . .'

Jacko could hold it no longer, a second later they were all laughing out loud and Len was glowering out of the window.

Danny steered Lizzy off the ship. As usual he was looking for the biggest wreck he could find to get behind, anything would do, car, van, whatever. He grinned, there it was, heaven sent, the nastiest, rustiest, old red Ford Escort van he'd seen in a long time: amazing that it could run at all.

'Jesus, look at that,' Brian said. 'It's just fucking rust that's holding it together . . . Get behind it mate, go on, go for it . . . But watch this big bastard on me right, he'll have us over if he's not careful . . . Twat.'

Brian snarled at the driver of the large grey truck, who lobbed two fingers up at him.

'Not just a twat but a cheeky twat an' all,' Brian remarked, looking around at the others for confirmation. They all nodded their heads in agreement.

Danny went for it, and they fitted in nicely behind the van. Only there seemed to be some sort of hold-up: everything in front of them was slowing down.

Not again, Jacko thought, with a terrible sinking feeling in the pit of his stomach.

'What's the matter?' Len voiced the question for everybody as they all strained to see out of the windows. He was visibly on edge as he pushed Adam out of the way.

'Oh for fuck's sake,' Danny said.

'What's the matter?' Adam demanded.

'Looks like they're pulling just about everybody in,' Danny answered, his heart plummeting to the floor as sweat popped out on his brow.

Brian shook his head. 'Never seen it like this before . . . We're hardly off the bloody ship and we're right into a traffic jam. Something serious this is.'

'What we gonna do about the baccy?' Jacko asked.

'Oh God, the flaming baccy.' Danny felt as if his life was coming to an end. There was a huge black hole in front of him filled with customs men, all with eager little faces, and he was close to falling over the edge. It just wasn't fair: he had always stuck to the rules, every man to his limit. But today of all days he had to be greedy.

'Damn.' He punched Lizzy's steering wheel. *Please God,* he prayed silently, *don't let them take me bus.*

Adam stared silently ahead. Jacko didn't even dare look up: he was sitting with his fingers crossed, praying like mad, then crossed his ankles for good measure.

As they crawled towards the bays they could see customs men all over the place. 'Must have called for reinforcements from all over the fucking country,' Brian muttered. 'The bastards.'

Danny's mouth went dry as they reached the first bay. It was packed with three times as much traffic as he had ever seen it before. Sniffer dogs eagerly padded from van to car to bus. Beaten, Danny sighed, patted Lizzy's steering wheel and prepared to pull in.

Then a customs man stepped in front of them. It seemed as if everyone in the van was holding their breath as they stared at him. The man was tall and powerfully built. His face was stern as he gave the bus the once over, before waving them on.

'Jesus!' Danny gulped. 'Thank you, God.'

'I thought for a minute they'd imported that bastard from Belgium,' Brian said.

Jacko, his heart still skipping beats, laughed nervously, 'Aye, he does look like him an' all.'

They were waved on again at the next bay. When they were waved on from the third bay Danny dared to hope that all the bays were full up. At the fourth and last bay the red Escort was waved in.

'Oh God, oh Jesus,' Danny whispered as the customs man, this one small with dyed blond hair, loomed close in the windshield. He stared at the bus then lifted his arm.

This was it. 'Merry Christmas everybody.' Danny said as the customs man dropped his elbow to his waist and waved them through.

'Bloody hell!' Danny gasped. He was so giddy with relief that he stalled the bus.

'Don't stop, for Christ's sake,' Jacko snapped, gripping the edge of his seat.

Danny smiled his best smile at the customs man and quickly got Lizzy underway again.

Overwhelmed with relief they drove out of the bays only to find as many policemen crawling about the street as there had been customs officers to welcome them off the ship moments ago.

'Same shit, different clothing.' Brian muttered, the

worry that had momentarily lifted from his face descending once again.

Cars, vans and lorries were pulled over on each side of the road for as far as anyone could see. A huge Alsatian raised its head and sniffed the wind as they passed.

'Shit, shit, *shit*,' Jacko yelled his frustration. 'The nasty interfering sly bastards. If one doesn't get yer then the other one does. Fucking hell.' He punched the back of the seat, his eyes bulging. 'Sly bastards.'

When they had gone nearly the length of the street without being pulled over, and just a moment before they dared start to breathe easy again, a tall policeman with a huge beer gut put up his hand to stop them.

'Well, this looks like the end of the line, guys,' Danny said. 'Just leave the talking to me, and remember our story, if he questions yer. It's all for me birthday party and New Year's Eve.'

'Like I'm gonna talk to a copper,' Adam said, while the other three nodded.

Jacko had gone quiet, worrying about Christmas and the last minute shopping he had planned for Melanie this afternoon. It was an unwritten law that if the boss loses his load, you don't get paid.

Only one of the five had any idea of just how much trouble they would be in if they were caught with the drugs that were secured beneath their feet. The black car which had kept close to them since they left the ship, scooted past.

Danny, his heart beating loud enough to be heard

back home, pulled into the spot indicated by the policeman. Hand shaking, he switched off Lizzy's engine, then wound down the window.

'Can I help yer, officer?' he said, trying hard to smile but only managing a painful grimace.

The policeman ignored him and looked through the windows, first counting the men then counting the slabs. He frowned for a moment, then scanned the bus once more. This time he spotted the boxes.

'Been to Belgium?' he asked with a smile as he rocked back on his heels.

Danny hesitated, then thought. When in doubt always tell the truth. At least they can't do yer for lying. 'Yes, officer.'

'What's in the boxes?' he demanded, with the satisfied air of one who has captured his prey.

Brian, with a fixed smile on his face, nodded as Danny hastily said, 'Oh, ornaments officer, just ornaments. Yer know, the kind of things yer put in windows and places, like . . .'

'Ornaments?' The policemen's tone was sarcastic as he repeated, 'Ornaments,' then said in a no-nonsense manner, 'Open them up.'

'But they're presents, officer, and I'll never be able to . . .' The policeman was staring at him in such a way that said, in no uncertain terms, shut the fuck up now.

Len was the nearest and the policeman glared at him. For a moment Len just stared back then, as if 3000 volts had just passed straight through him, he shook himself and hastily reached over to the back and grabbed a box.

'One's for his girlfriend and the other's for his ex-wife,' Len babbled as, all fingers and thumbs, he proceeded to wreck the box as he opened it. 'Shocking, isn't it, sir?' he nodded at the policeman. The policeman tore his eyes from Len and glanced at Danny and gave him a look that made Danny feel as if he were a serial bigamist. He swore under his breath that if they got out of here in one piece he would personally murder Len with his own two hands.

'There yer go sir, a pig!' Len announced, holding up a large pink pig for the policeman to see . . . 'Do yer like pigs?'

Just about everybody on the van cringed when Len came out with that one.

Adam and Brian were staring straight ahead, backs as stiff as pokers. The back of Danny's neck had grown three inches trying to see everything the policeman did, while Jacko prayed hard for them to be let go intact.

The policeman looked at the pink pig, looked at Len and said, after a long drawn-out moment, 'I haven't got much choice, have I.'

There was complete silence in the bus, as Jacko and the others, even in the depths of fear, struggled not to laugh out loud.

Then the policeman said, 'Yer free to go.'

26

Carter knocked on the door, then opened the letter box and shouted through it, 'It's me, Luke.'

Luke heaved a sigh of relief and rose from his position on the floor. His joints creaked from keeping watch over Selina, and he took a moment to stretch his muscles out. Rubbing the knots out of his neck, he walked down the hallway and opened the door.

'Yer all right, mate?' Carter asked, although he could see that Luke was anything but. He looked like he hadn't slept for days. His eyes were bloodshot and ringed with dark circles, and he sorely needed a shave. Carter still stood at the doorway, but from here the house seemed eerily quiet, as if its inhabitants were elsewhere.

Then the banging and screaming started.

'Jesus,' Carter exclaimed as he stepped over the threshold. 'How long has that been going on?'

'Best part of four days, on and off.'

'Christ, yer right. Yer do need help, man.'

'Yeah, that's why I sent for you, Carter.' Luke ran tired fingers through his hair. He had explained everything to Carter earlier today when he'd picked him up from the hospital, knowing he could not go on any longer without help. Luke had left Selina locked in her room, and the whole time he was away from her, he worried about what he'd find when he came back. He dreaded leaving her alone for even five minutes when he went to the corner shop to pick up food. Thank God Carter had agreed to help out.

Luke led Carter down the corridor. Having him here reminded him that there was life outside these four walls; that he had a job to go back to. It was easy to forget that when he was living on tinned soup and next to no sleep. Luke sighed when he thought about work. He knew that he owed Lorraine an explanation in the morning and he dreaded it. He knew he should have told her straightaway. Especially as she had really opened herself up to him in the pub. She would think that he didn't trust her.

But that wasn't the case. How could he have just come out with it? It was bad enough trying to get his own head around the fact that he had a daughter. A daughter that was a drug addict.

They stopped outside the door to Selina's room. She seemed to have given up hitting the door. Carter wondered whether she had fallen asleep. He turned to Luke with real concern in his face. 'Have yer eaten . . . the pair of yer?'

'She's just about thrown up everything I've offered her and what she hasn't she's thrown at me.'

'OK, I'll make dinner, then you can get to bed and I'll take over. Then you do a stint while I sleep, then I'll be up for the day shift tomorrow, OK?'

'Yer sure yer up to it?' Luke looked concernedly at the younger man.

'Yeah, I'm fine.'

'Thanks, mate. I owe yer one,' Luke said, clasping Carter's shoulder.

Carter beamed. Luke was his hero as much as Lorraine was his heroine. Feeling like a dog with two tails he made his way to the kitchen while Luke took a shower.

Then the banging started again.

As Luke showered he thought of Lorraine.

What's her reaction gonna be when I tell her?

He knew that he wanted more than just a friendly, working relationship with Lorraine. There was something between them; they both could feel it. He knew she would be good for him and he would look after her as much as he could. He thought about the present that he was going to give her on Christmas Day. A sweetheart locket on a gold chain. Old fashioned, but he thought she would love it. And he loved the thought of her wearing something that he had given her.

He leaned against the shower wall, and let the hot water run over his head.

But how can we have a relationship now? Now when I come with baggage.

No woman in her right mind would want to deal with such a mess. And mess is what that poor kid is, nothing but strung-out misery.

He reached for the towel, roughly dried himself then looked in the mirror.

God, he so loved Lorraine. She made him laugh even when she wasn't trying.

She's beautiful.

She's everything.

300

But my duty's to Selina.
Tomorrow I'll tell Lorraine everything.

After Luke crawled into bed, Carter went to make himself a cup of tea and went to the living room to sit down for a few minutes. It was the first time he'd been to Luke's house. Oh yes, wooden floors, leather three-piece, tasteful, just like he had imagined it.

Blimey, is that a guitar? Didn't know he played.

'What a beauty,' he murmured, gently stroking the guitar.

I bet he plays real good an' all. Wonder if he'll teach me?

He looked at the music centre in the window. *Bet it's the Eagles he's got on.* He laughed gently when he was right. He would love a flat like this. From there he wandered back to Selina's room and sat in the chair that Luke had recently vacated. He could hear her moving about.

Wonder if she wants to read some local history books?

Saturday 23 December

27

Niall reached for the cornflake box and looked steadily at Kurt as if daring him to say anything.

Kurt stared back and shrugged.

'What are you doing today, boys?' Niall's mother asked, as she came into the kitchen, her flip-flop slippers smacking the tiled floor.

She had been very happy to allow Kurt to stay. Niall had told Kurt that she thought he was a saint.

'That boy doesn't take drugs,' she'd heard her telling his father.

Wake-up call, mam, he'd thought at the time, *neither does your son.*

'Ah, thought we might go to the movies.' Niall surprised himself, how easily the lie just rolled off his tongue. But then he shrugged. He was guilty of worse.

'The movies,' she echoed. 'Oh, how nice. Anything good on?'

'Um, we don't know. Thought we'd see what was on and make our minds up then,' Kurt said.

With a smile at Kurt, Mrs Campbell walked out of the kitchen and into the sitting room, where her husband was sitting watching telly.

'She's gone to tell Dad that at least I'm not hanging

out down the Beck, scoring drugs,' Niall said with a snort. 'Come on, let's get outta here before she calls in a brass band and awards us a major prize just for going to the movies.'

Kurt ran upstairs for his blue hoodie, then they set out. Niall was walking with his hands in his pockets. 'Look, it's snowing.' He stuck his tongue out and caught a few flakes.

'It's not gonna last though, just a flurry.'

'Wonder where Melissa is?' Kurt worried, as the snowflakes disappeared as quickly as they came.

'We wondered that yesterday.'

'Aye, but that bastard Adrian had us clearing a pitch at the Seven Sisters most of the day . . .' Niall sighed. 'We have to get away, yer know that. God only knows what he's got planned for tomorrow night . . . Fucking creepy that's what he is, and that brother of his is worse. We could get the girls and fuck off to London; nobody would ever find us there, would they?'

'That's not gonna happen, mate. We'd just be living on the streets. Rachel wouldn't come with us; she's too much in love with Marcel for that. And Melissa, well,' he looked at Niall side-on. 'She doesn't exactly blend into a crowd, does she.'

Niall stopped dead, 'I know, I know. Only day-dreaming. Trust you to burst the bubble.'

'Yeah, well, yer not the only one who can daydream yer know, but that's not getting us any fucking where, is it. For two pins I'd go to the coppers. We should, 'cos Rachel might be happy to be there, but Melissa isn't. What if he's keeping her prisoner, have yer thought about that?'

'We can't go to the coppers. We were there when the night watchman fell off the roof. Marcel might talk about destiny, but I don't think the coppers will fall for that one.'

Kurt sighed. 'That was a horrible accident. How the hell did we know that he was gonna follow us up there, eh. How could we know?' He shuddered at a picture in his mind of the night watchman struggling on the spikes for what had seemed ages at the time, but could have been no more than thirty seconds. His right arm, which wasn't impaled, waved violently around, then suddenly dropped, his fingers spreading wide then closing. Kurt took a deep breath, then for a moment closed his eyes tight against the horror of it all.

'We just get deeper and deeper every day . . . Every fucking day . . . And we still don't know where Melissa is.'

'Why do we do it, Kurt?' Niall said. 'Why do we keep on going when we know what Marcel is expecting us to do?'

Kurt ran his fingers through his hair and he sighed. He sat down on a nearby bench and rested his elbows on his knees. Niall sat down beside him.

Kurt said, 'I felt like I had finally found a family, yer know? People who I could trust. I've spent my whole life, it feels like, walking on eggshells around me mam or waiting for me dad to come home from abroad. Well, walking on eggshells didn't help me mam – she still found excuses to hit me. And when me dad comes home, it's great, but he makes all these promises that he doesn't keep, and after a few days he's gone again, and it doesn't even feel that he was there at all.' Niall looked at his friend. Kurt's eyes were red and he angrily wiped away tears from his face. He carried on, with a catch in his throat, 'The first time I met Marcel I thought that he loved me – like a father, yer know? – and I felt, for the first time in my life, totally accepted. And then Richy and me became friends with you and Melissa and Rachel. I have a laugh with all my other friends but I only really talk with you guys. Now Richy's dead, you're my best friend, Niall, and nothing's gonna change that.'

Niall nodded his head. 'There's something about Marcel, isn't there? Something that makes you think that he's gonna make everything all right. I never felt like I had to eat or make excuses for meself with him. But now, now I'm really frightened.'

Kurt was silent while he waited for a couple, arm in arm and laughing, to walk past them. When they were out of earshot, Kurt said softly, 'It's been a week since we broke into the warehouse.'

Niall smiled sadly. 'Feels like a lot longer.'

'This time last week, I was so sure that Marcel was right about everything. I thought he would take us away with him. I would have followed him any-where. Now he's got all this stuff on us – he could throw us to the dogs, if he wanted to.'

They sat in silence for a moment longer until Niall said, 'Be cool. It's Katy Jacks.' Katy was walking by herself, with her hands deep in her pockets. Seeing the boys, she went up to them and said, 'Think the police are going to want to speak to youse two.'

Both boys paled. 'Why?' said Kurt. 'What do you mean?'

'Haven't yer heard? It was in last night's *Echo*. Melissa Tremaine was found, drowned.'

The boys just sat, staring up at Katy, looking horrified.

'Don't look at me like that. I'm just the messenger.' And with a snort, she moved off.

Niall dropped his head in his hands. 'Oh Christ, Christ, Christ.'

Kurt took a deep breath. 'Look, it's just Katy Jacks, yer know what she's like. Let's go to the corner shop, grab a paper. It might be nothing.'

'Oh shit, Kurt, what are you talking about? We haven't seen her since Wednesday. Of course it's her.'

'Look, you wait here. Don't move. I'll be back with a paper in a couple of minutes, and then, at least, we can be sure if Katy Jacks is right, or if she's talking out of a hole in her arse.'

Kurt stood up and started sprinting back the way they came. He went into the first newsagent's he saw and asked the girl behind the counter whether she had last night's copy of the *Echo*.

As she talked, she chewed gum noisily. 'We usually send back yesterday's papers. But I'll see if we have one out the back.'

She shuffled out the door in the back of the shop, leaving Kurt hopping on the spot in anticipation.

'Yer in luck,' she said. 'He hasn't collected this yet.' She handed Friday's *Echo* to Kurt.

Kurt scrabbled in his pocket for change.

'Nah, don't worry,' said the girl. 'They're not gonna miss one. It's yesterday's news anyhow.'

'Thanks,' Kurt said, and ran out the shop. He had the newspaper folded under his arm and dreaded opening it. *Let's just hope Katy Jacks was winding us up*, he thought, but in his heart he knew that she wouldn't lie about something like that.

Niall looked up as Kurt approached. Worry was etched into his face. 'Got the paper,' Kurt panted as he sat down beside him.

Niall nodded, chewing his lip.

As Kurt unfolded the paper, they saw a colour shot of Melissa staring up at them from the paper. It was a school photo, taken only a few short months ago. Melissa was smiling; she looked happy. Niall's chin started wobbling. 'I can't look at it. Read out what it says.'

Kurt took a deep breath. 'The body of Melissa Tremaine, 15, was found in the Fatfield river early this morning. The teenager was last seen by her parents late on Wednesday evening. While the police have declined to comment at this time, sources say that they are treating the death as suspicious.'

Niall looked pale, and then he stood up and walked over to the hedge behind the bench where he was sick. Kurt sat staring at the ground in front of him. 'It's true,' he said quietly.

Niall made his way back to the bench. Kurt put his arm over Niall's shoulder. Niall had his elbows on his knees and his hands over his face, but Kurt could hear him sobbing, as if his heart was breaking. His own tears he kept in check. He needed to be there for Niall.

'The bastards, the bastards,' Niall kept saying over and over. Kurt rubbed his shoulder. 'Listen to me, Niall. Richy died after he went to talk to Marcel. Now Melissa is dead. She wasn't happy with the way things were going with Marcel; we know that. It's just too much of a coincidence, man. Two of our friends are dead, Niall, and Rachel is up there without a clue. Who's gonna be next?'

Niall chewed on his nails, then raking in his pockets he found a crumpled cigarette. While Kurt stared at him, he straightened the cigarette out, lit it, took a draw, then finally looking at Kurt, he said, 'We have to get Rachel outta there before that fucking ceremony tomorrow night. God knows what he's got planned, but I'll tell yer one thing, nowt the mad bastard comes up with now will surprise me . . .'

Kurt said, with a cold, calm rage, 'I wish to God I'd never listened to Richy in the first place. Come along for a laugh, ha, look where his laugh got him. He's dead. Dead, dead, dead.' Kurt punched the bench. 'And so's Melissa . . . Oh Jesus . . .'

'What the fuck are we gonna do, Kurt?' Niall said. 'What the fuck are we gonna do? Jesus Christ, I'm so scared . . .'

'We have to get Rachel out. Before the ceremony tomorrow night.'

'But she won't want to come with us,' Niall said. 'She's so loved up with Marcel, she won't believe anything we say.'

311

'There must be something we can do,' Kurt said anxiously. 'We have to find a way, have to convince her of what we know and get her the hell out of there.'

Niall shook his head, his eyes still full of tears. 'Easier said than done,' he said. 'And we will have to be careful. If Marcel or that other creep Adrian suspects that we're onto them, God knows what'll happen. 'Cos we'll be on our own yer know, just me and you. Not one of them up there will help us. Not even Rachel.'

28

Doris was making tea in the kitchen for Vanessa and Sandra who were in the sitting room. Doris looked out the window while she was waiting for the kettle to boil. She spied a robin sitting on one of the branches of next door's apple tree. She watched its funny antics until she heard the kettle whistle, then filling the teapot and putting her best cups on a tray, she carried the lot through into the sitting room.

Vanessa had stood up to get yesterday's *Newcastle Journal* out of the paper rack when she caught sight of Debbie Stansfield scooting past the window. Quickly, watched in amazement by the other two, she ran outside.

'What the . . .?' Doris said.

Sandra got up and moved to the window. 'Ah.'

'Ah, what?'

'It's Debbie. Vanessa must have spotted her . . . I have to say she looks awful, poor soul.'

'God, she must be going to that cop shop again. Bet they're pissed off with her all right.'

After a few minutes Vanessa came back in. 'She says she's only going to Houghton for shopping. I told her one of us would pop up for her but she won't have it. Said she had to get out of the house for some fresh air. I said OK, I'll go with yer.' Vanessa shook her head, 'She wasn't having that either.'

'Do yer believe her?' Sandra asked.

'No. We all know where she's going.'

'What can we do?' Doris said. 'Short of tying her to the kitchen chair or something, like.'

'Poor thing,' Sandra said, still looking out the window. 'It's time somebody got their fingers out, if yer ask me, and let the poor lass bury her dead . . . And it's cold enough for snow out there an' all. She'll catch the 'flu, you mark my words, 'cos she's fairly run down at the moment.'

'Aye,' Doris agreed, glancing out the window. 'It's freezing out there. And it doesn't look like she's dressed for the cold. Anyhow, it's bloody shocking if yer ask me . . . Never known a funeral take so long. It's gonna be after Christmas now before the poor lad's in the ground . . . Bloody disgraceful if yer ask me . . . I mean, what could be taking so long? It's obvious the poor lad hung himself. There must have been something that he was worried about.'

'That's not what Debbie thinks though, is it?' Vanessa murmured. 'She thinks he was murdered. Never heard her sound so certain about anything in her life. I know if it were one of mine, though, I'd be thinking exactly the same way.'

The other two shivered in unison at the thought.

'What the hell's going on there?' Doris shrieked a moment later, nearly choking on a mouth full of hot tea as she pointed at the television.

'Oh my God,' Sandra gasped.

'Turn it up, quick, turn it up.' Doris panicked as Sandra looked for the remote.

The screen was showing warehouse after warehouse full to the brim with cartons of cigarettes and pallets full of lager cans. The three of them stared intently at the screen as the announcer informed the nation that the government was cracking down on alcohol and cigarette smuggling, Then the camera moved to Dover, panning over a shot where dozens of vans, cars and minibuses were pulled over by customs officials.

'No.' Doris put both hands over her mouth.

'Oh no, right on bloody Christmas an' all, the nasty bastards,' Vanessa practically shouted. 'What we gonna do? None of us can afford the price the shops charge.'

Doris, who'd had to pack in smoking years ago because of continued chest infections, ignored her. She was on her hands and knees in front of the screen looking for Jacko.

29

It was mid-morning. Lorraine had only managed to grab a quick cup of tea and a slice of toast before running out the door and into the office. She couldn't remember the last time she'd had a weekend at home. And now, with Carter recuperating from his operation, and Luke God knows where, she was even more run off her feet as usual. She heard a knock on the door and looked up from her paperwork.

'Thought you might do with one of these, boss.' Sanderson waved a package at her. The brown paper bag was stained with grease and the smell of freshly baked pasties wafted into the office. Lorraine's stomach rumbled in response. Sanderson balanced, in his other hand, two take-out coffees.

'Sanderson, you're a lifesaver. This is exactly what I needed. Come in, sit yerself down, we'll have a breather.'

Sanderson sat on the other side of the desk. He passed a pasty over to Lorraine, and gave her a cup of coffee, throwing the small packets of sugar on her desk. They ate their pasties in silence for a moment, then Lorraine cocked her head to one side and looked at Sanderson. The sly, appraising look she cast at him made him uneasy.

'What?' he said, in the middle of a mouthful.

'You like dogs, don't yer, Sanderson?'

'Hmmm, yes,' he said guardedly.

'How about Joan? Wouldn't she like a dog to keep her company? Yer know, on those dark nights when yer out keeping the streets safe.'

'Joan's a cat person.'

'Is she now?'

Jacobs came in then and Lorraine gave her the same look. 'Do yer like dogs, Jacobs?'

'Oh yes, what kind?'

'What do yer mean, what kind? A dog's a dog.'

'Well, not exactly . . . Some dogs are pedigrees, yer know, like poodles, and Dalmatians.'

'How about a mix of . . .' Lorraine thought for a moment, as Sanderson looked the other way trying to hide a grin, 'Alsatian, Labrador, collie?'

'A mongrel!' Jacobs declared as she screwed her face up in disgust.

'And what's wrong with mongrels?' Lorraine demanded. 'I'll have yer know Duke is every bit as good-looking as yer average poodle or bloody Dalmatian.'

'OK, boss, whatever you say.' Jacobs put the letters on the desk and backed out the door.

'The cheeky stuck-up madam. As if I would even let her anywhere near the dog.'

'OK,' Sanderson scrunched his paper packet into a ball, 'what's the newest member of the Hunt household done now?'

'He's shedding. I've never seen anything like it. He's been in the house, what, three days? And everything's covered in the mutt's hair. The settee, my coat . . .'

'Lorraine, yer can't give the dog away because yer had some hairs on yer jacket. Besides, how would yer get it out of the house? Mavis and Peggy would never speak to yer again.'

'Yer say that as if it's a bad thing.'

'I know yer, Lorraine, and yer more likely to get rid of yer left arm than yer are to get rid of that dog. Admit it, he's got yer wrapped right round his little hairy paw . . .'

Lorraine was just about to raise her voice in protest when she heard a commotion outside in the corridor.

'What the –?' Lorraine put her cup on the desk and went to open the door to see what was happening outside, only to come face to face with Debbie Stansfield raising her fist to knock.

'Debbie, what's the matter, love? Come in.'

She led Debbie to her desk and sat her down in the chair that Sanderson had quickly vacated. Gone was the grieving woman of a couple of days ago. Debbie Stansfield looked like she was simmering over with anger and frustration. But she also didn't look well, and her voice, when she spoke, sounded as if she had the beginnings of a bad cold.

'When are yer lot gonna release my son?' Debbie said, her voice a cold growl.

'Debbie, are yer OK? Don't yer think yer should see a doctor?' Lorraine asked quietly.

'Don't talk to me about doctors,' Debbie spat the last word out. 'What do they know what's good for me? All they want to do is give me pills to sleep and pills for the anxiety and pills to calm me down. Well, don't you understand? I don't want to feel numb. I want my son back, and I want to give him a decent funeral. It's what he deserves.'

'Yes, Debbie, I can understand that. But our investigation into his death is ongoing. But I'm going to see the pathologist after I talk to you, and then I'll ring you and let you know whether Richard's body is ready to be released.'

'That's not good enough,' said Debbie suddenly. 'I want my Richard and I want him now.'

'You're going to have to wait, Debbie,' Lorraine said. God, she felt so sorry for the poor woman, but her patience was wearing thin. 'You've got to let us do our job. I know it's hard, but you've just got to trust us.'

Debbie stood up suddenly, scraping her chair across the floor. 'How can I trust yer?' she almost screamed. 'How can I trust anyone again? I know that Richard didn't kill himself and you lot are just dragging yer feet.'

Lorraine tapped her fingers on her desk. 'Look, I promise yer, if Scottie has anything I'll come right to your house and let yer know what's happening . . . Now, why don't yer go home get some sleep, before yer collapse, eh Debbie?'

Debbie stood with her head hanging. When she looked up a moment later Lorraine could see that all of the fight had gone out of her. Her eyes were full and when they spilled over she made no effort to wipe the tears away.

'I want my boy,' she mouthed silently.

'I know yer do. I'm doing my best, Debbie.' Lorraine's voice was firm but inside her heart was hurting for the broken woman who stood in front of her.

Debbie gave in then and nodded slightly at Lorraine before silently turning and leaving the room.

After she'd gone, Lorraine sat down. 'Jesus, Sanderson, that poor women's got me all wrung out, never mind herself.'

'Yeah I know . . .' Sanderson looked down the corridor after Debbie, then snapped his attention back to Lorraine. 'So, we're going round to Scottie's then?'

'Yeah, we'll go and see what he's got. By the sound of the message he left on my phone, he's got some exciting news.'

'Right, what yer got?' Lorraine said, as she and Sanderson walked into Scottie's domain. As usual he was standing over the autopsy table and Edna was swinging on her stool.

'Have youse two moved at all since the other day?' Lorraine gave them a mock frown.

'Yer know us, Lorraine, no rest for the wicked. Now,' he said, coming round to the other side of the table, 'have I got some news for you. I think yer going to be very pleased. Very pleased indeed.'

Edna snorted. 'He's been bursting to tell yer all morning.'

'Well come on then, Scottie. Don't hold me in suspense. What have yer got?'

'I have found evidence that Richard Stansfield could not have killed himself.' Scottie smiled as he saw Lorraine's expression change from confusion to dawning comprehension. 'I'll show you.'

Scottie went to the bank where the bodies were kept. With a grunt he pulled out a drawer. Lorraine and Sanderson stood on either side of the large, metal casket that held Richard Stansfield's remains.

'Poor lad,' said Sanderson with feeling.

Richard's body was a blueish white, with dark purple marks around his neck.

'After we found the same fibres on Melissa's body, I took another look at the pattern of the marks around Richard's neck. Now, I assumed that Richard killed himself, not by climbing up the tree and leaping off, which would have broken his neck immediately, but that he was more cautious. In other words, that he slid off the branch, rather than jumped. So it was a slow death by strangulation. But see here,' Scottie pointed at the bruises on Richard's neck with a ballpoint pen, 'if he had slid off the branch, you'd expect rope burns to run from the base all the way to the top of his neck.'

'Well, yeah,' said Sanderson, 'isn't that what these are?'

Lorraine shushed him. She knew that Scottie had more to say, and she was starting to get that feeling in her stomach that meant that finally they were on to something. 'Go on, Scottie,' she said softly.

'Yeah, well, as I was saying, yes, these are rope burns. But these are far more extensive than what you'd expect if Richard had jumped off. In fact, I think he was pulling the rope down as it was being yanked up. There are marks on his neck from his fingernails, but I assumed that these came from when he was trying to get the rope off his neck. Yes, he was trying to get the rope off, but I firmly believe now, and will swear in court, that he was, in fact, strung up.'

Sanderson let out a slow whistle, but Lorraine didn't hear him. Her mind was working in overdrive. 'How many people would it take to do this to someone?' she asked.

'A struggling young boy in the peak of health? I'd say two, probably three,' Scottie said.

'So, he was taken up to the Seven Sisters,' Lorraine said slowly, 'probably in the boot of a car. He then had a noose thrown around his neck, and tried pulling it off, while two, at least two, people threw the other end of the rope around the branch and hauled him up.'

'There would have been at least one more person making sure he didn't get away,' added Sanderson.

'And once his feet left the ground, he wouldn't have stood a chance.' Scottie said gravely.

Lorraine had a mental picture of four figures dressed in black, watching as the young boy they had strung up tried to get the rope off his neck while he kicked out futilely in the air. She wondered whether they had watched him in the last throes of death, or whether they had simply turned and walked down the hill.

'What do yer want to do now, boss?' Sanderson said, his voice breaking into her reverie.

'I want to find out who would have wanted Richard killed. Sanderson, at this stage we tell people on a need-to-know basis. I don't want anyone telling Debbie Stansfield what we've found out until we've filled in some of the blanks.'

Sanderson nodded, but then his face clouded. 'But if we told her, she might be able to help us, tell us who his enemies are.'

'No, Sanderson,' Lorraine shook her head. 'She would have told us by now who his enemies were if she knew. I think we need to go back to his friends now, find out what they have to say about this, and about Melissa Tremaine too.'

30

They were less than an hour from home. Brian was in the driving seat with Danny sitting next to him. Unknown to any of them they had already passed three weigh stations on the road where the police were pulling in the traffic which had escaped Dover.

Each station had been full to overflowing, with the excess waiting on side roads. Danny and co had escaped Lincoln by a hair's breath. Three minutes earlier and it would have been them instead of one of the Hetton-le-hole vans.

Danny's mobile had died with a loud beep six hours ago, so although both his girlfriend and his ex-wife had tried to get in touch with him to warn him what was going on, both of them had failed, and so the gang sailed on in total ignorance of the situation.

'Ah need a piss,' Adam announced suddenly, fidgeting in his seat like a small boy.

'Thought we agreed to go straight home, no stops,' Len growled, glaring at Adam.

'I could do with stretching me legs an' all.' Brian put in. 'Me arse feels as if it's melding with this bloody seat. I'm sure the springs have gone.'

Danny glared at Brian. How dare he criticise Lizzy.

'I know the springs have not gone.' He spun round

to Jacko. 'You need to go an' all?' Jacko shrugged, 'Five minutes won't hurt. There's a service station just up the road. Actually, I'm more in need of a drink.'

'Aye, that one'll do,' Adam nodded eagerly.

They all fell quiet again. Danny put it down to tiredness, two trips in one week was what they usually did, but this last one had been nearly a double one. Even so he had never known them be this quiet before. No jokes from Adam, very little whingeing from Len. Now *that* was heaven. But Brian had been edgy as hell with just about everybody.

Fifteen minutes later, and about forty miles from Durham they pulled into the service station. Behind them, a black car which had used lorries, car transporters and many more large vehicles to hide from them most of the way, swung off the motorway and followed them into the service station.

Adam stood up ready to jump out, but Brian didn't stop. Before any of them could react he drove out the other side of the garage and stopped in a lay-by behind the garage which was hidden from view by a long line of pine trees.

'What the fuck yer doing, Bri? If yer think for one minute I'm pissing in a field when there's toilets back there, yer can fucking well think again.'

'Uh oh,' Len said, his eyes growing wider by the second. Mouth hanging open in shock, he tried to flatten himself against his seat as he watched four men jump out of the black car and run towards the minibus.

'What the fuck?' Danny gasped in amazement as

Adam, who had been standing at the door, was yanked out by a tall, thin, auburn-haired man in a red tartan shirt, then dragged yelling and kicking to the ground.

'Hey,' Danny yelled, jumping out of the minibus. 'What the fuck do yer think yer doing?'

He was followed immediately by Jacko, who without hesitation launched a heavy fist at the man who was now kicking the ball that Adam had become. The fist landed square on his chin and rocked the man on his heels, the left hook which came next knocked him flat on his back.

Danny was boldly squaring up to a blond man twice his size, while the other two men grabbed Jacko's arms. He managed to shake one of them off at the same time as he recognised him as the short bald man who had nearly had him bouncing from deck to deck on the ship. His partner was tall and very dark, both in skin and hair, and close to losing an ear when Jacko bit into it a moment later.

Danny had managed to jump up and nut his opponent, who was bent in half holding his face, but unknown to Danny the auburn-haired man who had scrambled to his feet, although unsteady, was ready to pounce on his back.

Len gallantly realised that this was not the best time to turn the other cheek. He grabbed a slab of lager, jumped out of the van and, grunting and heaving, brought it crashing down on the head of the man who was stalking Danny, 'Take that, yer villain,' he said as half of the cans burst wide open and lager sprayed everywhere. As if in slow motion the man folded and fell at Len's feet. 'That'll teach yer,' Len yelled, shaking his fist at him.

Brian finally climbed down from the van, but it was to go and help the blond man that Len had floored. At the same time the small bald man had made a run for the black car. Jacko made a run for him but stopped dead when the bald man swung round from the open boot with a sawn-off shotgun in his hand.

Len immediately held his hands up.

Danny poked him in the back and he dropped them as quickly as he'd put them up, then they all watched silently as Brian helped the blond man onto the minibus.

'Judas,' Len muttered, when Brian was out of earshot.

'What yer doing this for?' Danny asked the bald man.

'Obvious, don't you think? Pretty valuable cargo,' came the reply as the other man got into the black car and started it up. 'It was touch-and-go for a while back there. I don't think any of you realise just how lucky you were.'

Jacko spat on the ground and took a step forward.

'Just stand still, and no fucking funny business. By the way your friend had the right idea. All of you put your hands on your heads . . . Now.' He waved the shotgun at them.

One by one they did what he told them, as the bald man and the redhead backed towards the car. Before he got in he said with a smirk, 'By the way, you were carrying more than you knew. Something that brings a heavy jail sentence in more countries than one.'

Without looking at any of them, Brian drove the minibus back into the garage, then onto the motorway followed by the black car.

'Bastards, bastards.' Danny stomped around, as reaction set in and, tears streaming down his face, he sat down on the ground.

Jacko went to Adam, who was still curled in a ball and groaning softly.

'Are yer all right?' Gently he tried to turn him over, but Adam groaned softly and huddled in on himself.

'They've took Lizzy, the bastards. The ugly fucking twats. I'll fucking kill that Brian when we get home, fucking kill him.'

'It's all right, we'll get her back.' Len tried to console Danny. But Danny was inconsolable.

'Me fucking bus, man, they've took me fucking bus. What am I gonna do?'

Len nodded his sympathy, then said to Jacko, who was on his hands and knees trying to see how badly hurt Adam was, 'How is he?'

'Can't get him to turn over. He's bleeding from somewhere.' Jacko wiped blood from his hands onto his jeans. 'Adam.' Gently Jacko touched his shoulder. 'Come on, mate, turn yerself over so we can see what's wrong.'

Danny sighed, shook his head, then moved over to where Adam was lying. Carefully, with Jacko's help, they managed to turn him over.

'Shit!' Jacko said, shaking his head.

Adam was bleeding from his left eyebrow which

was split wide open, a deep gash on his left cheek and a burst lip.

'The bastards, the lousy stinking bastards,' Danny said as they helped Adam to sit up.

He groaned and clutched at his chest. 'I think one of me ribs is broken,' he whispered.

Len was on his hands and knees now. He examined Adam's face, then felt around his ribs, 'No, probably just bruised, mate. He gave yer one hell of a going-over.' Len took a handkerchief out of his pocket and mopped as much blood off his face as he could. 'Yer face looks a canny bit worse than it really is. Do yer think yer can stand up now?'

They helped Adam climb to his feet amidst protests and groans. He took a deep breath, then another. 'Any pain then?' Jacko asked.

'No.' Adam looked at Jacko and slowly shook his head. 'Tell yer what though, if I meet the bastards again I'll make sure I've got the dogs with me. Oscar will show them the road home all right. Fucking bunch of creeps. I'm gonna be stiff for days now. Twats.' He spat blood onto the ground.

'Good, yer'll be right as rain in no time.' Len nodded, then went on with practically a wail, 'What we gonna do? How on earth are we gonna get home?'

Danny patted his pockets. 'I haven't got a cent. Everything's in the van in me coat pocket.'

'Mine an all.' Jacko looked in the direction the van had gone, then suddenly, as if just realising how cold it was out here without a jacket, he started to shiver.

'Looks like we're gonna have to use Shanks's pony. There isn't anybody gonna give a lift to us,' Len jerked his thumb in the direction of Adam, 'especially with him looking like he's just walked out of three rounds with Tyson.'

Adam groaned, 'Sorry.'

'It's not your fault, mate,' Jacko said, looking at the blood that had dried on Adam's face. 'It's them bastards. Wish I had me hands on them now . . . Then I'd give them what for.'

'Better start walking,' Danny said, 'or it'll be next Christmas before we make it home.'

Jacko sighed. 'Yeah. And I'm fucking freezing.'

Half an hour later they had reached a truck stop near Scotch Corner. Exhausted, Adam sat down on the grass; the others followed.

'Thirty miles to go,' Len said.

Adam rested his head in his hands. 'Seems like three hundred and thirty the way I feel . . . We might as well be on the fucking moon. I mean look at them bastards whizzing past, not a fucking care in the world. We could die out here.'

Jacko was staring at the busy road, then he turned to Danny, 'Do yer think that slimeball Brian was carrying the drugs for them?'

'Not on him, that's a fact. I know what's happened: one of them in the black car has tied them underneath Lizzy, probably in that café we called into or the warehouse in Belgium . . . That way he would have appeared as innocent as us. Then they probably followed us from there . . . If we'd been pulled into the customs, the dogs would have gone mad.'

'How do yer know that?' Adam asked.

Danny sighed, 'A couple of weeks ago a few blokes were talking about it on the ship, said they knew of a van that had been used that way. Customs actually believed that they were innocent an' all. Seems it's an old trick, been done a few times . . . I should have took more notice of them and checked the bus out now and then.' He groaned, 'What the fuck am I gonna do now without Lizzy? We'll all starve and that baldy twat will probably sell it on. Bastards.'

'How sly's that, eh, I ask yer, how sly's that?' Len shook his head in disbelief, then opened his eyes wide with surprise and delight as a huge red tractor stopped beside them.

The driver, an oldish man in a brown corduroy jacket with a matching cap, said in a singsong voice, 'I'm going as far as Durham, if that's any good to yers.'

'You bet yer life.' Jacko jumped up and helped Adam onto the trailer that was fastened onto the back of the tractor. 'Thanks mate,' he shouted, to be echoed by the others as they climbed on board.

'Oh, what's that smell?' Len wrinkled his nose.

'Hoss shit,' Jacko replied.

'What?'

'Yeah well, it's better than walking. Home's only four or five miles from the roundabout at Durham . . . Much better than walking thirty.'

It was dark when Jacko finally walked down his street. Doris had been checking out the window all day. Adam's mother had been down twice, Danny's girlfriend had sat here for hours and his wife had called once. None of them had any news, and all the television kept showing was the same scenes from this morning.

She heard the gate open and hurried to the window, but Melanie had beaten her to the door.

Flinging it open, she threw herself into Jacko's arms, then a second later begged to be down.

'You stink, Dad,' she accused, backing away from him.

'Aye, I can smell yer from here, what the . . .?'

'It's a long story, Mam. A bath, food, then I'll fill yer in. In that order, OK.'

Later, sitting in front of the fire with Melanie on his knee, Christina by his side, Jacko filled Doris in, leaving out the bit about the sawn-off shotgun.

'So, are yer gonna tell the coppers?' Doris asked.

'How can we? Technically we were breaking the law.'

'Aye, but . . .'

'We had two cartons of baccy on the bus, Mam. That's way over our quota.'

'What the hell were yer doing with baccy? I thought Danny stuck to the rules?'

'We took a risk, Mam, all of us. If it had paid off we would have had a Christmas we would never have forgotten.'

Doris pulled a wry face. 'We're not gonna forget it in a hurry anyhow.'

31

Sanderson drove to Kurt Allendale's house while Lorraine sat in the passenger seat in silence, staring out the window. She was thinking of Debbie Stansfield, and how she was going to take the news when Lorraine told her about her son. Perhaps one question would be answered but surely a whole raft of other questions would follow? Lorraine knew in her heart that Debbie never could be satisfied, but maybe knowing that he hadn't wanted to die would help, even in just a small way. Lorraine chewed her lip before turning to Sanderson and saying, 'Yer think I'm doing the right thing? About not telling Debbie about Scottie's findings, I mean.'

Sanderson nodded his head slowly. 'It's a difficult one, boss. But yeah, I think yer right. Not until we can go to her with some of her questions answered.'

Lorraine nodded slowly. 'That's what I thought you'd say.'

'What are yer planning to ask Richy's friends? What's your strategy there?'

Lorraine thought for a moment. 'I'm not going to tell them about Richy at this stage, but I will tell them what we know about Melissa, and let them draw their own conclusions. See what their reactions are.'

'Do yer think they're involved, boss?'

Lorraine sighed. 'My gut says that they're not directly involved, but my instincts haven't exactly been on the money lately.'

Sanderson shook his head. 'Yer being too hard on yerself, boss. Yer will get to the bottom of this, I know yer will.'

'Hopefully before another teenager turns up dead.'

Sanderson didn't reply to this and they remained silent for the next few minutes. Pulling up in front of Kurt's house, Lorraine gave a watery smile to Sanderson, undid her seat belt and got out of the car. Followed by Sanderson, she walked up to the front door of Kurt Allendale's house.

Mrs Allendale answered Lorraine's knock with a curt 'Yes?'

'Mrs Allendale?' asked Lorraine, flashing her identification at her. 'I'm Detective Inspector Lorraine Hunt. Is Kurt in?'

Mrs Allendale didn't move to allow them to enter the house. Lorraine's first impression was of a hard-faced, bitter woman who thought the world owed her a living. Given that she was manicured, coiffed and plucked to perfection, and her gym-hard body was encased in designer jeans and a Whistles top, Lorraine thought that she hadn't done too badly by the world. She had her arms folded across her chest and a smile that was more akin to a sneer curled her upper lip.

'So,' she said. 'What has he done this time?'

'This time, Mrs Allendale?' Lorraine looked at Kurt's mother questioningly. 'My understanding was that he's a decent boy. Never been in trouble at school, not known to the police. Would you like to explain to me what you mean by that?'

Mrs Allendale dropped her smile. 'Yer better come in,' she said. 'But wipe yer feet before you do.'

Lorraine glanced at Sanderson who looked back at her expressionlessly as he deliberately wiped his feet on the mat. They followed Mrs Allendale into her house. She led them through a pristine hallway that smelled of cleaning products into a kitchen that was so clean that it seemed no one had ever cooked there. Mrs Allendale motioned them to sit at the kitchen table.

'So, Mrs Allendale. Can we speak to Kurt please?' asked Lorraine, with more than a hint of impatience in her voice.

'Kurt's not here, Inspector,' Mrs Allendale said smugly. 'In fact, he's run away.'

Lorraine and Sanderson glanced at each other. 'Mrs Allendale, are you aware that Richy Stansfield was found dead almost a week ago? And another of Kurt's friends, Melissa Tremaine, was found drowned in the Fatfield river just yesterday? Aren't yer concerned about yer son?'

'Concerned? About Kurt?' said Mrs Allendale with a snort. 'That boy can look after himself. Look at this,' she pulled up the sleeve of her top to reveal a faint bruise, 'this is what he did the last time I saw him. Had a good mind to report him to yer lot an' all.'

She's making a great deal of fuss about nothing, thought Lorraine. *I wonder what she's hiding.*

335

'Mrs Allendale, when was the last time yer saw yer son?'

'It must have been Wednesday night,' she answered. 'The school called to say that Kurt hadn't been to school that day. I decided to confront him about it. After all, it's up to him to decide whether he wants to waste his education or not, but if he thinks he's still gonna be sponging off me once he's over eighteen, he's got another think coming.'

Sanderson shifted uneasily in his seat. Although he hadn't said a word since he entered the Allendales' house, Lorraine knew that he was horrified by this woman's attitude towards her son and she couldn't blame him. She felt pretty much the same way.

'Mrs Allendale, yer *son*,' Lorraine placed an emphasis on the last word, 'has been missing since Wednesday evening. The same night that Melissa Tremaine went missing. That's the Melissa Tremaine who is now dead. Her parents were round at the police station first thing on Thursday morning to report her missing. But we've heard nothing from you, Mrs Allendale. We had no idea Kurt was missing until yer told us just now. Aren't you worried about yer son?'

Disconcerted, Mrs Allendale blinked at Lorraine and said nothing. Lorraine stood up with a sigh. 'We'd like to take a look at Kurt's bedroom, Mrs Allendale. See if we can find anything that might give us some clues as to where Kurt is.'

With a single, acknowledging nod of her head, Mrs Allendale led Lorraine and Sanderson upstairs to

Kurt's bedroom. 'I'll leave you to it,' she said, and Sanderson waited until he heard her walk down the stairs before saying to Lorraine, 'What a cold, hard woman. To talk about her lad sponging off her like that. He's only fifteen, for God's sake.'

Lorraine nodded, but didn't reply. She opened Kurt's wardrobe, and then went through his drawers. 'Looks like he's taken quite a few of his clothes. When the uniforms went through Melissa's bedroom, it didn't look like she took anything.'

'So he was actually intending on going somewhere.'

Lorraine thought for a moment. 'When did I pick up Duke? Wednesday night, wasn't it?'

Sanderson frowned. 'I think so.'

'Well, Kurt Allendale and Niall Campbell helped me with the dog. Perhaps he's at Niall's place now.'

'Hello?' said the woman who Lorraine took to be Mrs Campbell, Niall's mother. She had opened the door with a smile on her face that became fixed when Lorraine showed her her identification and introduced herself. 'What's the matter?' she said, her smile gradually fading and replaced by worry. 'It's Niall, isn't it? Is it drugs?'

Lorraine smiled in what she hoped was a reassuring manner and said, 'Could we talk inside, Mrs Campbell?'

Niall's mother said, as if just remembering her manners, 'Yes, of course,' and stood to one side to let Lorraine and Sanderson inside.

Sitting at the Campbells' comfortable kitchen

table, Lorraine assured Niall's mother that her son was not a known drug user. 'That's not what I've come to talk to him about. Did yer know Melissa Tremaine?'

Niall's mother nodded her head slowly. 'Unfortunately, her body was found in Fatfield river yesterday morning. As Niall was one of her friends, we'd like to talk to him to see if he can give us any idea of Melissa's state of mind.'

'Oh, poor Melissa,' Mrs Campbell said. 'But Niall and Kurt can't help you at the moment. They're gone to the movies. I don't think they have any idea what has happened. And coming so soon after Richy Stansfield too,' she shook her head. 'They're going be devastated, poor lads.'

'So yer know where Kurt Allendale is?' Sanderson leant forward in his chair and regarded Mrs Campbell seriously.

'Oh yes. He's been staying here with Niall since about Wednesday night, I think.' Niall's mother looked as if she was counting back days in her head. 'Yes. Definitely Wednesday. I was happy to have him stay. He's a really decent lad.'

'His mother didn't know where he was,' Lorraine said. 'Didn't report him missing either. Does that sound strange to you?'

Mrs Campbell's usually sunny countenance clouded over. 'When Kurt came to stay, his lip was cut. He said that he'd had a run-in with a tree. I didn't believe him.'

Lorraine nodded her head. She remembered Kurt saying that he'd got it from fooling around with

Niall. 'I saw him that night,' she said softly. 'That's not what he told me.'

The two women looked at each other. They were both thinking the same thing: *Kurt's mother did that to him.*

'Do yer know when Kurt and Niall will be back?' Lorraine asked.

'No, they didn't say.'

Lorraine and Sanderson stood up to leave. 'Here's my card, Mrs Campbell. I'd really appreciate it if you could ask Kurt and Niall to call me when they get this. They're not in trouble; we just want to ask them a few questions.'

Mrs Campbell took the card and walked Lorraine and Sanderson to the door. 'I've been worried that Niall has been on drugs for such a long time,' she said, looking close to tears. 'I think worrying about him so much has made him keep me at arm's length. But now with everything that's going on with his friends, I'm just terrified that he's into something that I can't help him get out of.'

Lorraine smiled at the other woman. 'Yer have my number. Call me if there's anything yer worried about.'

Walking down the path to the car, Sanderson said, 'Nice woman. But we haven't found out anything new here, have we?'

Lorraine waited at the side of the car while Sanderson unlocked the door. 'We've found Kurt, thank goodness. And we think that his mother has been laying into him, poor kid. And that Niall's mother is obsessed by the idea that her son is on drugs.' Lorraine got into the car. 'OK, so nothing that we didn't already suspect. But we're getting a better picture of Richy and Melissa's friends, and I think that they're into something much bigger than what they're telling us.'

32

Kurt and Niall stood at the gateway to the house on Daffodil Street. Kurt looked at his friend. 'You OK, Niall? We don't need to do this; we can go to the police and take our chances.'

Niall shook his head. 'We'll go to prison, Kurt. Marcel will make sure of that. And Rachel will be stuck with him forever.'

Kurt took a deep breath and nodded. He clutched his friend's shoulder for a moment and gave him a weak smile. He was glad that they were together on this. The two boys passed through the gate and walked up the steps to the house.

The house was buzzing with activity. Some girls were passing through the corridors with bundles of washing, others were carrying cutlery from the kitchen to the communal dining room. Kurt and Niall realised that they had arrived at the house in time for dinner. They looked at each other. It would mean that all the Blessing Guides, including Marcel and his brother Adrian, would be gathering to break bread together, as the custom of the house dictated. It wasn't going to be easy to get Rachel by herself. A blonde girl, tall and willowy with big green eyes passed by Kurt and Niall carrying a large tureen of what smelled like pumpkin soup. 'Blessed be,' she said to them with a smile.

Kurt flashed her a quick half-smile. Not in the mood for smiling, Niall nodded at her. As she walked away, Niall whispered to Kurt out of the corner of his mouth, 'What's her name again?'

'Inge. She's Swedish, remember?'

But before Niall could reply Marcel and his brother Adrian came down the stairs, followed by someone Niall didn't recognise. That didn't mean anything; there were often followers who Niall couldn't be certain of, but had Marcel's eyes lingered on him and Kurt longer than they had on the others? He felt as if someone had just poured a bucket of ice down his spine. When Niall had first come to a Blessing Guides meeting, Marcel had clutched his hand and told him that he could look deep into his soul and see the good that lay within him. Niall had the crazy feeling that Marcel was looking into him now, and knew exactly what he and Kurt were planning. He shook his head to rid himself of the thought.

Why didn't we suss him out in the beginning?

He swallowed hard against the lump forming in his throat.

Can't afford to be weak now. Gotta save Rachel even if she doesn't want to be saved.

Niall took a deep breath and looked into Marcel's eyes. He had now reached the bottom of the stairs and had paused there, looking at the two boys, his hand on the rail of the banister. Adrian stood behind him, his eyes blazing into them. 'The two prodigals.

It's good to see you, Kurt, Niall,' he said. 'I was beginning to think you had forgotten us.'

Kurt cleared his throat and squared his shoulders. 'We're sorry, Marcel. Will you forgive us?'

Niall glanced at his friend and then back at Marcel. Kurt's tone wasn't sarcastic, but Niall thought he saw a flicker of something – what? – in Marcel's eyes. Could it possibly have been suspicion?

Marcel lifted his face into a smile. 'Of course. But see me after we eat. We must find you both appropriate roles for the ceremony tomorrow.'

Kurt nodded. As Marcel and Adrian passed them, Kurt deflated, as if he had been holding his breath. 'I haven't seen Rachel yet,' he whispered to Niall.

'No, me neither,' Niall whispered back. He looked at Kurt. 'I'll tell you something for nothing though. I'm fucking scared. I'm not backing out but I'm fucking scared.'

'Me too,' said Kurt. 'Come on, let's go.'

They filed into the room. There were around a dozen Blessing Guides milling about the room, but no sign of Rachel. A large pot of rice was placed on the table, next to the tureen that had been brought in by Inge, and a few mismatched plates were on its other side. Marcel stood at the top of the room, smiling and nodding to his followers. As Niall was about to give up on seeing Rachel, she entered the room, along with Mary and the small, plain-looking girl who had joined the Blessing Guides after them. Rachel was smiling, glowing with happiness and pleasure, and she looked at Marcel as if he was the only person in the room.

Marcel looked round the room and motioned for them all to join hands. Niall grasped Kurt's hand, and the hand of a brown-haired girl whose accent gave away the fact she came from Liverpool. Everyone bowed their heads.

'We give thanks for the food, for the company and for our health.' Marcel stopped speaking for a moment as if he was in silent prayer. 'Amen,' he said quietly.

The group murmured 'Amen,' in response, and everyone dropped their hands, although they remained standing in a circle. Marcel looked around the room with a soft smile on his face. Niall found it difficult to meet his gaze; inside, his stomach was churning with anger and fear. When Marcel spoke, his voice was warm and tinged with happiness. 'As you know, tomorrow evening marks a new beginning, for us and for Mary. She will travel in the world, spreading our word of hope and happiness and peace. And so I am calling a new Mary, Louise, to be my wife.' Marcel held a hand out to Louise and she went to stand beside him. 'But I am happy to be calling another, Rachel, to be Louise's handmaiden and to help us on our journey.' He held out his other hand to Rachel who, beaming happily, moved out of the circle and stood beside Marcel. 'The ceremony tomorrow night will be an affirmation of our principles and will bring our initiates into the circle of the Blessing Guides.' Adrian came up behind Marcel with a steel box that he held open. 'And now, before we break bread together, please hand over your daily tithes.'

The Blessing Guides formed a line and each of them dropped an envelope into the box, before moving to the table and dishing themselves out a bowl of rice and vegetables. Kurt and Niall held back at the end of the line. As they approached Marcel, his benign expression changed and his face became much darker. 'You have nothing to offer us, do you?' he said as they stood before him. 'You know the laws of our community, you know I ask little of you in return for the wonderful gifts I offer you. You come back asking forgiveness and yet you've neglected to bring me even a small offering?' Marcel shook his head. 'I am disappointed in you both. Come with me.'

Kurt was about to speak but Marcel silenced him with a glance. 'We will discuss this separately,' he said firmly. 'There is no need to trouble the faithful with this. You will come with me into my quarters.'

Niall and Kurt glanced at each other and then Niall looked at Adrian. He had closed the steel box, and locked it, and was now looking at them both with an expression on his face that Niall couldn't read but definitely didn't like. Reluctantly, the boys followed Marcel out of the dining room and into the room that he used for his private conversations. Marcel motioned them to sit on the sofa in front of his desk, and once again Adrian stood at the door so that no one could enter or escape.

'So, Niall and Kurt,' Marcel began. 'Can I ask you a question before we begin? Why did you come back?' He leant back in his chair and regarded them both. There was no warmth in his eyes.

Kurt took a deep breath. 'We realised where our

true family is. It's here, with you. We're sorry that we disappointed you but we were weak and frightened. The night watchman –'

Marcel sighed. 'For those of us bound to the earth, there's always weakness and fear surrounding the most natural thing in the world. Death. You are showing no faith, not in me, nor in God. For didn't He send His only son to give those who believe eternal life? And hasn't He blessed me with the gift of bringing His son back into the world? This is what is important, not the passing of those who don't believe.'

Kurt dropped his head down and was staring at the floor as if ashamed. Niall noticed, though, that Kurt's face was burning and that he was clenching his fists hard. 'And you, Niall.' Niall's head snapped up as Marcel turned his attention to him. 'What do you have to say for yourself?'

Niall took a deep breath. 'All yer say about us is true. We're weak, we're tied to the earth and we've let you down. But please,' his voice took on a pleading tone, 'we want to prove to you that we're worthy. Give us one more chance. We'll do anything.'

'Are you sure that you deserve this second chance?' Marcel put his palms together and leant his forehead on them as if in prayer or deep in thought. After a few moments, he said, 'Our God is one of forgiveness. You shall have your second chance, but I need to be shown that I can trust you. Tomorrow night, after the ceremony, you shall escort our old Mary back to this house where preparations will be made for her to spread our word. This shall be your task.'

The boys nodded.

'Now go. Ask Inge what you can do to help prepare for tomorrow night. And remember – I will be keeping an eye on you.'

Adrian moved from the door so that the boys could leave. After they had gone, looking at Marcel, he said, 'So you really trust them?'

'No,' Marcel replied starkly. 'It's obvious that they're here out of misplaced loyalty to Rachel. It's better that they're here so that I can keep an eye on them.'

'You need me to speak to Rachel?'

Marcel shook his head. 'No. I'm not worried about Rachel. She has proved herself,' he paused and looked his brother straight in the eye, 'faithful.' Adrian sniggered. 'But tomorrow night. You've made the plans for Mary?'

Adrian nodded his head.

'Good. Let's give Kurt and Niall the chance to join her on her journey.'

A look of understanding passed between the two men. 'I shall make the arrangements,' Adrian said.

33

Luke tossed and turned, muttering loudly. His dreams were tormented, guilt-ridden horror stories, dreams where he tried to grasp something important just outside his reach, dreams where he was chasing someone elusive down blackened corridors. Dreams where he felt like he was doing something wrong, dreams where he was the villain of the piece.

A loud scream caused him to sit upright. Heart pounding he shot out of bed, pulled on some pyjama bottoms and threw open the door. Carter was in the position where Luke had left him last night, sitting in front of the door to what was now Selina's room. 'You all right?' Luke asked.

Carter looked up from the book he was reading and smiled weakly. 'Yeah, I'm fine. That's gone on all night. I'm beginning to get immune to it. Yer must have been dead to the world.'

They fell silent as fists pounded on the door. 'Let me out,' came a muffled voice from behind it. 'Yer wankers, yer've got no right to keep me here.'

Luke shook his head and sighed heavily. 'I'm going to get dressed. What's the time?'

Carter looked at his watch. 'It's half one. Doesn't time fly when yer having fun?' he said wryly.

'Jesus, I had no idea it was so late. Sorry, mate. I'm going to have to ask yer to hang on a bit longer. I need to talk to Lorraine. I told her yesterday that I was going to talk to her today; I can't let her down again.'

Carter nodded. 'That's fine. Slept plenty in the hospital. You go and talk to the boss. She'll understand when yer tell her the truth. Yer know she will.'

Luke sighed again and ran his palm over his head. 'Càn't say I'm looking forward to it though, Carter . . .'

Luke went back into his room and shut the door. Slowly he began to dress. He thought through how he would approach Lorraine; what he would say to her. Start by apologising for the time off and offer his resignation. God, that was the last thing he wanted to do. He couldn't imagine not being a police officer. And he knew Lorraine; he knew she'd be angry about him not telling her the truth. She'd probably expect him to resign. He sighed as he slipped on his jeans and pulled a dark red jumper over his head. This was a complete mess. Just as he was starting to get close to Lorraine, too. But if he had the choice, he wouldn't do a single thing differently. There was no way he could have ignored Selina's plight. He hadn't known her for sixteen years; there was no way he was going to abdicate his responsibilities as a parent now.

Once dressed he left his bedroom. Passing Carter on his way to the kitchen he asked, 'Toast, coffee?'

Carter stretched his stiff limbs. 'Don't mind if I do.

Heavy on the butter and the sugar.' He tapped on the door. 'Want some brekkie, Selina?'

'Fuck off.' The voice tried for defiance but just sounded sulky and tired.

Carter looked at Luke. 'Don't think she's slept a wink.'

'Think she's still wired.' Luke smiled ruefully and walked into the kitchen.

When was it all gonna end?

What state was she gonna be in when it did?

The toaster popped at much the same time as the kettle blew steam, startling Luke as he swung his head from one noise to the other. He decided to try and feed Selina first, get it over with.

He made milky tea for her and buttered two slices of toast. Over the last few days she had managed to swallow small portions of food, some of which had come right back up but, judging by the energy she still had, she must have kept some sustenance down.

He walked back down the hallway, carrying a plate and a big mug of tea and gestured with his head for Carter to open the door.

'You sure?'

Luke nodded.

Apprehensively, not knowing what to expect, Carter opened the door and stepped inside the room. It had once been a beautiful room. Carter could still tell that from the lemon-yellow walls and the matching curtains that gave the room a lovely glow. Luke had obviously decorated the room with care. But the curtains were shredded and the bedspread looked as if Selina had taken offence to it and ripped it out of spite. Carter wrinkled his nose. The smell was terrible.

Selina was sitting cross-legged in the middle of the bed, wearing a frown that cut deep lines into her forehead. Even so, Carter thought she was the most beautiful girl he had ever seen.

Next to Lorraine, of course, he hastily told himself.

'Close the door, Carter,' Luke said as he stepped through. 'And stand beside it.' Carter hastily obliged.

'What, yer think I might do a runner?' Selina asked, a smirk in her voice.

'I know yer will.'

'Huh,' she shrugged, looking at the breakfast offerings. 'Don't want that shit.'

Actually, she was starving, and wanted nothing more than to grab the food and eat and eat. Her mouth was starting to water at the smell of toast and rich butter. Trust him to make perfect toast. Looking up at her father's face, the father that she had never known she had, she had another thought. She wanted something more than food, she wanted to ram the toast in his face, the bastard who had put her through this hell that was only marginally starting to recede.

She folded her arms across her chest. 'I want to go home.'

Luke shook his head. 'This is your home. From now on, the only home yer have.'

'I'm not staying here . . . I've got friends. They'll be wondering where I am.'

'Yeah, needle buddies.' The disgust showed on Luke's face. He couldn't help it. He hated drugs, had seen the effects that drugs had on families time and time again. Had carted kids off the street and straight into the mental hospital from the effects of dope. Some had made it back onto the streets, a couple had made it home and some of them were still in overcrowded mental wards years down the line.

'You need to have something to eat. I've brought you this.'

'Don't want any food,' Selina snarled, but the way she was looking at the plate belied her words.

Luke weighed her up. She needed to eat. He might be exhausted but he wasn't going to give up. 'If I give you this,' he looked sternly into her eyes, 'yer have to promise that you won't throw it at me, or at Carter or the floor.' Selina didn't say anything, just looked at the plate hungrily. 'You promise?' he asked.

Selina raised her eyes to his and then sullenly nodded her head. Luke handed her the plate with the two slices of toast and waited to see her reaction before he passed the tea over. She stared at the plate for a moment, then slowly reached out and took it. She nibbled into the first slice of toast, then reached out for the tea.

Warily and, with the undeniable impression that somewhere deep inside herself she was laughing at him, Luke passed the hot tea over. He fully expected to be doused with it at any moment. Why should today be any different?

But Selina surprised him. Still looking him straight in the eye she took the tea and drank.

Inwardly Luke breathed easier. Carter, who had held his breath without knowing it, let it out noisily. 'So,' he turned full on to Luke, 'what time are yer gonna see the boss?'

'What about me?' Selina said around a mouthful of toast.

'I'm babysitting.'

'God,' Selina said sarcastically. 'Yer not much more than a baby yerself . . . I bet you're a pushover an' all . . . What are you gonna do, Ginge, when I just get up and walk out? Eh, what can you do?'

Carter shrugged. He would do what he had to do. Luke was depending on him. 'Me name's not Ginge. You can call me Steven, or Steve, or Carter, everybody else does – call me Carter, that is . . . But if me mam's there yer have to call me Steven 'cos she goes mad if anybody calls me Steve.'

Selina spread her hands wide, and curled her lip. 'Like I needed to know all that.'

Luke felt his hackles rise. Both he and Lorraine were very protective of the young policeman 'That's enough of yer cheek. He was only trying to be friendly.'

Selina snarled. 'Who gives a fuck?'

'And we'll have enough of that street talk in here. This is my home and you'll learn to respect it.'

'So,' she shrugged, then rose up off the bed as if she were sizing up to him, 'what are you gonna do about it, eh? Yer gonna get the coppers? Ha, I think that's up to me, isn't it? I mean, keeping people against their will, isn't that called kidnapping or abduction? You can get years for that, clever bastard.'

Luke looked at her, then turning he ushered Carter out of the door. Putting one hand on the knob he said, 'Something I forgot to mention before. Carter and me – we're coppers!'

Satisfied by the look on her face he closed the door.

'Well done, Luke. That fairly took the wind out of her sails,' Carter grinned.

After Luke had left to see Lorraine, Carter went into the sitting room and turned Luke's Eagles CD on.

'Good, that'll drown out her wheedling voice,' he muttered as 'Hotel California' immediately filled the room.

He had managed to keep a casual front with Luke, but in reality, the night he had spent outside Selina's room had been a trial for him in more ways than one. She had tempted him with things through the night that he would never dare in a million years repeat to Luke. He could stil feel his face burning now, just thinking about it.

My God! . . . Some of the things she said.

Half of which he had not understood, but he had made a good guess at.

'Bloody hell,' he said as he heard her yelling again, 'does she never stop?'

'Turn that shit off,' Selina yelled.

'Why, don't yer like it?' Carter shouted back from the kitchen where he had found a jar of beetroot. He collected a fork from the cutlery drawer and trotted back to Selina's room.

'Fuck off,' she said when she heard him sit back

down in the chair outside her room. 'Who the fuck likes that kind of noise anyhow?'

'Yer dad, he loves it. It's his favourite group, and he would love to see them live, if he ever could.'

'Who the fuck asked for a conversation? And he's not my dad.' She went off on one then and Carter could hear her stamping about the room and throwing things off the wall. A loud crash and he guessed that she'd pulled the wardrobe over or, at the least, the set of drawers.

Carter sat patiently while Selina worked her way around the room, wreaking as much havoc and destruction as she could. Suddenly she calmed down. Carter could hear her laboured breathing through the door.

'Yer all right now? Yer've not hurt yerself or anything?'

But Carter's concern only set her off. 'What the fuck do you care? Are you round the fucking bend or what? Who the fuck wants a copper for a father, eh? How uncool is that? Bastard . . . What the fuck am I gonna tell me friends? How can yer say your father's turned up after all this time and guess what, he's only a fucking copper! A fucking copper . . .' she raged. 'No way . . . Do you think I'll have any friends when I finally get to go home and they find that out? Fuck, I wish that bastard wasn't me dad.' She went quiet then, as if she was thinking. Or perhaps she was just listening to the end of 'Hotel California'.

Carter made himself comfortable on the small red armchair. His back was to the door, and he was thinking, *I bet poor Luke wishes with all of his heart that he wasn't yer dad.*

'Hotel California' finished and then, as if coming out of a trance, Selina shouted, 'I hate you!'

'Really? Well, I don't care what yer think of me. Me mam says everybody gets what they deserve, but yer dad deserves much better than you, and that's a fact.'

He listened to the indignant silence that seeped through the door, and contentedly plunged his fork into the beetroot.

Fifteen minutes later, having scoffed most of the jar, he moved his chair uninvited into her bedroom, then proceeded to bore her into submission with numerous details of the history of not only Houghton-le-Spring but the whole North-East.

'Have yer heard about the Lambton Wyrm?' Carter asked. Selina had seemed to have calmed down and was regarding him warily.

'What the fuck's the Lambton Wyrm?' she asked, interested despite herself.

'It's a legend. There's even a song about it.' Carter started to sing, but after a few bars. Selina put her hands to her ears and rolled about the bed as if in pain.

'Enough, enough, for Christ's sake . . . You so cannot sing.'

'Well, that's not very nice,' Carter said, looking at her with a hurt expression on his face.

'Are you for real or what?' she replied, 'Don't say you're taking the huff, geez, a babysitter that takes the huff.'

'Can you sing, like?'

'Well,' she hesitated, then burst out with a genuine laugh. 'No, not really.'

Carter laughed with her. She had a beautiful laugh and he liked her much better now than when he had first met her. He had no delusions about his singing voice, he knew that he couldn't sing and had just pretended to take the huff. It seemed to have done the trick though – she was a lot calmer and friendlier, gorgeous now that she was smiling – but he knew that she was volatile and needed careful handling, and would do for a while yet.

'Tell me about him,' she said suddenly.

'You mean yer dad?'

She shrugged in non-committal sort of a way.

'OK, well, what do yer know?'

'Nothing . . . I was dragged off the street into a police car and told I was going to meet my dad.'

'Big shock, eh.'

'You bet!' She sat quiet for a moment, a wry smile on her face, before going on. 'I thought he was dead, like my mother . . . I don't know why, it just seemed the easiest way to think . . . Gran never mentioned him . . . Then he turns up out of the blue, and he's a copper. Now that's hard to swallow.'

Carter nodded. 'Tell yer one thing about yer dad, yer might as well give up, and start toeing the line now, 'cos if yer've got plans to run, he'll find yer wherever yer are and drag yer right back, and yer'll have to go through the last few days all over again. It'll be a bit like spending yer life in hell, know what I mean.'

Selina shuddered as Carter went on, 'He's one of

357

the best, your dad. A really good and kind man . . . The best.'

'Has he got any . . .?'

'What?' Carter asked.

'Yer know, a squeeze.'

'Oh, yer mean a girlfriend?'

Selina nodded slowly, looking at Carter as if he was a dimwit.

'Well, yer see it's a bit like this, he loves the boss and she loves him. The thing is, everybody knows it but them two.'

'Oh.' She thought this over for a few minutes then said, 'I would like to take a bath now.'

'OK, yer do look a bit scruffy, like.'

'Well, that's not very nice.' This time Selina pretended to take the huff, but she couldn't keep up the pretence for very long and they both laughed. Then Selina swung her legs off the bed and headed towards the door.

'Hang on, just a minute,' Carter said.

She turned, and watched Carter rise to his feet.

'I have to go with yer,' Carter said, with an embarrassed look on his face.

'What! Into the bath?'

'Well no, oh my God.' Carter blushed a deep scarlet colour. 'Not exactly into the bath, that would be, oh dear . . . I'll, er, I'll stand outside the door, but,' he reached over and took hold of her elbow, 'sorry, but I have to do this.'

Selina looked at Carter appraisingly, smiling that slow, gorgeous smile at him. 'Are you a virgin, Carter?'

If it was at all possible Carter blushed on top of his blush, and Selina grinned, mischief dancing in her eyes.

'I, I . . .' he couldn't go on. Shaking his head, Carter ushered her to the bedroom door. 'Luke says there are some clean clothes in the bathroom.'

'He's a mind reader or something?'

'What do yer mean?'

'Forget it.' She allowed Carter to guide her up the stairs.

Outside the bathroom door, she turned, glanced quickly to each side, as if weighing up any possibility of escape, but Carter was blocking every angle.

Sighing, she said, 'So what's she like, this boss?'

'Sparkling.' Carter smiled.

'Sparkling,' Selina repeated softly. She walked into the bathroom. At its threshold she stopped and turned round and smiled that smile at him. 'Want to come in? It's boring taking a bath by yourself.'

Carter pulled the sternest face he could, even though it had turned red again, then gently pushed her inside the bathroom, and quickly locked it so she couldn't get out.

'Yer dad says there's some clean clothes in there. He says that if yer complain about them it was you who picked them at the Metro centre the other day. But he says yer were as high as a kite. So what yer got, yer got.'

He heard her groan and guessed she didn't like the clothes.

34

The sun was very low in the sky and, despite the central heating, Lorraine felt a chill run through her body. *Fuck, it's cold*, she thought. She looked in her drawer for a cigarette substitute, but finding none, sighed and pushed the drawer back in its place. Sanderson had volunteered to get sandwiches for lunch and Lorraine was looking forward to having something in her stomach.

Lorraine uncapped a pen and starting making notes on the pad in front of her. It wasn't working; there was nothing new that she could think of that would actually help the investigation. 'Jacobs!' she yelled as she noticed her pass by her door.

Jacobs came in, looking frazzled. 'Yes, boss?'

'How are you getting on with the missing persons register? Any luck on the girl with the port-wine stain yet?'

Jacobs sighed. 'Nothing within the last six weeks. Sorry, boss.'

Lorraine felt the frustrations of the last week build up within her and explode. 'For fuck's sake, Jacobs! I asked yer to look back five years, not six weeks! What the fuck have yer been doing?'

'It's been busy out there. I've had to man the desk

as well as look after Carter's work –' Jacobs said, her excuses made all the more annoying by the high-pitched whine in her voice.

'We're all busy,' said Lorraine, her temper rising. 'We're always busy. We're the police, for God's sake, and we work outside the 9 to 5 and we don't do things half-arsed because there are people out there who actually count on us. I shouldn't need to have to tell you that. Now get the fuck out of here and do your fucking job!'

Sara Jacobs looked at Lorraine as if she couldn't believe her ears. Turning red she mumbled, 'Yes, boss,' and stumbled out of the room, only to walk straight into Luke.

Surprise at seeing Luke certainly registered itself on Jacobs's face, and Lorraine could only wonder whether she looked just as shocked. She readjusted her features into a neutral expression. *Fuck, get a grip, he told me that he was coming in today to tell me why he's been away.* Jacobs, glancing between both of them, scuttled out the door and down the hallway.

Lorraine drew herself up to her full height. Now, with Luke in front of her, she didn't trust herself to say anything. They looked at each other for a long moment, Lorraine taking in his comforting familiarity while noticing that his face had a slightly different cast to it – he looked tired, worn out, troubled. Luke was the first to break the silence. He smiled, looked down at the floor and then up again at Lorraine. 'Sounds like you were finally giving Jacobs what for.'

Lorraine smiled. 'Lost my rag a bit. Shouldn't let the little bitch get to me, but at least I don't have to hold Carter's hand while he's doing the job. Just told her a few home truths, that's all. And if Clark has a problem with that, well . . .' Lorraine thought for a moment, 'he can bite me.'

Luke laughed. But then there was another moment of tense silence. 'Um, well, do you want to sit down?' Lorraine said, pointing to a chair. *God, how fucking formal does that sound?*

Luke took a seat, and Lorraine sat behind her desk. *This is ridiculous. He's obviously come in to talk, and that's the last thing we're doing.*

Lorraine took a deep breath. 'So, how've yer been, Luke?'

'Quite well, actually,' he said, looking up at Lorraine, his face deadly serious.

Lorraine fought to keep her expression neutral. 'So, if yer were feeling well, why did yer not come in? It's not like you, no explanation, no nothing.'

Luke let out a deep breath. He leant his elbows on his knees and washed his face with his hands. He then looked back up at Lorraine and regarded her. It seemed to Lorraine that he was weighing up something, something about her.

'This is harder to say than I thought it was going to be,' he said finally. 'So I'm just gonna tell yer straight.' He took another breath, straightened up and looked Lorraine directly in the eyes. 'I have a daughter. She is sixteen years old and a drug addict. Until a few days ago I never even knew she existed,' he sighed. He put it as simply as he could.

Lorraine stared at him. This was the last thing she expected him to say. *Bloody hell. You poor sod, a teenage daughter.*

'What, er, what's her name?'

'Selina.'

'That's a very pretty name.'

Luke nodded in response. Lorraine knew she was making small talk, but her mind was reeling. *A sixteen-year-old daughter who is also a drug addict, Christ!*

'She's a very pretty girl,' Luke said after another awkward moment. 'The double of her mother when she was that age . . . She's dead now.'

Lorraine had now run out of words, she simply didn't know what to say to him. The silence between them was becoming uncomfortable, until Luke broke it by saying, 'If you want my resignation.' He shrugged his shoulders and held his hands out in front of him.

Lorraine shook her head. 'What?'

'My resignation . . . It's my own fault, I should have told you earlier, not just stayed off work . . . The least I should have done was give you a proper explanation. But I just didn't know how to tell yer.'

Lorraine looked steadily at him. 'I think yer should've told me, but I think I can understand why it might have been difficult for you. As for yer resignation, I can't accept that, Luke. Yer the best policeman I know.'

Luke smiled sadly and said, 'But I let you down, boss. I can understand it if yer don't trust me any more.'

Yeah, Lorraine thought. *Like yer trusted me. Like you trusted me with yer secret. After what I said to yer in the pub.* But instead she said, 'I do trust yer Luke. But what about Selina? Who's with her now?'

'Carter. He agreed to help out to give me a rest and to come and talk to you. Hopefully she'll be better in another few days.'

Yeah, and that's when the problems will start, no shortage of what she's addicted to up here, she thought, but said instead, 'So this daughter, yer never knew about her at all?'

Luke looked her in the eye, 'No, her mother was my first girlfriend.' He shrugged and then was silent for a moment as if remembering. 'She moved away, probably before even she knew . . . I never saw her again . . . We were just kids.'

'Rotten way to find out.'

Luke nodded again, and she could see he'd been really embarrassed to lay this at her door. She sighed, feeling sorry for him now. *Why the fuck was life so complicated? Just when I decided I really do love this man, just when I was certain that he feels the same, just when I was about to give in and go with the flow, this happens.*

'She's gonna take some watching, Luke. Even when her system's clear the temptation will still be there. It's everywhere . . . She'll be going ape shit at the moment, eh.'

'You bet yer life . . .' Luke said with feeling.

'Well, yer gonna need more than one babysitter to see yer through this. Or maybe yer can go on shorter hours, though I really do need yer here.'

And what about us? she wondered. *Will there ever be an 'us' now?*

'She should be on the mend soon enough. It's just keeping her off everything until she's completely clean. At the moment she'll do a runner as soon as me back's turned.'

'How about Dinwall and Sanderson? I'm sure they'll offer their services, plus I don't mind doing a spot of babysitting now and then.'

He smiled with genuine warmth. It was his first real smile since he'd entered the room. 'Thanks, boss. Yer a gem. And I want to get back to work full time. It'll do me good to get me mind off things.'

She smiled back. 'Good. It's good to have yer back. Go and sort yer babysitters out, then we need to get to work. There's a religious group living up at the Seven Sisters in caravans and using a house in the Seahills as their base. There is certainly something dodgy going on there.'

'What? Yer mean a cult group?'

'Yeah. Picks on young people by the look of things. I don't know what they're involved with, but there's nothing that we can pin on them at the moment.' She sighed. 'And then there's Debbie Stansfield. We've just had word from Scottie that Richard's death is suspicious – we're looking at a murder investigation now – but I don't want to tell her that until we've got some more answers. She's been round here every morning since it happened, and the gutless wonder through there, Jacobs, has just been letting her walk on through. So, to say I'm missing you – and Carter,' she hurriedly added, 'would without doubt be an under-statement.'

Luke looked as if he was going to say something, but then changed his mind. 'So tell me more about this group, then. Seems a bit strange. They're not known to the police?'

'I wouldn't say that exactly. They were based in Europe for some time and there was some trouble there. But it seems that this group, since they have been in England, have been very quiet, very well behaved. In fact they do nothing at all to draw attention to themselves. But why did they wash up on my shore, and why are they so quiet? What are they hiding?'

'Well behaved or just better at covering up trouble?'

'That's the thing,' said Lorraine. *God, it's good to be able to bounce ideas off him again.* 'Just don't know. But two kids – Richy and Melissa Tremaine – have died and . . .'

'What?' said Luke. 'Melissa Tremaine? The big girl? The one we saw at school?'

Shit. Of course. He hasn't been here. He doesn't know. 'I'm afraid so. She went missing on Wednesday, found yesterday morning in Fatfield river. It turns out that both of them were connected to the religious group – they call themselves the Blessing Guides by the way – but nothing sticks. And get this, a coin with the same symbol that was carved into Manners's body was found in Melissa's pocket.'

'Have you discovered what it means yet?'

'The fish and the circle? It's an ancient Christian symbol . . .'

'Surely that's enough to bring in the leader . . .' Luke interrupted Lorraine but she stopped him from going on with a glance.

'There's so many threads here. I'm sure they're all connected, but I want to tread very carefully. We can't say for sure whether it's the Blessing Guides, we can't say for sure whether the leader – his name is Marcel Gottsdiener – is involved, whether it's another individual or whether it's the whole group. If I'm going to bring them in I want it to be very clear about why. They've slipped through the fingers of the police in other countries before. I don't want them to slip through mine.'

Luke nodded. 'I can understand that.'

Lorraine sighed. 'What really gets me is Melissa. I know she wanted to say something to me – I picked her up to take her to school on the day she went missing – but she didn't.' Lorraine lifted her eyes to Luke. 'There was something about Melissa. She wasn't the hard girl she made herself out to be. It was all a front. And I feel that I let her down somehow. That if only I had pressed her more she might have said something; she might still be alive now.'

'It's not your fault, Lorraine.'

There we go. He's saying my name again. I wish he wouldn't do that. It sends goosebumps up my spine.

Luke leaned back in his chair. 'I don't like these cults, even the quiet ones. Something spooky about all of them if yer ask me.'

They sat in silence for a moment, each lost in their

own private thoughts. To break the ice, Lorraine said, 'So, Mavis told me she had invited you over to Christmas dinner. Are you still going to come?'

Shit, why the fuck did I ask him that?

He's got more on his mind than bloody Christmas dinner and that's a fact.

'Well,' he hesitated, wondering how to put it, then said gently, 'I'd love to come, Lorraine, but in the circumstances, I can hardly bring Selina, can I?'

'Ohh, er, course yer can. Two coppers, the Hippy and the Rock Chick – Selina doesn't stand a chance.'

Luke smiled sadly. Although he would dearly love to go to Lorraine's for dinner, Selina was his main priority at the moment. He owed it to her poor mother, who had been so, so . . . he struggled to see her face. It was strange to find that his heart could ache so much for a girl of so long ago.

'I don't really know,' he shrugged. 'God only knows what sort of mood she'll be in.'

Lorraine stood up. He was just pussy-footing around and she'd had enough. 'OK, Luke, we'll leave it for now . . . We have work to do.'

Luke, feeling like he'd missed a golden opportunity, but in his mind still adamant that Selina must, for the moment, come first, stood up as well. 'If yer don't mind, I'd like five minutes with Sanderson and Dinwall.'

'Sure.'

She watched him go, nibbling at her lip in frustration. Had she botched it up again?

Oh hell.

35

Jacko knocked on Danny's door. The lights were out. There wasn't even a flicker from the televison. It was gone eleven but he had to talk to Danny. He knocked again, not too loud – he didn't want to wake the neighbourhood up – and was rewarded by the landing light flashing on.

'Good,' he breathed, his breath rushing out into the night, highlighted by the light coming through the door.

Danny opened the door. 'What? Can yer not see we're in bed?'

'I need to talk to yer.' Uninvited, Jacko stepped over the threshold.

'Come in, why don't yer,' Danny said, his back to Jacko as he walked along the hallway to the kitchen.

'Sorry, Danny, but I couldn't rest . . . Not with the thoughts of all those drugs on the streets, drugs that we brought in even if we didn't know anything about it. We have to go to the police as soon as possible.'

Danny spun round in the kitchen doorway, then walked backwards into the centre of the kitchen. He rubbed his face with his hands then said, 'How the fuck can we go to the coppers, eh? Yer saw the fucking gun didn't yer?'

'We have to.'

'Look the others agree, no coppers . . . Do yer not think I'm pissed off as it is, they've got me fucking bus for God's sake. Do yer know how much buses cost? I can never in a million years replace Lizzy . . . I'm fucking gutted here, man.'

'Lizzy's in Brian's yard.'

'Fuck off!'

'Straight up.'

Danny grabbed hold of Jacko's arm. 'Is she all right, no dents, no bits missing?'

'Looked fine to me. The cargo's still there an' all.'

'Yer've had a good look then?' Danny turned to the kitchen drawer and raked around. 'Where the fuck? I put 'em in here, I know I did.'

'What yer looking for?'

'The spare keys.'

'Can't drive it.'

'But yer said . . .'

'There's a big yellow clamp on the front wheel.'

'Shit, shit, shit.' Danny thumped the breakfast bench.

'I reckon we go in the morning and talk to Lorraine Hunt. We can trust her.'

'A copper's a copper, yer can't trust none of them. For fuck's sake Jacko, that's basic, even yer idiot kid on the street knows that.'

'This one's different, she's straight as a die. I know her mam. She'll help. She helped with Melanie.'

'What, help us get stuff the customs are gunning

for, after that huge sting they've pulled today. She had to be in on that yer know . . . Are you for real or what?'

'No, yer've got receipts. Everything tallies.'

'What about the baccy?'

'Bin it.'

'What? After all the trouble we went to going all the way to Belgium? And do yer not think the coppers are gonna go over everything before we even get a look-in?' Danny shook his head. 'Yer not thinking straight, Jacko.'

Jacko sat down on one of the breakfast stools. 'Well, you think, then, 'cos I reckon we should go. Look, Inspector Hunt's a good 'un, she's straight up, honest. I reckon we've got a good chance – if we help her she'll help us . . . There must have been a good quantity of drugs under the van for them to do what they did. The coppers are gonna love us for that.'

'Don't want no love-in with a pile of coppers.'

Jacko grinned. 'Look, I'm off. But yer know I'm right. I'll come round in the morning when yer've had time to think about it, OK? And we'll go in together.'

Danny saw Jacko out and, as he climbed the stairs to his bed, knowing that his girlfriend would, by now, be snoring her head off, he realised that what Jacko had said made a lot of sense. He might even get Lizzy back.

36

It had been three hours since Adrian had, with a smirk, led Kurt and Niall into the freezing cold. He pointed around the backyard that was overgrown with weeds and grass, and had rubbish lying around the place. 'If you can't provide us with a tithe, you are to clear this ground,' he ordered. 'I expect this to be cleared in time for the ceremony.'

'But we'll never get it done by then . . .' Kurt had complained.

Adrian looked at him without emotion. There was no anger, no hatred in his eyes, not even annoyance. Somehow, the way he looked at him, blankly, as if Kurt was little more than an object he passed on the street, made him more nervous than if Adrian had looked at him with real malevolence. Adrian said slowly, enunciating each word carefully as if he was talking to someone of little intelligence, 'This is a community. Everyone in a community has to contribute to it, otherwise it fails. This is what you need to contribute, in lieu of a tithe. Do you have any money?' Adrian barely waited for a response. 'Didn't think so. Now get to work.'

The ground was frozen, the wind biting and, although the hard, back-breaking work warmed the boys up a little, their hands were soon numb and raw from the cold. Niall had had to sit down and rest from exhaustion more than once. Kurt leant on his spade and looked at his friend worryingly. 'You OK?'

Niall nodded, breathing heavily. He rubbed his hands together. 'I can't feel my fucking fingers.' He looked up at Kurt. 'What's the point of doing this anyway?'

'Didn't you hear Adrian? It's for the good of the community,' Kurt said sarcastically. 'More like punishment, I'd say.' He turned his head to look up at the house. 'We've got to go and find Rachel. We've got to tell her about Melissa. We've got to get her out of the house. And then I think we have to go to the police.'

'But what about the night watchman?'

Kurt sighed. 'I've been thinking about that.' He paused, looking down at the ground, the muscles in his jaw working. He then looked Niall straight in the eye. 'We have to come clean. We have to own up and face the consequences.'

Niall didn't look convinced. 'But what will happen to us? Won't we go to prison?'

Kurt shrugged. 'I've thought about that too. Maybe we should. OK, we didn't push him off the roof, but he wouldn't have gone up there if it weren't for us. And he's dead now. And Richy's dead, and Melissa . . . Don't yer feel guilty?'

Niall sighed and nodded his head. 'But jail . . .'

Kurt laid down his spade. 'Let's not think about that now. We need to find Rachel and get her out of here. Come on.'

Niall stood up stiffly and followed Kurt into the house. They shut the door quietly behind them. There were sounds from the kitchen next door where dinner was being prepared, but otherwise the house seemed deserted.

'Where do yer think she'll be?' whispered Niall.

Kurt shook his head. 'No idea.'

'Should we split up? I could check out downstairs, you could go upstairs . . .'

Kurt thought for a moment, and then shook his head. 'That's probably the right thing to do, but I don't know whether I really want to do this by myself.'

Niall nodded. Secretly, he was relieved.

'I think we should try upstairs first,' Kurt said. 'Let's go.'

Neither boy had ever been upstairs before. Upstairs was where Marcel's inner circle slept – most of the Blessing Guides shared caravans on the Seven Sisters – and the top floors were out of bounds. Kurt and Niall knew that if Adrian found them there, there would be hell to pay. So they took the stairs carefully, wincing each time the boards creaked under their feet.

The last vestiges of winter light fell on the red, threadbare carpet on the first floor. They could hear a conversation coming from a room at the far end of the corridor. Kurt looked at Niall and they walked towards the sound. The door was slightly ajar, and through it, Kurt could see Rachel sitting cross-legged behind Louise on a single bed with a pink candlewick bedspread, smiling as she wove Louise's hair into a plait. Louise was talking animatedly, but Mary, who sat on a chair at the foot of the bed, was staring sullenly at the floor. Kurt pushed the door open further, and the three girls looked up. Rachel's face fell when she saw Kurt and Niall standing on the doorway. She jumped off the bed and walked towards them, hissing, 'What the fuck are yers doing here? Don't yer know yer not allowed here?'

Kurt grabbed her wrist. 'We need to talk to yer, Rachel. We need to tell yer what we know.'

Rachel jerked her wrist away from his grasp. 'Don't touch me, yer have no right,' she said with venom. Kurt looked taken aback, as if he had been slapped.

Niall noticed that Mary had snapped her head up and was looking at Kurt with a strange expression on her face. It wasn't anger or fear. Niall thought that Mary looked at them with a mixture of curiosity and – was he reading too much into this? – hope. But she wore that expression for only a moment; in a split second she had replaced it with her usual impassive mask.

'Listen,' Kurt whispered, 'we need to speak to yer. Please. Let us just speak to yer for five minutes. That's all we ask.'

Louise sat on the bed looking at them, her pale face shocked and worried. 'Rachel?' she quavered.

Rachel turned round. 'Don't worry, Louise.' She turned back to Kurt. 'OK. Five minutes.' She pushed past them and opened a door on the other side of the corridor. 'In here.'

The room was cold and dark. Sparsely furnished,

bunk beds were arranged against three walls. Niall closed the door behind him. Rachel stood in the middle of the room with her arms folded across her chest. 'OK, out with it.'

Kurt glanced at Niall and then took a deep breath. 'Rachel, have yer heard about Melissa? She's dead.'

Rachel put a hand to her mouth. 'No,' she said quietly. 'How?'

'She was drowned in Fatfield river,' Niall answered.

'Oh God,' Rachel said, her eyes filling with tears. 'Oh my God. Poor Melissa.'

'Look, Rachel,' Kurt said, stepping up to her. 'We think it's because she wasn't happy here. We think it's too much of a coincidence that she's dead, and Richy's dead, and both of them wanted out of the Blessing Guides . . .'

Rachel took her hand away from her mouth. She looked at Kurt with contempt. 'Yer can't possibly be saying what I think yer saying.' She looked between Kurt and Niall, horrified. 'Oh my God, yer are. Yer think Marcel had something to do with this, don't yer?'

'Think about it, Rachel –' Kurt began, but she quickly interrupted him with, 'Think about what? Marcel has never, *never*,' she emphasised the last word angrily, 'shown us anything but kindness and love and trust. He accepted yer back and this is how yer repay him?'

'Rachel,' said Niall warily, 'this is dangerous and weird. What's this ceremony tomorrow all about, anyway? He's "marrying" that little girl who's what? Thirteen? Isn't that a bit sick?'

'Yer know nothing, yer both know nothing,' said Rachel. 'She's fifteen, same age as me. And she's blessed, she's pure like the Virgin Mary. She's going to be the vessel for Marcel's divine seed.'

Kurt and Niall passed a look between them. 'Yer can't actually believe that bullshit, can yer, Rachel? He's not whatever he says he is, he's a dirty old man who's manipulating yer into staying. But yer don't need to stay here. We can leave, now, just walk out the front door. Take yer back home.'

Rachel's voice was calm, controlled, but the boys could feel the anger that lay behind her words. 'Youse two are ignorant. Yer ignorant little shits. Do yer know who the real dirty old man is? Not Marcel, who loves me. Not Marcel, who treats me with kindness. No. The real dirty old man is my step-father. Oh,' she snorted, 'he loves me all right. He's loved me ever since Mam died and he first came into my bedroom at night. He's loved me so much I'm bruised and bleeding the next day.' She folded her arms across her chest and smirked at the horrified expression on her friends' faces. 'That's what I've got to go back to. That's my "home".'

Niall said softly, 'I had no idea.'

Rachel looked at him. 'Well, Marcel knew. I don't know how, he just did.'

The three of them stood in silence for a moment. Finally Kurt said, 'I'm really sorry about yer stepdad. But yer've got to see that this isn't right. It's not good for yer here.'

377

Rachel shook her head. 'Yer just like Richy and Melissa. Yer have no trust. Yer weak.' She walked past the boys and put her hand on the doorknob.

'Stop, Rachel,' Niall said. Rachel turned and regarded him coldly. Niall swallowed. 'Yer right. We are weak. And we're scared. We know that Marcel is right, that's why we came back, but we don't have faith. Please Rachel,' he pleaded, 'don't say anything to anyone.'

Rachel didn't say anything. She looked at them disdainfully, opened the door and stalked out.

'What the fuck are we gonna do now?' Niall looked at Kurt with fear in his eyes.

'Get the fuck out of here. And then we have to go to the police. We have to tell them what we know.'

Niall took a deep breath and nodded his head. The boys walked towards the door but stopped as a man in a dark suit blocked their exit.

'And what exactly do you know, Kurt?' asked Adrian, his mouth turned up in his customary sneer.

Sunday 24 December

37

Lorraine stalked into her office. She'd had a horrible feeling when she woke up that morning, a horrible feeling that she still couldn't shake. *What's wrong with me?* she thought as she hung up her coat behind the door. She ran her fingers through her hair and then tied it up in a ponytail. *I know what's wrong. I know that there's something going on up at the Seven Sisters but I can't pin anything on anyone. Two young kids have been killed and there's nothing I can do about it.* She sighed. *But at least Luke's back. At least I know what's been going on with him these past few days.*

As if she conjured him, Luke appeared at the doorway, carrying two steaming-hot cups of take-out coffee. 'Here yer are, boss,' he said, smiling so she could see that glint of gold. 'Thought I'd get back in the habit.'

'Thanks.' Lorraine took the coffee and took a sip. 'How was last night? How's Selina?'

Luke's smile faded. 'Better, I think. She was up and down all night though. Carter's been amazing. Really great. He's tougher than he looks. Don't know what I would do without him. And,' he smiled wistfully, 'he gets on with Selina better than I do. Came home

381

last night and they were sitting at the kitchen table, chatting away like long-lost friends. When I came in she went to her room, without anyone having to drag her there this time, and slammed the door behind her.'

Lorraine sat down at her desk and put down her coffee. 'It's bound to take time. She probably blames you for everything that's gone wrong in her life right now. I'm sure she'll come round.'

Luke looked as if he didn't believe her. 'Well, if yer say so, boss. At the moment, I'm not convinced.'

'So, do yer think she's over the worst?'

Luke nodded. 'She's still got some way to go.' He sighed heavily. 'And I don't know whether or not she's gonna stay off the junk.'

'I don't know what to say, Luke.' Lorraine looked at him with concern. 'She's gotta want to stop. I hope for yer sake she does. But yer can't watch her 24/7. Speaking of which, who's looking after her now?'

'I sent Carter home to rest. It's Dinwall's shift now. Anyway,' he said, changing the subject, 'Jacobs wanted me to tell you that she's got a match on the missing person.'

'Well, that's good news,' Lorraine replied. 'But why didn't she tell me herself? I saw her on the way in.'

Luke smiled. 'Think after yesterday she's too scared to mess with yer, boss.'

'Oh for fuck's sake,' Lorraine said irritably. 'What am I running here? An investigation or a kindergarten? Get her in here, now.'

Luke threw his now empty cup of coffee in the bin

and went to fetch Sara Jacobs. A moment later they appeared, Sara Jacobs looking sheepish. 'I printed this out for yer, boss.'

Jacobs handed Lorraine a sheaf of papers. On top was a picture of a very young Mary. It was definitely the same girl; on her right cheek was the same tear-shaped port-wine stain. But her name was different. 'Janice Nichols,' Lorraine said.

'Yes,' said Jacobs, 'from Somerset. Was reported missing by her parents three years ago. When she was fourteen,' she added.

'And that creep Marcel called her his wife.' Lorraine shook her head before letting a slow smile cross her face. She looked up at Luke and Jacobs. 'I think we've got him. That creep is a fucking paedophile. Jacobs, the Detective Inspector in Somerset,' she looked down at the papers, 'a David Murdoch. Could yer see if yer can get him on the phone for me, please?'

'Sure thing, boss.' Jacobs left the office and Luke watched her leave the room before saying, 'She's lost the attitude, that's pretty good.'

Lorraine sighed. 'We'll just see how long that lasts, shall we?'

Luke smiled. He sat down on his usual chair and stretched his legs out. Lorraine suddenly felt very self-conscious. She rummaged around in her desk for a pencil to chew before realising that if there wasn't one in there yesterday there wasn't going to be one in there today. *Yeah, but looking for something that isn't there is better than sitting in silence with the man of yer dreams.*

Then her phone rang, and Lorraine snatched up the receiver. 'Detective Inspector Lorraine Hunt.'

'It's Jacobs, boss. I've got Inspector Murdoch on the phone.'

Lorraine thanked her and then waited until Jacobs transferred the call.

'Detective Inspector,' Lorraine said. 'I'm sorry for calling yer on a Sunday.'

The man on the other end had a pronounced Somerset accent and a gruff but warm voice. He laughed as he said, 'Well, if yer job is anything like mine, yer might as well set up a bed in yer office for the amount of time yer get home.'

Lorraine smiled as she agreed with him, then said, 'Well, I know yer must be busy, but it seems we've got a girl up here who went missing from your area three years ago. Name of Janice Nichols. Do yer remember her?'

The voice on the other end became immediately serious. 'Yes. Afraid I do. Her mother works with my wife at the local school – they're both teachers. Kid had a run-in with her parents, something to do with a party that she wanted to have. Her parents put their foot down, but then she ran off, wasn't seen again.'

'Well, she's up here now. Along with a group called the Blessing Guides.'

There was silence on the other end of the line.

'Inspector Murdoch,' Lorraine said, 'are you there?'

'Yes, yes. Just that I was a bit surprised to hear that name after all this time. They were in our area for a while.' He snorted. 'That Marcel Gottsdiener, butter

384

wouldn't melt in his mouth. All peace and love and harmony, right, but getting his followers to pan-handle on the street. And there was a rash of thefts while he was there too –'

'Sounds very similar to what's been going on here,' Lorraine interrupted him as she saw Jacobs standing in the doorway. She motioned her in. 'Inspector, would you mind if I put yer on speaker phone? I want the officers working on this with me to hear this.'

'Of course.'

Lorraine pressed a button on the phone and replaced the receiver. 'So Inspector,' she carried on, 'just to recap, there were a number of burglaries there when the Blessing Guides were in your area.'

'More than usual. And then when they left, the burglaries dropped off. But all circumstantial, we couldn't pin anything on them.'

'We've also had two deaths. Two teenagers were killed but staged to look like suicide. Anything like that happen while the Blessing Guides were with you?'

Murdoch sighed on the other end of the line. 'Of all the young men who die, a quarter of them kill themselves. It's a terrible statistic, and no different here than the rest of the country. I can't remember any deaths that were suspicious during that time, but I'll get my sergeant to go over the files.'

Lorraine nodded. 'Back to Janice Nichols, did you ever suspect that she went off with the Blessing Guides?'

Murdoch cleared his throat. 'Look, Janice dis-appeared about six weeks after the Blessing Guides left. We never put two and two together – we assumed she had gone to London. Easy to get lost up there.'

'Could she have met up with them later? Do you know where the Blessing Guides went after they left your area?'

'Frankly, I was pleased to be shot of them.'

'Out of sight, out of mind, eh?' Lorraine said. She shot a look at Luke. He looked worriedly back at her.

'Anyway, Inspector Murdoch. Back to Janice. Yer wouldn't know that she seems to be a leading member of the Blessing Guides now. Marcel is calling her his wife. She's taken the name of Mary, which may be why yer lost her scent.'

Murdoch sounded as if he had just sat up in his chair. 'That makes things a lot more serious. Janice is what, sixteen now?'

'We realise the seriousness of the situation,' Lorraine said dryly. 'But thanks for yer time. Yer've been very helpful.'

Lorraine rang off. Just as she was about to speak, a WPC knocked on her door. 'Sorry to bother yer, Inspector, but we've got a Mrs Campbell on the phone – she said that her son Niall and his friend Kurt didn't come home last night. She's beside herself with worry.'

Lorraine looked at the young WPC, speechless for a moment. 'Fuck,' she said.

Luke looked at her. 'Do yer want me to talk to her?'

Lorraine shook her head. 'Jacobs, you take this call. Try to reassure her, but after our visit yesterday she's bound to be upset. Has Sanderson come in this morning?'

Jacobs shook her head. 'His mother-in-law is in town. I think they're planning a day out.'

'Well, after you talk to Mrs Campbell, bring him in. He won't mind – he's been avoiding his mother-in-law all week. Then go round to the Campbells'. Search Niall's room, see if yer come up with anything.'

'Yes, boss.' Jacobs walked out of Lorraine's office and past the WPC who was still standing in the doorway.

'Luke, you're with me. We're paying a visit to Daffodil Street. We're taking Marcel Gottsdiener in for questioning.' Lorraine got up out of her seat and went to her coat. 'Anything else?' she said to the WPC.

'There's a Jacko Musgrove to see yer. Something about a stolen van.'

'Well, can't he see someone else about that?' Lorraine said irritably.

'I asked him, but he's insistent. Won't see anyone but you.'

'Oh, for fuck's sake. He's just gonna have to wait. Come on, Luke.' Luke stood up and followed Lorraine out the door.

As Lorraine walked down the corridor, she saw Jacko Musgrove and a man she didn't know sitting on the plastic chairs in the waiting room. When Jacko stood up to speak to her, she put her hand up to silence him.

'I know what yer in to talk to me about, Jacko, but

I'm afraid now's just not a good time. Yer can make a report to the duty sergeant, I'm sorry.'

The man Lorraine didn't recognise said, 'I told you that this was a waste of time,' under his breath. Lorraine pretended she didn't hear him.

Jacko looked agitated. 'Look, Inspector, it's important that we speak to you and only you. I don't trust anyone else.'

'Well, yer just gonna have to.' Lorraine sighed. 'Look, Jacko, I know yer van is important to yer . . .'

'It's my van –' the other man said.

Lorraine acknowledged this fact with a nod and then said, 'But there are other things going on that are important too. I'm sorry, Jacko, we've got to leave. But trust me. Someone else can help you find yer van.' Lorraine turned on her heel and started walking to the double doors that led outside.

But she and Luke stopped in their tracks when Jacko called after them, 'But I know where the van is. It's parked on Daffodil Street.'

Lorraine and Luke were outside the interview room. Jacko and his friend, who he introduced as Danny Jordan, sat nervously on plastic chairs on one side of a formica-topped table. Lorraine knew how hot it could get in there, so she and Luke had got some water. Also, it was a chance for Lorraine to talk to Luke about the situation, get his take on it.

'Daffodil Street,' Lorraine said. 'It's coming up again and again.'

'It's strange all right,' Luke replied. 'Looks like

there's all sorts going on there. But the van thing strikes me as really strange. It's not as if they're trying to hide it either – Danny and Jacko found it straightaway.'

'If nothing else, it gives us more ammunition to use against the Blessing Guides. But yeah, they don't seem to worry about getting caught.'

'Yer not worried about Marcel leaving town?'

Lorraine shook her head. 'God knows, I want the bastard. And I want him fast. But it's a big operation he's got up there. He can't leave without us finding out. We'll see what Jacko and Danny have to say, then we're straight up there. If we can bring him in on receiving stolen goods, we can charge him on the more serious offences once we've gathered more evidence and talked to Janice Nichols. Come on, let's go in.'

'OK, Jacko, Danny,' Lorraine said as she took a seat. 'Why don't yer tell me what happened.'

Jacko glanced at Danny before saying, 'Inspector, is this confidential? I mean, it won't go further than this room, will it?'

Lorraine shook her head. 'I can't promise yer anything, Jacko. Yer know that.'

Jacko nodded and took a deep breath. Danny stared at the table, not meeting Lorraine's eyes. 'What I'm gonna say is probably gonna land us in a whole heap of trouble,' Jacko began. 'But there's more to it than yer think. It's like this . . .'

With occasional interruptions from Danny, Jacko told Lorraine and Luke everything that had happened since leaving Dover. The black car that followed them into a lay-by. The revelation that there were drugs planted on the van. The fight. Adam lying bruised and bleeding on the ground.

Jacko said to Lorraine, 'They're relying on our silence. Brian, that bastard, knew that we were smuggling in smokes.' He glanced up to see Lorraine's reaction, but she kept her face impassive. 'So he thought we won't go to the police. He thought he could do what he liked, take the van, all our money, everything, beat Adam within an inch of his life and then leave us to find our own way home, and we would keep quiet. But,' he shifted uneasily in his chair, 'I hate drugs. They're disgusting. They burn up all the good in the young 'uns who take them and leave them hollow . . .' Lorraine glanced at Luke who was staring straight at Jacko. 'And we both hate it that Lizzy –'

'That's the name of me van,' Danny interrupted.

'We hate it that Lizzy was used to ferry drugs across the Channel. That we became involved, against our wills and knowledge, in drug smuggling.' Jacko shook his head. 'It makes me feel sick.' He glanced up at Lorraine once more, and then dropped his eyes to the table.

Lorraine sat back in her chair, looked at Luke, then nibbled at her lip before saying. 'Trust you, Jacko. How the hell yer even got that close to home's amazing. Devil's own luck you've got.'

'So yer reckon the van's parked on Daffodil Street?' Luke asked.

'Aye, but we want to make a deal.'

Luke raised his eyebrows, but kept silent as

Lorraine said, 'Yer've just admitted to smuggling in ciggies. I'm not sure yer in a position to make a deal, but let's hear it.'

'Once yer get the drugs off the minibus then it's ours again.'

Lorraine snorted. 'Only a little thing, then?'

Jacko looked at her for a moment, then swung his head to Danny, who suddenly found something very interesting on the floor to absorb his interest. Jacko looked back at Lorraine . . . 'Please.'

'Yer rich, you are, Jacko.'

'Told yer, didn't I.' Danny finally found his voice. 'Told yer it would be a waste of time before we came.'

Lorraine looked at him. 'Yer've both been very helpful. I'll give yer that. OK,' she looked from one to the other. 'Tell yer what I'm gonna do . . . Go home, guys, but before yer do, leave yer mobile number. I'm not promising yer anything, but if I can get yer van back to yer in reasonable nick, I will.'

Danny's mouth fell open, 'Yer mean it?' Suddenly, in the depths of winter, the sun was shining again, just for him. His Lizzy was coming back home.

'What about the smuggling thing?' Jacko said.

Lorraine took a deep breath. 'Yer bloody lucky yer insisted on talking to me and not to someone else. I'm not gonna throw the book at yer. This time I'm gonna turn a blind eye. But,' she said as Jacko's face lit up with relief, 'I warn yer, yer better be careful. 'Cos, get caught by customs or by us, and I won't be able to stop them from prosecuting yer to the full extent of the law. Got that?'

'I told yer she's a good 'un,' Jacko said, smiling at Danny.

Lorraine and Luke, as they pulled out of the car park for the Seahills, didn't notice Debbie Stansfield walk into the police station. She looked wild and dishevelled, the result of nights spent tossing and turning in her bed, or wandering through her near-empty house, or just sitting in Richard's bedroom, staring into space. Sandra Gilbride, who had taken to spending nights with Debbie, made sure that Debbie washed, put on clean clothes, ate good food. In a small corner of her mind, Debbie recognised that Sandra was a godsend, a good friend and neighbour, who would never want the favour to be repaid. But Debbie resented Sandra too. She resented the fact that she had a family while Debbie had no one. She resented Sandra's cheery tone as she put yet another plate of food in front of her. But most of all, she resented Sandra trying to distract her from her grief. Trying to distract her from thinking about Richard. Trying to stop her from going down to the police station, so that Debbie had to sneak out, as if she was a prisoner in her own house. Sandra didn't see that Debbie had to go down to the police station, she had to. Who else was going to look out for her Richard?

'I'm here to see Inspector Hunt,' Debbie told the duty sergeant.

He looked at her slightly impatiently but said to her as kindly as he could, 'Ms Stansfield, Inspector Hunt isn't here. And unless yer've got something new to say to us, I'm afraid we can't help yer.'

'My Richy didn't kill himself,' Debbie said plainly, no hint of emotion in her voice.

'Yes, Ms Stansfield, I know that's what yer believe.' The duty sergeant sighed. 'Look, sit down for a moment. I'll get a car round to take yer home.'

The duty sergeant picked up the receiver and punched in a few numbers. 'Lynchy?' he said to the police officer at the other end of the line. 'How busy are yer?' He was silent as he listened to the response. 'Good. Need yer here to take Debbie Stansfield home, OK? See yer in five.'

But when the sergeant looked up, Debbie Stansfield was gone. He looked at the CCTV screen. Debbie was walking down the corridor that led to Inspector Hunt's office.

'Shit,' he said. And picking up the phone, he dialled another number.

Jacobs had called Sanderson who, as Lorraine had said, was happy to forgo his visit to the Metro Centre with his wife and mother-in-law and come in to work. She had filled him in on the missing boys, Kurt Allendale and Niall Campbell, and had been surprised when his tone became more urgent. 'Fuck,' he said. 'We should have fucking guessed this would happen.'

Jacobs had shrugged when she put down the phone. She couldn't understand how Luke, Sanderson, Inspector Hunt, and even Dinwall, got so caught up with their cases. 'Maintain a professional distance' – wasn't that the advice that they gave you at the academy? *Then why*, Jacobs thought to herself, *am I the only one who seems to be able to follow that advice*? 'Cos if you couldn't maintain distance, then you couldn't see the big picture, and in Jacobs's opinion, that was where Inspector Hunt went wrong. She got so caught up with the detail, with people and their petty problems, that she had lost sight of what her job was, which was to put criminals behind bars, not to pander to the public.

Jacobs made a neat pile of papers on her desk as she waited for Sanderson to arrive. The doors swung open, and she looked up, only to suppress a groan as she saw Debbie Stansfield walk towards her. 'Yes?' she said curtly.

'I want to see Inspector Hunt.'

Jacobs looked at the woman standing in front of her. She sighed impatiently. 'Ms Stansfield, Inspector Hunt isn't here. I don't suppose there's anything I can help yer with?'

'I need to see Inspector Hunt,' Debbie said, again with that blank, automaton tone. It was really winding Jacobs up.

'As I told yer, she's not here,' Jacobs didn't bother keeping the irritation out of her voice. 'Yer wasting police time, Ms Stansfield. Please, just go home and let us get on with our jobs.'

'My Richy didn't kill himself.'

Jacobs let out a deep breath. 'Yeah, well we've known that for some time, Ms Stansfield.' She went back to shuffling paper on her desk and didn't notice the shocked expression on Debbie's face.

'Yer know my Richy didn't kill himself?' Debbie said in a whisper.

394

'Like I said,' Jacobs replied brusquely, 'we know it's not suicide. Something to do with that cult that's up at the Seahills.' She looked up at Debbie, whose face had drained of colour. 'Don't tell me yer didn't know?'

Jacobs got her answer when Debbie turned her eyes upon her. Her eyes were stony, cold, with a new purpose in them. For a second, Jacobs felt cowed. Just at that moment, PC Lynch, a young man with mousey-coloured hair, came through the double doors, followed closely by Sanderson. Sanderson looked between Jacobs and Debbie and raised an eyebrow in question. Jacobs shrugged in response. The young PC took Debbie by the elbow. 'Come on, Ms Stansfield. I'm to take yer home.'

Coldly and clearly, Debbie said, 'I'm OK. Leave me alone.'

PC Lynch gripped Debbie's arm more firmly. 'Come on then, Ms Stansfield. We've got a car waiting outside.'

'I said, leave me the fuck alone!' Debbie yelled, and wrenched her arm out of the policeman's grip. With more determination than she had shown all week, she walked through the double doors, which swung wildly behind her.

'What the hell?' said Sanderson.

38

'It's no good, Kurt,' Niall said in the semi-darkness. 'There's no way out.'

Kurt took no notice of his friend. He was getting more and more irritated by Niall. Niall seemed to have given up. He seemed to accept their fate, which was what? Kurt thought. Hanging from a tree in the Seven Sisters or pulled from Fatfield river? *Yeah,* he thought dryly to himself. *Take yer pick.* He rattled the door of the cellar again. Nothing. But perhaps if he could slide a piece of plastic between the door and the frame, maybe he could jemmy it open.

'Niall?' he said. 'Any thin strips of plastic around yer?'

'Can't see any. Can't see much of anything,' Niall said.

'Well, try. Feel with yer hands if yer need to.'

Last night they had been led downstairs by Adrian and a new guy that Kurt had never seen before. He was strong, and had black hair pulled back in a ponytail. Adrian, after finding them upstairs, hadn't said a word to them, and had pushed them down the cellar steps so that they stumbled and fell at the bottom. The man with the black ponytail stood in front of the door with his arms folded across his chest. He stared at them disinterestedly as he chewed gum. Adrian looked at them both, still with that contemptuous smile before saying finally, 'You think you can stop the ceremony, don't you?' He shook his head. 'Well, you thought wrong. Tomorrow night is not going to be ruined by a couple of stupid kids. We'll deal with you later.'

Adrian took a handkerchief out of his pocket, reached up and took the light bulb out of its socket so that the room was plunged into darkness. They could hear Adrian walk up the steps. As the guy with the ponytail opened the door to let them both out, light from the corridor fell across Adrian's face, giving his face an evil cast. 'Oh, and I forgot to mention. It's been decided that the duties of the handmaiden shouldn't just be to service Marcel.' Adrian smiled malevolently. 'Rachel will service Marcel, and me, and Brian here.' Brian smiled widely as he chewed his gum, which made a loud cracking sound in the quiet. 'In fact, Rachel will service anyone we want her to.'

Both men laughed as they closed and locked the door behind them. At the time, it had been Kurt who had broken down, who had cried, shaking uncontrollably. 'Oh my God, Rachel,' he said over and over again. Niall had rushed up to the door and had tried the handle. 'It's locked,' he confirmed. 'And they haven't left the key in the lock either.'

It had been a long, dark, cold night and Kurt had spent it in fear. He guessed that it was now sometime in the afternoon. Light that came in through the cracks in the door cast a greyish pallor around the room. Somewhere, in the middle of the night, when he had got through the fear and the dread of what was going to happen to him, he had found new strength. He knew he wasn't going to be locked in the room forever. That even if they didn't get out, someone was going to come for them sooner or later. And when they did, he wanted to be prepared. He wasn't going to go down without a fight.

'Niall,' he said, 'we need to find weapons, anything, something that we can use so that we can get out of here and find Rachel.'

'What's the point, Kurt?' Niall replied. 'They've got us beaten. Oh Jesus.' Kurt could tell from his silhouette that Niall had dropped his head into his hands. 'I don't want to die.'

'We're not gonna. We're not gonna let them beat us.' Kurt went down the stairs. 'Come on. There's gotta be something that we can use on the fuckers.' Niall didn't move. 'Come on!' he yelled at his friend.

Niall raised his head. 'Shush,' he said. 'I think someone's coming.'

The two boys stood as still as statues as they heard a key turn in the lock. The light blinded them momentarily but then the door was quickly closed. They heard the soft, rounded tones of a Somerset accent.

'Kurt, Niall?' said the voice. 'You down here?'

'Mary?' said Kurt.

There was no acknowledgement, but the voice said, 'You have to leave. You have to leave right now. There's no one here, they're all up at the Seven Sisters preparing for the ceremony.'

'Aren't you supposed to be up there?' Niall asked.

'I slipped away, but I'll be missed soon, if not already. That's why we have to leave now.'

Kurt and Niall looked at each other in the darkness. 'Where's Rachel?' asked Kurt.

'She's up at the Seven Sisters too. Come on,' said Mary. 'If they catch me –' She didn't finish her sentence.

'When does the ceremony start?' Kurt asked.

'Are you stupid or something? What are you doing asking questions? What do you think they're going to do to you after the ceremony? Let you go? I don't think so.'

Mary opened the door and the boys ran up the stairs. 'Why have yer done this?' said Kurt as they were in the corridor. 'Yer gonna get into trouble, yer know that. They'll know it was you.'

'They don't care about me. I'm not important to them now that they've found the new Mary.'

'Come with us to the police, Mary. They'll help you. You can tell them what you know,' Niall urged her.

'You have no idea, do you!' Mary yelled. 'As if the police will help me. I'm in it, right up to my neck. Marcel and Adrian have made sure of that. I can't go to the police, they'll never believe me.'

Kurt and Niall looked at each other despairingly.

'And anyway,' Mary said, defeated, 'it's going to be over soon. The ceremony starts at sunset. We've got less than an hour.'

'What about Rachel?' Kurt clutched her arm. 'What's going to happen to her?'

Mary shrugged. 'What do you care what happens to her anyway? She's happy. At least for now.'

Kurt released Mary's arm and ran his fingers through his hair. 'We've got to get her out of there.'

'She'll never come with us, Kurt,' Niall said. 'Yer saw what she was like last night.'

'I know, I know.' Kurt looked down at the floor. 'But I can't leave her up there.' He looked at Mary. 'We're going to come up with you. We'll hide or something. We'll try and get Rachel alone and talk her out of it.'

'That's not much of a plan, Kurt,' Niall said worriedly.

Kurt took a deep breath. 'It's the only one we've got.'

39

Lorraine and Luke parked outside number 66 Daffodil Street and got out of the car. They paused for a moment, while they looked at the imposing façade, the overgrown bushes and the rusty gate. 'So this is it, boss,' said Luke. 'Do yer think it's one of those places where you'll receive an inheritance if, and only if, yer survive one night under its roof?'

'Very funny,' said Lorraine. But she felt daunted, despite herself.

'No lights are on, and it's nearly dark,' said Luke. 'Looks deserted to me.'

'Go and get the torch from the car, we might need it,' Lorraine said, and waited while Luke fetched the torch from the glovebox.

As they walked up to the front door, Lorraine said, 'So that must be Lizzy.' She pointed over at the white van that was parked beside a black car with a flat tyre. 'Did yer get the licence number off Jacko?'

'Yep, boss.' Luke pulled a slip of white paper out of his pocket. 'He left it with his mobile number.' He looked from the paper to the number plate. 'That's the one.'

'Good. We'll have Marcel Gottsdiener up for receiving stolen goods at least.'

They walked up the white steps to the front door. Lorraine pressed the button. They could hear a loud buzz, but no one came to answer the door. Luke cupped his hand, put it to the windowpane, and tried to look through the frosted glass. 'It's hard to tell, but it doesn't look as if there's anyone in there.'

Lorraine pressed the bell again. There was no answer. Lorraine turned and stared at the black car. Something was tugging at her mind.

Suddenly she snapped her fingers. 'I'm sure that's the car that followed me the other day. The day I picked Melissa up.'

Quickly she and Luke walked over to the car. She glanced into the minibus first. 'Looks like the guys are gonna be lucky. Everything seems to be there.'

'Well, that'll make them happy.' Luke grinned.

'Yeah, Dinwall an' all. Guess where he gets his ciggies. Not down at the cash-and-carry for sure.'

'Yer going to let them keep everything?'

Lorraine looked at Luke. 'Cigarette smuggling is the least of my worries at the moment. I'll let Jacko off, this one time, but I'll send him on his way with a flea in his ear. Besides,' she grinned wryly, 'they'll only be sitting in the station, tempting fate, and especially me.'

They turned to the black car. Lorraine looked in the back window while Luke walked around and examined the front.

The windows were tinted but Lorraine could just make out the empty back seat. *Hang on, not quite so empty.*

What's that?

Something white was poking between the seats as if it had been hurriedly pushed out of the way and forgotten about. 'Luke,' she called, then louder, her heart beating faster.

Luke came round to her side of the car. Lorraine pointed to what she saw on the back seat. 'Does that look like a hairband, yer know, an Alice band, one of the ones they're all wearing now.'

Frowning, Luke picked a brick up from the edging around the path. 'Sharp find out, boss . . . Turn away.'

Lorraine quickly spun round and hunched her shoulders against flying glass. A moment later Luke had fished out a white hairband using a twig to stop him from handling it.

'Looks like a hairband to me,' Luke said.

Lorraine took a plastic bag out of her coat pocket and Luke put the hairband in it. She knew instinctively who it belonged it. She looked at Luke. 'It's Melissa's. I know it is . . . We've got to show it to Scottie. Hopefully he'll be able to pull some DNA off it.'

'Yer sure it's Melissa Tremaine's?'

'See this,' Lorraine showed Luke the edging that was sown to make the band into a circle. A good quarter of an inch was fraying away. 'I noticed that on Wednesday when I offered her a lift to school. I thought about telling her, but then I thought that she had enough to worry about.'

Luke nodded gravely, then his expression changed. 'We'll need Scottie up here to check through the boot too. A struggling girl with her wrists cut from plastic ties, there's bound to be some DNA evidence too.'

'It's too late for her now, but thank God she was a fighter.' Lorraine thought with sadness of the last time she saw Melissa, of how scared she had been. Again that feeling was upon her – if only she had been more observant, if only she had read the signs properly. But she shook those thoughts out of her head. There would be time to go over the whys and wherefores later. Right now all she wanted to do was get her hands on that evil scum, Marcel Gottsdiener, shove him in a cell and make sure that they had enough evidence to ensure he'd never get out of prison again. She looked at Luke. It was getting darker, almost sunset. 'Right then, use the same trick to get inside the house. We'll come up with something to explain why we had to break in later.'

'There's a better way than a brick, boss.' Luke took a credit card out of his wallet. 'Don't tell me you don't know this trick?' He grinned, but it didn't make his eyes. He knew the seriousness of what they were about to do.

It wasn't as easy as all that though. Lorraine had the uncomfortable feeling of being on the other side of the fence as she stood look-out for Luke. It took him five minutes to jemmy the lock. 'We're in, boss,' he said, sucking his thumbnail, which he had managed to split with the exertion of getting into the house.

Lorraine turned round. Luke pushed the door open, but each paused for a moment before crossing the threshold. The house was very dark and very quiet. There was a faint smell of overcooked vegetables. Lorraine took a deep breath and entered

404

the house, Luke close behind her. 'OK, Luke, yer take the upstairs. I'll look around down here.'

Luke nodded his head and walked quickly and carefully up the stairs. Lorraine walked across the hallway. A door was ajar and she peered through it. Stairs went down to what Lorraine assumed was a cellar. She turned her attention to the room opposite. She opened the door and surveyed the room without going in. She had been in here before, and it was very much the same as the day she had sat in the chair opposite the desk, trying to contain her anger at Marcel's smug and patronising demeanour. She noticed that the flowers on the table were no longer fresh, they were wilting and sad looking, and a few petals had detached themselves and were lying beside the base of the vase. She shut the door on the room. There would be time to go through it in fine detail later.

Lorraine had never been in the next room she entered. It was huge; it looked as if two rooms had been knocked into one. She walked round the wide empty space. Some trestle tables were set up at one end of the room, and there were cushions scattered opposite them. She suddenly realised what the room was used for. *It's a meeting place*, she thought. *It reminds me of a village hall, or where I used to go to youth club.*

Lorraine knelt down. There was a stain on the wooden floor, half covered by a rug. She threw the rug to one side and was studying it when Luke came in.

'Deserted up there, boss. Looks like they got

dressed in a hurry. Clothes strewn here and there, all sorts of things lying about. Untidy bunch if yer ask me.'

'Take a look at this.'

Luke knelt beside Lorraine and regarded the stain on the floor for a long moment. He looked at Lorraine. 'Scottie's gonna have a field day in this house,' he said. 'I bet yer anything yer like that's blood.'

Lorraine stood up. 'I wouldn't bet against that, Luke.'

'So where now, boss?'

Lorraine strode across the room, not waiting for Luke to catch her up. 'I know exactly where they are – they'll be up at the Seven Sisters.'

'It'll be dark soon.' Luke caught up with Lorraine just as she was walking out of the front door. She had taken her mobile out of her bag and was dialling a number.

'Yeah,' she said as she put the phone to her ear. 'I'm calling for back-up at the Seven Sisters, Luke. I want Sanderson and Jacobs up there and also an armed response team. Remember, Jacko said that they have guns. We're gonna need all the people we can spare on this. I have a feeling we might need them, now that everything's coming to a head.'

Debbie had managed to shake off the young PC, who had followed her out of the police station insisting that she should be driven home in his squad car, by turning round and screaming in his face. She'd had enough of the police. She knew what she had to do.

406

Calling in at her house first, she was walking fast, almost running, right up to the Seahills. Night was falling and there was a chill in the air but Debbie didn't feel the cold. The heat of revenge was coursing through her veins, boiling her blood. She had never felt so angry, nor had she ever known so clearly what she needed to do. It was simple, really. Obvious. She didn't know much about the Bible, but wasn't there something about an eye for an eye? Surely any religious group, any *cult*, should know about that.

She didn't know where to start looking for the house. The rude policewoman didn't tell her where. But Debbie had the feeling that she would know. There would be pointers, surely. A cult stands out in a community, doesn't it? She pushed down a treacherous thought that sprung into her head and whispered, *But how would yer know? Yer didn't know the trouble Richy was in when he was alive.* She shook the thought out of her head. She was prepared to knock on every door if she had to, prepared to ask the inhabitants, 'Did you kill my son? Was it you who took him from me?'

But then, for the first time in a week, luck shone down on Debbie Stansfield. A car that she recognised was parked outside number 66 Daffodil Street. A car she recognised as belonging to that bitch Lorraine Hunt. That bitch, with her kind words and false promises, that bitch who didn't even have the decency to tell her that she was right, Richy did not kill himself.

She came up to the car and looked in the window. It belonged to Hunt all right. An envelope with her name and her address on it lay crumpled on the passenger side of the car. Debbie straightened up. She turned around, and scuttled behind a tree for cover. There was Hunt on the front steps of the house, with that black copper, who had just pushed the front door open. She watched them as they hesitated for a moment before entering the house. Then, walking through the gate, she crouched behind a tree and waited for them to return to their car.

She didn't have to wait long. Five minutes later, Hunt was tearing down the front steps with the black copper fast behind her. She strained her ears to hear what they were saying, but she couldn't quite make out their words. But then Hunt stopped as she talked to the person on the other end of her mobile. Debbie held her breath as she waited to hear what Hunt had to say. She caught the words *back-up* and *Seven Sisters*. She watched Hunt and her partner walk through the gate, get in the car and drive away.

Debbie's grip tightened on the knife that she was holding by her side.

40

The wind whistled through the Seven Sisters, causing them to sway and creak in the breeze, as if dancing to some unearthly music. The sun had almost set, and in a circle twelve fires were burning, tended by two male Blessing Guides, who ensured they were kept alight.

Niall and Kurt were bunched up together behind a bush. They had hidden themselves a fair distance from the camp, but their vantage point meant that they could see everything that was going on.

'Don't think I'm ever gonna get warm again,' Niall said. 'And never thought I'd say this, but I think I actually want to eat. Steak and kidney pie.'

'Shush,' said Kurt, whose own stomach was rumbling noisily. 'We don't want anyone to look our way.'

Kurt felt his insides twist as he saw Adrian and Brian come down the steps of a caravan. The Blessing Guides, who had been milling around the caravan, laying out food and jugs of liquid on the table, or raising up flags with a circle enclosing a fish upon them, or just standing around talking to each other, looked up and walked towards Adrian and Brian. Inge, the Swedish blonde, actually clapped her hands as she skipped her way to them. When each of the cult members stood in front of Brian, he placed something on their tongue.

'What are they doing?' whispered Niall to Kurt.

Kurt shook his head. 'Dunno. Looks dodgy to me.'

'Can't see Rachel.'

Kurt sighed. 'No. I don't expect to right now. She's with that new Mary, remember, anointing her body or something.'

Niall shuddered. 'We're not gonna get to her in time, are we? She's gonna . . .' Niall swallowed, 'have to "serve" those bastards tonight, isn't she?'

Kurt didn't say anything, just stared with renewed anger at the two men standing in front of the caravan. Both boys were silent for a while. Then Niall said, 'Mary, I mean the old one, ran off quite quickly when she left us, didn't she?'

Kurt shrugged. 'Not surprising, really. She's terrified, and she thinks there's no way out. Not for her, anyway.'

'Kurt,' Niall said in a quavering voice. 'I'd like to try to get her out too. I know she thinks it's pointless going to the coppers, but she did help us. She did get us out of there.'

Kurt shifted his body so that he was staring straight into his friend's face. 'Yeah, but if she hadn't approached Richy and me in the shopping centre, we wouldn't have joined the Blessing Guides in the first place.'

'But two wrongs don't make a right. She was terrified; yer saw what she looked like. What's gonna happen to her, now that she's not gonna be Mary any longer? Listen to me, Kurt,' Niall's voice became

410

stronger. 'We don't have a plan. We're waiting for something to happen – we don't know what – so that we can find a way of getting Rachel out of there. Well, if we can, why don't we try to get Mary out of there too?'

Kurt thought for a moment then said, 'Only if we can. We need to think of Rachel first.'

Lorraine and Luke parked at the bottom of the Seven Sisters. They got out of the car and Luke gave a low whistle. 'Look at that, boss.'

The Blessing Guides' numbers had swelled to about twenty or thirty people. They were all inside a circle that was encircled by at least a dozen fires. Some of the Blessing Guides were dancing; others were locked in embraces. All looked wild and abandoned. One tall, willowy blonde was twirling slowly around, waving her arms high in the air, her head thrown back. Just outside the circle, but clearly shown by the light of the flames, were two large flags.

'A circle enclosing a fish,' said Lorraine. 'We've got them now on the Manners murder too.'

Luke nodded, his eyes still on the group of people dancing inside the circle. 'They're on something. Look at them. That's not the way people behave when they're straight,' he said, his tone chilly.

'Haven't yer heard of religious ecstasy?' Lorraine said wryly.

'Think we're looking at the kind yer buy on the street, boss.' Luke finally turned to Lorraine, concern etched on his face. 'This could be what was smuggled over in Danny Jordan's van.'

Lorraine hugged herself for warmth. 'Back-up's taking its time to arrive.'

'Sanderson and Jacobs on their way too?'

'Yeah, caught them just as they were driving to the Campbells'.'

'What do yer think has happened to Niall and Kurt?' Luke asked. He looked towards the circle. 'Don't think they're there. Don't recognise anyone.'

'Wish I knew.' Lorraine looked down at her feet. 'Feel I've let all of them down, in some way.'

Luke touched her arm lightly. 'Yer didn't. Yer've gotta believe that. Yer beating yerself up about this too much when, if it weren't for you, Richard Stansfield's death would have been written off as a suicide.'

Lorraine lifted her face and looked up into Luke's eyes. 'Yer've gotta be kinder on yerself, girl,' he said as he went to brush a strand of hair away from her face, but then, almost as if he realised that this was neither the time nor the place he let his hand fall to his side.

A pair of car lights swung around the corner and instinctively both Luke and Lorraine took a couple of steps away from each other. The car pulled up alongside them and Sanderson and Jacobs got out. But before anyone had a chance to say anything, a police van came around the corner and parked next to Lorraine's car. A sliding door opened and half a dozen armed policemen, in black helmets and flak jackets, jumped out. A medium-sized policeman walked towards Lorraine, a rifle under his left arm. He held out his hand to her. 'Detective Inspector, I'm

Sergeant Tom Davis. We've met before, I think?'

'On a training course in Sunderland,' Lorraine took his hand and shook it. 'I remember. Thanks for coming. This is my sergeant Luke Daniels, and these are Sanderson and Jacobs.'

Davis nodded to each of them. He turned round and looked at the Blessing Guides campsite. 'What the hell is this?'

'Religious group,' Lorraine answered. 'Not like any Christians you or I know, however. More like a cult really. We know that their leaders have smuggled drugs into the country and that they are armed. We can pin three deaths on them already. But yer need to be careful with those things.' Lorraine pointed to the gun that Davis was holding. 'We have no reason to believe that any of the followers are to be considered dangerous. I want this take-down to be as clean as possible.'

Davis, who had been listening to Lorraine with his eyes on the campsite, turned to her and said, 'Understood. We'll establish a perimeter around this area.' He swept his hand, indicating a semicircle. 'We'll make sure yer covered. But yer will all need to wear flak jackets. Turner, Evans.' Two of his team looked up. 'Get these people fitted up.'

As they were eased into the tight-fitting and heavy flak jackets, two more paddy vans turned up to escort the Blessing Guides to the police station for questioning once they were arrested. Lorraine had requested that the drivers should arrive with the lights turned off in order to avoid the Blessing Guides seeing the police and doing a runner, but seeing as all of them were off their faces, Lorraine didn't think they would notice. 'Do yer think there'll be enough room for everyone?' Sanderson whispered to Lorraine as he tightened his flak jacket around his body.

'Touch-and-go, Sanderson. Hope so.' Lorraine pulled the flak jacket down and shifted her shoulders so that it was sitting more comfortably.

'Boss, I've gotta tell yer something. Yer not gonna like it,' Sanderson whispered. He looked meaningfully at Jacobs, who had enlisted the help of Turner, who put his gun down to help Jacobs tighten the buckles on her jacket. Lorraine and Sanderson walked a few steps so that they were standing just outside the group.

'What is it, Sanderson?'

Sanderson took a deep breath. 'Well, it's like this. Debbie Stansfield came into the station earlier. Fine, except that Jacobs told her that we know that Richy was murdered.'

Lorraine looked at Jacobs who was looking over her shoulder at Turner and laughing. 'Shit.' She folded her arms across her chest. 'What the fuck was she thinking, Sanderson?'

'I know, boss,' Sanderson said. 'I know.'

'Well, we can't do anything about it now. Do yer know where Debbie might be?'

'No idea, boss. Didn't know what had gone on until we were on our way to the Campbells'. Jacobs told me in the car just before you called.'

Lorraine closed her eyes and let out a long, deep breath. This wasn't the way she wanted Debbie to find out. She wanted to tell her herself, when she had more information, when she could say that she was, in fact, closing in on the killer. Lorraine opened her eyes and turned to Sanderson. 'I'll deal with Jacobs later. I just hope Debbie's coping with the news OK, that's all.'

Not far from where Kurt and Niall had hidden themselves, Debbie Stansfield looked down on the Blessing Guides who danced in a circle before the Seven Sisters. Was this what her son, her Richy, had been into? She couldn't believe what she was seeing in front of her own eyes. Although the group was only dancing, there was a frenzy about it that made her uncomfortable, something almost sexual. A very pretty, tall and slender blonde girl danced in the centre of the burning circle, and two boys had started to come in from its edges, staring at the girl. They reminded her of nature programmes she had seen, with two predators, working in tandem to catch their prey. She shuddered.

On the very fringes of the group, outside the circle, standing just in front of the caravans, were two men. Both tall, both dark-haired, they were looking at the group and whispering to each other. The one with the ponytail let out a bark of laughter at what the other had said to him, and whispered back. Debbie read something malevolent in the way they stood looking on at the group and commenting on it. Were they responsible for Richy's death?

A shaft of light was suddenly thrown out on the ground as the door to one of the caravans opened.

The dancers were immediately still, standing as if suddenly turned into stone, and they gazed at the open door. Debbie noticed the two men had also turned and looked at the caravan, but there was something less urgent about their movements, as if they weren't participants in whatever it was that was happening.

A man stepped out from the light, followed by three girls. They were all dressed in flowing white robes. The man had tousled, curly hair and walked at the front of the group; the three girls walked behind him in a straight line. Suddenly, as if they had picked up on some sort of signal, the dancers took their places along the edges of the circle while the man stood at the top of it, the girls close behind him. Even though he stood with his back to her, Debbie could clearly make out his ringing tones. 'Blessed be,' he called out.

'Blessed be,' the group answered back.

Suddenly Debbie knew for certain who was responsible for the death of her son. With a patience born out of necessity, she waited for the right time to strike, the moonlight glinting on the steel of her knife.

'Look,' Kurt said, and nudged his friend in the ribs. He pointed over to one of the caravans. 'It's Rachel.'

Marcel had led the three girls out of the caravan and they now walked behind him. Rachel stood at one end, Mary at the other, and the girl that would soon take her name was walking, smiling broadly, in the middle.

'Do yer think Rachel knows what Adrian's got in store for her?' Niall said.

Kurt sighed. 'Let's hope she doesn't have to find out the hard way.'

Marcel called out the blessing, and the Guides responded in kind. The three girls passed into the circle, and knelt in front of Marcel.

'Boss,' Luke said in a loud whisper. 'Something's going on.'

Lorraine, who had been talking tactics with Davis, stepped away from him and looked to where Luke was pointing. Davis came up behind her. The three police officers saw Marcel at the head of the circle, with three girls kneeling in front of him.

'This looks dodgy,' said Davis. He motioned to his team, and they moved silently into position.

'Luke, I want yer beside me. Sanderson, Jacobs, you follow behind. I'm gonna arrest Marcel Gottsdiener and his associates before this farce goes any further.' Lorraine gave her orders in a steady, calm whisper, but inside she felt sick with fear. She could only hope that Davis and his team were as reliable as they seemed to be. She glanced over at Luke. He gave her a reassuring smile and put his thumb up. Lorraine nodded and stepped out.

Debbie was looking with repulsion at the scene in front of her. The girls were kneeling in front of Marcel and he had placed his hands on top of the heads of the two girls with the dark hair, while the pretty, red-haired one knelt to one side, her hands clasped as if in prayer. The two men who had stood in front of the caravan had now moved to stand just behind the man in the white robes. But there was an opening. If she sprinted straight down the hill, she could ram the knife into the man's back. She had the element of surprise on her side, she calculated, but what she really needed was a distraction.

For the second time that day, luck was on her side. There was a movement outside the circle and Inspector Hunt stepped out of the darkness, flanked by three police officers. 'Marcel Gottsdiener,' her voice rang out just as clearly as his had done only moments earlier. The Blessing Guides turned as one towards the voice, and the pretty, red-haired girl stood up, although the other girls that had knelt before Marcel remained on their knees. Debbie noticed that the two dark-haired men put their hands inside their coat pockets and were staring at the policewoman.

'Put yer hands up,' shouted the black copper. 'Now! We have yer surrounded.'

And all of a sudden dark shapes emerged out of the darkness to become helmeted, black-uniformed policemen, their rifles trained on the three men at the top of the circle. Marcel's followers were turning slowly round, but there was nowhere to run. There was a gunman blocking every possible exit. The two men took their hands out of their pockets and slowly raised their hands in the air. Marcel just looked horrified, and stumbled backwards.

Debbie rose to her feet and shook the stiffness out of her joints. The time to act was now.

Kurt breathed a sigh of relief when he saw Inspector Hunt. There seemed no need to hide behind the bushes now. 'Looks like the cavalry's arrived,' he said to Niall with a smile, and motioned for him to stand up. 'I knew she'd come through for us, I really did.' They crept out from behind the bush.

'Do yer think Rachel's in any danger?' Niall whispered.

'Nah, they're not after her. It's obvious that they're after Marcel,' Kurt answered.

'We're still gonna have to go to the police though, aren't we?' said Niall.

His smile fading a little, Kurt nodded. Then it brightened again. 'But it's over, Niall, it's really over.'

The two friends looked at each other, and grinned.

Then a figure just across from them ran down the hill with a bloodcurdling scream.

It happened in an instant. First, Lorraine had everything under control. Adrian, and the man who must be the Brian Jacko had mentioned, had their hands in the air. Marcel was flailing uselessly in his robes, but he was no threat. The rest of the Blessing Guides were huddled together in small groups, terrified of the policemen who had their guns aimed in their general direction. Then a figure had come out of the trees directly behind Marcel and had sprinted towards him, screaming like a banshee. It was Debbie Stansfield, and she had caught Marcel, holding him

419

to her. She had one arm around his midriff, the other held a knife to his neck. Marcel's eyes were rolling wildly; a drop of blood rolled down his neck onto his white robes. Lorraine noticed, out of the corner of her eye, Davis's rifle drop for a moment as he assessed the situation, then he lifted it again, pointing it, this time, at Debbie's head.

'Debbie, no,' Lorraine said, as calmly as she could. 'There is no need for this. We're gonna take him away, lock him in prison. We have enough to keep him inside for a very long time. He's not worth it.'

'What the fuck do yer know!' Debbie screamed at her. 'Richy was my only family, my only child! He killed two people that day – Richy and me. He doesn't deserve to breathe the air that Richy would have been breathing.'

Lorraine walked towards her with her hand out-stretched and tried to continue talking in that calm voice. 'Just put the knife down, Debbie. We'll look after yer. We'll make sure he gets what he deserves. But trust me, this isn't it.'

'Trust you! You!' Debbie's voice was a mixture of torment and rage. 'Yer didn't even bother to tell me that I was right, that Richy was murdered! Yer let me keep on thinking that I was going crazy or something just because I believed what yer knew. That Richy didn't kill himself, some other bastard did. This bastard here!'

And with a roar that seemed to come from some-where in the depths of her soul, Debbie plunged the knife deep into Marcel's neck. She let him go. Marcel staggered backwards, his eyes wide. Everyone stood stock still and shocked as Marcel raised his hand to the knife and pulled it out of his neck. A gush of blood spurted out of his wound, spraying Debbie on her face and clothes. She shrieked and reeled away from him. For one split second, Lorraine felt Marcel's eyes on her, in the next he was down on the ground, his blood pouring out of him, one leg twitching helplessly.

Lorraine went to run towards him but was stopped by a snarling voice. 'I don't think so,' it said. 'Stand back.'

Lorraine turned round. In the horror of Marcel's stabbing, Adrian had grabbed Rachel and had one arm round her neck. He pointed his gun at the top of her head. 'One wrong move from yer, and she gets it.' He looked up at Brian, who had taken his gun out and was pointing it at Lorraine. Luke ran up beside her. 'Don't yer fucking move!' screamed Brian. 'Stay the fuck where yer are!'

'Yer fucking arsehole!' Luke screamed back. 'If yer want to aim yer gun at anyone, aim it at me!'

'Happy to,' said Brian, and aimed the gun at Luke.

Suddenly a shot rang out and Brian crumpled to the ground. Davis had taken aim and fired, and Adrian, surprised, had taken his gun from Rachel's head and was pointing it wildly in in the general direction of where the shot had come from. The Blessing Guides scattered like frightened sheep.

Up on the hill, Kurt looked at Niall. 'You grab Rachel and get her out of there. I'll try to grab the gun.'

Niall, pale, nodded.

They ran towards Adrian as fast as they could. Kurt was aware of time slowing down, of people screaming, of Adrian looking over his shoulder with a horrified expression on his face, of him thrusting Rachel away from him so that she fell on the ground, of raising his arm, of Niall hoisting Rachel to her feet and pulling her away, of a shot ringing into the air as Kurt barrowed into Adrian, throwing him off his balance. Somewhere a girl screamed.

Kurt lay on top of Adrian. He looked up. Suddenly, six guns were pointed at him. Inspector Hunt was standing over him, shock and surprise etched into her face. But Kurt didn't feel scared. Just a powerful feeling of relief.

'It's over,' he kept on repeating. 'It's over.'

41

It was the second time in a week that yellow police tape marking a crime scene had cordoned off part of Copt Hill, and the Seven Sisters in particular. After the shooting, the Blessing Guides had been escorted off the hill in police vans and were probably now, Lorraine thought wryly, sitting in jail where at least it was warm. The last of the ambulances had left, taking the wounded to the hospital and the dead to the morgue.

'All right, Scottie?' Lorraine wandered over to Scottie, clothed in a white forensics suit like the rest of his team. He looked around and smiled when he saw Lorraine.

'It's a mess, that I can tell yer. We'll go through the cabins later but the ground here has been churned up by people's feet. Not sure that I'm gonna get much out of this.'

'Well, anything yer can, Scottie, that would be great.'

Scottie smiled in response, then, his face suddenly serious, said, 'And that lad's mother, how's she?'

Lorraine shrugged. After Kurt and Niall had been led away by a couple of uniforms, she had walked up to Debbie, who was sitting, huddled on the ground, with no concern for the cold. 'Debbie?' she had said gently.

Debbie looked up at Lorraine. She smiled. 'I got him,' she said quietly. 'I got the bastard what took my Richy away from me.'

Lorraine squatted down so that their faces were on the same level. 'Yer know I've got to charge yer with Marcel's murder, don't yer?'

Debbie shook her head. 'I don't care about that. I don't care what happens to me. Two people died when Richard was murdered. The only difference is that I'm still breathing, still . . .' she sighed heavily, a tear rolling down her cheek, '*existing*. The only thing left for me to do is to count the days until I see my Richy again. And I can do that in prison as easily as anywhere else.'

Lorraine stood up silently. She waved Sanderson over. 'Could yer take Debbie down to the station and put her in a cell.' He looked at the woman sitting on the ground and nodded gravely. 'Oh, and Sanderson,' Lorraine said as an afterthought. 'I don't think there's any need for cuffs.'

'Right yer are boss,' he replied and gently raised Debbie to her feet. Taking her arm he walked her from the Seven Sisters.

'I don't think she's gonna be fine,' Lorraine said, snapping back to the present. 'I don't know how someone like her is gonna last in prison.'

'Reduced sentence perhaps?' Scottie suggested.

Lorraine shrugged. 'I'll recommend it. But it's out of my hands now.'

Luke walked up to Lorraine and Scottie. 'Not a great start to Christmas, is it.'

Lorraine nodded. 'Well, we'll leave yer to it, Scottie. We've got a long night ahead of us.'

Lorraine and Luke looked across the desk at the girl with the tear-shaped birthmark on her cheek, who was sitting opposite, hands clasped together. 'So, Janice, are yer prepared to tell us what yer know?' Lorraine began.

She nodded and looked up at Lorraine. Her face was expressionless, except for a tic in her cheek. 'I haven't been called that in three years,' she answered. 'It sounds strange.'

'I'm going to have to record this,' said Lorraine. 'Yer understand that this might be used in a court of law.'

Janice nodded, dropping her gaze to the table.

Lorraine gave Luke a nod and he started the tape. 'This is Detective Sergeant Luke Daniels. Present are Detective Inspector Lorraine Hunt and Janice Nichols, who has waived her right to an attorney. Time of interview is,' Luke looked at the clock on the wall, 'ten thirty-two.'

Lorraine began the interview by asking Janice how she came to be involved with the Blessing Guides.

'It was three months before my birthday,' she began. 'I was about to turn thirteen. I've never had many friends; I was teased because of this,' she pointed to her birthmark, 'but I had always been close to my family, especially my grandma. One day

I was walking through our village when I was stopped by a girl who told me that I had pretty hair and asked me where I got it cut.' Janice smiled at the memory. 'I realise now that was an opening. She didn't really like my hair, she wanted to recruit me into the Blessing Guides. Marcel told me how to pick out targets, look out for the vulnerable, anyone who could be manipulated. Tell them that you like something about them; their hair or the way they dress. Flatter them. Bring them to the meetings. And then Marcel did the rest.'

'We'll ask yer about that later,' said Lorraine. 'Go on.'

'Well, Mary, that was her name, took me to some meetings.' She shook her head. 'Marcel gave me special attention. He told me I was beautiful, that I was chosen. He tried to get me to leave my family and join him, spreading his word.' She swallowed. 'I believed him but I didn't want to leave my mum and dad. The Blessing Guides were being moved on – the police didn't like them in our area – and I told Marcel I couldn't go with them. He told me that they were moving to the South Downs and that if I changed my mind, I could find them. I'd always be wanted. Then they left.'

'So why did yer change yer mind?' asked Luke.

Janice smiled sadly. 'Six weeks after they left was my birthday. I had made some friends through the Blessing Guides and most of them, like me, stayed when Marcel left Somerset. We used to get together and talk about Marcel all the time. We missed him. So I wanted to throw a party but my parents didn't want me to. They didn't trust my new friends. But they didn't understand,' Janice raised her voice slightly, as if reliving an argument. 'These were the only friends that I had ever had at that time. I was furious. And,' the muscle in her cheek twitched again, 'I screamed at them. Slapped my grandmother. She wasn't very well . . .' Janice stopped and rubbed her eyes for a moment. 'And then I left. Middle of the night. It was summer, but it was still cold at night. I had no one else to turn to. The Blessing Guides had gone to the South Downs, so I hitched a lift and met them there.' She stopped speaking, and fiddled with the cuff of her shirt.

'And then what happened, Janice?' prompted Lorraine.

'I became Mary,' Janice replied simply.

'I don't understand. What does becoming Mary mean?' Lorraine asked.

Janice took a deep breath. 'Marcel believes – believed,' she quickly corrected herself, 'that he was a direct descendant of Mary and Joseph, from one of the children they had together after Jesus was born. He believed that Mary was impregnated not through the Holy Ghost but through Joseph, who had divine seed. Marcel believed that he was the new Joseph, and that through him a new Christ would be born. I was to be,' Janice stopped speaking for a moment then said quietly, 'his vessel.'

Lorraine shot a glance at Luke who looked back with a slight frown on his face. 'So Marcel slept with you?'

Janice swallowed hard. 'Yes,' she said quietly. 'He

slept with me because I was a virgin. But I couldn't give him the children he wanted.'

Lorraine sat back, horrified. Luke leant forward. 'What about the other Mary, Janice? What happened to her?'

Janice shook her head. 'Marcel said that she was out in the world, recruiting others to his cause, but I never heard from her again.' She stopped speaking for a moment, then said, 'He was going send me out into the world this evening.'

'Can you tell us when yer last saw the other Mary?' Lorraine asked.

Janice nodded.

'Good. Now we need a little more from yer. Marcel had his fingers in all sorts of pies, didn't he?'

Janice nodded. 'We all had to supply him with a tithe if we lived in the community. But no one had any money, so he'd send them out to beg or steal. There were also drugs involved. Most of the Blessing Guides are hooked on something. Brian ran that side of the operation. How is he?' She looked up at Lorraine.

'Shot in the shoulder. He's going to be OK though. So is Adrian,' Lorraine answered.

Janice deflated a little. 'Everyone was scared of them, scared of the both of them. But it was Marcel who gave the orders.' She swallowed again. 'He was the worst really. Because he also gave everyone hope. Made everyone think they were special. But then he'd play favourites, set people up against each other.' As if that prompted a memory, Janice asked, 'What about Inge?'

Inge had been shot when Kurt had tackled Adrian.

'She's in the operating theatre now,' replied Luke. 'But it doesn't look good.'

'Poor Inge,' Janice replied. 'She was OK, really.'

A WPC came to the door. Luke stopped the tape. 'I'm sorry for interrupting,' she said, 'but Niall Campbell's parents are here and really want to take their son home.'

'I need to speak to Kurt and Niall first though,' Lorraine said. 'Luke, are yer OK to continue questioning Janice? I'll go and speak to the boys.'

Luke nodded and as Lorraine left the interviewing room he spoke into the tape once more.

Both Kurt and Niall looked up as Lorraine entered the room. She looked sternly at both of them. 'What yer did up there was very, very stupid. Yer could have been killed. A girl is shot because of yer. What the hell did yer think yer were doing?'

Kurt's face was rigid, as if he was expecting nothing less from Lorraine. Niall shifted nervously in his seat.

'Well?' said Lorraine. 'Are yer gonna give me an explanation?'

'It was Rachel,' said Kurt. 'We found out from Adrian that she was gonna be used for . . . you know . . .' his face reddened. 'We wanted to go to the police, but we only had an hour. We had to get her out of there.'

'You mean used for sex, don't yer?' Lorraine said. 'Tell me more.'

'Marcel had brainwashed her,' Niall added. 'She

thought he treated her OK, much better than her stepfather –' He stopped, realising that he had, perhaps, said too much.

Lorraine sighed. 'Are yer implying that Rachel was abused by her stepfather?'

Niall nodded, his gaze on the floor.

'Did she tell yer that?'

Niall nodded again.

'OK. We'll look into that. But still, it was a bloody stupid thing for yer to do.'

Kurt took a deep breath. 'There's something else we have to tell yer.'

Lorraine sat in silence as Kurt told her of the night that he, Richard, Rachel and Niall had broken into the warehouse while Melissa stood guard. As he started talking about when the night watchman had surprised them, and they had all ran up onto the roof, his voice started wobbling, as if he was about to break down in tears. 'We didn't mean it to happen, the night watchman, he came up on the roof and came towards us but then he slipped and . . .' Kurt's voice faltered.

'Richy was gonna go straight to the police,' Niall added. 'But we stopped him. We told him to go and see Marcel first. And then the next thing we know is that he was found up at Seven Sisters.'

Lorraine sat still for a long, quiet moment while the boys looked worriedly at her. 'Yer realise,' she finally said coldly, 'that if yer had come to me earlier, Melissa would probably still be alive.'

Kurt nodded his head. 'We know. Niall and I realised that. And we were gonna come to yer the day before the ceremony, but Adrian locked us in the cellar.' He looked Lorraine straight in the eye. 'We know that we have to face up to what we've done. We know we're probably gonna go to prison. We've accepted that.'

Niall looked down at the table, but nodded too. Lorraine suddenly felt a wave of pity for the two boys. They had been picked up and used because they were vulnerable, and the prison system was just going to pick them up and use them too, spit them out once they were harder and tougher and a real threat to society. She had seen it before, young lads who had gone into prison having done something stupid and had learned nothing except how to be a less stupid criminal. She didn't want that to happen to these two boys.

'Listen,' she said at last. 'It's up to the court to decide what's gonna happen to yer. But if yer co-operate fully with us,' she pointed a finger at them, 'and I mean fully, yer to tell us everything, then I will recommend a non-custodial sentence. I can't promise yer anything more than that.'

Kurt and Niall agreed.

'Well, the cells are full tonight. I've got nowhere to put yer so I'm gonna let yer out on yer parents' recognisance, Niall, but I want both of yer back here on Boxing Day at nine in the morning. Yer got that?' The boys nodded. 'Put one foot out of line, and I swear, I'll have yer up for the worst I can throw at yer.'

Lorraine got up out of her seat and left the interview room. She met Luke in the corridor. 'I cut the interview short, boss,' he said. 'Janice is willing to tell us everything, but she's tired. We'll get more out of her in the morning.'

Lorraine looked at her watch. 'It's morning now,' she said.

Luke nodded. 'Christmas Day. One hell of one, isn't it? How were Niall and Kurt?'

'Well, I've found out what happened to Eric McIvor.' Lorraine filled Luke in on Kurt and Niall's explanation of the break-in at the warehouse.

Luke let out a low whistle. 'They were in it up to their necks.'

'Yeah,' agreed Lorraine, 'but they were vulnerable. They were just after something that they couldn't find at home. Except for Richy. Sounds like he was just along for the ride. He wanted to come to the police after the night watchman died. That's why he was killed.'

'And probably why Melissa was killed too,' Luke replied. Then he said, 'Have yer seen Debbie Stansfield yet?'

Lorraine shook her head. 'Sanderson charged her with murder when he got to the station. She's been fingerprinted and photographed. She's been perfectly co-operative. But I think it's better that I talk to her in the morning.'

'Mavis and Peggy are not gonna like that, yer working on Christmas Day,' Luke said, with a ghost of a smile.

Lorraine ran her fingers through her hair. 'Oh, they're used to it by now. Hopefully it'll just be the morning though. Yer'll be here though, won't yer?'

'Of course, Lorraine. I'll need to check on Carter though. Make sure Selina's OK.'

'You go do that now. We're just about finished here anyway. I'll see yer in the morning.'

Luke smiled a goodbye and was just walking down the corridor when Lorraine called after him, 'Oh, and Luke?'

He turned round.

'The invitation's still good, for Christmas dinner, that is,' Lorraine said, her face flushing. 'That is, if we make it out of here in time. Selina too, of course.'

Luke smiled warmly, 'No promises, Lorraine. But sounds good.' He walked down the corridor, leaving Lorraine feeling deflated. But just as he reached the double doors at the end of the corridor, he turned back. 'Tell yer what,' he said, the gold in his smile glinting, 'I'll bring the mince pies.'

Lorraine smiled back. 'It's a deal.'

Debbie sat on the bed in her cell, looking straight ahead of her, at the grey brick walls. She pulled her legs up to her chest and smiled to herself. Her son was dead but she had made it better, she had put things to rights. She leant her head against the cold brick wall. At last she was at peace, with herself and with the world.

Every Breath You Take

He hates them, but he loves them too. Those gorgeous, cruel young girls. That's why he worships them from afar: sending them flowers, following their every move, discovering their secrets. And that's why, when it all goes wrong, when they fall, inevitably, from the pedestals he's erected for them, he kills them, cutting out their hearts and leaving, in their places, single, perfect white roses.

Everything is getting too close for comfort for Detective Inspector Lorraine Hunt. A killer is stalking the streets of Houghton-le-Spring, targeting young women and killing them brutally, and without mercy. Selina, the daughter of Lorraine's partner, DS Luke Daniels, is a beautiful and wilful sixteen-year-old with a dark history. Just as it seems she's finally getting back on her feet, she's attacked. Is Selina's past catching up with her? Or could it have been the White Rose Killer?

The closer the killer gets, the more elusive he becomes. Lorraine faces her toughest case yet as her resources are tested to the limit by a killer with no conscience, no remorse. Just a pitiless hatred for the girls who inspire desire within him . . .

Available April 2007 from Century

C

Century · London

Prologue

It was a dark night, dark and cold, colder than usual, even for early February, even for Dublin. And quiet, too. It was that dead time of night, that time in between the last stragglers being thrown out of pubs and the first early risers, getting out of bed and heading for work. But Dublin is never really quiet, never really still. There were a few people about still on the streets, some in better states than others. A drunk tried to hail a cab, and swore at it as it sailed past him. Muttering to himself, the drunk pulled his coat around him and walked in the opposite direction from the cab, which had stopped at the lights and was now inching down a cobbled street near Temple Bar.

Freezing fog had rolled in from the rugged North East coast and, even though the temperature was well below zero, there was an ethereal, almost soulful beauty to this usually vibrant city. The hard frost gave everything it touched a shimmering cover of tiny pinhead diamonds that glowed in the light from the streetlamps. The fog had turned the hard edges of the buildings soft and muffled noise so that footsteps sounded dampened and far away.

He was breathing heavily as he walked down the road and into a narrow alleyway. He knew he needed to control his breathing, but knew too that this always happened at this point of the proceedings, every time. It was his only weakness. But it was only the anticipation of what he was about to do that made him breathe so hard, and his breathing, just like everything else, could be controlled. And once controlled, he knew the rest would fall into place. In fact, he felt calm, purposeful. Warm breath hurtled out of his mouth, creating a fog of his own, streaming from his lips like ribbons and ribbons of ectoplasm.

He closed his eyes and took another breath, this time deeply, filling his lungs to their full capacity. He counted to ten and released the breath, and with it his tension. It was a simple trick he'd learned years ago, and just this uncomplicated act made him feel better, alert and clear of mind, his muscles tensed but prepared.

It smelled here though. It smelt of discarded trash, of vomit and urine and of things much worse. It smelt as he imagined it smelt years ago, back in the olden days, when it was supposedly less clean. But some things, he mused, never change. People never change. No matter how many chances you give them to prove that they can. And anyway, he had become used to the smell. He had walked down streets just like this one many, many times before.

He closed his eyes, once more regulating his breathing, in through the nose, out through the mouth, in through the nose, out through the mouth. He clenched his fists and released them in time with his breathing, digging his fingernails into the soft flesh of his palm. It was just another aspect of his preparation, it was meditative, calming, readying him for what he was about to do.

Opening his eyes, he surveyed the narrow cobbled street that he had just walked down. It was almost laughably perfect; he couldn't have chosen a better place, not even if he had drawn up the plans and constructed it himself. The alleyway was narrow and dark, two thirds of the way down its length there was a broken bit of wall that stopped short just below his chest. He had no idea what it had been built for, but nowadays it was used as a rubbish receptacle for a greasy spoon that had closed for the night. He knew this because he had been prepared. He knew where she walked, where she went, and the shortcuts she took to get home. This was one of them. The best.

A sudden crash broke into the fog-dampened silence. He spun round, his heart beating hard in his chest; it couldn't be her, it was too early, he wasn't prepared. He breathed a sigh of relief when he saw it was just a cat that had jumped on top of a load of rubbish, only to lose its balance and fall to the ground. It ran away, tail to the ground, as if it sensed that something bad was about to happen here. He smiled to himself. He was taking risks by standing in the alleyway, he could be seen by anyone passing its entrance, but what would they assume? Probably that he was just a drunk, taking a leak on the side of a wall. But still, he shouldn't tempt fate. He moved into his hiding position.

The wall really was perfectly positioned. There was even a chunk bashed out of it at his eye level, which meant he had a perfect vantage point; he could see without being seen. Reaching inside his black jacket, he pulled his black polo neck jumper down over his slim waist. It had risen up over his trousers and was exposing his bare flesh to the elements. He pulled on his gloves more firmly and took a large leather pouch from the inside front pocket of his jacket and weighed it in his hands.

This was not the first time he'd hidden. Not the first time he'd been snubbed and suffered rejection.

How dare the bitch think she was better than him? How dare she, that stinking little tart?

A dark red mist of hatred threatened to overwhelm him. With a tremendous effort of will he pushed the anger back down inside him. Now wasn't the time to lose control. To focus himself, he opened the leather pouch and laid it on the ground.

Four very sharp knives of different weights and sizes lay comfortably in their sheaths. A pair of long handled autopsy scissors snuggled next to them.

He ran his fingers gently, almost reverently, over the instruments. They were beautifully made, worth every penny of the considerable amount of money he had spent on them. There was something in their cool precision, in their heft and their perfectly balanced weight, that brought him back to his senses, calmed him down, prepared him for what he was about to do.

And then he heard her. She was clattering about in those ridiculous high heels that girls insisted on wearing these days. From his hiding place, he watched her walk unsteadily towards him, his green eyes becoming calculating slits, measuring the distance between them. Even now, even after her cruel rejection, he still desired her. Five three and slim boned, she was fashionably dressed in clothes that were much too light for the freezing weather. Even from this distance he could see she was shivering, her lips trembling with cold. Her shoulder length brown hair had blonde streaks and he noticed it was frizzing at the ends in the damp air. He had once supposed her beautiful, now he could see that she was merely pretty. Her nose was too long. Her chin too sharp. And from this angle he could see an incipient heaviness at her hips. He shuddered, but not from the cold.

A tease. That's all she was, that's all she ever would be. A vicious tease. Not worth his love, not even worth his regard.

She stopped for a moment, drunkenly rooting around in her small bag. Tottering on her yellow heels, she took out a mobile phone. His heart stopped in his chest. After all this preparation, all this work, was it all going to be ruined? Was she going to call someone to pick her up, or walk back down the alley away from him?

Luck, however, was on his side. He saw her press a few buttons, then heard her mutter 'fuck' under her breath. She gave a deep sigh and continued down the narrow alleyway, not paying attention to her path as she put her mobile back in her bag. She drew closer to him and he jumped clear over the wall and stood in front of her. 'What the fuck?' she gasped, her face registering surprise, then recognition, and then incomprehension as he lifted his arm and struck her, bringing her to the ground.

She landed on her back. One of her shoes had come off her foot and was lying on the ground next to her. She was too shocked to react, and she stared at him, her terrified eyes locked on his. Finally she said, 'I know you, don't I? You're . . .' as she tried to scrabble to her feet, but with a callous sneer, he pinned her down, and just as she managed to pull herself together enough to scream, his right hand smashed into her mouth snapping her front teeth.

She retched and spat, bits of her teeth landing in the gutter along with her blood and vomit. He grinned. She didn't look so pretty now. He took her long dark-brown hair in one hand and pulled her head back tight. Her pale neck looked vulnerable, fragile. She yelped and kicked out at his legs ineffectually. He laughed, and then slapped her across the face with the back of his free hand. Suddenly, she went limp, doll-like. She must have fainted. Good. That made things easier.

He picked her up, her petite frame limp and almost malleable in his arms. Carrying her the few short steps to the wall, he tossed her over as if she was nothing more than a heavy laundry bag. Again she landed on her back. Quickly he followed her and a moment later he was astride her with his tools next to him.

With practised ease he unzipped her leather jacket and ripped open her pink cotton blouse, exposing her chest. She wore a flimsy bra of almost the same shade of pink as her blouse, which he easily tore away. Her breasts spilled out into the freezing air. He caught his breath, staring at her for what seemed like the longest time.

Then he sneered. She was beneath him in more ways than one. Quickly, he turned his back on her, and went to his tools. The third one from the right was the sharpest; it was also the longest, and his favourite. Smiling, he picked it up and ran his gloved finger along its edge.

When he turned back, her eyes were open and she was cautiously moving away from him. Suddenly he realised that her limp body had been a trick, she had lied to him. She had only pretended to have been knocked out – a futile, desperate attempt to escape. This knowledge of her deceit, even in the face of death, made him angry, but it was a cool sort of anger this time. It was anger he could use. It was anger to make him strong. He grasped her ankle, pulling her back towards him with a sudden jolt. She hit her head on the dirty ground – her face was now a mass of blood, bruises and vomit. He smiled. 'Please,' she whimpered, 'I don't know why you're doing this. I'll do anything you want, just please let me go, please . . .' she sobbed over and over again, 'please . . .'

She saw the knife as slowly he raised it above his head and she knew her fate. Her body shook with terror and her eyes pleaded with his, as her ruined bleeding mouth hung open in a silent scream. She watched helplessly as her death, now only seconds, away began to descend.

He plunged the knife into her heart, felt the

resistance of rib and muscle for a moment, but the blade had been honed to a brilliant sharpness. Viciously he twisted it round. Blood spurted out of her body, spraying his face and chest and then slowing, as the life ebbed out of her. He watched her face as she died, his eyes locked on hers. This was intensity, this was passion, this was love. He caressed her cheek with his gloved hand as her eyes finally glazed over and her body went limp. It had taken her only moments to die, but her eyes remained open. He ran his hand gently over her face and closed them.

Calmly, his face devoid of any emotion at all, he pulled the knife out, wiped the warm bloody blade on a piece of litter beside him, and replaced it in the sheath before drawing out the smaller cutting knife. Quickly and expertly he opened her body from her throat to her navel. One by one he snapped the top two ribs on each side of her chest, the sound muffled by the fog.

A few minutes later he was staring at her ruined heart. He lingered only a moment though, then with his autopsy scissors cut the blood vessels. The aorta – the largest artery in the human body – had a slight, slippery resistance to the scissors, but it was only slight and the rest proved easy. In just a few moments he held her treacherous heart in his hands.

A cool, calm contentment washed over him. He placed her heart on her stomach between her navel and her pubic hair. Thoughtfully he studied the placement for a moment, committing it to memory. He never took pictures. Pictures would be incriminating.

Once again he wiped his tools on the detritus beside him before removing his rubber gloves and stuffing them into a pocket in his tool kit. From a lower pocket he took out a clear pair and snapped them on before taking a white envelope from his jacket pocket. Inside it was a delicate white rose, only marginally bruised from the efforts of the kill. It had a delicate luminosity in the winter air. He looked at the girl lying there before him one last time before he placed the rose gently, tenderly, almost with love, into the bloody cavity from which he had ripped her heart.

Bad Moon Rising

Sheila Quigley

A young woman walks home by herself, the tapping of her high heels the only sound. At two o' clock in the morning, it's cold, the streets are deserted and she thinks she's all alone. Waiting for her, sleeping soundly in his bed, is her baby son. When he wakes the next morning his mother still isn't back. She's never coming back. Because the streets weren't as deserted as she thought.

Three women are dead and Detective Inspector Lorraine Hunt is searching for a serial killer. In Houghton-le-Spring it's Feast week, a time when all hell is let loose as the fair comes to town, and a frenzy of celebration and decadence provides a temporary distraction from the grim realities of everyday life. It's not a good time to be searching for a stranger. It's not a good time to be a woman alone . . .

arrow books

Run for Home

Sheila Quigley

1985: a man runs for his life – wounded, exhausted, hunted remorselessly by a woman assassin known only as The Headhunter.

2001: sixteen-year-old Kerry Lumsdon runs across the same terrain. She runs to win and she runs to forget.

When a headless body is found in the wastelands of the Seahills Estate, Detective Inspector Lorraine Hunt is called in to investigate. But then a more urgent case lands on her desk when Kerry's sister, Claire, is violently kidnapped . . .

arrow books

The Rottweiler

Ruth Rendell

The first girl had a bite mark on her neck but they traced the DNA to her boyfriend. But the tabloids got hold of the story and called the killer 'The Rottweiler' and the name stuck.

The latest murder takes place very near Inez Ferry's antique shop in Marylebone. Someone saw a shadowy figure running away past the station, but the only other clues are that the murderer usually strangles his victims and removes something personal – like a cigarette lighter or a necklace . . .

Since her husband died, too soon in their relationship, Inez has supplemented her income by taking in tenants. The murderous activities of the sinister 'Rottweiler' will exert a profound influence on the lives of this heterogeneous little community, especially when the suspicion emerges that one of them may be a homicidal maniac.

'In the world of contemporary crime fiction, Rendell really is top dog'
Sunday Times

'In Rendell's expert hands, you'll want to keep reading until dawn – with the light on'
Red

'Rendell skilfully crafts her characters and they breathe feverishly through her imagination'
The Times

Road Rage

Ruth Rendell

A by-pass is planned in Knightsbridge that will destroy its peace and natural habitat for ever. Dora Wexford joins the protest, but the Chief Inspector must be more circumspect: trouble is expected.

As the protesters begin to make their presence felt, a young woman's badly decomposed body is unearthed. Burden believes he knows the murderer's identity but Wexford is not convinced. Furthermore, having just become a grandfather, he is struggling to put aside his familial responsibilities and emotions in order to do his job.

The case progresses, the protest escalates. And alarmingly, a number of people begin to disappear, including Dora Wexford . . .

'One of the greatest novelists presently at work in our language . . . a writer whose work should be read by anyone who either enjoys a brilliant mystery – or distinguished literature'
Scott Turow

arrow books

The Last Juror

John Grisham

In 1970, one of Mississippi's more colourful weekly newspapers, *The Ford County Times*, went bankrupt. To the surprise and dismay of many, ownership was assumed by a 23-year-old college drop-out, named Willie Traynor. The future of the paper looked grim until a young mother was brutally raped and murdered by a member of the notorious Padgitt family. Willie Traynor reported all the gruesome details, and his newspaper began to prosper.

The murderer, Danny Padgitt, was tried before a packed courtroom in Clanton, Mississippi. The trial came to a startling and dramatic end when the defendant threatened revenge against the jurors if they convicted him. Nevertheless, they found him guilty, and he was sentenced to life in prison.

But in Mississippi in 1970, 'life' didn't necessarily mean 'life', and nine years later Danny Padgitt managed to get himself paroled. He returned to Ford County, and the retribution began.

'*The Last Juror* sees Grisham at the absolute peak of his form . . . page-turning urgency'
Mail on Sunday

'*The Last Juror* does not need to coast on its author's megapopularity. It's a reminder of how the Grisham juggernaut began.'
New York Times

arrow books

ALSO AVAILABLE IN ARROW

Murder Artist

John Case

**Magic, voodoo and death – the electrifying new thriller
from the bestselling author of *The Genesis Code***

There's nothing in a glorious summer's day to suggest anything
even remotely sinister. In fact, Alex Callahan, a news correspon-
dent, surprises himself by enjoying the Renaissance Faire that
his six-year-old twins, Kevin and Sean, have dragged him to.

The boys are delighted by the jugglers and magicians, jesters and
foodmongers dressed in full Elizabethan costume. But it's the
joust that the boys have really been waiting to see. Alex takes a
break to watch, while keeping half an eye on the twins, but when
he turns to see how they are enjoying themselves, he can't see
them at first. And then: he really can't see them at all.

The perfect day has turned into every parent's nightmare.
There's no sign of Sean and Kevin, and eventually the police
arrive. They're initially suspicious of Alex but no one can explain
the bizarre origami figure he finds after he returns to his empty
house. Or the bowl of water that has been left on the top shelf of
the wardrobe. Or, more sinisterly, the T-shirt soaked in blood.

'John Case is a confident master writing at peak performance'
Lorenzo Carcaterra

'Grips the heart and gut with equal force'
Guardian

arrow books

The Genesis Code

John Case

Italy: a dying doctor makes a chilling confession to the priest in a remote hillside village.

Washington DC: a mother and her young son are savagely murdered. Their house is then burned down.

Joe Lassiter, the woman's brother, discovers a chain of similar killings around the world.

What is the link? Who are the shadowy, merciless killers? And what is the Genesis Code, the secret so unthinkable that powerful men do anything to make sure it remains in the grave?

'Impeccable in plot, immaculate in story resolution, moves with high skill from locale to locale and from suspense to suspense'
Norman Mailer

arrow books

The Eighth Day

John Case

An explosive, compulsively readable novel of suspense that plunges a clever young man into a web of mystery and international deceit, bringing him face to face with the ultimate evil.

Danny Cray is a struggling 28-year-old sculptor/video artist who lives in Washington DC. To make ends meet, he does occasional freelance work as a researcher for a large firm of private detectives. When one of their most powerful clients approaches him with a job, the money is too good to resist. All he has to do is learn what a recently deceased university professor was working on when he died. But Danny stumbles on far more than he expected when he discovers that the professor was in touch with the Vatican about a remote tribe of Kurds who worship the Peacock Angel – Satan. (This tribe does indeed exist.) After others connected to the professor start to disappear, Danny finds himself in great peril and must travel into the ancient land where this tribe still lives in order to discover what is truly at stake in his investigation.

A mesmerising blend of science, religion, history and suspense. *The Eighth Day* confirms John Case's position as a master of intelligent commercial fiction.

arrow books

THE POWER OF READING

Visit the Random House website and get connected with information on all our books and authors

EXTRACTS from our recently published books and selected backlist titles

COMPETITIONS AND PRIZE DRAWS Win signed books, audiobooks and more

AUTHOR EVENTS Find out which of our authors are on tour and where you can meet them

LATEST NEWS on bestsellers, awards and new publications

MINISITES with exclusive special features dedicated to our authors and their titles

READING GROUPS Reading guides, special features and all the information you need for your reading group

LISTEN to extracts from the latest audiobook publications

WATCH video clips of interviews and readings with our authors

RANDOM HOUSE INFORMATION including advice for writers, job vacancies and all your general queries answered

Come home to Random House

www.randomhouse.co.uk

arrow books